FROM SOMEWHERE
TO NOWHERE
THE END OF THE AMERICAN DREAM

THE UNBEARABLES PRESENT

FROM SOMEWHERE TO NOWHERE
THE END OF THE AMERICAN DREAM

EDITED BY JIM FEAST, RON KOLM & SHALOM NEUMAN

AUTONOMEDIA

Autonomedia
POB 568 Williamsburgh Station
Brooklyn, NY 11211-0568 USA

www.autonomedia.org
info@autonomedia.org

ACKNOWLEDGEMENTS

"Burning, Burning — September Eleven" by Breyten Breytenbach is from *A Veil of Footsteps: Memoir of a Nomadic Fictional Character* (Afrikaans Edition, 2007). "The Collector" by Ron Kolm is from *Night Shift* (Unbearable Books/Autonomedia). The excerpts by Basil King are from *Twin Towers/Learning to Draw/A History,* published by Skanky Possum, 2005. "Requiem" by Janet Hamill is from *Body of Water* (Bowery Books, NYC, 2008). "Parks" by Martha King is excerpted from her not-yet-published memoir, *Outside Inside.* Max Blagg's "Tenth Between Fear & Trembling" is from *101 Nights* (Shallow Books). Thaddeus Rutkowski's story "Loft Living" appeared in *Home Planet News Online* and in *Guess and Check* (Gival Press). "Kathy's Street" by Karen Lillis was originally published in the *LadyFest East* anthology, 2004. Samuel Delaney's excerpt is from *Times Square Red, Times Square Blue,* New York University Press, 1999. William Considine's excerpt is from *Times Square Taxi.* The excerpt by Floyd Sykes is from the unpublished manuscript *I'm Your Man.* Alfred Vitale's "8-border dispute" is excerpted from his unpublished manuscript *Yorkville.* "Going into Harlem" by Tim Beckett is from his unpublished manuscript *Pilgrims.* "Raden in Woodheaven" is from bart plantenga's *Beer Mystic: A Novel of Inebriation & Light.* Larissa Shmailo's "Nora at 13" is an excerpt from *Patient Women* (BlazeVOX, 2015). "The L" by Bradley Spinelli is excerpted from *Killing Williamsburg* (Le Chat Noir, 2013). "I Drink Your Milkshake: Chaos and the Cloud of Unknowing" by Carl Watson is from the *Williamsburg Observer.* A slightly different version of Matthew Flamm's "The New Co-op Owners in Their Living Room" was published in *Poetry East.* "God Bless America" by Jerome Sala, originally appeared in *Look Slimmer Instantly* (Soft Skull Press, 2005). "Why I Support Occupy: What Happened on L.E.S." by Clayton Patterson was originally published in *The Villager,* October 20, 2011. Gary Shapiro's "Shakespeare, Proust Join the Protests" appeaared on nysun.com, October 27, 2011. Peter Werbe's "Occupy Confronts the Power of Money: The Encampments as Anarchy in Action' is from *Fifth Estate,* Spring 2012. "The Return of the Frog King, or Iron Henry" by Peter Wortsman is excerpted from *Ghost Dance in Berlin, A Rhapsody in Gray* (Travelers' Tales, 2013). Maria Lisella's "Trumped Over the Moon" is excerpted from *Conversations with Mom.* Any credits overlooked will be corrected in future editions.

TABLE OF CONTENTS

THERE GOES THE NEIGHBORHOOD

FUSIONISM CENTERFOLD,

IT'S THE ECONOMY, STUPID!

O.W.S.

POSTSCRIPT: TRUMP

FOREWORD
RON KOLM

When we started putting this book together, we were operating under the notion that 9/11 in New York City was somewhat akin to the sacking of Rome in the year 410 — kind of high-water marks for two similar empires — and that these events presaged the eventual decline of both. We felt that, in the West, Rome's fall led eventually to the rise of the British Empire, and then, inevitably, to the American imperium, with New York City becoming the new Rome. I now think we were wrong to equate the two events. Several thousand people died in the World Trade Center attacks, but many more died in Rome during that particular sacking. Also, America is still vaguely preeminent among the current megaliths, whereas Rome had already lost much of its luster by 410.

We are still using 9/11 as a starting point for our project, though, as it is a commonality for the contributors, many of whom live in New York City, and 9/11 leads, more or less, to where we are today. It is a shared fact of our lives; one that we continue to talk and create art about — it is a communal memory we can't forget.

The second section of this book, "There Goes the Neighborhood," is a digression of sorts, a kind of paean to the mean streets where most of the contributors came to live or work; i.e., the Lower East Side, Times Square in the bad old days, Brooklyn — even Detroit! These "neighborhoods" have changed greatly since 9/11 — gone out of focus, if you will — and the reason has to do with where the American economy has gone. The gap between rich and poor has increased exponentially, making paying the rent a monthly high-wire act. Because of this, many of the folks we know are leaving New York City, or planning to in the near future. Gentrification is a daily fact of life.

And this leads us to the third section of the book: "It's the Economy, Stupid!" This section provided a chance to vent our collective anger at the 1%, the top tier of the *übermeisters* who make our lives, and the lives of so much of the world's population, miserable. And so the rants and screeds ensued!

The original ending section of this tome was called O.W.S. (Occupy Wall Street). We felt that the O.W.S. actions, and the theories that arose from them, seemed to provide one way out of the dilemma in which we find ourselves. The basic problem, of course, is how to redistribute the world's wealth, and end racism and sexism at the same time.

This version of our book was all well and good, but then the American presidential election of 2016 happened. Bernie Sanders — who seemed to understand the problems we are facing, and who had come up with some solutions to them — was put out to pasture, and the mega-huckster, Donald Trump, has become the head honcho. In this position of power, Trump is smashing everything in sight like a retro-nightmare, taking us back to a regressive past. So the new last section of this volume, one we added in retrospect, deals with our reactions to this new, unbearable, reality. Should he be pensioned off, we will still have to deal with the fact that he existed at all — and that some folks felt, probably sincerely, that he was the correct answer to the questions we all are asking. Should he vanish, done away with by the "deep state," we must still try to describe the stain on the wall with all the energy we can muster, before they rub it off and say it never existed.

9/11

BURNING, BURNING — SEPTEMBER ELEVEN
BREYTEN BREYTENBACH

A t last, at the end of that day, darkness came over the city. And with it an eerie silence. In the south the sky was clogged and burning angrily. Strange: one had become so accustomed to living in a growling, hooting, whirring, pinging, beeping, jostling, bustling, hurried environment, and now there was stillness. But "the city that never sleeps" wasn't asleep. One knew that behind those darkened windows and the flimsy walls (all walls had become flimsy) there were millions of people, tense but tired, numbed by the viscid and flickering flow of horror imagery flooding their living-rooms through TV consoles. Or perhaps they were shouting at one another or at the ceiling or phoning frantically or just weeping.

> *I have shut my balcony because I do not want to*
> *hear the weeping, but from behind the grey walls*
> *nothing else is heard but the weeping.*
> (From Federico Garcia Lorca's *Casida of the Lament*)

(Breyten Wordfool and Golden Lotus were exhausted too. They were depressed and irritable and it had become difficult to concentrate. They slept long hours hooked in heavy dreams of anxiety and woke up drenched in perspiration. I tried working on Breyten's book, this anatomy of days and nights. It was no good. I'd become dissociated from myself. Then I looked back and remembered how twins had emerged from the text in various guises. When you write something in the way I'm now trying, in long prose, in a ping-pong game with events as they appear and with the environment, you don't plot beforehand and you don't stop to confront and understand the symbols. Words are the little hooks holding the sheer and rotting cloth of reality together. True, the word bird had wondered once or twice what the twins were doing in our story. Until now, suddenly: the Twin Towers! Everything had become portentous, at least in retrospect, blackened by "meaning.")

> *he says he woke up*
> *it was the night of the day*
> *when airplanes exploded in fiery stories*
> *and the towers of this world city's*
> *skyline crumpled*
> *and a big seamless naked and slithery*
> *white body was pinning him down*
> *he says it was he and not yet he*
> *for the corpse was bloated with death*
> *and he trying not to be smothered*
> *but he also says he is not I*

Continuous TV coverage was spitting and spilling the events through 'live images' (in opposition to dead ones?) as they occurred; reactions and commentaries very soon were spinning them. You could even say this "being told what you should know" happened instantaneously: On CNN, while an official addressed a press gathering, snipped phrases summarizing and bowdlerizing and *editing* the contents would scroll on the screen as he or she spoke. In a sense, this shallow but never-ending ribbon of visible consciousness, like the madman's stream of mouth-runoff with neither rhyme nor reason, was first dissolving the fabric and then displacing and replacing "reality." But the language was inadequate. Years of inflation and flatulence had distended its ability and usefulness for us "to get our arms around it." The happening was too big.

Wall-to-wall dramatization and sentimentalizing will end up trivializing everything, making a soap opera of even the most shattering event, effacing the lines between commercials and reporting.

And then, along comes something momentous and the adjectives pack no punch anymore, they've become too flaccid and reamed out to be of any effectiveness. Anchormen and -women now looked for the historic clutch, groping for the sob in the throat, essaying their hand at dooms-daying. Poor Dan Rather who'd been waiting for this day all his life (he said) was reduced to facing the camera like a solemn ox and slurring at each of his interviewees: "Did you *ever,* sir, expect that one day…?" And proud they were, these stations, that they broke all records in going on the air uninterruptedly without any commercial breaks, losing millions in revenue.

It went further. Larry King, that insatiable glutton for base emotions and tear-jerking confrontations, had on his 'show' the freshly bereaved who still clutched photos of their loved ones. What, he wanted to know, were the last intimate messages exchanged seconds before death? And then (one sensed it coming with a lurch in your stomach): "How does it *feel?*"

"How does it f-e-e-e-e-e-l, to be all a-lone?"

Perhaps one shouldn't hold it against him. He presents us with the present-day Punch and Judy spectacle that people secretly crave. We all have a hunger for drama, we all identify with the victim, we personalize the performance we watch and we cry under cover of darkness in the movies — maybe as an attempt to preempt the impact and steer it away from us. Do we not *need* these strong emotions so as to *feel* ourselves alive still, appreciating our luck?

In this the journalists were not alone. Politicians and officials were all at sea for words but this didn't stop anyone from yacking. Time is money, so any unoccupied space is a loss. Don't give way to doubt! Talk the motherfuckers down! The president of the country himself was singularly inept at finding the right expressions, seemingly at a loss for understanding. It looked as if he was not so much stunned by the magnitude of what was taking place as scared witless, and now — impaled on a lexical and emotive inadequacy — he could only muster some lame phrases and bluster. The suit was too big for the man. At one point his eyes were visibly stiff in his head, his hands shook. Then he tried to cry.

In the beginning he referred to both the good and the bad 'uns as "folks." Then, as the nightmare kept expanding, excesses in verbal commerce kicked in and new cowboy raciness was introduced. *Attack on America; The First American War of The 21st Century; An Attack on Civilization* (Whose civilization, Mr. President, pray? This drug-guzzling, polluting, gun-toting, child-killing one? And only one? Are other peoples elsewhere not civilized? Later he would change tack to make it an attack on the land of "freedom and opportunity" with the inference that terrorists just cannot abide the notion of opportunity); *America Will Lead The World To Victory Over Terrorism* (What "world" has mandated you to do this, Mr. President?); [We Will Be] *Ending Countries* (no less: one marveled at the manly resolution!); *No Middle Ground; Those Who Aren't For us Are Against Us; "smoking out of holes, putting on the run, binding and delivering... all those who don't have the same god we have"; A Crusade Against Evildoers; Operation Noble Eagle.*

Other terms quickly gained currency and were suitably apocalyptic. "Ground zero," for instance. And "this is the worst day in human history." Behind the fundamentalist discourse there was a quick reach for extended arbitrary American power worldwide in defiance of existing treaties or customs or international law. Global capitalism was to be rapidly equipped with visible imperial clout. The unilateralist and over-bearing stance of the United States in the world, which may well have been one of the root causes for the attack, was to be reinforced.

The planes with their load of absolute and final anguish had torn into the soft flesh of the collective imagination.

Some of the public utterances spluttered by lawmakers were unintentionally ironic. Square-jawed middle-aged white gents would step up to the camera — often flanked by a phalanx of clones in similar suits arranged like a badly composed Rembrandt "Night Watch" — look it straight in the lens and proclaim "Make no mistake!" when all the possible mistakes had already been made.

Breyten Wordfool was wondering about the reactions of the African-Americans. Of course, many of them were also victims of the aggression and their weeping relatives were likewise walking the streets to look for any sign or news of survival. But where were the community's spokesmen? Had this happened years ago there certainly would have been a Martin Luther King finding singing metaphors to rise to the occasion? And Malcolm X might unhappily have said something about "chickens coming home to roost." But these here were BIG chickens, dude. And now?

> "Cry Havoc, and let slip the dogs of war;/ That this foul deed shall smell above the earth/ With carrion men, groaning for burial." — Shakespeare

Now the dogs of war were already inside the house and breeding fast, salivating and grinding their hips to the dance of death. Some, it turned out, had lived for a long time in this middle-class and provincial civilization, smooth-faced, walking their kids to school, mowing the lawn and exchanging howdy's with neighbors, before tying red bandanas around their heads and flying their human bombs (with innocent people trying to phone loved ones one last time) into the giddy towers and squat fortresses of America's symbols of wealth and power and arrogance. War dogs know neither nationality nor fealty.

How puny and inadequate my reflections on the interaction and the overlapping of 'fact' and 'fiction' now appeared to be! How the events of the past days had torn a gaping hole in my ivory tower and crumpled it, scattering the dainty thoughts! It was my turn at present to be pronged on the sophistry of twisted solipsism. It was as if real death and its mirrored relay through monitors or interpreters could no longer be disentangled. The screen itself was a mortuary with dead heads talking (their heads off). The released force of reality came like a boiling cloud up the streets from the south, burying in dust and ashes (as if of the cremated) my delicate distinctions. You could push your TV set to the window and see both the real thing smoking out there like a blown volcano, maybe with plunging bodies still as lesions on the retina, and the packaged and thus distancing image crackling on the screen.

We were breaking through the pellucid skin between phantasmagoria and phenomena. "Just like in the movies," one was to hear again and again. Salient frames — a homing aircraft, a bursting fireball, a roiling cloud at street level, people greyed by the grit of death and disintegration — were projected so relentlessly that they became everybody's story. And from this igneous litany of repetition it was no longer possible to draw the line between what we *actually saw* and what had now been internalized as communal nightmares. For this must be the way a shared subconscious is forged and images of terror shaped to be embedded in the dreams of generations to come. Like Hieronymus Bosch's renditions of Inferno, which may well have started from memories of burning barns. Is this how we came by our archetypal figures of hell and dragons, is this why we dread the flames of damnation so?

Who was to stop us now from veering to implosion? Already technology and "progress" run mad had made us lose the delicate balance of "controlling" nature and the environment. And what little hold our better thoughts would now have on the play of events! What dereliction! (A sign on the door of the grocery story downstairs announced: "This establishment is closed because of circumstances beyond control.")

Osama Bin Laden appeared in our living rooms as a fallen angel of the light, Lucifer with the sweet face and the soft eyes and the reassuring beard of absolute evil, and now he was to be the sacrificial goat we were going to stone to death outside the city.

Evil, somebody suggested, is the incapacity of seeing the other (the enemy) as human. This, it would seem, is also the way Bin Laden looks at Westerners. The unbeliever (or believer in a false god) will be a factor to be considered dispassionately, a number, a cog, a dog, an ancient undertaker, a statistic, potential collateral damage — but not human the way you, Reader, and Breyten Wordfool and Golden Lotus and Gogga are. Evil then, would be the lack of imaginative identification with the human.

And then nothing was left but the rites. Days resumed their pattern of passing; nights were getting longer and cooler. For a nation with such a notoriously short attention span ("the minds TV-fried"), there's forever the meticulous and pious commemoration of something or other, and as forever the celebration of individuals and events going back over a considerable length of time. In the process the dictionary meaning of words will be gutted and turned inside out: "victims" will become "heroes" by the mere fact of dying, and most all Arabs will be "terrorists." The rites and props were poor: the stars and stripes (meaning nothing and everything), God (meaning everything and nothing), candle-lit vigils, holding one another, bagpipe music, someone croaking "God save America", bunches of flowers and then the heart-rending pictures with descriptions of the missing on pavements and against wire fences. They were shamelessly intimate, sometimes corrected in spidery annotations, that the tattooed dragon was on the right buttock, not the left. At first one felt like a voyeur, too embarrassed to look, but then you let go and realized that this was a form of communion. Looking is already a grieving solidarity. Also the strive for "normalcy," which mostly meant re-opening the stock markets, presented as starting up again the economic engine of the nation, which meant trading — but not of goods, only puff money, a wind of dust coming up the street. For a while quite fat but very attractive black ladies would be getting the opportunity to publicly and *a capella* sing patriotic songs in angelic voices. Later on chesty guys with tattooed biceps and double-breasted politicians belching off key will relay them.

At home mysterious phone calls started coming in: Breyten Wordfool would be woken in the middle of the night by the ringing, somebody would then ask him something (a woman with intense anguish in her voice, speaking in what sounded like Spanish), she'd mention a name, there'd be a lot of noise in the background, he'd answer in Spanish that she's got the wrong number, that she's making a mistake, or that this is a private apartment (with death in the soul, because he knew what she was after), and then the line would be cut. Was she calling from over or *down* "there"?

This is however New York, a vibrant city of incongruent diversity where all want to "belong" — but not everybody was going to fall for the beating of patriotic drums of war. Nearly immediately another language (a *patois*?) was showing up, warning against the perils of fighting the shadows in your own mind, reminding one another of the causes of tragedies and the consequences of ill-considered posturing, trying to broaden provincial America's perceptions to what had been and was still happening elsewhere in that world which now, finally, had to be merged with this the Other World. Some balconies of the building facing ours across the gardens and the alley with the plane-trees were festooned with American flags or garlands of colored bulbs in red, white and blue, but then a big calico banner painted with the peace sign also was hung out. Not all languages are verbal.

Already, on the very first morning after the strike (12 September) as Breyten Wordfool made his way out of our cordoned-off quarter to look for a newspaper, he came across wisdom flowers crayoned on the concrete. DONT TR UST YR TV ABT WTC. And a little farther along: RACIST PATR IOT ISM IS COWARDICE. And then: CAPITALISM=CANNIBALISM. And: AN I FOR AN I LEAVES EVEN YO U SIGHTLESS. Then he saw a moving drawing, still in white chalk on the sidewalk, of the two towers now with big wings, as protecting angels of the mutilated city. And written just a yard or two away: CRY MORE.

Up by Union Square the signs of mourning and the manifestations of a mute debate were multiplying rapidly. A 'Mural of Hope/ Mural de la Esperanza' was soon plastered with the photos and particulars of missing persons in a pathetic homage to love and as affirmation of the refusal to accept the horribly inevitable. Fuck off, Death! No time, no time. Take your fetid face elsewhere! Just show me the body! Maybe he's still alive in some air pocket. He was always a hero. Cell-phones were heard to be ringing from under the rubble....

Scrolls of paper were laid down on the ground and people wrote messages. (To whom? The living? The dead?) *My cousin is one of the missing firemen. Keep all trapped in your prayers; 15 minutes from losing my father — 15 minutes!; Yesterday we were strangers on the street. Today you look in my eyes; Where love's gone? Where peace's gone? Don't forget evils, But no hate, No War. We do want peace. No more tragity; Wake up to the inequalities that exist in the world; Wo iss Gott?; We will not turn the other cheek; We have been too Disne(y)fied. Too many yellow smiley faces. Wake up now. Complacency is lethal; The Naked City has had its soul beared; Stand as one or fall apart; It seems as if we have disappeared into thin air... lost we are in the madness of this day; Enjoy your life cause you never know what may happen; I miss those I will never know; Don't let CNN define your world; Palestinians are dying and nobody cares; I care; Fuck you!*

On his haunches an intense young guy with tresses and a handful of coloured markers was moving from roll to roll and writing carefully: *Balance x=y.* And: *Asymmetry.*

By the second day candles with thick tears of spilled wax were like a gathering funeral crowd who'd been out in the naked sun for too long, improvised statues were going up, flowers and mementos piled in heaps, the square was turning into a huge open-air chapel. On the morning of the third day when a smell of burnt plastic (and what else?) was hanging like a shroud over the city, Breyten walked with Chuck Wachtel toward the scene of smoking devastation. We couldn't get beyond Canal Street. This is Chuck's town. His eyes saw things and buildings and perhaps people who were no longer here. Our conversation ranged wide. He told Breyten Wordfool how New York is a working class city, of how his mother was trying to make a phone call back into the past — 'hello? Hello, New York?' — but the past was receding rapidly, of how peasants mostly stay out of history, including those who were now going to be killed, for they will not be remembered.

We spoke much about how writing is also a way of becoming better-equipped and more aware citizens. About how writers, except for those ideologically motivated, do not normally blow on the coals — rather, they bring understanding and nuances, pages of doubt, so few answers, a recognition of shared humanity, a warning of the implications of policies and what the songs of blind leaders really mean. About how birds know many things in advance. About how it is up to each generation to find its own forms for the reaffirmation of humanism.

And already some enterprising and patently poor Chinese, recently peasants, were on the streets flogging t-shirts embroidered with the American flag or eagle or colors (how quickly! Done overnight in sweatshops?) and with slogans like: "Evil will be punished" or "I was there and lucky to survive." My wife, Golden Lotus, said they were priced at only five dollars each. The mayor had been on the air to warn against gougers, hustlers, and those stealing donations to sell them elsewhere, leeches, crooks, dealers, scam artists, maybe even looters. Breyten didn't know whether to be angry or to cry. Here were people feeding off the event but also trying to turn their own pain into a quick buck. And then he thought: but this exactly is an affirmation of the American dream, this is why they sacrificed and endured much to get here, *anything* can become money! Within a generation they will have saved enough to send a daughter to university, and she may well want to study writing, that art of decadent distancing.

Two women were holding up gold-framed, black-bordered, cheap Xeroxed reproductions of the New York skyline the way it was when the twin towers were still gloriously present. They were selling these souvenirs — or *ex votos,* or holy images — in sing-song voices. The only American they knew was the price of the pictures. The images had a glow and a halo, as you'd see in pictures of temples or portraits of Bodhisattvas, or maybe just the ancestors. Yes, this was it. Already these towers were ancestor spirits. We have to invoke their benevolent protection. Perhaps we'll have to bring little presents as sacrifices on the altar. Breyten Wordfool will offer these pages, and I'll help him. Soon there will be small statuettes. We'll prostrate ourselves and burn incense sticks. Somebody will compose a song. Tales will be told. Chunks of concrete, stained a permanent grey by the ashes of death, will be collected and sold religiously. Small leftovers of human parts have by now been gathered in bags, but thousands of bodies will remain there and become part of the foundations of the new buildings. The cellphones and the pagers will fall silent.

A young man thrust a hand-stencilled flyer in Breyten Wordfool's hand:

THIS IS AN AFFIRMATION OF
MY *LOVE* FOR YOU AS A HUMAN.
WE ARE *ALL ONE*: *HUMANS*.
THIS IS AN OPPORTUNITY FOR *PEACE*.
CHANGE THE VISCIOUS CYCLE OF
THE EGO, TO A CYCLE OF *LOVE*
PEACE FOR ALL;

THEY EXSIST AND AWAIT
YOUR HAND. TO BE ONE
WITH PEACE PLEASE
SHARE THIS, AS AN ACT
OF LOVE FOR YOUR FELLOW
HUMAN LOVE.

MIRROR NOTE 2

What I remember now from these days: a lone saxophone crying in the park, two young black girls making clumsy but fervent
love to one another on a bench behind some bushes, the unbearable
sight of a man very high up the smoking glass cliff face with its
gaping black mouth waving his shirt from one of the windows
("goodbye, goodbye New York"?), a Mexican midget with straw
sombrero and poncho and beard solemnly watching a Chinese
hunchback doing tai-chi, people holding down their lips with trembling fingertips, the two Asian girls buying souvenir postcards of
the Twin Towers and in the background the towers are blazing
beautifully as in a Bosch painting, the drunken black guy with the
embroidered Muslim hat screaming obscenities, the second black
guy on Union Square in a circle of Philistines hoarse from shouting
his hands trumpeting his mouth going on about a day of reckoning
and doom and God casting down flaming arrows of destruction repent! repent!, the third black man walking purposefully reciting
repeatedly to no-one in particular: "You never know, you just never
know," pigeons rising from the street as the plane ploughed into
the first tall building (foreshadowing the fluttering departure of
souls?), the awesome picture of the wingless angel plunging head
first a hundred stories down the gleaming facade, at red dusk the
circle of Zen practitioners (some shaven heads) cross-legged on
the grass hearing that perhaps (surely) this too is the dharma, people wearing small nose-and-mouth masks against the slightly acrid
smoke moving uptown through deserted streets and some have
them perched on their heads like minute clowns' caps, an old man
doing slow exercises with a wooden sword, on the second day the

pall still rising like a footnote left by an absent god, on the third day the pall still rising like a footnote left by an absent god, my conviction that the enormity can be approached in words paralleled not too close so as not to burn, my conviction that I wished to believe this like a footnote left by an absent god....

LAWRENCE SWAN

AFTER THE ASH-WIND
ROB HARDIN

9/11/01: 8:54 a.m.

My shift has ended and I'm sitting at my computer, finessing a letter to Swedish musician, Tomas Pettersson. Looking out of an eighteenth-story window off Maiden Lane, I notice what might have passed for falling snow if not for the flashes of sunlight caught by strips of plastic as they flex and shiver in the sky. Their sinuous glitter seems indicative of mischief. Is this confetti dropped from a helicopter, some prank by Howard Stern? The detritus of a bon voyage party on the roof of an adjacent high-rise?

I exit 110 Maiden Lane to find a group of lawyers lingering on the marble steps just under the awning. They're chatting about their case and staring at something overhead. I glance in the direction of their stare, expecting some aerial anomaly. Instead, I see flames aslant, a tower set afire.

I squint at the scene to focus. The damage seems oddly contained. What appear to have been the sixty to sixty-fourth floors are now rings of glowing metal, their windows, slots that spume fire and curlicues of smoke.

Flashes from the slots merge and descend like searchlight beams filled with coruscating minutiae. The effect seems almost whimsical. This spotlight, this anachronism, might have framed a glittery-tuxedo'd Marlene Dietrich, or a wand-shaking Tinker Bell trailing pixie dust.

The beam flows down to my feet. Its contents are singed paper.

I open my satchel. Remembering the way they glittered, I shove the pages inside.

31

I hear labored breathing and turn to my left, squinting to see through the haze. A heavyset African-American woman emerges and struggles to keep walking. None of the lawyers seem to notice. Sweating and wheezing, she pulls herself up the steps.

"Hey," I call after her. "You have asthma?" She turns but doesn't nod.

I pull out my inhaler and tell her to open her mouth. She does and I dispense three pumps of synthetic adrenaline. Then I tell her I'm going to walk her into the building.

Two of the lawyers notice her at last, freed from the spell of shop talk and gossip. They take her upstairs to enjoy their fastidiously circulated air. It makes me feel useful to think I might have saved her a trip to the hospital.

I decide to walk toward whatever had left the lady unable to breathe. Someone else might need a few puffs from my inhaler.

I head up Fulton Street until I come within yards of the burning building. Nearly there, I gaze upward: Someone jumps to her death.

Wave upon wave of jumpers follow the first. The heat's unendurable for them. The band of fire pushes out to the ledge and then the street. Next to me, a middle-aged black woman with a shopping bag is weeping so hard her body jerks. She's hiding her face and gripping the handle of her bag. It feels like the end of the world.

Yet I don't weep as the people fall and flatten. *This is what happens to us,* I think. The Tower looks like the paintings of Kali I've seen all my life, only vast and real. She's coming for us. She's scorching and slashing us all.

In the course of an hour, I watch a dozen people catch fire.

People rush down the street sobbing and exhorting everyone else to pray. But for some reason, I don't break down or turn away from the carnage.

Perhaps the reason I'm able to stay objective is because I've lost a lot of people. Perhaps lack of attachment and not wisdom affords me the luxury.

Someone nearby explains that terrorists have attacked the building. Someone else says that the Pentagon was attacked. I wonder where people are getting their information — how do they know for sure? No one's cell phone works. No headlines crawl across the LED displays in gadget store windows.

I start walking again. I'm just about to cross Broadway when a plane flies around the Second Tower in a half-circle, slanting down toward the base of the building. Then its thunderous impact: The report of a god-sized gun.

People run frantically, as they do in disaster movies. They look like they're fleeing Godzilla. I turn, then stop. *What am I running from?*

Behind me, an oblivious twit compliments the ingenuity of the terrorists. "They knew what they were doing, you gotta hand 'em that." A middle-aged man in a brown suit gives me a look of exasperation. Then the first man praises the sturdiness of the buildings. "Look how well they're taking it," he tells us. "Those things are built for it. They're never coming down."

On cue, the Second Tower collapses. I tilt my head and see the entire structure begin to sink, and the tiny figures on the edges of the floors and the roof enter their free-fall. Some hang from the unmoored ledges until the initial shift of the collapse wrenches them free. Others seem to let go voluntarily. As the building crumbles, two figures embrace for the last time before floating apart in midair. You can't see their faces and the space is like silence around them. I'm with them when it happens. My eyes say goodbye as they disappear into wreckage.

Stravinsky once said that the most heartbreaking artwork from the ancient world depicts lovers who are faceless, whose individuality remains hidden from us, but whom the story destroys. Falling people look that way, too — like doomed Cycladic figurines.

Smoke comes rushing out from the base of the falling structure, overtaking us.

Waves of people rush toward the river—many of them weeping, most of them panicked by the falling monolith and its onslaught of smoke and debris.

White wind chases me down a sloping alley and into a ten-story building, where the air grows so opaque I have to run back into the street. A group of us try to force our way into another building that seems more airtight, but the people on the other side of the glass won't unlock the doors and we refuse to break the windows. It would be cruel to expose the people who are shunning us to the poison the rest of us are breathing.

None of the little shops, which have depended on Wall Street customers to survive for all this time, will open their doors to the rushes of coughing people. Storefronts become fallout shelters guarded by survivalists. The clerks stand at the backs of the stores, safely distanced from the locked glass doors which the crowd could shatter so easily. *This is how they've always seen us.*

Police herd us down Water Street and past the Brooklyn Bridge. I'm coughing the whole way there. Someone actually collapses and I right him until he's standing again because he doesn't have time to stop. For a long time, I breathe through my collar and can't see the sidewalk in front of me. Then some of us move to the street to make room for three people in wheelchairs. A policeman stops and tries to help them embark a parked bus. By the time I reach Bayard Street in Chinatown, the air has cleared. I'm standing outside the school where I used to teach English. Old people smile out of obligation and watch me turn toward the entrance. The door is locked. I walk down to the park, where tourists and business people on breaks used to wait in lines that stretched into the street for a woman in a cart to make tiny pancakes. The cart's locked and no one is there, not even old men on benches. There's a space where the street veers downward and the buildings ahead aren't as tall as the drop. I get there in time to gaze toward the horizon and watch as the First Tower disintegrates. An invisible hand presses down on it, grinding it into powder. Fire swells behind rising smoke trails that arc and thicken. Anything can happen now. Anyone might die.

I keep walking until the smoke clears and I'm close to my neighborhood. The whole way there, I smell the taint of burning chemicals. I arrive at Rivington and Bowery, where a singer I know lives, and try to get buzzed upstairs. Her husband leans out the window and waves. He claims to be having a problem with the door, but the problem with that door is me. I continue walking to Houston Street and buy things to chew and swallow, perhaps to weigh myself down: Lox from Russ & Daughters, an Excedrin from in Panjali Deli. The turbaned cashier looks miserable and tells me how sorry he is.

I go to a Polish diner on Second and A and order coffee. The analog TV's tuned to a news loop on New York 1. I'm the only dusty person in the place—the only person who's come from the site—but I don't look bereaved, so the female waiter concentrates on a man in a gabardine sports jacket who trembles and says he "doesn't want to hear about it." His reaction doesn't seem selfish to anyone else, but it's hard for me to understand why I'm supposed to care how he feels. He and I are both still alive and sitting in a diner, but I'm pretty sure that whatever I inhaled on the way there will impact on my lifespan and he won't bother grieving for me, let alone, for the ones who jumped.

After I leave, another guy on the street notices my cremains-dusted satchel. "Hey! You're covered in ashes! Did you just come from the WTC?"

I look at the man, who, like so many others that morning, is in his thirties and dressed formally. In this case, he's wearing a white summer suit.

"Yeah, I did come from there. I even grabbed some of the papers that floated down from the Tower and stuffed them in here. Not sure why."

He peers at my satchel hesitantly. "Hey, you wouldn't let me buy that from you, would you? How much you want for it?"

"Want for what?"

"How much you want for the bag?"

I tell him no and keep walking home. As I reach the front door, I realize I should have blown ashes all over his suit. *Now you don't need the bag.*

* * * *

I turn on the television in time to hear Bush shout, "This is an act of war!" After ten minutes of news, I turn it off. My phone rings twice, but I don't pick up. An ex who broke up with me the year before leaves a message asking if I'm OK.

I call a co-worker, Roy, to make certain he's safe. He tells me he had to walk so close to the Second Tower to get to home he was hit by debris. He saw flames shooting from the clothing store, Century 21. He saw the people jumping.

THE COLLECTOR
RON KOLM

I'm a collector. I hunt down runs of literary magazines and signed first editions, and place them in university library archives. I collect comic books and the Jokers from decks of playing cards. I also lust after die-cast model cars; mostly Hot Wheels. I have hundreds of them — maybe thousands — some on display, but most of them stashed away in boxes.

As I've gotten older, it's become more difficult to compete with younger Hot Wheels collectors. They line-up outside the doors at Toys R Us and, when the store opens, they shove the mothers with their kids aside as they race to see who can get to the pegs first. I usually come in last. So, in order to get the newest releases I've had to hook up with a 'dealer' — a guy who spends most of his waking hours tracking down product; some for himself, some to list on eBay, and the rest for schmucks like myself.

My dealer's name is Ken, and he's a prison guard who works the night shift at Rikers, which means he just barely makes it to the store before it opens. But he's buff, so no one fucks with him — he always gets to the Hot Wheels display rack first without having to hustle — the other collectors part like the Red Sea when he walks by.

Anyway, I took the day off from work and made plans to meet him on the Toys R Us parking lot in Long Island City on the morning of September eleventh, 2001. My wife and I sent our two sons off to school and then walked across Northern Boulevard towards the store. His car was parked pretty far away from the entrance, even though the lot was mostly empty. We noticed as we approached that his car doors were open, and his car was surrounded by several young girls all wearing red t-shirts, who seemed to be listening to the car radio, which was turned up real loud. Then we saw in the distance a plume of smoke rising into the sky from the city's skyline; more specifically, from one of the World Trade Center towers.

"Seems to have been hit by a small plane," Ken told us when we got to his car.

"Man, New York City firemen are the best," I enthused. "They're probably inside putting it out right now."

Moments later a manager came charging out of the store, shouting, "I don't give a fuck what's going on! If you don't get your asses inside and punch in I'll fire all of you!" which quickly dispersed the crowd.

I looked back at the skyline — one of the towers had disappeared and smoke was now pouring out of what used to be its twin. When we heard on the radio that planes were flying into things, my wife left to get our youngest son, while I flagged down a car service to Astoria to collect our oldest.

9/11
RONNIE NORPEL

A t P.S. 166, Monica, Grace and I were finishing with the last few parents signing their children up for the after school program, when Antonio and Asako (Francesco's parents) came whooshing through the doorway and stopped in their tracks in front of our table. Their faces were oddly flat as they asked us, "Did you hear about the accident?"

"No, what accident?" The three of us ask in unison. "Two planes have hit the world trade towers," Antonio explained.

"Oh, my God, I'm going to have my baby," Monica moaned. She is due on November 12.

"Are you kidding?!" I asked, knowing that it had to be an impossible joke and that, of course it was true, Antonio's being a rather sober guy, even under normal circumstances.

Grace's cell phone rang as we were listening to Antonio's quick explanation.

"A plane hit the Pentagon too?" she responded in disbelief to her caller. It was immediately clear that none of this was an "accident" and that the US, us, we were under siege.

Another mom walked in and told Monica, "My son called me at 9:30 and said 'Mom, do not come to work!' If I hadn't been delayed to speak to my younger son's teacher and the principal, I would've been going right through there!"

Kaye's near-miss was the first of many we would hear about over the next days. Her face was blank. I watched from my side of the table and then heard myself ask, "Do you need a hug?"

Her tears welled at my question, and I leaped from my chair and around the desk and put my arms around this person who two minutes earlier had been a stranger. It was the first of my attempts to comfort a fellow human on a day when many strangers would fall, some literally, into each other's arms.

"What sign are you?" Kaye asked me.

Such a funny question at a time like this, but I answered like it was my name, "Cancer."

"Oh, Cancer, of course, they are so nurturing."

"Well yeah, but crabby too."

"Don't tell me about that," she replied. "I'm dating a Cancer, and boy, can he be mooo-deee!"

We chuckled despite ourselves, our new reality.

CATASTROPHE
ELLEN AUG LYTLE

It's Tuesday, September 11, 2001. How could you not remember such a warm sunny morning with hardly a cloud floating about the painterly sky? I hurry to open the porch door which is off Mike's small studio, in our four room flat in Tribeca. Oh! Let this air wash over me! I had, as usual, a list of errands to finish, but no teaching today, so yay! Free for a change!

About 8:30 a.m. I'm gladly done feeding Oddie and Twill, and Mike's off to his gardening job. But my joy is interrupted by a loud wide, droning noise above our building; an airplane I suspect, is flying dangerously low. My landline rings: Stacey, my daughter: harried and hurried like always, but yes, her birthday yesterday was fine, and she's too busy to talk, but... I'm breathless, hearing a chaotic, crashing coming I think, from right downstairs.... there's been an accident, I tell her, and she's suddenly all ears. Sounds like a plane crashed into four trucks or fifteen dumpsters, something very big... call you back.

Suddenly, the rushing rubble noises abate and for one or two minutes there's dead silence, just the sun burning onto the balcony. I can't see the immediate street because of scaffolding, we're only nine floors up, but facing the huge courtyard of our thirty-nine story building, I watch the tenants' dogs come on the terraces and immediately some begin to howl, then others catch up, and in unison, they tell us something ominous is happening.

Minutes later my sister calls from Florida: Turn on your TV — a plane hit the World Trade Center! Oh yes — flew over our building, pilot must have been drunk, small plane, hah? TV shows

40

an enormous Boeing 767 stuck through high floors of One World Trade Center, aka the North Tower. I shiver. So that's the loud sickening noise I just heard.

Of course I'm not prepared for what happens next: another explosive noise — sounding slightly farther away than the plane that flew across our roof — the second plane knifing through the South Tower. I grab onto one of our bookcases, thinking I might fall thru the floor. Our phone rings, call waiting, even on the Sprint cell phone Jimmy bought me for my last birthday, ringing, ringing... daughter-in-law, daughter, in-laws, friends.... I've got to leave our flat, they say, Come to our place; Upper East or West Side — someplace safe... What? Never!

We are staying right here, I say to Oddie, our corgi, and to Twilly, our cat. Right here until I bathe and then we'll go out and I'll see for myself. I'm near the coat rack on my way to bathe, clean clothes in my hands, when a third frightening explosion sends me onto the floor. OMG, I think, we need to leave. A fifty second bath and into bra, panties, jeans, a t shirt, and shoes — harness on Oddie — grab a leash! We'll be back right away Twill, I lie, as I straighten the bed and shut the porch door.

Andy, my oldest, a farmer in upstate New York, somehow gets through to my cell. O, the fire is contained now, I say, in the street, knowing now the explosion before my bath was the South Tower crashing. I can see blinding flames in the North Tower from here; they are rising up to higher floors, but it's nowhere near collapse, though I'm six or seven blocks away. Let you know more when I get my camera! And though I don't know exactly what's happening, I run with Oddie back to our place.

All the neighbors clot in front, pouring out of the lobby in droves. The word is: No one gets back in for anything except maybe a pet. I know Twilly has to stay, a skittish cat can't possibly be outside with this. I prayed quickly. A few people talk about Afghanistan and bad US policies, and what did we expect?

Quickly word spreads: Terrorist attack. We had one before, and I remember our bathroom floor moving and a muffled sound of an explosion coming from deep down; earth's basement. That was Feb. 26, 1993. So, no surprise, some were saying, but determined to get my camera, I shake off anything being said, and try squeezing between the throngs to get back in. Too late! The loudest explosive rumble shakes the ground in front of our building: it's a volcanic rumble like a thousand boulders sliding down a mountainside, and waves of hysterical people rush up West street along the Hudson, looking for safety. I grab Oddie and try to cross the wide N. Moore Street for the grassy lawn outside The Shearson–Lehman offices, a bevy of motorcycles roars inches from us... fuck you! I scream and fall face down onto the grass alongside my dog. The North Tower doesn't withstand the force of the fire and comes toppling down. Medical triage is setting up along streets in Tribeca and trucks are unloading hundreds of black, zippered, body bags. Gradually we're led off the patchy grass onto a sidewalk packed with people, and told by loudspeaker to wait for and follow all instructions.

*****

Somehow, after a couple of hours, we make it up to Greenwich Village, a mile and a half north. I find my favorite outdoor cafe and try phone calls, no service; land or cell. Around 3 p.m. at a friend's on Christopher Street, I get through to Stacey who tells Mike, when he calls, we're ok — but we aren't — none of us would ever be ok, in the same way, again. We spit smoky snot from our nose and throat, the sky over Tribeca is dark for days, uniforms are everywhere checking ID for months, some streets closed to vehicular traffic till after Christmas, weeks later downtown shops and cafes are still deserted, smoke from the fires last well into 2002. At 5:30 p.m. that same sunny afternoon, World Trade #5 falls to the ground and a dusty cloud of what's left of it rolls like a tumbleweed up Greenwich Street, past our windows, caught in the late summer breeze.

WITNESS
TSAURAH LITZKY

> "For transgressions against God, the day of
> atonement atones, for transgressions of one
> human being against another the day of
> atonement does not atone until they have
> made peace with another." — *Midrash*

In Union Square after the tragedy, thousands of people are trying to dispel the darkness, lighting candles, clasping hands, singing "Give Peace a Chance," while the devil does the tarantella through the heavens holding the earth in his hands like a giant orange. At any second he may pop it into his mouth and grind all our unfinished lives into a bloody pulp.

Although I believe in the word of the Hindu sage, Marahanda, to kill one is to kill ten thousand, my gut is screaming, an eye for an eye, a tooth for a tooth, get Osama and his hellions, decimate the Mujadhin. When I tell my Catholic friend, Mary, this she says I feel this way because I am Jewish, part of an ancient, primitive tribe. She says it is more evolved to turn the other cheek, there is nothing more evolved than world peace. I get furious at her and yell, "When have the Catholics ever given the world peace? What about the inquisition? What about the popes who believe women don't have the right to control their bodies? The Jews," I go on, "have given us Freud, Marx, Einstein."

She laughs, "Yeah, Einstein," she says, "the father of the atom bomb."

"What about Ghandi? Don't you know that Ghandi was really Jewish?" I scream.

She tells me I am insane and she is right. I AM insane. Whether my eyes are shut tight or open wide I see, running over and over in my head, the news clip of the people jumping out of the windows of the World Trade Center, their bodies falling like ticker-tape.

I go down to Maryland to spend Yom Kippur with my father. I sit in the auditorium of the JFK High School among a thousand, well-scrubbed, earnest Jews dressed in their holiday best. These Jews are not from my ancient tribe, they believe in the rule of law — the *Torah,* the book of laws. With the rabbi, they bow their heads in a silent prayer for peace. I hold my head high, savage in my nose ring and designer knock-offs from H&M, and think that all I believe in is sex and death. Yet during Kol Nidre, the whisper of wings, I find myself reaching for my father's hand.

Back in New York I prepare for the second session of the erotic writing class I teach. For the first time in years the course is filled up, eighteen students. During last week's introductions,, half of them said they took the course because they wanted to lift their spirits.

I advised them to go out and have some sex. It would both lift their spirits and give them something to write about. I stop my preparations for Class Two: "The Petunia and the Pussy — Erotic Language." I decide I have to practice what I preach.

I call up a man I have just started to date but have not yet slept with. He is as battered as I am but also, astonishingly unbroken. I tell him I have to come over right away. When I get there, I stand in front of him as he sits down on the couch and slowly take off my clothes. He seems startled and lights a cigarette, but then he gets into it. He takes his cock out. I like it. It is solid, thick with desire, upstanding, a tree of life. He reaches his fingers up and pulls me down onto him by my nipples. He has a dog named Abraham Lincoln he has locked in his darkroom because I am allergic, still at the moment of penetration I feel that itch sensation all over my face that means I'm breaking out in hives, but I don't let this interrupt our ride. I concentrate on the heat between us, the building, cleansing fire. The *Midrash* says to search for the sudden light that lights up the heart. I do not know about the future of the earth, I do not know if this sorrow can ever be healed But at least for this little while I have found what I was hoping for, there is still miracle and wonder this is the day of awe.

JOURNAL ENTRY OF AN EYEWITNESS, TUESDAY, SEPTEMBER 11, 2001

BARBARA ROSENTHAL

Sept. 11, 2012. Below is my Journal entry for Sept. 11, 2001. I was on the Staten Island Ferry, in the middle of the harbor, writing in my Journal, looking directly AT THE TOWERS when the plane hit. I jumped up when I saw the smoke, yelled "It's a terrorist attack!! Take photographs!!" but everyone on board thought I was just another crazy. No one else there knew what to think until they were told what to think, later in the day. Here are the exact words as they came out of my pencil. (I wasn't wearing a watch, though, and I might not have had the times really right. And I did not have any camera-device, and didn't think to make a drawing, so I won't post any images today.)

4 a.m. Awoke to usual pre-dawn panic attack gasping for air, no dream, just patternless profusion of words screeching silently, extreme and intense. Head throbbing, aching anxiety, wrenching gut, retching and gagging, palpitations, tremors, three rounds of diarrhea. Doc gave Klonopin, but don't want take: seems stupid start day with med Gil given as sleeping pill. Took Bob's advice, jumped up down 200 times dissipate tension before shower; helps somewhat few minutes. Waking earlier every morning, two to four hours of broken sleep, can't swallow food, too restless even to use time meaningful work, and four hours to kill til leave teach Staten Island. Looking forward ferry, calmed by lapping water, big sky, receding view lower Manhattan from back deck always sit. Open water soothing and good: went beach over weekend, not any beach, but belated birthday outing with family to seedy old grandeur of Asbury Park, Jersey, a few sad salt-water

taffy stands and broken amusements still open along splintered boardwalk. Came as kid sometimes, when now crumbling beach architecture then full sandstone splendor, arching glassed casino now every pane shattered, ornate stonework haphazardly graffit-tied, parking lot trashed and overgrown. Shot many pics. Is it per-verted to think decay or tragedy picturesque? Beach, though, clean enough, and other families picnic, too, in post-summer warmth. Can't write anymore, pencil trembling, will try some deep breath-ing, tai chi, more jumping and another shower.

8 a.m. On 7th Ave subway downtown catch Staten Island Ferry teach fourth session Eng 111, Freshman Comp. Truly love subway, way it so homogeneously mixes and transports this international city, like ancient Alexandria, still people costumed in native or religious dress. Everyone has intricate life story, intense motivation to be here in stew of cultures where, despite our undeserved reputation as rude, New Yorkers most tolerant, most helpful, most deferential people. Everyone equal on subway. Sit body to body, touch hands along pole, all nationalities coming and going in morning rush.

8:30 a.m. Got favorite seat on back deck, crisp, clear sky blue sky blue sky blue sky, sunny and warm, just hint of light cool breeze, perfect day, perfect view. Battery starting to recede. Teal and steel blue water fresh and glinting, white wake churning, gulls circling, pigeons along for the ride. Empire State just barely visible now far up on 34th St, World Trade Center so disproportionate as architecture, but so grand a symbol of America's gigantitude, filled by family wage-earners. A few artists have studios there: such per-meating light, air, magnificent elevators must make them want work large-scale. Don't know anyone. Oh My God! Flames just burst, trailing black smoke westward, 2/3 way up left tower, 8:45!

9:10 a.m. On bus from ferry to college. No camera with me today, shit! Stopped writing when flames burst, jumped up, yelled, pointed, made everyone look. "Terrorist attack, terrorist attack!" Pas-sengers looked at me, not at skyline. Maybe ten people on deck, so blasé, some tourists with cameras, no one shooting. I kept yelling, "Take pictures! Call The Times when we dock or by cell phone. They'll pick up your film. You'll get it back!" "It's just a fire," a woman said. "No, no," I yelled, more frantically, "don't you remember the garage bomb in '93? Please take pictures! The view from the bay is remarkable! You're bound to hit the papers!" No one shooting, everyone edging farther from me, Statue of Liberty, which they came to photograph, floating up starboard. One dubious couple snapped a few frames toward the Battery, each one, of the other in front of the shot. "Take some of just Manhattan, of the burning tower in the scene. Please call *The Times* Metro Desk, tell them you have film!" They said they might, and politely left toward Statue. A few people came on deck from inside; their radios had no news.

11 a.m. Met confused 10:10 class. We sat out on lawn. News confirming terrorism still conjecture, but I am certain, and angry. Where CIA, FBI, Military, Coast Guard? The primary function of government is to protect its citizens. For years I've asked in class for essays: What are the rights of citizenship and what are its duties? Talked together for awhile, then let students go. By now more news: Islamic suicide pilots hijacked four fully fueled American planes within our own borders, and piloted them like bombs into each Tower, the Pentagon and The White House, which was spared because passengers aboard wrestled hijackers and crashed near Pittsburgh. I hadn't seen planes because they came from north. Grizzly news from city. People seen jumping from the fiery Trade Center! Faced with such enormous choice, overwhelmed by helplessness, know about to die and choose jump 100 floors rather than burn alive. Were flames lapping their bodies? Air impossible breathe even one more breath? A horrid death so immanent that so many jumped, convinced they could not be saved or save themselves, or even live through it, unwilling to hang on another minute, without any hope that rescue could come the next second? What was it like on ground, live bodies hurtling, smacking and smashing to instantly dead bloody puddles of dresses and business suit rags on the sidewalk?

2:20 p.m. Went to second class in case anyone showed up. No one did, although all commuters stranded, no traffic permitted in or out Manhattan. Will amble over my office and see what's going on.

3:40 p.m. More news. Both towers collapsed, pancaking storey after storey down and down; other buildings falling all over area. 500 firefighters lost. Death toll may reach 5,000, although earlier rumored 25,000! Large-scale plot of Islamic militants in the works for months, apparently. Cliché's are so fitting here: We were caught with our pants down; asleep at the wheel. W, I hate you! How could our agencies have been so lax? I repeat: the primary function of government is to protect its citizens! Waiting for phone lines. Have to stay here tonight. Staten Island Red Cross setting up cots in Student Center for those of us from other boroughs. Red Cross quite admirable today, as usual, but I harbor animosity toward International Red Cross for recognize all nations' Red Crosses and Red Crescents, but not the Hebrew Red Stars. (And in back of mind is fear that somehow, no matter what the facts, someone will get twisted idea to blame it on Jews, and we'll be in for another wave anti-Semitism.)

4 p.m. Got phone call through to Bill at home. Everyone's been worried about me! Had no idea! People we know from all over world been phoning! He and kids frantic because I took subway to Battery this morning. I've been so perfectly safe, while so many perished horribly. Never thought think anyone worry about me. Wish family could be together, but have to stay cots, no telling how long. Whatever will this barracks think of my pre-dawn panic attacks? How will I be able jump up down 200 times? Images of burning people leaping to their death, buildings collapsing all around them, are seared into my imagination; memory first burst of flames and wisps black smoke as I watched from the ferry, branded into my mind.

Midnight. Unexpectedly home! Police escorted chartered bus from college to a #5 subway stop in Brooklyn, the only train into Manhattan. On this ride, people seemed less united, multiculturalism seemed more suspect. From Union Square walked west across 14th St down through the Meat Market. I live less than one mile straight up West Street from site of Towers. Air is thick with vaporized bodies and eye-burning, unbreathable, dark, acrid filth. There's a ghostly vacancy in the foul sky when I look south from the door of my building. Tomorrow I'll donate blood at St. Vincent's. Tonight, tomorrow's pre-dawn panic is already rising. There are a lot of TV images and early news photos, all of them ghastly, but none of them show the very first layer of fire from the 23rd floor drifting westward across the Battery, from my vantage in the bay. The decay of Asbury Park is neatly lined up in latent images from my camera, but no pictures from this devastating day.

FROM *TWIN TOWERS* /
LEARNING TO DRAW / *A HISTORY*
BASIL KING

T he Twin Towers had replaced the Statue of Liberty. They were capitalism's welcoming committee. Everyone, no matter where they came from, was welcome. Get rich, be rich, stay rich. Poverty's face is ugly. It is also sick and has learning problems. There are good guys and bad guys, good girls and bad girls. It's too hard to think anything else. It's too difficult to think what it would be like to be without possessions. No possessions, no self-worth. Not to have MONEY. It's too difficult to think of. What would it be like if everyone had as much as you? If no one was considered less than you?

I insist light abstracts the smallest thing.

Manet and Franz Kline are crying. David Hockney is crying. The animators and the cartoonists and their comics are crying. Philip Guston is shaking his head. The towers have imploded and there are heaps of rubble. More than Guston's junk yard can tolerate. There is so much to internalize and process. Why did American turn its back on all the events that had taken place in the Mid-East leading up to this huge happening? This happening that wasn't an Art Happening outdid all the Art Happenings of the past century. A cast of thousands couldn't have accomplished what those two plane did. Two planes crashing into the Twin Towers have shown the whole world that everyone is vulnerable. Not just Americans, but everyone in the world is at risk.

HILL BY THE RIVER
BUD SMITH

On a steep hill, carefully rolling boulders to the bottom. Building a wall — cut in with shovel — cementing things together, to look pretty for the boats coming in and off the dock.

This rich, empty house, vacant till next summer. Me all alone. Birds the only noise, landing on the river, floating, landing on the dock, watching.

A Tuesday. New Jersey. The morning ending and me drinking out of the garden hose, thinking about breaking into the house and walking around on the tiles worth more than my life. No one would know. Heave a boulder through the sliding glass door. Maybe I'd find money for college in a drawer somewhere.

Also, I'd have loved to simply shove the boulders down the grassy hill, but I couldn't. The boulders would tumble across the dock and crash into the river, frightening the birds to death, scattering them. Boulders sunk into the mud on the bottom of the river wouldn't help me finish any quicker.

Rick, who'd dropped me off at 7, wouldn't be back until 4, or later. And all this hush on the lonely block. I had no radio. I had no phone. I began singing to myself.

The sun got higher. Indian summer. 85 degrees. Sweat came. I took off my shirt. I took off my shorts. I gently led the boulders down the hill in my underwear and Nikes. Singing. Thinking about my date that night with Shannon. It was her eighteenth birthday and she'd decided to share it with me.

I sang my songs louder, thinking about going to buy a new shirt after work. One without holes in it. And about buying Shannon a book to read. But which one? And about walking up the block, towards the highway. There was a deli. I really liked their turkey sandwiches. Good pickles too. They made their own chocolate chip cookies.

Then there was a horn, the birds on the dock looked over, nervous. Rick pulling up in his pickup truck. Brakes screeching.

"You're early!" I shouted.

"GET IN THE TRUCK!"

"Get in the truck?" I almost laughed.

"We're leaving."

"Early!"

I didn't even ask why. I sprinted down the hill, so happy. Kicking off my sneakers as I ran. I dove into the river. Cool water. Dirt washed off. Cement dust washed off. I climbed back onto the pier smiling. Home early!

I grabbed my shirt. I grabbed my shorts and sneakers, and ran barefoot towards his pickup.

"Something happened," he said.

I dried my body off with the shirt. I climbed inside the truck.

"Something happened, yeah, I just got happy as hell. That's what happened. I've got a date tonight."

He turned the radio on. I dripped. I listened to the radio. I dripped. I leaned in closer to the radio. He leaned in closer to the radio. Everyone did.

I SAW IT ON THE RADIO
JAMES DUNCAN

I t was a Tuesday, if I recall, about fifteen miles from the border Vermont shares with New York, between Bennington and Albany. I'd always scheduled my classes so the earliest one starts just before lunch, followed by a mid-afternoon course or two, creating a lazy-man's busy day with large empty pockets of time for sleeping in, casual lunches, and early dinners. I slept in a bit that morning, then shaved and showered and had just mixed up some pancake batter while listening to Howard Stern on my Walkman when someone mentioned the first plane.

I poured the batter into the frying pan and the batter spread into a wide oval as steam rose up and I set down the mixing bowl and walked into the next room to turn on the television, as Stern had done the same in his studio. They were talking in awed wonder at how such a terrible accident could happen and I went back and forth for ten or so minutes, scraping up the pancakes and flipping them, and pouring new ones before going back to the living room to see the smoke and flames and listen to Robin and Howard trade stories about — and then they saw it just as I did, perhaps on a two-second delay as they shouted just after my knees went weak, having already witnessed the second plane; the impact and the widening of eyes; the stunned panic of disbelief; watching and feeling it together, alone; thinking: this was no accident.

I couldn't rise from the coffee table and only heard voices in my headphone create a jumble of sounds that no longer made sense. I pulled the headphones away and stared at the television, two flaming towers in a city I'd never seen with my own eyes, and yet a profound emptiness overcame me — not fear or anger, but the sensation of standing in a drained pool at night, reaching out with fingers and unable to reach the sides, unable to discern the abnormality of where I'd found myself.

The stench of burning brought me back to reality and I ran to the kitchen and turned off the stove, threw the burnt pancakes and pan into the sink and doused it with cold water as steam and sizzling joined the haze in the kitchen. It was only then when I thought to call my girlfriend in St. Louis. The lines were all busy: to St. Louis, to parents in Albany and San Antonio, to friends on Long Island and Los Angeles. I set the cordless phone down on the kitchen table and opened the patio door and stood in the bright sunlight as birds called out in the autumn morning and a light breeze played with the ferns in their ceramic pots on the railing.

Nothing had changed out here, nothing had really changed inside either, but it would...in time. It was like being shoved off a cliff. The sensation is new but nothing really changes, until you hit the bottom. And when the news came about the Pentagon a few minutes later, the thought came to me that the bottom will be farther off than we might imagine, and not in a good way.

A call finally came through, but it was from the campus. Classes were cancelled but they were having students gather to discuss what was happening, to watch TV together, to console each other and what have you. I didn't really want to do any of that but I couldn't stand the feeling of being alone, and so I gave in to that animalistic instinct to gather and began driving into Bennington, listening to NPR on the way, pulling over when the towers began to fall.

I turned off the radio and stared out across the Vermont countryside, watching cows slowly tread across the mud in a farmer's field. A tiny tractor rolled across a dirt road in the distance, hardly moving at all. I didn't want to, but I started the car again. This time I didn't head toward campus, or home, but I took the 279 bypass and drove north, driving anywhere I'd never been before with the radio off. I didn't want to hear anymore. I didn't want to see. Instead, I tried to remain in that countryside stasis in rural Vermont, knowing that when I finally did go back, the dour realities of what we'd soon become would be waiting — the bottom of the cliff always in sight.

FLY

WTC HAIKUS
KATHE BURKHART

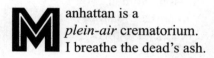anhattan is a
plein-air crematorium.
I breathe the dead's ash.

I always knew that
something like this would happen
here. And now it has.

Vast coalitions
of the oppressed attack us
when we're not looking.

Fundamentalists
in search of eternity
are the new rock stars.

Suicide bombers
Bioterrorism. Now,
what the fuck is next?

Rich conservatives
play Cowboys and Indians
with vigilantes.

The callousness of
the privileged unsettles
me and makes me sad.

Low flying planes jerk
me out of my reverie
Please do not crash here!

Stop the violence!
Osama bin Laden, just
go fuck your four wives!

Muslim women, won't
you pull a Lysistrata?
Put an end to this!

WHEN THE SKYLINE CRUMBLES
ELIOT KATZ

W as sitting Astoria kitchen chair about to vote mayoral
primary, then would've hopped subway to work
Soho's Spring Street —
turned TV on for quick election check when CNN switched
    to picture of World Trade Center #1
with surreal gaping hole blowing dark smoke out a new mouth.
Witnesses still in shock were describing a plane flying
    directly into the building's side
when a second plane suddenly crashed Twin Tower #2
and orange flames & monstrous dust rolls began replacing
    the city's world renowned skyline.
Soon the city's tallest buildings crumbled, one at a time —
with 50,000 individual heartbeats working in Twin Bodies,
    it was clear this horror going to be planet-felt.

I stared stunned at TV another half hour, called Vivian working
    Canadian summer forest job to assure I was physically okay
& mourn together, then wandered my Queens neighborhood —
almost everyone walking mouths open silent, eyes unblinking.
Two women & two men on 31st Street cried into cell phones,
    trying reach loved ones working the WTC,
a mover moaned Age Old Prophecy to his buddy loading the van:
    "The world has changed, bro."

Wednesday I subway'd into Manhattan looking to volunteer
    with bad back,

only found location to leave a donation check, all other slots
    remarkably filled for the moment —
also wanted to sense the air fellow Applers were breathing,
smoke that torched bodies now tangibly coating tongue &
    nostrils, dust burning all three eyes —
7th Ave above 14th St almost empty rush hour so our dead
    could be counted, a clear road to the next realm,
perhaps a friend's friend miraculously uncovered alive,
    given space to speed St. Vincent's Emergency Room.

Thursday I sat half-hour Union Square with a Tibetan group
    meditating for peace
as mainstream TV helped lubricate America's war machine
    hosting Flat Earth hawks urging 80% toward retaliation
against Bin Laden or any country harboring Bin Laden's cells —
even as academic analysts noted moments before those cells
    now spread to thirty countries including U.S.
Fox News had hosted a discussion between the far right
    & further right —
Newt Gingrich: The terrorists should be found & crushed —
Jeanne Kirkpatrick: We already know who they are, why wait —
a procession of military experts advocating carpet bombs
& napalm.

On Friday night, 3000 New Yorkers, mostly young,
    candlelit Union Square
to mourn the victims & stand for peace with signs like:
    "War Is Not the Answer" &
"Honor the Dead; Break the Cycle of Violence" —
CBSTV covered the event as another cute show of
    the city's spirit of togetherness
sandwiched between two dozen stories of a flagwaving public
    meathungry to support Bush Jr's rush to war.

After years of U.S. missiles flying into outward shores,
a decade after dozens of thousands of Iraqis cruise missile'd
    to death under Father George

the war has now come home, where it's apparent to all
what a senseless random murderer
is the one-eyed giant Terror
how it eats its innocent victims screaming alive, feet flailing
how it breaks the strongest of backs, rips flesh wide open
how it tosses arms East, legs South, skull & genitals
    North & West
how it forces hardened athletes to dive head first 99 floors
    to a concrete death softer than its iron teeth
how it leaves no paperwork behind to comfort the living
how it answers pleading mothers & weeping babes
    with a knife to the belly, glass shards to throat
how it burns a skyline of fresh bones to fragile white ash.

Now, we walk memory's long marathon to honor our dead
now we watch a million New Yorkers work courageously
    to meet the initial test,
daily tasks small to heroic, delivering socks,
    pulling two-ton girders
    off fallen firefighters atop creaky broken floors,
ignoring fear everpresent, unknown particles filling the air.
Now we see whether Americans can meet the next human challenge:
Protect the innocent & reject Terror in all its disguises,
    even strutting on TV in our own leaders' garb?
Or merely act a mirror of its latest high-rise profile?
The sometimes bitter juices of justice, law, human rights, & peace?
Or shot after shot of eternal bloodthirst?

GLOBAL TRAGEDY

MICHAEL LA BOMBARDA

I was sitting in my hotel room
Watching "Superman."
Then I decided to walk downtown,
Even though the episode was not over,
And out on Sixth Avenue
I saw people listening to car radios.
I heard something about a plane
Hitting one of the Twin Towers,
But I kept walking, switching avenues
And then I saw a tremendous ball of fire
On the side of one of the Towers
And half-jokingly, half-seriously
Wondered where Superman was and
How nice it would be if he could save
Some people and the building, too.
But of course, there is no Superman.
By the time I reached the Village,
My destination, I was just in time
To see the second Tower go down,
And I wondered where the next
Plane was coming from as I have done
Every day since then waiting for greater
Destruction than I can imagine.

THE FALL OF THE FIRST TOWER
BOB QUATRONE

Yes this is an action of history. These two blazing towers, falling with folk flapping from the windows. These masses leaping to their deaths, never before, like bugs flushed out of a carpet. Flushed out like the merest beetle larva, yes, flushed out by supreme natural forces from which we have our being, utterly and obsequiously dependent. Like the chaos of billiard balls on the pool table at the break, the shock of hard ivory cues. And then we who are the more fortunate, smile that smile of complacency, that grin or smirk depending on contending forces, that moronic smile of presidents and foreign ministers, of heads of state, of secretaries of state, that shit-eating grin from ear to ear, that little school-girl grin, as if she had never grown out of her dependence on momma, that is, the cornhuskers-, school boy-son of a president-grin, the stand straight up grin, the trying to con his audience grin, with no matter what he thinks, says, or does, because he cannot get past trying to con himself, having never risen to the level past natural necessity, if there is a level, having never surrendered to that redeeming tool of the intellect, at work against the forces of humiliation, against the forces of luck and fortune itself, as the ancient philosophers have said, yes with that grin of the clownish thug, no sorry, but not exactly thug, for those are the wife-beaters and police mongers, the squad car mickeys, and plenty of those arrived on the tragic scene, for once in their lives made heroic, ascending the lower stair, out of the fullest ignorance, out of the fullest duty, driven past all caution with reference to self, these hustlers, these unseasoned, unspiced, undeveloped, the puniest seeds imaginable, and the president himself picked from among these skinny weaklings on the beach, the skinniest of all, speaking in the personified average of clichés, comfortable with his task, at ease, lost in a life, of rich boy necessities, pulled in and galvanized by the first great strike, almost drawn to wisdom, as we were all almost drawn, forced out of his little window too, like the merest beetle larva, oh, we were all the lucky ones who drew a pass or a bye for that day, not forced out into the incredible, inebriating sky, into the heady wonder of the heavens, with fear reaming our private parts and, excuse me, running up our asses, and yet there were some. true philosophers, who, by a miracle, standing on the verge of imminent death, felt happy and loved the spectacular view, brought to the summit by destiny and the heavens, and must pass now into the void below, yes vermin squeezed out of a carpet, yet far above that, far better than that, vermin who by the sheerest miracles transcended themselves and put the face of humanity on all they did, comforted their buddies, helped the clueless, and the utterly wasted to put in their turn the face of dignity on all they did as well, these were squeezed out of the windows, but need not have ejected themselves, waiting in a sublime haste, all the action slowed to something utterly comprehensible, as the inferno roared and the unprincipled screamed, their crimes rebounding on their heads, the greatest crime of all, not to be aware, to be entirely without awareness, coming alone, or living their lives, in their voices programmed for success. Yes, utter dismal failures.

MEGALOPOLIS IN APOCALYPSE
VALERY OISTEANU

B etween the belching smoke,
Ground Zero looks like a spaceship crashed.
As if a meteor struck Manhattan
As if a nuclear bomb went off on the edge of Purgatory
Smells like an incinerator of 3000 corpses
And computers, ratio one to ten, twisted metal
Pulverized towers hang in the air, like two phantoms

Can't bring it back or re-make it
Thirty years of memory erased in one hour
These are now the gates to Hell & Temple of Divine Inferno
Releasing the imagination of the nuclear war
The Church of Inevitable: "Let's bomb somebody"
Smoldering spirits drift with the wind

Here is the holy ground for
The museum of destruction and crime
Welcome to Underground Zero
Descending to the lower levels of Inferno
Where PATH "ghost train" stopped at exactly 10:05
Take a helmet! Take a mask! Take a picture!
Welcome to the new lookout point of the New Millennium!

A TAXI DRIVER'S *DIE GÖTTERDÄMMERUNG* SEPTEMBER 11, 2001

DAVIDSON GARRETT

My downtown passenger, a banker from Barcelona —
we spoke of my love for soprano Montserrat Caballé
that pristine day, driving this — Senor Financier
to the brass portals of American Express,

temple of commerce on Hudson's shore.
Early in the morning, I yawned tired air,
he paid the meter's fare and said *adios.*
Zooming across the Westside Highway

in my yellow zephyr —
time for tourists at the Marriott Trade Center Hotel,
renovated midget adjacent to the looming twin giants.
Respite in the hack stand, I waited for an anxious hand

to hail my trusty Chevrolet
and whisk me away to another part of the island —
hopefully, filling my poor palms with crisp bills.
Feeling a whiff of the almost autumn breeze,

my bald crown hugged the headrest,
lids lightly closed for a needed snooze.
Without warning, an earth-shattering — BOOM
sounding like a million tympanis,

magnifying into decibels of Wagnerian proportion.
At first I thought it a bomb — like the assault of '93 —
leaping from the cab, heart drumming,
eyes glanced toward heaven.

Elastic flames like a snake's tongue
lanced through North Tower's steel skin
as a new epoch of terror fermented in fire.
Beams ripped amid primal screams,

sparkling glass rained down on my head
like waterfalls made of crystal confetti —
fumes of sulfurous clouds sparked fear,
the world shifted, seared in a crimson blaze of hate.

Like a mortal fleeing an incinerated dragon,
I escaped into my idling car — dented by debris —
explosions cracked like operatic thunder
while frantically clutching the steering wheel

for blessed life, afraid of what might come —
numb and dumbfounded in my own Immolation Scene.
A frightened foot pushed pedal to gas,
the auto dashed like a frenzied Valkyrie

toward Midtown, amid nervous skyscrapers.
In the rearview mirror, Valhalla
of the gods of gold and power
burned behind. No lyrical Rhinemaidens

or Brünnhilde's heroic high C
soaring over symphonic orchestra —
only my sea of briny tears, *pianissimo,*
accompanied by sirens.

JANET RESTINO

BLACK BEHIND BLUE
(A RESPONSE TO 9/11)
MAGGIE DUBRIS & ELINOR NAUEN

❊I am presently in love with Leonardo DaVinci.
I understand that he's gay.
I also understand that he's dead.
And that he was a paranoid dyslexic who wasn't the first man
to invent a flying machine. In fact, he was a great pretender compared to the three Banu Musa brothers of Baghdad (9th Century)
and their Book of Ingenious Inventions.

But everything was burned in the Crusades.

*** The Brethren of Purity, often referred to in medieval the-
ology as the 11 heads of cabbage, lived as one, choosing mute-
ness, communicating only by lengthy letters, one of which
argued that the animals of the world mirror the stars in the sky.**

* Whose notebooks will survive? snickers Leonardo, behold-
ing himself in the mirror as he writes. Would you choose to swim
in a pool made of mercury, drifting among the golden boats with
the barbaric Banu Musa Brothers, or would you put your money
on me? (I have invented a parachute, but no plane.)

*** He who journeys without companions can send his
thoughts to dwell in the eternal blue sky or to fall like a stone
into turbulent waters.**

* He lived on a star called Earth with Water. A star that twin-
kled like every other.

*** I fancy the stars are made of garbage, silence, soap and
heavier-than-air vegetables. I fancy purity is much the same.**

* Think how small my world would be, he wrote, if instead I stood on another star. The light would cast a different shadow, and my eyes create a different sky.

   * **Holding my long skirts high, I walk through hundreds of adventures. I dream of a sailor—Baghdaddy-o, a donkey, a raw unoriginal sin.**

* The sky would be true-blue. There would be no darkness beyond it.

   * **Come with me and I'll make you forget the world you live in and know. I'll carry you out to that strange land where the game of life is played by different rules.**

* On that star, would the sea demand souls?
Would a man make a sword from a meteor, or fill an egg with straw, and light it, and watch it fly away?

   * **That star is very well & quiet, & stones — worn out by history — fall into the air.**

* The earth is full of bones of people killed with meteorswords. They bleed like every other. To die from a bit of the sky, or to die from time passing, what does it matter?

   * **A dog growls. We can but fear. The dogs have howled—**

* I live on a star called Earth with Water. A star is just light. And the speed of light, time.

   * **When a dog howls, the stars above his head howl with him.**

* I go back into the shadows, where Leonardo lives. I bring him crackers, and tell him that he'll live forever. I bring him bright red ink for his pens.

THE STRENGTH OF TRAGEDY

BRENDALIZ GUERRERO

And so
I end my night next to my beloved
In awe of how
Resilient
And hungry we are
For the justice of our dead
As New Yorkers
As humans
And citizens of this world.
We WILL forgive
But we will NEVER forget

THE DAY AFTER 9/11
GIL FAGIANI

Ninety-one-year-old Mrs. Higgins
enters a Latino-owned Dollar Store,

I want an American flag, she hollers.
Sorry, mam, we don't sell flags.

What's the matter,
don't you love America?

.

RESPITE #1 AT GROUND ZERO
HOLLY ANDERSON

ARC Mass Care volunteer Sept–Dec. 2001

RESPITE #1 PT. 1

I thought I'd try and write briefly about first encounters with the enormity of Ground Zero where I'm working 1 or 2 shifts per week at an American Red Cross center they call Respite #1. This past Wednesday (9/26) we provided meals and snacks numbering roughly 1700 between 8 am & 4:30 pm for everybody working recovery down there: that means cops, firefighters, iron-workers plus all the other union trades, ATF, FEMA, FBI, CIA, Army Corp of Engineers, Nat'l Guard, you name the organization we feed them all good catered food from a huge company called Great Expectations that normally service Lincoln Center, BAM & our other high culture NYC environs. The Southern Baptist Church generally contracts for a lot of American Red Cross long-term disaster feeding across the US but the 2 days they provided down at Ground Zero had EVERYBODY bitching about a mystery dreck known as "beanie weenies" & "turkey" roll in gravy w/ canned grey veg. You simply cannot feed that sort of "food" to NYC firefighters who everybody knows are some of the great, great cooks in the metro area. It is forbidden. So now it's lots of fresh salad, fresh fruit & better quality carbs & proteins. There's never quite enough of everything but all those serviced are much happier w/ the chow now. There are also parked semis out front w/ hot showers, cots for 52 upstairs in the classrooms (we put thank-you letters from school kids & a chocolate on each pillow on day 2) new donated clothes, donated boots, underwear etc. This center which took over the downtown branch of St. John's University should be running for a year but it's not known if ARC can occupy the facility for that period but that's how long Guiliani says it will take to clear the pile…. The pile.

When I was first bused in last Mon. (9/24) morning (security is incredibly tight — we have to arrive at ARC Brooklyn staging area at 6:30 am every shift to receive picture ID that allows us access on the bus & through the numerous military checkpoints which means I leave home at 5:30) I saw what looked like a monstrously filthy closet flung open and spilled into the street. The shock of that 7 story much too quickly familiar image viewed again and again on videotape VS the utter ugliness of its actuality froze me. You think you are looking at some hideous, bile-pocked indigestion vomited up from the cramped bloody bowels of the earth. The mind refusing to receive what the eye is showing it. The colorless color and unrecognizable forms of the wreckage and all the while that particularly acrid smoke never before encountered snaking into your mouth & touching your lungs as you stand on a chaotic corner looking nervously over your own stiff shoulder. Unwilling to face it squarely. It is ugliness of the most profound sort and at the same time it is holy ground.

I am honored to work like a dog down there whenever the call comes. The only way to grieve is through direct action like this.

RESPITE #1 PT.2

Well forget about last week and the 1700 meals we served day 4. The joint has most definitely been discovered. Word of mouth travels fast. Last Tuesday the 2nd October 15,000 meals & snacks were served in a 24-hour period according to Claude, the towering ARC national member who has been our kitchen maestro since day 1 at Respite #1. The sublime David Bouley took over catering last Monday so the food has gotten better and better. Salmon steaks and lovely baked potatoes, swimming pools of salad greens, brownies and rolling carts full of apple tarts. Starbucks coffee that's actually being prepared at its proper semi-burnt industrial strength unlike the bilge water that's being served out at ARC Brooklyn. No complaints except that some of the guys now claim they're eating too much.

I did the meet and greet out front of Respite last Wednesday — cajoling all to hose off their boots before they could come inside and have breakfast or lunch. Told everybody that passed by that they'd better not forget the fresh fruit or salad either, that I'd be querying them on the way out and immediately phoning wives or mothers if they hadn't complied. Also told lots of dusty, disheveled groups how much I really, I mean REALLY enjoyed bossing guys around and that always got some laughs. The impulse is to flirt as much as you can manage and try and keep it light when they're coming in for a break from that hallowed hellhole, the pile. There is too much pain in some of those faces. But more heartbreaking are the few that have gone utterly blank. Teddy bears and dry socks and loving letters from school kids aren't help enough.

These guys are in need of direct, immediate counseling that may well alleviate the Post-Traumatic Stress Disorder that could bury them later and destroy the remainder of their lives. Who can do this work? Without help?

The air was bad again, because of flaring fires, but how can you say 'hello' and ask people to hose off their boots when you're wearing a dual-chamber respirator? I just ate a lot of Tylenol for the headaches and was happy my lungs didn't hurt. Every time the winds shifted it would always let up for awhile anyway.

The real problem was with what was being seen in my peripheral vision off to the right — about a block away from all the meeting and greeting I could see the guys from the Medical Examiner's office in their paper hazard suits combing through a massive dumpster's worth of small rubble looking for body parts. All the various ambulances were parked in a ring, waiting. Evidently they were finding quite a bit because many ambulances were leaving the hot zone that day, driving slowly past Respite #1 with no lights. No sirens.

There's no writing "well" about any of this. I can't find the necessary language or tools but these quick notes might be helpful because later I'm afraid we could try and forget that something so piercingly cruel and chaotic ever came out of the sky right here at home on a spotless day in early September.

ONE MONTH LATER

October 11th. There's no predicting what sets any of us off in the aftermath of early September. Last week, 2 days after a shift at Respite #1 it was a trumpet player and a saxophonist on a southbound F train. I was reading a *NYT* article on the newer dilemmas affecting burial rituals. For instance: with the advent of DNA testing does a grieving family disinter the remains of an already buried beloved if more bits are discovered later on in the WTC pile? Should anyone ever have to make decisions like this? Christ.

So then along come these 2 familiar Russian fellows with their blaringly loud boom-box back-up performing "In the Mood" and people on the train begin to smile because they're not bad and their patter is funny and rambunctious but when they segue into "New York, New York" at a blistering decibel count I start sobbing immediately and uncontrollably behind my stupid Jackie O. sunglasses. I can't stop. I'm soaking the newspaper, my shirt, the front of my pants. The tears just rolling down down down and then there's the stop — Lafayette & Houston and an appointment at Fotofolio. And what to do then? You walk right out of your private 'event' fully functional again and resume your day. It still stinks downtown but everyone must be used to it by now. Yesterday's shift at Respite was more daunting than those in past weeks.

This newer weird familiarity with the crime scene seems to make the entry worse. ARC volunteers with current ground zero ID have the option of taking the subway in and not deploying as a group from the Brooklyn office. Now walking in past the police and National Guard on Broadway is like passing through the dusty back-lots of some lowball movie studio that cranks out apocalyptic thrillers. Over there are the banks of work lights just switched off after a long night and there are the guys in the rubber suits hosing down the emptied streets and the endless line of open-box semis and dump trucks topped up with perpetually smoking rubble headed straight for Fresh Kills on Staten Island or the barges. There's the "set" off to the left and the crumpled, cathedral-like form the whole world knows. Now it oversees a massive job site that workers trudge in and out of to a soundtrack of belching diesels and murmuring or muttering or occasionally laughing guys. There is an orderliness and an efficiency, a sense of spirit that buoys you up as you shiver in the stiff, early breezes off the Hudson welcoming everybody inside for an enormous, heart-stopping breakfast of bacon and eggs and pancakes.

But some of these guys, the iron-workers and steam fitters could be dying before our eyes. Already there are some ghosts walking in their lug-soled boots. Their faces blank under battered hardhats. Goggles and particle masks at their throats. The impulse is strong to take them in your arms. Say something. But what?

So instead you touch a shoulder. Pat the hands that all need washing.

Just some small simple contact because no one should have to see what they're looking at 12 hours a day. At least the firefighters have their fellowship, their tight bond of brotherhood. A Queens cop told me *"We're all lab rats down here anyway, no matter what any agency says."* He was referring to physical health concerns but what about the mental health crisis that's brewing as we feed those grumbling bellies full of rich, marinated beef and chili and stew over rice? God help us all.

RESPITE #1 PT. 4

Every night since that day a chain of *Hail Marys* pulls me towards sleep. Eros is elsewhere as Charon oversees the lines of trucks full of rubble bound for a Staten Island landfill called Fresh Kills.

Some of those working down there will survive the endless, smoking aftermath more intact than others. One officer comes immediately to mind. Part of his (self-directed) job description is loaning out hugs with the admonition that they be passed on as soon as possible. This guy hugs everyone including the former national director of ARC when she came breezing through from D.C. shortly after Respite #1 opened, a 350 lb. ferociously scowling 6 ft.+ EMT worker who hadn't slept in many days, various clergy, nurses of both genders, CSWs, Red Cross grandmothers working the dining room and on and on. He's hugged them all. So as I'm getting my own weekly allotment I'm thinking that with the bulletproof vest he's wearing it's a lot like clutching a torso encased in a canoe. Hugging him brought back what another cop from another precinct had told me earlier in the day.

That guy's an officer with an EMS unit and his current detail goes like this: 12–14 hours per day he's got an ambulance parked at the edge of the Pile. He and his partner wait to drive the remains of the uniformed to the city morgue. More days than not he does plenty of sitting. He says he feels useless much of the time. When there are identifiable remains often times the ladder companies insist on sending their truck to transport one of their own. It's a way of honoring the fallen brother but it can take hours if the vehicle is coming in from the Bronx or Staten Island. So this officer sits once again and waits or comes across the street and talks to me doing the boot wash detail out front of Respite. He says that when he is finally called on to carry someone out and drive them away he feels privileged and connected to the arduous work at hand. He described a recent recovery as not much more than a torso that looked like something from an archeological dig and surely not a hardworking, breathing body just 6 short weeks ago. There was the now familiar stench of utterly desiccated skin and bone burned colorless. A charred parchment that he gently zippered into a body bag for transport. The oxygen canister recovered beside the remains was put into a separate bag because the smell of fluids on it was so powerful. When I asked him if he's talking to a professional, getting any help at all he said *"Of course not. Nobody wants to lose their shield or their weapon and that's what happens if you go in for psychological help."* So there's also no helping the cop at his stationhouse who went off — screaming and crying about all the wives and children who will never again see their mates, or their fathers after someone else innocently mentioned how hard it is for their own wives and kids to be dealing with the 14 hour shifts 6 days a week.

Men are coming undone now. Daily. There was the crane operator who came stomping in in an absolute fury because he'd been asked to show ID at another location serving meals south of the pile. When I told him he was always fine by us at this end and grabbed his hands and asked him how long since he'd had a day off he said "Never." He said he's been down there since 3 hours after the towers fell.

We have to ask ourselves where will someone like this go after his work is finished? What kind of life and with whom will he be capable of living?

GROUND ZERO VOLUNTEER
AT HOTEL RESCUE CENTER
PETER BUSHYEAGER

Hardhat with your name in black marker on
the Red Cross bus to the hotel a lecture:
don't look to either side from bus to hotel backdoor
don't breathe deeply stay inside
extreme times extreme upset don't
have sex in the elevators

Rows of cots mounds of donated jeans food line dish out
green beans for the workers eight hours empty out
trashcans in this thrown-together
village you break the rules walk on
the roof by the air conditioners see
the giant pile tiny men scaling the top

Think something like feel the world against
your skin rotate in every direction freeze the
scene gray dust garage sad coated cars desk papers
strewn still-on blue-light office overheads the rescue workers
restless someone says someone
found something in the pile

Some give shoulder hugs to strangers
some say eat your green beans some
sing something like Working on the Railroad
some want to genuflect under
some brightly colored
hanging lights

Bus home past site in high-intensity disaster light
a deep busload moan then quick thank-you patter
stop at the lavish park trees inappropriate
the subway entrance a welcome mouth
your name on the hardhat
smeared and can't be read

SOME NOTES ON THE UNSPEAKABLE
Thomas Zummer

11 September, 2001

What recourse do we have, we who work embedded so deeply in language, when words fail? When they fail so completely and utterly, in confronting tragedy of such proportion. Is there anything which authorizes our speech, we who remain outside the hole, the blank, utter, negation of those voices who could speak, but cannot? No. That is impossible. For us and for them. There is no possibility of speaking but from that position, and those voices are silent. Where might hope lie for us? Circumscription, writing around a wound, forms a cicatrice, a scar that forever marks the place of absence. And yet there is the constant reflexive urge to fill this metaphoric hole with language. Never mind that it cannot support such language, and that at the same time such language occludes the space of horror, take its place, and that this pure negation frames every language. Even our perceptions, as they are before — or at least different from — language are compromised. I stood on my roof watching through binoculars the fall of the northernmost tower. For some minutes before it collapsed I saw what looked like dust. Like there was dust crumbling from the edges of the building. It wasn't until four days later that I realized that it was not dust, but people. So even at the very moment of perception, or perhaps it is in that gap between perception and cognition, where pure perception has not yet made itself into the world, not yet entered into a relation with the possibility of knowing — when it is attenu-

80

ated, momentarily absolved from commitment to the horror —
that we are closest to the event. And for the rush of language that
inundates that space, how much of it is *cliché,* familiar tropes,
truisms that order not the event itself — which cannot be domes-
ticated — nor even our relation to it, but rather our protection
from it. When the first airplane hit, it was broadcast almost immediately. Young children in one of the schools closest to the site
cheered and laughed, applauding this incredible image — how
could they not? The only precedent for such an image was in cinema or on television, where everyone tacitly knows that, with all
of the weapons fired, all of the explosions, no one is really killed.
Moments later these same children witnessed, out the windows
of their classroom, the bodies of people who had jumped hit the
ground, literally exploding on impact. There is no way to suture
these two events together in any sensible way. They remain an
aporia, an impossibility that one cannot, and yet must, work
through. The work of mourning. One of my students asked if,
within the framework of this intentional act of terrorism, whether
the composition of the act — a plane flying down 5th Avenue
into the first tower, with a second plane, from another direction,
hitting the second tower half an hour later — was not also intentional, so as to have produced the clearest images of terror. I
didn't know how to answer this. Our city is already composed as
an image, in a sense, there is something cinematic from the start.
Perhaps terror always composes itself as an image, and that this
was an opportunistic instance of that reflex. How many times did
we hear that it was "like a movie," or a "special effect?" And how
was it like a movie in the very moments that it unfolded? It is as-
tonishing to think of the network of people, stationary, fixed, in
whatever proximity to the event, in front of their television sets.
It was a movie, coextensive with the horror of its actuality, a film
or covering membrane, something with which one could think,
because any closer and thought too disappears. The question of
the precessionary comes up here. "America has had its 'wake-up
call'" is another statement that we continue to hear. What does it
mean? That we have finally learned, in the worst way, the meaning of "globalism," and the hegemonic phantasm of our daily life

now has to admit that other hells punctuate the world, and have done so for a long time, whether it be the thousands of people "missing" in Latin America, or fear and atrocity in Burma, or Algeria, or a hundred other places. Have we backed into a world different beyond our imagining? I don't know. The world is different, to be sure. The etymology of the word "aftermath" is useful to note: moving away, or moving on. Isn't there also a resonance of mathesis, of working through, making (an image)? And not only in images, but in judgements and acts? The word theory in its original sense authorized the passage from event into language so that the truth of an event could be ascertained, judgements rendered and appropriate actions taken. Our task is to think outside the event — there is no other place — and to think through our judgements and actions so that this sort of thing, on any scale, in any place, for any reason, cannot happen again. There will be the inevitable retaliations, there is no question. And there will be retaliations to retaliations. We have not only found ourselves within a probabilistic total war — where unspeakable things can happen anywhere, any time — but we now recognize that we have been within a probabilistic total war for some time now. What do we do? Adorno's chilling question, how does one write lyric poetry after Auschwitz, has haunted the last century, and has not passed away. Lyotard speaks, and then writes "Discussion, or how do you phrase 'after Auschwitz'?" It is in the phrases which circulate around negation that the work lies. Discussion, *dialektiké,* is the ground for community, and it is within communities that the phrasing of events takes place, takes up the task of mourning, which must be a positive task. Phrases are mediated. One has only to reflect on the order of repetitions of images, statements, phrases, to see an emergent pattern, a possible, and perhaps at times opportunistic, form of persuasion. We must be careful of an opportunism that merely determines other targets and agendas. Politics organizes language; language orders perceptions. The image of Americans detourned, used as living bombs against other Americans, has wrought an agony of signs and phrases, mapped and remapped into the contours of our anxieties. Constructed as a mediated event, not before, but as it occurred, within the global public sphere, the event persists continuously reshaped and deployed, analyzed and revised. It cannot have been anything else, and such continuous signification, and the perceived requirement of its symmetrical inversion, a commensurate response, accomplishes the preservation of terror. Language shapes response; response reflects interest. The notion of a "cell structure" for example, dates from the period of the Russian anarchists of the late 19th century. Is this really an accurate and useful representation of how the perpetrators of this inhuman act worked in our world (it would seem to operate more on the analogy of a metastasis)? Or is it to enable, authorize and legitimate forms of response? Under the necessity of our covert forces "getting dirty" in a commensurate fashion with the other denizens of the twilight world of terror/counter/terror, have we instituted a structure of secrecy which will thoroughly deconstruct the traditional freedoms of the press? Does the reflexive anxiety about this event, so close, produce a more and more normative discourse about fighting another "good war," one to "rid the world of evil," a phantasm which is greatly at odds with the world as it is? What do we do now?

SEPT. 22 (SAT) 2001
YUKO OTOMO

My journal entries had stopped on Sept. 11 (Tues). I could not come back to it until today. Finally, I opened the book & started to fill it in. I almost forgot what day it was....

This is how my re-entry to the journal began 11 days after the event. It took more days to pass till I started to write detailed descriptions of what happened on the subject titled WTC911 on Oct. 2 (Tues). Below are the minimized excerpts of the massive entry.

WTC911

It happened 3 weeks ago on Tuesday. The day was clear, beautiful & bright, just like today. The blue sky opening up infinitely — it was a perfect end of summer/beginning of autumn kind of day. I got up around 8:30 am. I made tea as I always did. Helicopter noise was booming outside the window busier than usual. But I ignored it as part of city life in my half-awake/half-sleepy mind. Then, the phone rang. I heard the familiar voice of Alexandre in Paris where we just left after enjoying a long visit a few days earlier. I usually don't answer phones right away. I screen all calls. Especially not in the morning. I listened to the incoming message. The voice kept saying, "Are you OK??? Are you OK??? I just heard that the plane crashed into the World Trade Center..." Instead of picking up the phone, I ran to the bedroom to wake Steve up, repeating what Alexandre said. In a few seconds, he called us again. This time we picked up the phone. He told us to turn on the TV. We did....

The plane crashed into the 2nd tower as we watched it in disbelief. The shock was so huge & indescribable that I felt like I was in a warped vacuum of Time/Space. I felt no sense of the weight of what had happened, although I clearly knew it was something extremely heavy. I was suspended in a weightless void. I got frozen & everything halted for an instance. The visual image of the plane crashing into the clear-cut Minimalist building with a superbly clear blue sky as its backdrop was so impactfull that we literally lost our words. I don't remember what our reaction was following the initial shock that literally took our breath away.... Regaining our senses, we got dressed & rushed around the corner. There, with a small group of passersby & neighborhood residents, we saw tower one crumble. We were all totally dumbfounded. In the fragile silence, someone, in a flat voice, said "It's like a movie...." Everything seemed to be moving in extra-slow-slow motion. But it was not a movie. It was REAL.

It took 3 weeks for me even to gain the feeling to write about what happened. The shock took words & spirit away from me. I was mute for 3 weeks although I resumed my general journal entry on Sept. 22. The whole event destroyed my system of "language". I started to doubt words in general since every word I used seemed to lose its prevailing meaning or to shift the content of its meaning. The first & most immediate word to describe what happened was "tragedy." But it could not describe my feelings & thoughts of the moment. The sudden withdrawal of words scared me. The most ironical thing was the fact that I kept talking; talking more & faster than usual expressing my anxiety. In the wordless void, I tried to search for some words that could describe the exact shape & the content of my thoughts & feelings. I kept talking in order to grasp my own mind in vain. It was not just me. The whole event made us talk more than usual. Everybody was talking & talking as if talking was the only salvation & substitute for mourning, crying or shouting. Strangely, I don't remember seeing anyone crying over the event. A big silence & the sudden burst of talking as if talking can put us back in the right position on the tightrope. We were all like tightrope walkers that lost balance. As we lost our words, TV kept pouring out their words: words such as "tragedy," "attack,"

;edented," "unbelievable," "heroes," "cowardly," "God," ," "hate," etc, etc...

Grand total silence, muted & muffled by the shock; a void devoid of words; a disconnection between mind & language; a flood of talking/chattering; trembling excitement over the "spectacle"; a deep dive into horrified TV viewing; a sudden erasure of the value system you believed in; thoughts on "God".... I asked Steve "Do you think God did this?" I was shocked to hear me saying such a question. "What do you mean by 'God'?" He asked back. One of the escaped said to the TV reporter that he was saved by the grace of "God." "God Bless America!" one side sings as the other side prays "in Allah (God)" This public talk on God intrigued me. We were all talking of the same different God....

It's interesting to reflect on how we came back to reality. Right after the shock, I could not take music at all. Music was the furthest thing I wanted to relate to. For a few days, I let myself soak in TV news instead. Gradually, my appetite for music came back. The first music I listened to was Count Basie on a cable TV jazz history show I saw accidentally. The tempo of his music was perfect to lean on at the moment. The second music I listened to was Verdi's arias. Soon, we let ourselves roam to see some "silent" films @ Anthology Film Archives to cure our damaged spirit & to change our mood. The first film was a 1922 German silent film *Othello*. I managed to watch it through without breaking down since it was silent. As I watched it, I finally understood the point of the play. It's not about "love," "jealousy" or even "betrayal." It's about "faith." Othello loses his faith in his love toward Desdemona. The lost "faith" induced the tragedy. The second was the 1921 classic *Manhatta* by Charles Sheeler & Paul Strand. Manhattan seen from the ferry in pure silence. Indescribable emotions & thoughts went through us watching this beautiful work. We knew that things would never be the same as we stared at the screen with our blank eyes. A few days later, Steve played Monk's "Alone in San Francisco" on CD. How nurturing his music was! It enveloped us & helped in healing our spirit....

All of sudden, before doing anything else, I wanted to clean my habitat. First, I started to sort out my personal possessions. I kept cleaning & cleaning & cleaning. This time, my desire to clean the house & to simplify my life was naturally motivated without any force or willed intentions. It was my WANT; not my MUST....

The writing ended with some blank pages & scattered descriptions as below.

These pages were kept blank to be filled in to describe every detail of after effects of THE EVENT: THE FALL OF WTC. I thought I was going to keep writing minute changes happening to our daily life & our states of minds. But life kept moving fast & the states of mind kept changing as the world kept shifting to become more FEAR based. At the same time, my own emotional & sentimental elements kept changing & I felt bothered by the idea of keeping THE EVENT (now officially called "911") journal. Politics are always politics in the most horrifying debased sense. As my desire to fill the "blank" space faded away, I decided to keep the space <BLANK> on purpose. War & Peace are always TWIN bastards of Humanity. What's so different of what happened in our back yard from that of others'? Sentimentalizing political energy is the worst solution to the problem we face now.

END/BEGINNING

REQUIEM

JANET HAMILL

New York City, September 11, 2001

The precious skyline of glass and steel remains.
Of all that's lost.
And flowing into the sea
At the end of the island where the rivers meet

The candles burn for so many
Doves crowd the branches
Of the blue garden tonight

In every park on every corner a fine curtain of dust
Settles on the altars
Of the open city
Photographs and the sweet heavy fragrance of flowers

The candles burn for so many
Doves crowd the branches
Of the blue garden tonight

So many wings rising from so many lives ended
In the collapse of the towers
A common prayer
Scribbled on scraps of paper blows through the streets

The candles burn for so many
Doves crowd the branches
Of the blue garden tonight

Beneath the bridges the rivers flow as sorrow into the sea
Of all that's passing
Innocence and ashes
The precious skyline of glass and steel remains

The candles burn for so many
Doves crowd the branches
Of the blue garden tonight

"IT CAN'T HAPPEN HERE"   Bill Anthony

POETS AGAINST THE WAR
SUSAN BRENNAN

We stood at the Capitol
forever in the snapshots.
of curious tourists

our rumpled posters reflected
in the officer's shades as he spoke
so softly it surprised me

asking us to step off the sidewalk
his voice as a shepherd beckons
his flock, his accent sunned in Southern

syllables. Maybe "sheep" is not the most
likeable metaphor for human protestors
but clumped with the others I could

let go of my small life and be a cluster
warmed by fellow shoulders
our faces a brief constellation of togetherness.

We made a silence that mushroomed
in the February chill as the Capitol
glowed lunar behind us, our silence

arched over us and I sensed the vortex
of a great ear hinged to the cold skull of the sky.
In the togetherness of strangers you forget

what you have chosen to be seen as. The poets,
the watchers, the news camera, the officers,
the residents hurrying by on their cells, the callers

on the other end of those phones — the minutes
we're pinched together as a potter coerces clay
formed then de-formed. From the far end

of Lafayette Park a flock of starlings twist and wheel
their under wings silver flashes, their black top feathers
sweep the space between us and the sun —

How many people have been killed in this war?
Killed in blood. Killed in spirit.
What, from my small life, could I bring to this silence?

A silence that has now wedded to the silence
of bones worn to dust.
I'm not listening to the birds now clamped

to a single tree top, chattering whether
to stay or move on; I'm not listening to the listening,
the fruit of silence; I'm not listening to the deaf bell
stamping its hard thick notes to the downward wind —

I'm listening to the war. To its silence.
It sounds like peace, it sounds like rest;
but it is hollow, it is the whole endless groan
of mothers who have lost their motherhood.

I DO NOT LIKE THOSE SKINNY LIGHTS
EK Smith

This time I forgot what day it was
  and was happy.
    I put on my new necklace
and my new dress
and even took a photo before I knew.

I took off the necklace and
put on something somberer — olive green with black.

I saw a big old red convertible with too many American flags.
I crossed the street and went the other way
past all these people posing for pictures with their phones
the new tower in the background.

I walked uptown to the local stop
farther from home.

THERE GOES
THE NEIGHBORHOOD

THE EAST VILLAGE: AN INTRODUCTION
GREG MASTERS

America doesn't treat its artists right. Intelligence and feelings are treated as accoutrements in this country. It's almost un-American to value depth over gain, to explore and decipher rather than accumulate. It's practically un-American to make the choice to be an artist or to be involved somehow in the creation of art. It simply isn't valued or respected in the overall culture. Blues singers, jazz musicians, poets, dancers proceed in their crafts despite the small and often inattentive audience. It's a calling to forge some sense for oneself out of the proceedings of the day.

I remember an event by performance artist Charles Dennis that took place at Danspace in the mid-70s. Dennis bisected the Parish Hall of St. Mark's Church with a chain-link fence and strew garbage around. The audience had to creep through a break in the fence to reach the seats. It's this sort of urgency that typifies the best East Village performance. The audience is challenged to forgo a separation from the art occurring. It is invited close and given the opportunity to experience the art's street credentials.

East Village art exalts in the personal. It's not trying to mine the archetypes for some universal significance. It looks to the ordinary daily experience for its material. It's a choice to honor the normal transaction with its connection to what poet Lewis Warsh calls "immediate surroundings." This focus on the common moment confines its appeal to a smaller audience, but an audience that's passionate in its appreciation for small miracles. Think of the moment a favorite song starts playing from a jukebox, or a film-maker focuses on a sidewalk moment. It's an attentiveness, a noticing of incidents we may fail to pay attention to otherwise, disregard in our travail through the day.

Art is a solution. And the East Village community takes it seriously. Perhaps nowhere else is each individual's effort to communicate more respected. The artist's transformation of a response into an artistic expression is revered as a lay holy ritual.

DISPLACEMENT

Like seeing a guy in a tuxedo in the middle of the forest, East Village art plays with displacement. Performance artist David Leslie appropriates the glitter and dazzle of a Las Vegas show to surround his East Village events, whether a prize fight at Angel Orensanz, a converted synagogue on Norfolk Street or a rocket car event in SoHo. The point is to play with an audience's expectations by referencing archetypal social events and then smashing the expected outcome. We're drawn in by familiar conventions, but forced to stray from the usual route. Instead, we're led on a detour that brings us somewhere unexpected.

Allen Ginsberg taught us all to howl. He brought the Yiddish art of kvetching (vocalizing against absurd conditions) into the realm of public discourse. His act was not to whine about what he saw as wrong, but to mobilize with a sense of urgent rehabilitation. His belief that the immutable could be altered gave shape to his cause. Where mainstream America dismissed him as a mere "beatnik," others found in him a messenger who found enunciation for what had been silent.

His consistent hammering in verse, as well as his substantial participation in direct lobbying, established waves of activism for causes previously not participant in the global discussion. He forced his way in to question authority. Whitman's son, he made the personal public and demonstrated that love of oneself is respect for all. Ginsberg's voice attracted those of us who'd felt disempowered and alien in our disparate communities.

Every major city in America has its opera house, ballet theaters, symphonic music halls and high school gyms where culture is presented. The bigger cities support local troupes and bring in visiting troupes from all over the world. This provides a nice evening's entertainment, uplifts the spirit and ignites the minds of those patrons who can afford the price of admission, which is high. In fact, it's a class act to attend, a sign of achievement. The audience is a show of its own, each member there to be seen. The cultural presentation is an act of enrichment, but it's primarily an entertainment for the leisure class.

At the same time, there are alternative cultural presentations occurring on a smaller scale in churches, schools, social centers, Ys — groups presenting dances and songs of the old country, teenagers rocking out or singing folk songs, theater groups reviving everything from Agamemnon to Thornton Wilder to Woody Allen.

This is closer to what the East Village is, except that the East Village is in New York City so it's simply better than anywhere else. Why? Because people here have had their eyes open, and their spirits have been hungry for meaning and they've known where to look for it. They found a way to catch a ballet growing up by either sneaking in or ushering. Eventually they made their way here if they were seriously hungry for more and could escape the hometown inertia.

And the reason the East Village is such an unknown entity to the popular culture is that most of its artists do not aspire to communicate to an audience broader than the art school types found in every high school. The goal is not to become famous, but simply to put on shows for friends and a few paying customers. The dream is not to take bows on Broadway — well, maybe for a few drag queens.

I think there's an understanding that the presentations are provincial in the sense that they're intended for an audience of the initiated, an audience hungry for what hasn't been available in movies, on TV, or even in books. Those are products of the mainstream. Sacrifices and compromises had to be made to accommodate the producers whose job it is to reach the broadest audience possible.

The East Village aesthetic may be to investigate further and to present the unspoken and the unimagined. It's a world where not only is anything permissible, but more is demanded and expected. The already seen is yesterday's news. We don't want revivals here. It's not a museum. It's a pulsating life form.

It may not be the greatest art, but being great is not the point. It's perhaps more vital to be pertinent to the moment, to make people laugh, to titillate, to point something out not noticed before, to offer a point of view not experienced before, to make it worth coming out for the evening.

And to validate feelings not addressed in mainstream media. Primarily, there's a sense that the world is nuts beyond the village perimeters — defined as the East River to the east, Broadway to the west, 14th Street to the north and Houston to the south. But there's credible evidence that worthwhile things happen beyond these boundaries. The point is, East Village sensibility has no fear of authority — whether government directives, parental control, *Bible* edict or good sense. I'm thinking of a play I saw in the '70s at the Poetry Project that was a takeoff on an episode of the '50s TV sit-com "Leave it to Beaver." This one was called "Leave it to Penis," and I suppose it had something to say about paternal oppression as it was presented by an all-female cast, but who can remember. The point is, like a skit from "Saturday Night Live," it took something familiar as its starting point and added its own spin.

It's all about emoting. And if you'd been silenced all your life, not invited to participate, there is a platform for you in the East Village. Whatever your peculiarity, whatever your particular suppression—minority and marginalized voices are not only tolerated but encouraged to emote. Because somehow we knew this was right. We hadn't grown up with these value systems, but had come to the East Village where it was celebrated. Growing up we were taught to objectify by race, by class. In the East Village you were given the chance to live among the classes and ethnicities spoken of in so demeaning a manner in your hometown. It was, in fact, a fiesta of possibilities. Here were Hispanic, Polish, Ukrainian, Jewish, Italian, German and enclaves. We had the richness of these ethnic specialties to choose from. The only conflict was whether to order the pierogis boiled or fried.

IT'S ABOUT REAL ESTATE

Ultimately it's about real estate. For alternative art to flourish, it needs to happen in a place where rent is cheap. The East Village has, until recently, always provided that. The cheap rent has drawn immigrants and artists. The architecture of the East Village neighborhood, comprised of five or six story tenement buildings, encourages small creative enterprises. With a 1,000 sq. ft. commercial space on the ground floor and apartments above, anyone with the energy can rent the storefront, remodel a bit and open for business. The size of these spaces has, over the decades, nurtured book stores, cafés, clothes designers, art galleries and performance spaces. Being that the entrance is street level encourages strollers to enter. The whole neighborhood is a bazaar, but the offerings will never be sold at a Wal-Mart. This stuff is unique, hand-made, out of range of safe mass market taste, meant for an elite substrata who have managed to make their way to the distant reaches to taste of the unique.

A variety of factors has drawn artists to the neighborhood. There had been a precedent of artists and social experimenters here — most notably reformer Emma Goldman, musicians Charlie Parker and Charles Mingus, writers Jack Kerouac, Allen Ginsberg, W.H. Auden, Miguel Algarin, Ted Berrigan and Alice Notley. But the primary reason artists flock here is because the rents were cheap. Artists in any discipline don't make a lot of money, so a low rent is crucial. The apartments are not luxurious. In fact, they're often fairly primitive with many designs left over from the turn of the 20th century. Tourists visiting the Lower East Side Tenement Museum on Orchard Street pay a few bucks now to visit a style of apartment many of us still occupy — a tub in the kitchen, small rooms, a trudge up five or six flights of stairs, toilets with "the thing... the chain," as Tessio describes it in "The Godfather."

But this lack of material comfort was and remains barely a consideration for those artists finding their way here. The point in being here is to be among a community of folks with similar pursuits in mind. Many of the new, young people moving into the neighborhood in the '60s, '70s and '80s, were coming from sub-urbs all across America where they'd grown up with the so-called comforts. By moving to the East Village one was making a choice to abandon that. It was a decision to abandon the elite, middle class or working class path we'd grown up in in order to pursue a path that freed one from a career objective or the restrictions of starting a family.

A major reason for coming here was to rebel. Many of us were in our 20s. The prospect of going to Vietnam was as deplorable as the prospect of beginning a 9-to-5 existence. We were privileged maybe in escaping those options, but it took a lot of guts to make it here. You had to deal with the derision of your family and the judgment of others who were committed to their paths and proba-bly envied your independence.

THREE ARCHETYPAL LOCATIONS ON THE EAST SIDE IN THE 1960S

ED SANDERS

AVENUE B FROM 10TH TO 12TH

Two blocks of Avenue B during the early and mid-1960s were seething with vitality. Strutting along those two blocks in the '60s was an ineffable mix of people from the Old World and people from the New World of the underground film, the underground press, the voter registration campaigns in the South, anarchists, jazz and folk musicians, genuine Communists, pacifist poets from the *Catholic Worker,* and communards sharing $31 dollar a month railroad flats over by C.

There were three bars in those two blocks that were always packed in the '60s. One was the Annex, another a bar called Mazur's, and the third was Stanley's Bar, located on the northwest corner of Avenue B and 12th. Stanley Tolkin, the owner, was a friend of many of the artists that mugged their livers there during long nights of drinking and debating. Stanley, who collected art, had a boat moored on the East River and artists would join him for sails on the weekend.

The Charles Theater, which featured underground films, was just down the street from Stanley's. It was there I first saw Jonas Mekas's film "Guns of the Trees" in early 1962, and I remember the filmmaker Ron Rice wearing bright green shoes at a showing of his film "The Flower Thief."

The Civil Rights marches were in full swing, and people left that small two block stretch fairly regularly to go south. The keys to its vitality were Idealism, the Rising Expectations of the era, Openness and Cross-Pollination. People were convinced the Kennedy era of "Rising Expectations" was going to last at least for thirty years. And there was enough sex and shaking of pot seeds down the jackets of jazz and folk albums those early years to fill a million lifetimes.

During the first few nights I went to Stanley's in early 1962 I met the magician/filmmaker/folk music anthologist Harry Smith, the novelist H.L. Humes, painter Larry Rivers, scads of poets and painters, and a bunch of people then writing for the *Village Voice*.

During the days of the Cuban Missile Crisis in October of '62, none of us had televisions so we gathered at Stanley's to watch Kennedy's utterly spine-trembling speech announcing the blockade. Two nights later we gathered again for an End of the World party at Stanley's. It was very unclear whether or not the Russians would run the blockade of Cuba and World War 3 would rain death down on Avenue B.

THE PEACE EYE BOOKSTORE

I rented a former kosher meat store on East 10th Street in late-1964, right around the corner from the Avenue B strip. The store had groovy tile walls and chicken-singeing equipment which I transformed into a vegetarian literary zone called the Peace Eye Bookstore. I left the words "Strictly Kosher" on the front window.

Next door above the Lifschutz wholesale egg market lived Tuli Kupferberg, a beat hero who was featured in anthologies such as *The Beat Scene,* and who published several fine magazines, *Birth* and *Yeah,* which he sold on the streets of the East and West Village.

The term "folk-rock" had not been invented in late 1964 when I approached Tuli, after a poetry reading, about forming a rock group. Tuli eagerly assented, and was the one who came up with the name, "The Fugs," borrowed from the euphemism in Norman Mailer's novel, *The Naked and the Dead*.

Tuli and I began writing songs at a fevered pace. We created at least fifty or sixty within a few days. Soon we asked a friend,

Ken Weaver, to join the Fugs. Weaver had been a drummer in his high school band, and brought fine song-writing skills and stage presence to our performances.

Steve Weber and Peter Stampfel of the Holy Modal Rounders were friends, and agreed to perform at the grand opening of the Peace Eye Bookstore in February of 1965. They also joined in with the Fugs, our world premiere, at that party. Peace Eye was very packed; Andy Warhol had done cloth wall banners of his flowers image, and literati as diverse as William Burroughs, George Plimpton and James Michener were on hand for the premier croonings of "Swinburne Stomp" and other Fugs ditties.

The Peace Eye Bookstore lasted for five years on the East Side. We had a mimeograph machine on which I printed hundreds upon hundreds of street leaflets, magazines, poem sheets and manifestoes free. We helped the Underground Railroad during the War, a system helping soldiers of conscience to get to Canada.

THE PSYCHEDELICATESSIN

There was an invisible moment, just about February of 1967, when people started saying "Far fucking out" and the derogatory term "beatnik" was set aside for a few years on the East Side to make way for "hippie." It was around then, just up the street at 164 Avenue A, between 10th and 11th, not far from the *East Village Other* underground newspaper office, that the Psychedelicatessin opened.

The Psychedelicatessin flourished for about two years, 1966–68. It provided employment and it fit in well with the East Side community. If the peacock feather in a vase in your living room should accidentally break, you could rush to the Psychedelicatessin to get an inexpensive replacement. Ditto for broken water pipes or lost hash screens. We regularly stopped by to check out its displays of incense, body lotions, body-revealing gowns, black lights, ever-burning candles, cases of love beads and *moiré* patches, standing close to fellow visitors sporting pantaloons, early tie-dyes and Afghan vests.

The Psychedelicatessin helped bring burning incense to the East Side streets as barefoot hipesses from Brooklyn or the Heartland bought sandalwood wands, lit them and then carried them down to Tompkins Park to listen to free concerts by the Fugs, the Grateful Dead, the Blues Project and other bands performing on the hard-won outdoor stage.

When it was busted in late June, '68, the Psychedelicatessin was thriving. The owners were adding a "Trip Room" and a room for free rock shows and jams. The two rivers of commerce, that of pot and acid, and that of flowing gowns, power sticks and flavored candles, were a bit too commingled at the Psychedelicatessin for it to survive, even in 1968, and so it faded into the flow of history, as did also Stanley's, Mazur's and the Annex.

USED BOOKSTORE LORE
ARNOLD SKEMER

I don't know how many readers have extensive experience of dealing with second hand bookstores. In the New York metropolitan area there are still quite a few and, being a book freak, I have had occasion to visit many of them. Sometimes I would get real bargains and sometimes not but I always found it a relaxing time, exploring the shelves and discovering unusual things. There are several aspects to used bookstore visits. One thing I find revealing is people bringing in books for sale. The encounters can be amusing.

There was a store called Discount Books, defunct for twenty years now, then located three blocks south of Queens Blvd. in Rego Park. It wasn't that far from the former location of my then place of employment and people did come in to sell their old books. Once a middle aged couple came in with that object in mind and laid their books on the counter for the examination of the clerk. I looked over my shoulder at what they put there and from 25 feet away just knew what was coming. I waited for the clerk to voice my thoughts.

"Aaaaaaahhhh! We don't want these. They're old paperback best sellers, mass market stuff. We don't need them!"

"Why? Is it because they're old?"

"Well, not so much because they're old. You see, we're looking for books that have stood the test of time."

The couple looked at each other in confusion. He tried to explain but they were incapable of understanding. They had twenty beaten up best sellers with raised cover lettering, garish illustrations, sex, wealth and power fictions, hot babes on the covers with lots of tit showing, standing next to big studs. Doubtless they had held them with excitement as they read them in their hot little hands. They had entered the store with big smiles on their faces. They probably thought they would get $10 for this claptrap that would pay for a nice lunch at one of the nearby coffee shops. They walked out stunned and confused.

I see this a lot. At 12th Street Books in Manhattan, also defunct, the obnoxious business owner saw a young fellow came in with a box load of the same. I, as usual, with prurient interest, looked over my shoulder and saw what was in the box. Once again, I knew what was coming. The owner, seeing at a glance what was there, peremptorily said: "I don't want any of these. I have no need for them! Thank you."

The man starred at him in amazement: "The books, dey new, dey new books!"

"I don't want them."

Most likely the fellow was a janitor in one of Manhattan's thousands of apartment buildings and he found these in the incinerator room. The books were new and had glossy covers. He reasoned there was money in it. Of course there was none, He couldn't understand that and neither can any of the others. Many people coming in have debased tastes, wallow in ignorance, read at an 8th grade level or less and have the mentality of grocers. Bookstore owners know what their customers want and they don't want schlock.

Guess what else they don't want. They don't want books on music. I overheard a conversation in Alabaster Bookstore, 4th Avenue at 12th Street in Manhattan. The clerk described a man repeatedly coming in with music books and having a hurt look when told that they didn't want them. Why? Because they just sit on the shelves and collect dust. Perhaps a music specialty store might make a market in these but not a general used book store.

1 had a discussion with a clerk at 12th Street Books who told me that they no longer stocked Italian language books because "nobody buys them." They only stock French and German. It's all about shelf space. It is valuable and they can't afford to have "dead space" in their stores. They want stuff to move. The discussion on shelf space started because I asked where the "classics" section

had gone. I'm very fond of Everyman's Library, World's Classics and I periodically check there for new acquisitions.

"Oh! The owner tossed all those... replaced them with mysteries."

"TOSSED THEM! Threw them out!?"

"I'm sorry. Yes, that's what he did. He's got overhead. He has to increase sales."

That hurt. It was one of my best sources for these.

I frequently go to the Strand bookstore at 12th and Broadway (the largest used bookstore in the country, or so they say). And frequently hear the voice of Fred Bass, the owner, deal with book purchases as I glance through bookshelves nearby. It's amusing to hear how he deals with sellers, firmly but politely. If they try to bargain the price up he says: "No! I won't pay that. I have given you a fair price. If you don't want it then you can go to another store."

Most amusing is when he selects three books out of a box brought in, tells the seller that he will pay, say $17 for the three and then says: "I don't really need the others but, as a courtesy to you so you don't have to lug them back home, I'll give you $3 for the rest."

There is a nervous pause as the seller cogitates, and then agrees. So it's $20 for the whole box. He has this line down to perfection; it always seems to work. He's so suave. If he comes across a group of high quality books he says: "...these books are exactly the kind of thing we're looking for, high quality volumes. We really want scholarly books like these. If you have any more like these and want to sell them, please bring them in and we'll give you a good price."

I've learned over the years that the price they offer is about one third of what the book will sell for. He doesn't want any "junk" unless he can get it for less than a quarter. These are rapidly sorted by store clerks, prices marked with stickers and placed in the junk boxes along the 12th Street side for $1, $2 or $3 (mostly art books).

The Strand began in 1927 in a little store front on 4th Avenue, a block away. I first encountered the business when I was a high school senior in 1964 when the store was, say, one third of its present area on the main floor.

The used bookstore trade is very precarious but the Strand has survived and they can't be forced out by a landlord massively increasing the rent (this last actually happened to La Librairie Française in Rockefeller Center; in their case it was tripled). Why? Because they bought the building in which the store is located.

PARKS
MARTHA KING

P arks are the joy of urban mothers — we get to be outdoors with others. Outdoors where screams and cries don't bounce off apartment walls. We get to let the alpha waves flow. Through eyelashes we keep gentle tabs on a scene glowing with all the stuff we know is good: sunshine and a precious lengthening of the physical space between us and our kids.

1966: in walking distance from 57 Second Avenue were four distinctly different open spaces. All shared soft worn-down Manhattan dirt. All supported big trees: London planes, locusts, oaks of several varieties. Some were twisted, ill-favored, and fantastically burled. Some were stately and gracious. But even the gracious ones were knowing survivors that had earned their age.

All the parks sported patches of shade-tolerant grass. All but one had a row or two of metal swings, two or three slides (called sliding ponds in New York City) and square cement pits filled with not very clean sand. They were enclosed by a circle of park benches, or a tall iron picket fence, or both.

West a few blocks from me lay Washington Square. Its near north side playground was used half by academic mothers and half by hired nursemaids. The mothers did a lot of high-pitched explaining about how important it is to share, watching their kids with the stressed attention of people attending a play performed in a foreign language.

The nursemaids were bored and perfunctory but very concerned to prevent the soiling of clothing, eating of dirty food, or risk of injury. Children in their care were usually confined, strapped in strollers or walked about in harnesses, until the required time in fresh air had elapsed.

All these children had thick, expensive toys. *New Yorker* toys, I called them. I was scolded for allowing my three-year-old to climb into the sand pit with a real kitchen spoon and a cheap plastic cup. ("Don't you know that cup could shatter?" an academic mother demanded.)

Had the scene been more carefree, I might not have minded. The Washington Square playground was closest to our apartment — and the playground itself was in good shape.

True, the big fountain in the center of the square was off limits for little kids. It was turf for NYU students, park drifters, street musicians, con artists, wandering dogs. The water supported cigarette butts and used coffee cups. On really hot days, shirtless young men and dogs roiled the fountain waters together, while children in the sweltering playground had their faces and hands mopped with damp washcloths.

Way up at 23rd Street was Stuyvesant Park, bordered on the west by the beautiful spare 18th-century Friends Academy school building. It was far cooler than Washington Square because the shade was deep and the grass less patchy and distressed. Here, nursemaids way outnumbered mothers. They spent their hours together chatting over coffee or sodas. The kids they cared for could dig in the dirt around the bushes, fill their pails at the water fountain, and drag their dolls and trucks into the sandbox. At this park, children arrived on riding toys, and occasionally a baby would have its diapers changed — right there on the park bench — something only I did in Washington Square. But it wasn't a place for friendships. This was nursemaids' turf and they liked it that way. It was also a hot twenty-block walk from our apartment on 4th Street.

First Houses, on the other hand, was only three blocks away, thus sometimes my first choice on oven-hot summer days. First Houses had been created from two rows of tenements in the 1930s. It was a LaGuardia administration demonstration of slum reform, the first-ever public housing, I believe. The buildings had been renovated, not built new. Behind them, a second row of tenements had been removed to provide open space. It was not really a playground at all, but a mini-plaza, reachable from the street by two narrow walkways. No one was ever there. The quiet was almost shocking. The London plane trees had had thirty-five years to grow. They dappled the octagonal paving tiles with cool shade. And it was so clean. Leaves were always meticulously swept away. Metal trashcans were empty unless I tossed in a cookie box or a used paper towel. But when we arrived on dog days, a sprinkler would mysteriously be on, plashing gently, making a circle of wet paving, a heavenly oasis. Unless it was not, and then, like as not, we would leave because there was nothing else to do at all. No swings, no slides, no jungle gym, no kids. In the space between the silent apartments and the tall brick back wall, the ghostly super of First Houses ordained peace. Peace and loneliness. Well, you can't have everything.

So by default, Tompkins Square was park central. It was not peaceful and not lonely and not at all well cared for. Moreover the territory was sharply divided on class and ethnic lines. The playground on Avenue A was a fort for Ukrainian and Polish mothers. They kept their overdressed sausage-like babies in huge black Cadillac baby carriages. The hoods always had pink or blue pom-poms attached to indicate gender of occupant. Older two- and three-year-olds were packed into snowsuits and hoods from the first cool of September all the way through May. In summer they were outfitted with shoes, hats, and cotton sweaters. Or they didn't appear at all. Winter or summer, they were barely allowed to move. It was their business to eat and their mouths were continually occupied with cakes, bottles, pacifiers. Occasionally they were pushed in swings or taken up to the top of a slide and allowed to ride a grown-up's lap sedately down.

I never quite figured what happened after that. Some of these Eastern European-American children went on to lead the tightly supervised lives that seemed inevitable. Some, mostly girls, were enormously overweight as early as age six, bulging out of their parochial school uniforms as they placidly walked the streets. But this same population also gave rise to wily neighborhood kids, universally boys, who were neither clean, overweight, nor overdressed. They were a tribe. They dodged traffic, dragged baseball bats, screamed to each other, and ran through the park in small packs.

With my kids in tow I passed Avenue A and continued down to Avenue B where in the Avenue B playground "the sixties" held sway.
"Scheherazade! I've got your lunch."
"Amanita, leave that dog shit alone!"
"Ocean, come here. I'll cut the dirty side off."

Our kids took off their shoes, made huge mud cities with trenches and dams where grass should have been growing but hadn't for years. They mixed sand and water into slurry in the sand pit. They ran without being ordered to stop and behave, they hung dangerously from the monkey bars, and somehow organized themselves, because we mothers were too busy bitching about our lives to bother if they shared any toys or not. We shared. We shared watching each other's children, giving each other leave for a dash to the bank, store, or laundromat. We knew each other mostly by our children's names. We shared bags of outgrown baby clothes, information about apartments, gossip about landlords, birth control methods, day jobs, day care. No one was horrified if a kid pulled another kid's hair. We'd intervene if someone was really screaming. We weren't aghast if a child ate a peanut butter sandwich that had fallen on the sidewalk. Our concern for safety was mostly focused on the foul public toilets over by 10th Street — a problem that had been solved by us ad hoc. An ancient locust behind the long bench where we all sat was the official pee-pee tree. But to shit, well, that was trouble. You could take a kid to 10th Street, a dark and smelly ordeal, but it was better to go on home.

Two park officials came by one day, doing a needs survey. They looked a bit glassy when we explained we wanted an open-sided pissoir. "No door, so grown-ups won't use it," one of us said. "If it's open it won't smell," another offered.

The recorder put his pen back onto his clipboard. The lead man thanked us courteously. And they fled.

My Tompkins Park friends hadn't read Jack Spicer, though most knew Allen Ginsberg and Ken Keasey. All of them would have laughed with recognition at Spicer's dictum: "Lie to your children. Teach 'em to be wary! Think they're gonna find a world of truth out here?" Our sense of reality separated us from the Barbie-doll world of the sanitary, racially segregated suburbs and from the over-controlled behaviors of Washington Square mothers. We were a bit smug about it.

I knew, my park friends knew, that the world contained the unpleasant, dangerous, and problematic and that our babies couldn't be insulated from it. The "everything is groovy" brand of the sixties was still a California phenomenon. The sandpit at Tompkins Square harbored bottle tops, chicken bones, occasional dog turds. It wasn't groovy, but it didn't outrage us. It was up to us to teach our kids to be wary — and occasionally to remove the worst threats.

As for money, working for money, holding down a paid job, well, there we were in the park. Church of All Nations Day Care Center wouldn't take kids under three, nor older children if there were younger ones at home. I'd have to wait till summer of 1967, when Hetty would be three and to be eligible. Until then, even a "good" job wouldn't net me more than what the sitter would get once I paid her.

We talked about this bind on the benches of Tompkins Square. Aminita's mother. Kali's mother. Dwywyn's mother. We knew what was possible. For working-class women there were pink-collar jobs. For educated women, like most of us, it was teacher, secretary, nurse, proofreader, fact-checker, or go-fer with some glitter. Either way women's work was low wage work, requiring money for good shoes, pantyhose, haircuts, make-up.

So we sat in the park and let the sun beat on our backs, watching the asphalt patches soften around the base of the ever-leaking water fountain. We mothers together were living a life of merriment and boredom, the life of young mothers everywhere who are lucky enough to have a daily gang to hang with. We felt sorry for suburban women, in their solitary homes, in their stark well-stocked kitchens, surrounded by cleanliness and convenience. Even across the park in the Polish-Ukrainian preserve, merriment and boredom collected among the women with the pom-pom bedecked black baby carriages. They had each other just as we did — all of us to glorying in a sunny day, and wiping noses and bottoms, merry and bored.

A few years later, hippie parenting was breathlessly chronicled in mainstream media. Magazines featured squalor-glamour photographs of young mothers nursing bare-breasted in public, their older buck-naked children clambering about in feather headdresses, with homemade swords. It became a thing to do — to live in a painted bus, to have fun. In 1963 and 64 and 65, when Mallory and Hetty were babies, things weren't that way. Cops would and did harass the women who nursed in public, with "public" defined as a park bench at the Tompkins Square Avenue B playground. I did it with a diaper over my shoulder to hide my baby and my open shirt. And with park pals who didn't have to be asked to ride shotgun for me.

It was radical to believe in children's innate good sense, as Paul Goodman's *Growing Up Absurd* proposed. It was radical to oppose white supremacy too. It was radical to recognize government lies, and radical to see the growing war in Vietnam as a possibly deliberate drain of energy and attention away from the fight for civil rights at home. All too soon, escalation was a way of life everywhere. TV news anchors were talking every night about "the kids," meaning people in their twenties, and claiming that their groovy idealism was changing America.

This sentimentality is going to breed reaction, Baz said.

But first it bred a prophetic decline on the Lower East Side.

SKETCHES OF TRIBES
STEVE CANNON

To begin at the beginning. The idea of starting A Gathering of The Tribes gallery and performance space was inspired by the Nuyorican Poets Café opening its doors on East 3rd Street in 1989. A writer from the *Village Voice* wrote a long-winded article in that paper about all the wonderful things that were in store for the new Nuyorican Poets Café and I was curious to see how it was all going to play out. Their main innovation was the slam poetry contests every Friday night, an idea brought to New York City from Chicago by the one and only Bob Holman. The café, under the direction of Miguel Algarin, also featured open mic readings on Wednesday nights as well as on Friday nights after the poetry slam. And since their building consisted of four floors, they also planned to have poetry workshops, publish a literary journal, and furthermore, have space for out-of-town writers to stay overnight. Unfortunately, the only parts of this ambitious agenda that came into being were the open mic readings and the slams. Every now and again, they would invite a guest poet to read. Still these activities were new and innovative and inspired me to open A Gathering of The Tribes at 385 East Third Street.

At about the same time I decided to start a literary journal that would be based in the gallery/performance space and use the same name, featuring writers and artists that read and showed their work there. I figured it would be wise to get two young writers to edit the magazine and I would act as their consultant, based on my experience of having worked on small literary magazines in the Lower East Side in the sixties and seventies. My original choices were Buddy Kold (Bernard Meisler) and Norman Douglas. They were in a position to do such a thing, since both of them were moonlighting down on Wall Street as IT nerds, and making oodles of money — in other words, they were making more than enough to pay for the cost of the magazine. Since they were half my age and palled around with a younger crowd, I would have to trust their judgment in choosing good up-and-coming writers for the magazine; poets, essayists and fiction authors. However, this never panned out because, among other reasons, they took off and went to Europe.

By the time they got back to the states, I'd already published the first issue of *Tribes* with Gale Shilke as the co-editor. She was half my age and was curating readings at the Knitting Factory and at the Nuyorican Poets Café. She showed an interest in older writers, by featuring them at her readings, as well as younger ones; this gave us a wider range of talent. Since the Lower East Side has always been famous as a multi-racial, multi-cultural and multi-everything else neighborhood, we had to make sure that the magazine reflected this diversity. We wanted to represent all the various artistic disciplines; dance, music, poetry, visual art, etc. from this inclusive perspective — that was our aim then as it is now.

The first patron of *Tribes* was Elizabeth Murray. And then David Hammons had an exhibition in Seattle, Washington. As part of the agreement he signed with that gallery he had to give a certain percentage of the money he made to a nonprofit, and the one he chose was A Gathering of The Tribes. David also put one of his images, a self-portrait, on the cover of the first issue of *Tribes* magazine. This issue included a round-table discussion with David and the editors of *Tribes* on his art-making process.

This first issue appeared in the fall of 1991. The release party, obviously, was held at the Nuyorican Poets Café. By this time, we'd assembled a group of writers, poets, fiction writers and editors whose job it was to solicit material that they thought would fit in the magazine: music, poetry, interviews, visual art and essays; the whole shebang. The idea at the time was to cover the Lower East Side and the myriad forms of art being produced here, in documentary format, and run it in the magazine. All decisions regarding the final product before publication were by consensus. The magazine never was and never will be dedicated to a single theme. What we wanted was to publish works of excellence with a focus on diversity.

THE TIME THAT JOHN FARRIS ALMOST GOT ME ARRESTED

B. KOLD

I was leaving my apartment in the Jacob Riis Houses on Avenue D and 7th street with two of my friends when we got stopped by a zealous cop. I was about twenty-five, and so was my friend Tim. My friend John was about fifty, a poet, and black. This was way back in the day, and I was the only white man who lived in the projects. Two young white boys with an older black man in the projects on Avenue D was not a good look, as far as law enforcement was concerned.

John didn't take shit from anybody. He'd done time for selling a kilo of pot back in the '60s, when he wouldn't snitch on his dealer. I didn't know it at the time, but he'd been one of Malcolm X's bodyguards, was actually standing next to Malcolm when he got shot, and felt guilty ever after about not stopping the bullet. Which might explain his love of whiskey and cocaine. Why we were friends, what we had in common, despite our age and demographic differences, was literature. And whiskey and cocaine. We had just left my apartment on the 14th floor and were taking the elevator down when it stopped on the seventh floor and a young black housing cop got on. Housing cops were real cops, sort of. They had low status in the cop world but they carried badges and guns and could arrest you. The cop gave us the once over. He didn't like what he saw.

"What's up fellas? Where you coming from?"

"We were at my house," I said.

"Uh-huh," he said, "sure you were." I'm nervous because I've got a quarter ounce of cocaine in my pocket. We had been doing blow all afternoon and were completely wired. We were on our way to Vazac's to get some whiskey. "Where's that?"

"14th floor, apartment C." I swallowed, hard.

"*Suuure.* C'mon, let's take a little ride." I'd recently been arrested for the first time and really didn't want to go through that rigamarole again: the thorazine tea, the baloney sandwiches, the poor choice of reading material. I looked away from Tim and John, who were suppressing smiles, amused by the cop's Shatneresque manner. The eager-beaver cop stopped the elevator, pressed the "14" button and back up we went. We got out and walked across the hall to apartment C. The cop cop-knocked on the door, BOOM BOOM BOOM, with the meaty part of the fist instead of the knuckles.

My roommate Tina, the only white woman in the projects, answered the door. Tina worked on 3rd and D as a teacher at the day care center. She got the apartment through one of her co-workers. Everybody in the neighborhood knew who she was. "Hi Miss Tina!" the kids would say while their parents beamed. Nobody knew who the fuck I was, and treated me accordingly.

Tina was no dummy. She saw us, saw the cop, and played it cool.

"Hey guys, what's up?"

The cop was taken aback to see a white girl open the door. "Evening miss. Do you know these gentlemen?"

"Sure."

"What are their names?"

"That's John, Tim and B."

"And which one lives here?"

Tina pointed at me.

The cop pointed at John. "What's his name?"

"John."

The cop pointed at Tim. "What's his name?"

"Tim."

The cop started to point at me again, but quickly reversed and pointed back at John, like he was trying to fake Tina out. It was

FROM SOMEWHERE TO NOWHERE

one of those moments where you really shouldn't laugh, like if somebody farts at a funeral, which of course makes it ten times funnier. It was one of the funniest things I'd ever seen. We were holding it in and dying.

"What's his name?"

"John."

The cop frowned. "All right miss, have a good night. C'mon fellas, let's go down." You knew he wanted to say "downtown" but "down" was as close as a housing cop was going to get.

We all got back in the elevator. The cop pressed the "L" button. "You know I know you guys are full of it. I don't know what you're doing here but...."

"Listen you punk," John said, poking a finger in his chest. "I'm old enough to be your father! Treat me with some god-damn respect!" He gave the poor cop a serious eyeball fucking.

I'm thinking holy shit, I am royally fucked. I told you I had a quarter ounce of coke in my pocket, right? But John was so damned intimidating the cop backed down. "Yes sir, you're right, I'm sorry."

John continued glaring at him the rest of the way down. The cop stared at his shoes. As soon as we reached the lobby and the door opened, he scurried off, tail between his legs.

"Jesus Christ, Johnny, you're gonna give me a heart attack! You know I'm holding!"

John laughed. "Fuck that little bitch. About time somebody taught him some manners."

Tim was laughing so hard he was holding his sides, like Felix the Cat, leaning against the back of the elevator so he didn't fall down.

DANIEL KOLM

LOISAIDA
JOHN FARRIS

The demographics of Third Street were in a state of convulsion of a magnitude not seen since that first great incursion from the other side of the Atlantic. It was the '60s and a renewed heroin epidemic came at a time the existing housing stock had become unprofitable to many of their landlords occasioned a spate of fires no one even bothered to deem suspicious though they did come at the expense of the occupants who were forced to move on.

Left in all this abandon was a plethora of rubble-strewn lots covered in a shower of loose bricks bristling with broken glass, worn automobile tires, motors, sinks, beds, couches, TV's, tables, chairs, various articles of clothing, dolls, books, tricycles — all lacking something — an arm or two, a leg, an eye, a back, a wheel, a handlebar; or burned nearly beyond recognition, the cotton stuffing of mattresses; exposed, blackened.

Dominating the few leaning tenements and puckered row houses was the towering housing project on the river known as The Lillian Wald Houses. Wolfie had lived in the shadow of these all his life. His young mother's body had been found in just such a rubble-strewn lot; her killer never found.

Whatever change that was taking place in this span of time was barely perceptible till now: cartoons bolted to the sign-posts of bus stops, shadowy human silhouettes brushed onto buildings next to the usual neighborhood graffiti.

One morning, out of nowhere, as Eddie, Ralphie and he were on their way to school a wheel of purple footprints led them farther and farther away from their destination until Eddie said they would

123

be late for class. Had they kept going the outsized purple footsteps that appeared to have been made by a giant would have led them to a lot on Rivington. Peculiar about this was the fence behind which it lay, freshly painted in a purple bold as the footprints themselves; the lot freshly planted in exotic flora laid out in perfectly geometric beds instead of the familiar dead or dying geraniums in broken plastic pots. The footsteps then led west on Rivington to where a group of hairy blanco youths dressed all in black had squatted a couple of buildings; they had scavenged car hoods, bumpers and grills, tricycles, dolls and bicycle wheels — all morphed into a couple of mountains resembling a roller-coaster in a zany, rusting carnival.

What these lots had in common with the purple footprints was that they were both gated and locked against casual intrusion. A gaggle of art galleries had opened here and there. There had been a gargantuan art show in a group of abandoned buildings on Delancey called "The Real Estate Show" though it was not too long after that event that the buildings that had been host to it were themselves reduced to rubble.

The Sailor arrived on his twenty-two incher, hands small as a child's gripping the handlebars, one foot resting straight legged on a pedal, the other knee bent to favor a hip.

Third Street, bathed in a golden glow, fascinated him as he steered past the torched carcasses of automobiles, the lots of struggling ailanthi, the tenuous strands of sumac tall as the leaning buildings they seemed to support.

All references to things maritime aside, it wasn't the sea he took his name from as much as the very air itself; the Sailor was a grifter whose nickname had been given to him by the Gypsies who had taught him their game; how to vault expertly into the air over the hoods of oncoming cars to claim insurance, the hip he favored the result of a terrible miscalculation he'd made at the most critical moment — that of contact — that had sent him sailing not under the power of his amazing gift of gymnastic powers, but that of the oncoming vehicle whose owner he'd thought to dupe, his repair leaving one leg shorter than the other. The practice of this subterfuge had not been his main vocation; it had been no more than a ruse to support the ever-burgeoning heroin habit he'd acquired and the art he made from whatever materials that happened to be at hand including his own blood — draining as much of it as was required each day, reintroducing the transforming, intoxicating powder he'd acquired from the proceeds of his extreme concentration and exhilarating moment of exertion into whatever vein that had not collapsed. As he was, however, stuck with no longer being able to support himself in the manner he'd trained himself to, he had drifted east, a light breeze — and the monkey on his back — blowing him here as it were in search of other opportunity.

Exulting in a ray of golden sunlight, a feeling of warmth and well-being settling over his clammy body usually felt only after he'd injected, the widening grin revealing a set of crooked teeth with most of the molars missing was prompted by anticipation of what he sought; what the light detailed outside of himself assuring him he might find what it was he was looking for, for so much poverty was wealth to him; it would not be long before he would be fixed. He felt it in his decalcified bones; the creeping effusiveness, the surge of joy he experienced at the sight of the torched cars wrought by his satisfaction that these could no longer thwart him, that he might sit as comfortable as he could given his fragile hip in any one of them and take off higher than the projects dead ahead, could get as high as the sun offering the gold of its warmth, could tumble over the moon without being gored except as he chose to gore himself. Alchemist as he was in the truest sense, he was sure he would find here the compounds mortared from that flower more passionately adored and sought after by its admirers than the rarest orchid that he craved for his transformation among the mostly struggling ailanthi, the sumac with their yellow pods, the spare green leafage of crown that hovered over them only half dead; and as he was transformed, he would transform every displaced stick of furniture — every book — every lost article of clothing.

Spying in his glittering eye a group of abject figures sallow and shivering like himself though it was a warm June morning and joining them, he shortly got what he needed. Directed after his inquiry to an unkempt gentleman huddled under an incongruous pile of blankets inside a cardboard refrigerator box on Avenue B, he purchased a set of works and in no time was back in the ravaged chassis of what looked like had been a brand-new Monte Carlo, fixed and dreamily nodding — it was then that someone had stolen his bike — sure it was this he later saw being ridden up and down the block one after another by a group of whooping neighborhood kids wild as Indians, he never liked them much after that.

Scouring the neighborhood lots between fixes with the hopping gait of a wounded crow he had soon assembled another; though as a rim was slightly bent it rode with a wobble. Finding some black paint and a bundle of brushes, he began to paint silhouettes on the sagging tenements, the walls of the nearly recumbent row houses.

THE LADY IN THE APARTMENT NEXT DOOR LIVES IN PERPETUAL FIRE HAZARD

MICAH ZEVIN

The Landlord hears complaints of smoke rising and infiltrating this is untenable. The lady says she is a woman of worship, that this is an attack on spirituality, her right to light candles and incense to the Virgin, and have messages travel in signals of Saintly fire rings and burning flesh erasing humanities sinful habits. This is the point, argue tenants, you can have your heaven or hell, just purchase some common sense.

"We don't all desire to voyage the way of the ashen, We do not all make fetish God's breath outside doorsteps. Here we pay rent, returning from fatigue ridden days for body and mind's renewal, time together or alone with ourselves, not to perish at frail hands of repentance, or a kingdom yet formulate its intentions...."

TENTH BETWEEN FEAR & TREMBLING
MAX BLAGG

We lived one floor up from a woodworking shop from which the tools had long since been stolen. It was on East Tenth Street, way over almost to the river, a view of the smokestacks of Con Edison's 14th Street plant painted that year in patriotic shades of red white and blue. Every night Sherillee went to 49th Street to sing her heart out in the schlock rock musical "Jesus Christ Superstar." I stayed home, studying the light of golden afternoons as the sun streamed over the towers of the Con Ed plant. We were just beginning to discover how little we had in common.

Unable to find regular employment, my only income was derived from the sale of my blood by the pint on alternate days to a clinic known as the Vein Drain on First Avenue. The first time I went there I recognized the nurse from the movie "Chelsea Girls." But she didn't give me a break, she probably wasn't a real nurse anyway. I thought she said ten dollars for that clean rhesus negative, and then after I had given my precious fluid she handed me a glass of milk and a cookie and six bucks, telling me it's ten the *second* time you give. New York, I was learning very slowly. It still wasn't as bad as the time in San Francisco when I gave plasma. They took the blood out then put it back in after they had extracted the plasma in some kind of centrifuge. It paid about $4 a pint. Horrible feeling to have the blood trickling back in because it was a lower temperature than the blood already circulating. I felt like Keith Richards in Switzerland.

Anemically strolling through the lower east side, I felt totally connected, the city streets more familiar than the streets of London had ever felt in the four years I'd lived there.

"See London's under the sign of Capricorn, but New York's under Cancer, and you're a Cancer, so naturally you fit here" somebody told me, and such pretentious celestial observations seemed perfectly acceptable. Every street looked like the cover of "Freewheeling," redbrick buildings and steel fire escapes. It was my neighborhood, though I didn't know it yet. Every day I roamed streets familiar from movies and dreams. I usually spent my blood money on a huge Polish loaf that would last for two days, a quarter pound of smoked ham, peanut butter. The rest was for thin tap beer at the St. Marks Bar and Grill, though I never saw any evidence of a grill, on First Avenue, where the old Polish ladies danced to Frank Sinatra at 3 a.m. and wept over their lost lives in Gdansk, the loved ones they had left behind in Cracow.

My initiation into dread soon occurred. It was a black and Puerto Rican neighborhood, and east of Avenue A there were very few white faces. Tenth between B and C was a particularly tough block, lots of prison fit youths hanging out on stoops, like coyotes circling the herd, watching for the weak, the unwary. I naively believed I had something in common with these people though. I was a bohemian, and like them I had no money. They could relate to that. Wrong. The bus cost 25 cents and it ran right by my door, along Tenth Street to Avenue D, but on this warm summer night I didn't have a thin dime.

I had nursed one drink for several hours at Eileen's Bar on Second Avenue, and finally embarked on the short walk home, more alert after I crossed Avenue A, the psychic borderline between the dodgy and the truly dangerous. I traversed the block between B and C without incident, crossed Avenue C and then walked at a casually rapid pace from the corner to my building, exactly in the middle of the block. I was opening the flimsy wooden door when somebody landed on my back and another pair of hands pushed me inside. As the assailant swayed around piggyback it dawned on me that this was my first mugging. Instead of being scared I became totally enraged at these cowardly scum attacking me in this chickenshit fashion.

"You fucking *patos,* I kill you quick" I screamed into the stairway, pulling my voice from deep within the thorax, a Viking technique to intimidate the enemy. In the confined space it bounced around like a sonic boom. Out of the corner of my eye I had seen the glint of white metal but it was too late to stop now. Armed response was the only response. I had read that on a bumper sticker. I pulled the small caliber pistol smoothly from my waistband, placed it on my left shoulder, wedged my jaw against my forearm and squeezed the trigger. I felt the muzzle flash burn my cheek and a violent ringing in my ear. The mugger's grip slackened and he slid down my back to the floor.

I turned to the other youth who was backing wide-eyed into the wall. His hand was open to show me that the metal was just a steel comb. There was a sharp reek of shit mingling with the cordite hanging in the air. I pressed the small gun's barrel against his thigh and pulled the trigger. His leg kicked spastically and he fell like a racehorse at a fence, his scream filling the echo left by the gunshot. I started kicking his good leg, his ribs and his head with those solid state Frye boots and I was still kicking him when the cops arrived.

No, that didn't happen.

The guy landed on my back and I automatically slipped my hand into my pocket, fingers sliding into the worn loops of the brass knuckles I always carried. I swung my fist back hard onto the top of his head and felt the brass knuckle bounce resoundingly on his cranium. Big headache coming up. He dropped off my back like a shot jockey. I turned and straight-armed the second youth as he came at me. My brass-covered fist smacked him square in the mouth. Teeth gave way as his lip, trapped between brass and bone, squirted blood onto my shirt in a furious arc. "Oh you asshole that's my best shirt" I screamed in a high thin voice and hit him in the chest. I saw the soles of his sneakers come up toward me as he went over backwards like a poleaxed chicken in a TV cartoon.

Was that how it happened?

I had the door open when somebody fell like an anvil onto my back. That triggered a simian rage. I nimbly swung around as his partner tried to push me inside the hallway and close the door behind us, kicking the partner in the shins with the toe of my heavy boot. He yelped and hopped backward. I pushed him outside and slammed the door. The other guy was still on my back, screaming at me to give it up. Give up what? I didn't have anything to give up. I backed into the brick wall as hard as I could. He half fell from his mount and I kicked his legs from under him. He obviously wasn't aware that until recently I had been a college soccer star renowned for the excessive violence of my defensive tackling. I ran up about five steps of the staircase, turned round and jumped down, landing squarely on his stomach and spleen, where I briefly but emphatically clog danced a victory jig. With a low moan, he turned his head to the side and puked. I would be sent off the field for this, but my opponent would have to be carried off, yes the referee was signaling for a stretcher....

No, that didn't happen either. None of these variations happened until after the real event, and then I constantly replayed these and other possible scenarios, the level of violence varying according to my mood.

What really happened: I opened the door and somebody landed on my back, pushing me inside. A second youth followed us and slammed the door. Then we were three in the small space at the bottom of a steep stairwell.

"Give us the fucking money, man," said the bigger of the two, a solid-looking brother with a gold earring that gave him a vaguely piratical appearance. The other kid was a light-skinned Hispanic boy and he looked more scared than I felt.

I was quite calm because I didn't have any money and that was that. And I was counting on the English accent to charm away their hostility. "I'm terribly sorry," I said, "I'm broke, I mean penniless, lads, why do you think I was walking home instead of taking a cab or the bus even?" The accent had no effect whatsoever, and they methodically searched my pockets, forced me to remove my boots, then checked my underwear. They became furious because I had wasted their time and obviously had no money. When someone decides, using their finely tuned instincts, to choose *you* as a victim, and then discovers you have no money, they become angry at their own ineptitude. Since they had seen me open the door they knew I lived here. I wasn't fast enough to bluff them into believing I was just visiting. They took the keys and we walked up one flight to the loft.

We went inside and I still wasn't too concerned because there was very little worth taking. But after they had secured me hand and foot with extension cords I started to become slightly alarmed. Jeeze, if they didn't get enough stuff, they might want a piece of my young ass, they might want some anyway, just for jollies.... The two began to load everything into a suitcase and the lovely old leather bag that had travelled with me from England, to the West coast and back again. When I saw that about to go I forgot myself for a moment.

"Aah, please don't take my travelling bag, you chaps..." I said, laying on the English accent as thickly as I could.

"Shut you' mouth muthafucka" snapped the pirate, sounding exactly like a character from "Shaft." That quieted me down and I lay there and watched as they loaded up. Everything must go: a two dollar alarm clock, an old steam iron, even my cumbersome manual typewriter which couldn't be worth more than five dollars on the street. When they had filled up the two bags and a pillowcase they took a sheet from the bed and loaded more stuff into that. How were they planning to carry all this junk? Did they have a truck outside? After they had trashed the contents of the desk I saw the pirate studying Sherillee's headshots. "Oh they'll see I'm shacked up with a black sister and let me go," I thought, for two seconds.

"Where the woman at?"

"Oh she's working late, she won't be home for hours..."

"Shall we lay up for the bitch, man?" The smaller one said, and I prayed that Sherillee would stay out late tonight, wouldn't just walk in the door in the middle of this and find me lying there helpless. There is a crucial scene in the movie "Performance," when three thugs have beaten and whipped James Fox and trashed his apartment and he gets his hands free and that big automatic is suddenly there, he's got the whole world in his hands and the power shifts and that's where I wanted to be just then, my finger on the trigger of a large caliber gun pointing at these two petty criminals. They had put murder in me, perhaps the fear of my own death had roused murder in me. I could have pulled the trigger without a second thought, first thought best thought, no problem. Put them in the stairway first so as not to mess up the loft with their punk blood. Momentarily transported into a dense red rage by this violent fantasy, I soon returned to the brutality of the fact I was bound hand and foot, trussed up like a pig or a chicken and if they wanted to eat me or fuck me or murder me after they had robbed me there was nothing I could do.

They decided finally to leave, carrying two loads apiece, looking like they had just been evicted. After a while I crawled over to lock the door in case they came back for the toothbrush. I managed to get my feet untied but I couldn't get the cord loose from my hands. I dialed 911 like a contortionist and gave the operator the address. Twenty minutes later the cops still had not arrived. Finally I walked down the stairs out onto Tenth Street with my hands still tied behind my back. A citizen was walking by.

"Excuse me, would you mind untying my hands?"

The man paused to untie the cord, handed it to me and walked on. Not his business.

The cops showed up just as Sherilee arrived home to a looted apartment. She began to clean up what was left while I rode around with them for a few blocks but they were more interested in my accent than in finding the perpetrators.

"They probably live right in the neighborhood, and chances are they'll be back." said one cop reassuringly.

"But they took everything already!"

"Don't matter, they've been once, they'll be back."

What if I'd had a gun?

One cop looked at the other and they both laughed.

"You'd probably be on your way to the morgue right now. But if you ever get the chance, just say there was a scuffle, you grabbed the gun, boom, it went off. You'll walk."

I was in New York City, I had just been bound and robbed, and now I was riding around in a cop car with a policeman telling me it was alright to kill somebody. I might get really scared if I stopped to think about it.

Three days later, as I rode the bus across Tenth Street, I recognized one of my assailants sitting quietly on a stoop between B and C. So he *was* my neighbor. I knew where he lived but he knew where I lived.

GREGORY KOLM

THERE IS NO GOD
ON THE LOWER EAST SIDE
Diane Spodarek

My husband lifted me off my feet and threw me across the room. "A man can only take so much," he said. "That's it. Get out," I said. "I really mean it this time."

He ran to the bedroom and locked the door. He installed the lock the first week he moved in. Everything he did pissed me off.

The back of my head was throbbing. I got ice from the freezer, the last cubes that didn't end up in my vodka.

I pounded on the bedroom door. "It hurts like hell. I have to go to the hospital."

He opened the door. His black hair was teased into a bouffant flip and he was wearing red lipstick. It wasn't mine.

"Take off my slip," I said.

"You provoked me."

I grabbed the doorframe to keep from falling.

"Lay down," he said.

"You're not supposed to with a head injury."

"I know that." He pressed his lips into a smirk. "Why you always tell me what I already know?"

I walked to the living room and sat on the sofa. It was white before he moved in. Now it was covered with his leavings: wine, semen, pasta sauce. I looked through the window; swirling blankets of snow obscured the brownstones on Essex Street. The twin towers to the south looked ghostly, their blight on the landscape muted.

He stood in front of me, legs spread, a half hard-on rising under my slip. His red-lacquered toenails on his big hairy feet were dull, the big ones chipped.

"You're ripping the seams. Take it off."

He waved his penis and said, "Big Jack's not talking to you."

He stomped away, like a petulant toddler, his flat feet slapping the wood floor. He slammed the bedroom door.

I rammed my shoulder against the door. It cracked. He swung the door open and rattled it back and forth until it broke away from the hinges. He raised it above his head like a surfboard and hurled it at me. I ducked. I could smell his Channel Number 5 as he grabbed me by the shoulders, growling. He lifted me up and flung me across the room. I felt the thrill of flying before I hit the wall.

I told the doctor I fell while washing the floor.

AA. Al-anon. Sobriety. Meditation. Yoga. Buddhist Chanting. Hindu Retreats. Past Life. Living in the Moment. Atheism.

I was in the bathroom when I heard the explosion that was the first plane. Through the window from the fifteenth floor, I saw flames and black smoke burning from a black hole in the tower. I turned on the radio. Breathless voices described falling debris, smoke, people running, body parts, a woman cut in half, a hand in the street.

The media called the site ground zero. Every day orange/brown smoke filled the sky, a sign of the underground burning, a rage that lasted for a year. I looked at the smoke every day, a symbol of violence and hate. But I could not look at it without thinking about the violence in my own home. Every act begins in someone's heart. Even in mine.

Sobriety is over-rated. I was living in a twelve-step fog when I said yes to a man in New Zealand, a former lover who said he had quit drinking. I sublet my apartment on Grand Street to Sheba, a born-again Christian real estate broker. While walking by the sea in Pukerua Bay, Sheba stole my apartment in New York City. She made a deal with the co-op board, reported its owner, Charlie, who had sublet it to me. The board fined Charlie thirty thousand dollars for illegal subletting and Sheba sold the apartment for seven hundred and fifty thousand dollars, the "market rate." I lost all my furniture, books, pots and pans, and sheets and towels. Shortly thereafter, Charlie died.

Sometimes I wonder if Sheba still cooks in my cast iron pot, still chops vegetables with my chef's knife, still dries her back with my bath towels. Perhaps she threw it all away like she threw Charlie and me to the street.

I don't believe in forgiveness. I hate Sheba like I hate my ex-husband. That feels right, more in the moment, more spiritual.

I went to see my dentist on Grand Street. When he told me his fee, I said, "Oh my god." He cut the fee in half. He is the last man standing on the Lower East Side.

After drilling out a cracked amalgam, he said, "You have a mineral problem in your saliva."

"What can I do about it?"

"Nothing."

"Where do the minerals come from?"

"They come from god," he said. *"If* you believe in god."

He swept his right arm out to his side and said, "But how could you? Just look around."

LOFT LIVING
THADDEUS RUTKOWSKI

My landlord invited me to a party in his loft. His place was in a fashionable neighborhood, and it was bigger than I'd expected. It had two floors and covered about 3,000 square feet. When I arrived, I stared at the fixtures and exposed wood. The appliances were shiny, and the railing around the balcony looked like it was made of oak.

During the party, my host pretty much ignored me, but when he noticed me, he took me aside. "You know," he said, "your rent is nothing, compared to what I pay."

I was the host's subtenant. I lived in a building that had been abandoned, then sold to a group of artist-entrepreneurs. It was a de facto co-op. "I'd like to have a permanent lease," I said.

"Don't worry," he said. "We're going to fix your place up; then we'll sell it to you."

"An option to renew my lease would be enough," I said.

He slapped me on the shoulder. "Buddy," he said, "you could be a friend of mine, except you're my tenant."

At the end of his party, he released dozens of balloons that had been held in a net near the ceiling. As the balloons bounced, he said to me, "I'll say one thing for New York. It's the easiest place to get laid."

***

I invited a young woman to my loft. She didn't seem to mind the fact that I had no furniture. After all, I had a big space.

She and I sat at a table made of two-by-fours and particleboard. Under the table, a split in the floorboards revealed a slice of the apartment below. Below us, the couple in residence was yelling at their dog. First the woman, then the man, would shout, "Klaus, no!" We could see them as they passed beneath the hole in the floor.

"You remember the party where we met?" my guest asked.

"Yes, of course," I said.

"It had a theme."

"It did."

"The theme was 'Say yes to love.' "

"I remember."

From below, I heard the woman, then the man, yell, "Klaus, no!" but when I looked through the crack, I couldn't see the people or their dog. I didn't know what Klaus was doing wrong.

"It was a nice party," I said, but I didn't really think so. I'd come there with a couple, and by the end of the party, they'd broken up. The man had met another woman and ignored his date.

"You have to say yes," my guest said. "You have to say yes to love."

Downstairs, my neighbors said "No" again.

Later, I walked my guest out to the street and helped her hail a cab. I must have been nervous, because when I shut the car door for her, the metal frame hit me on the head.

***

My landlord sent a man named Olaf to install a new wood floor in my place. Olaf had a routine: He would align a plank, then sink a nail into it with one blow of a hammer. He repeated this action hundreds of times. In two days, he was half finished with the job.

I noticed that the floor wasn't level. It swelled where the old subflooring was higher, and it dipped where the former floor had sunk. I pointed this out to Olaf. "The floor is curved," I said. "You have to level it out by using shims. You have to shim it up. Do you know how to shim?"

I couldn't tell if Olaf understood, because he didn't say anything.

I tapped the floor with my foot. "You call this a shim?" I asked. "I call it a shame."

Olaf left then and never came back. The floor remained as it was. Half of it was new, and half was the old, rotting wood.

***

At one point, I noticed that cockroaches were infesting my place. I sprayed with insecticide, but it didn't make much difference. So I called a phone number I'd found in a classified ad for extermination services.

Two women came to my place. They called themselves the Lady Killers. They blasted white powder from squeeze bottles into every crack and seam. "It's boric acid cut with baby powder," they explained.

At first, there was no change, except that the roaches ran around covered with white dust.

After a while, I saw fewer insects, but the powder stuck to everything. Whenever I picked up a glass, dish or utensil, I had to clean off a residue of roach dust.

***

The tenants in my building formed a group to fight against our landlords. None of us had renewable leases or predictable rent increases. We retained a lawyer, who advised us to put our rent into a bank account. The money would remain there and would show that we were able to pay, if we wanted to. We just didn't want to.

I was appointed treasurer for the group. I set up an escrow account, collected rent from all of the tenants and deposited the money each month. I kept a record of the amounts on paper.

***

One night, a couple of other building residents came to visit. We sat at my particleboard table and played cards. Now and then, the gas heater mounted in a nearby window kicked on with a bang.

"My heater doesn't do that," one of the residents said.

"Don't worry about it," I said. "When it restarts, it explodes."

People seemed startled every time the gas ignited.

Presently, we heard a knock on the door. I opened it and saw a young man standing in the hallway. I thought he was a friend of one of the other residents. "Do you want to come in?" I asked.

He handed me a paper document. When I asked what it was, he said, "Just read it."

I brought the document inside. It was a summons to appear in court. We had been subpoenaed.

***

One of my neighbors came back from a deposition. "I listened to the statement of one of the owners," he said. "She kept saying she was an artist."

He imitated her accent: "I am AH-tist! Give my space back!" The owner was Korean and spoke English with an accent.

"What are we?" my neighbor said. "We're artists, too. We're AH-tists. Artists don't pay rent."

***

I started working with a couple of guys to rehabilitate an abandoned building nearby. We planned to clean it up and occupy it. We were going to move in and take ownership.

There was a secret door to get to the stairs — it was a piece of sheetrock nailed to a frame. The three of us pried the board off the frame and went through the opening.

As I walked through the apartments, I saw rooms with different-colored walls. There were pink rooms, blue rooms, yellow rooms. I saw shelves with dishes still stacked on them, and floors covered with papers, clothes and plasterboard shards.

Using a broom and a shovel, I scooped up as much trash as I could—I worked hard.

After a few days, the three of us had made no dent in the piles of debris.

I called our housing lawyer — the one guiding the dispute with our landlords — to discuss the situation. "Maybe we could live in

this abandoned building," I said. "We would move in and just refuse to move out."

"Who owns the building?" the lawyer asked.

"The city."

"You don't own it?"

"No."

"Do you have a lease or any sort of contract?"

"No."

"What you're doing is tantamount to walking into a bank and
saying, 'We're going to break into the vault and take some money,
but it's for a good cause. We're going to give it to the poor.' "

***

Our landlords made us an offer: a four-year lease, or no lease
at all. If we moved out immediately, we could keep the rent we'd
saved in the bank.

Most of my neighbors chose to move out right away. I with-
drew money from the escrow account and gave them their portions.
One person, however, claimed I owed her for one month more than
I had recorded. "You have to give me another thousand," she said.

"I don't see it on my record sheet," I said.

"I'm not leaving until I get it."

I should have told her to sue me, that I wouldn't hand over the
money without a fight, but I didn't. I didn't have the time to argue.
I gave her the extra amount.

***

I chose the four-year lease. I knew I'd never be able to afford
a place as spacious as the one I had. I decided to live with the unfinished floor and the exploding gas heater and enjoy the loft for
as long as I could. Klaus and his owners were moving out. I could
still look through the floorboards to the apartment downstairs. Who
knew what I would see? It didn't matter. If a dog didn't move in,
things would be quieter over the next four years.

THE AMERICAN DREAM IN REVERSE
ROB COUTEAU

I n the spring of 1981 my friend Drew found an apartment in
the Lower East Side, and he asked if I was interested in sharing
it. A fifth-floor walk-up on East Eleventh, it was moderately
priced, so we decided to grab it.

At once, we set about to renovate the place: slapping up
sheetrock, coating the floors with polyurethane, and sealing cracks
along the baseboards. The latter task was of special import, because
so many roaches came crawling out at night that they would have
walked across our faces if we hadn't positioned the bed legs in sar-
dine cans filled with turpentine.

The building next door featured an Italian-American club, and
the cigar-chomping man who ran the joint, a short stout fellow
named Freddie, was our landlord. Although we didn't realize it at
the time, the real owner, a mobster, was locked away in a federal
penitentiary, and Freddie was merely fronting for him.

Freddie seemed to take an instant liking to us, and especially to
me, for some reason. At first we thought it was because, coming
from Gravesend, Brooklyn, Drew and I knew how to talk respect-
fully, and in a certain down-to-earth manner, to men such as Freddie,
even though it was obvious that we weren't quite like Freddie, being
a bit more schooled and polished. But we never acted pretentious,
or felt awkward in his company, something he appreciated since
there were so many yuppies scrambling to find apartments in the
neighborhood, which was rapidly changing. But as we eventually
discovered, Freddie's gregariousness had other, more sinister roots.

A few months after we'd installed ourselves there, I lost my job as a photographer's assistant, so now I was forced to quickly find work.

From that time on, we suspected that Freddie had planted a bug in our flat, because he always seemed to know when things were tight. Whenever I was about to have trouble paying the rent, he'd appear with some work. In fact, he soon hired me as his right-hand man, and together we'd renovate tenements in the building so that he could charge the yuppies even more as they moved in.

A typical day with Freddie would begin in his flat, the only one on the ground floor, where we'd devour a lumberjack breakfast of three or four eggs each, with ham, sausage, bacon, or all three, and topped with an espresso that would stiffen the hair on your nuts. All this *chez* Bonzet, a Sicilian word meaning "little fruit," for Bonzet — the only non-mobbed-up man around, as we later learned — was over three hundred pounds. A fair haired, blue eyed, slightly nervous fellow, Bonzet — or Jimmy — enjoyed the simple things, such as eating, relaxing in his folding chair in the sun, and chatting about whatever nonsense happened to be the order of the day. Jimmy possessed a charming sense of humor, and, more than anything, he loved to laugh. Only something stressful, such as Freddie's snide comments and gruff commands, could flip his switches and bring out his more anxious, jittery side.

In any case, well fortified by Bonzet's cooking, Freddie and I would clamber up the slate steps. Then he'd lead me into some ancient, dilapidated tenement.

These were the same apartments that the nineteenth-century immigrants had lived in, gaining their first foothold in America. And there we were, Drew and I, college-educated guys from solid, middle-class families, and what the fuck is wrong with you kids? It's as if your grandparents' American dream is running in reverse! And how on earth can you afford such astronomical prices? People are paying 750 bucks a month for these dumpy, roach-infested holes, Freddie would exclaim, all the while insulting us, berating us, and puzzling over why we'd let him take such advantage of us.

A classic Freddie rant, it was the kind of thing he pulled on everyone. He loved to break your balls; that was just Freddie. He was also crowned with a Napoleon complex, not just because of his petite stature but for some other, more mysterious reason: something I never quite fathomed and of course never asked about. But I suspect it had to do with the father that he never once mentioned.

Anyway, we'd work for a few hours, Freddie and I, perhaps down on our hands and knees as he taught me how to lay linoleum tiles.

"You heat the edges slightly, with this here blowtorch," pointing it directly into my face and nearly singeing my eyebrows. "Then they melt into place. When you trim them to fit all those oddball angles, it cuts like butter." Freddie loved his torch, and he would have made an impassioned Nazi storm trooper.

After a couple of hours, just when we were really kicking ass on the job, Freddie would suddenly say damn it, I forgot my Scotch. Robbie, do me a favor, go get it, it's in the club.

So I'd climb down the stairs, knock on the door, and tell Ralphie, or Nicky, or Harry that Freddie wants his Johnny Walker Black. And they'd let me in, the only non-mobster other than Bonzet who was ever allowed inside, and hand me a bottle. But always with some witty remark, such as: *ain't he had enough already, or that lush, or make sure he don't drink it all in one gulp!*

I'd smile and nod, never once talking back to these killers and maimers and torturers. Although, at the time, I didn't know what they were up to, I could sense these were men not to be fucked with. Unless you assumed the proper role — of being the younger, less experienced one, nodding with great respect to the elders — your ass was grass.

So I'd return with the Johnny, and then things would get a bit blurry, if I might call it that. Like a baby sucking on his mommy's tit, Freddie sucked on his bottle, and soon the tiles would have gotten laid sideways if I hadn't volunteered, in the most diplomatic manner, to take over:

Hey, Freddie, I'd say, save your knees, take a break. You're working your butt off; let Robbie take over. Come on, Freddie, relax, enjoy your drink. You did enough for one day. Besides, I appreciate how you're teaching me this stuff, so let me practice a bit, and get it down.

Freddie would stop, take a deep breath, and say, yeah, maybe yer right. OK, but do me a favor. Reach over there, on the floor, behind the toolbox. Hand me one of them cigars. So I'd pass along a cheap Denobili, and he'd offer me a slug of Johnny, and I'd say no, I'd better not; I can't handle it like you can. If I do that, the tiles will end up glued to the wall! And Freddie would laugh, especially since the joke was on me.

Then he'd drink some more, and start slurring, and that's when the day would end, the workday that is: about three in the afternoon when, suddenly, he'd announce: "OK, that's it; I've had too much to drink. We better call it a day."

We'd leave all the tools and half-cut tiles right there on the floor. I'd cover the can of linoleum glue, then we'd enter his flat, wash up, and go next door to the club.

Once inside, he'd hand me cash for a day's work, then insist that I join him in a drink. There was no way around that, so I'd sip a shot as slow as I could. Because if I downed it, Freddie would pour another one, and then I'd be unable to write for the rest of the night. So instead, I'd sip, and try to blend into the woodwork, as Nicky Joe "The Cook" turned on the espresso machine, and somebody knocked at the door, and Frankie "The Foot" slid open the curtain just a crack and said, *it's them fuckin' junkies.*

Two skinny scruffy beady-eyed guys in their late twenties or early thirties would step in, but no farther than the threshold, and open their long trench coats. Just like in a cheap B-movie, the linings were stuffed with filet mignon, nicked from a local supermarket. Freddie would offer them six bucks a steak, then settle accounts and say scram. Then he'd throw me a steak or two, and Nicky would hand me an espresso, and I'd thank them profusely, but not too profusely: just that right balance. For, as Walt Whitman says: *Be profuse, be profuse, be profuse. But be not too damned profuse.*

COLLECTOR'S ITEM
DAVID HUBERMAN

winter's day in NYC, as me and my younger sister are walking briskly through the cold downtown streets. On the corner where CBGB's punk club used to be, there is a man with a reddish face looking up at us. As we get closer, the smell of cheap alcohol reeks about this person. Immediately my sister says, "Let's cross the street". I look at her and just nod my head no. We continue to go past him, and then I look down on a grayish piece of rag, a chipped ashtray with the words "New York World's Fair 1965" lies on it. "Collector's item" the ruddy face stutters. I stop and then my sister stops beside me. Silence envelopes me, I don't move, I can't move. Like an echo I hear the man's voice again only weaker, "Collector's item." My little sister makes a face, and her eyes go upward. "Oh for god's sake, here we go again, that's why I don't like going out with you. You want to buy that piece of junk don't you?" Before I reply, she continues with her tirade. "I know you, you're thinking of buying that piece of trash, then you would scamper off like the packrat you are, bring it to your overcrowded cluttered studio apartment with junk piled so deep you can hardly walk in the place, then you'd stash that broken ashtray in some remote corner of the whole mess... and what about all those horrible germs, no wonder you have asthma!" She breaks my trance and we continue to walk but again we stop or rather my sister stops and says. "I'm telling mother." I don't say anything and once again we continue on our journey. Two blocks away and I swear that street person's voice is still with me, only now it's a whisper.

PLASTIC FLAMES
JENNIFER BLOWDRYER AKA
JENNIFER MEGAN BARING-GOULD WATERS

Theodora Baring-Gould Waters, my British Grandmother, lived in Alphabet City for forty years or more, bouncing around from Third Street and Avenue B to the 3 Haven Plaza, on 11th Street behind Avenue C. She was looking forward to moving into Szold Plaza, really just a dent of a cul de sac that caused visiting junkies to chuckle "Szold!" festively waving their tiny bags of dope in the air.

Presumably all the different rooms and flats Theo moved to became very cluttered, we all have so many interests down here and so so little room. When she died, about fifty contractor bags of stuff went in the trash, her friend's junkie son stole some Baring-Gould ancestral ephemera, and it was a massive purge but a little bit remained. I kept a little art deco mirror table. Inside its two small drawers I found wads of nasty human hair and a couple of cheap broken pins. I kept a black angora sweater, bolero style that only went down to the top of my ribs. It was too ridiculous to throwaway, and besides it was nice material. My own clutter bug future started right there and then, twenty-five years later I could describe half my 'collectibles' that way. Ridiculous, nice.

I lived in the place she was supposed to move into, and added to the fake fireplace that lit up a few too many items of my own, like a mostly used-up prayer candle with "Lovely Baby Spirit" and a bleeding heart crudely drawn on it, from when I had an abortion and had to emcee a show the same night. A huge novelty ring that's broken but I may crazy glue together one day, for a prop possibly. A jumble of jewelry and make-up I'll never and probably shouldn't use as it's inches away from a can of roach spray, a wig head, a

slightly torn American flag, a special basket for my large belt collection, and a stereo that pretty much works. A junkie friend once
fell asleep in front of the artificial fireplace, and I saw him actually
scooch up to the red bulb that lights up beneath aluminum stream-
ers, under the plastic log, for warmth. It seemed to work for him.

There's more, about a million times more. I sometimes wonder
if the way I have cluttered this apartment reminds my father of his
mother. Bag Lady II. I reassure myself that I have no torn vinyl
chair, no lumps of human hair hidden in drawers, that it's not that
bad. My mess is ironic. I wore the misshapen angora sweater to the
Life Cafe once, because I thought someone should wear it once and
honor it as a thing. I didn't want to deny its hideous reality. I wondered for a tiny second if she had ever actually worn it, if it started
out a normal size and shrunk, or if the unwearable sweater was just
part of a desire to fortress a nest with soft materials and shapes.

My grandmother belonged to a soup kitchen and barter project,
Everything For Everybody, on E. 3rd Street. She cooked muffins
in cleaned-out cat food tins, and left full tins at the edges of grown
over vacant lots for the street cats. She kept up her subscriptions
to the Ben Franklin Society and British Royalty Watch. She kept
lying about her age so she could keep working office jobs way past
retirement age. When she saved up, she'd take a cruise to Europe.
In a wooden bureau of hers I found about a hundred Cunard Line
postcards that she snatched, along with ancient Cunard Line stationery and matchboxes.

She liked the life on the ships, and entered mixers like the ama-
teur talent contests. Theodora was sparkly in a manic way on these
trips, I suppose. I know she got a lot of her cruise ship outfits from
St. Emeric, a thrift shop right behind Three Haven Plaza, near P.S.
34 and what was once St. Emeric Catholic School, now a bingo par-
lor. My first years in Alphabet City St. Emeric's thrift shop, which
was a repurposed Quonset Hut behind a usually locked chain link
fence, was still open — Mondays and Wednesdays from 9:30 to 3:30,
Saturday from 10 to 1:30. I'd go and buy torn-up fur coats, books
like *King: Hell on Women, King of the Dolls,* and beat-up trays for
my make-up. I knew the old ladies in there a little; they'd point me
to dresses and watch me try things on. I fit in pretty well, I like to

149

think. Sometimes I saw long tacky dresses with elaborate plans that I know my grandmother would have worn. Once one of them gave me a jolt, and I wondered if I actually did see her in it — possible.

Back in the Eighties you could live in the neighborhood and seldom had travel beyond Avenues B or C, and people there looked better, mostly. Bodies weren't photography model anorexic, or very fat, the elderly managed to get around, and we didn't look as wary. Strides were pretty steady, except for people who'd just copped on 10th & D, swaggering briskly while enjoying a blissful chemically altered state, trying to look normal ten years after they ever could. My father got mugged in the Szold Street building while visiting my grandmother, but she never did. She lived there.

I saw Theodora acting animated at my Father's second wedding. She had on a cheap, silvery brown wig that was on crooked so that some of the wig tape showed on one side, and a dress that was actually one piece but was styled to look like a black velvet blouse with a big splashy skirt. She couldn't get it together to belt it properly and maintain the two-piece illusion. It was probably from St. Emeric, she was pretty tied in with those nuns, even picking up duty free cartons of smokes to sell them. I'm betting they did favors for her. She was not one of those muddled, senile eccentrics; she was a bright, pushy eccentric. She probably got right in your face when she wanted something like a discount.

My grandmother went crazy when she was eight or nine, so intense delusion was home to her. Her father was a minister in a parish called Haverford West in Wales. He pounded on doors at six in the morning to get people to come to the Anglican Church where he preached for forty-seven years. The Baring-Goulds had once been aristocratic but we long since lost all, except for an ancestral home the inheritee rents out as a ghost hotel. Theo married an Irish Coast Guard drunk, who quickly got rid of her and their infant son. She then imagined an idyllic British childhood for herself, adopting an insanely perky British schoolgirl/flapper act as she straggled around the U.S. with her young son, trying to survive. She never admitted that she was not still married — it was just a sixty-year misunderstanding.

She almost lasted forever, despite her British belief in cigarettes, cocktails and starch. Those people do sometimes. It's been said they survive out of spite, but that's too simple. It may just be that the delusions of eccentrics drive them on more relentlessly, and a fully painted in alternative world eliminates a lot of stressful worry. Not having any delusions at all is probably the early killer.

She was all ready to move into this new place at East Village Towers, on 10th between C and D, when she died. She'd paid the deposit, signed the lease, made plans for the terrace to be fenced off so her big gray cat and her plants could go outside and flourish right near the Con Ed plant on FDR. She was in and out of Cabrini hospital until she was incredibly frail.

Leukemia, pneumonia, remission. She'd waited five years on the now very-closed-don't-even-ask East Village Towers waiting list. She achieved the ultimate secret luxury poverty tract deal, something families who've been here two generations often can't bluff their way into; and then she died. I left my 8x10 room at International House and moved right down to Theo's spot, between Avenues of C & D. I'd never spent much time with her in the neighborhood, or visited much. She didn't have a feel for children. The few times I saw her she acted like somebody in a bad play with a visiting granddaughter.

She and my father coexisted in a state of agitated hysteria that was painful — her loopiness, his rage. He had a point. He became a professor, settled in Rhode Island, wrote poetry and texts on French African theater, even his absentee father, Harold Waters, parlayed his own third grade education into published adventure books about Prohibition booze runners and the Coast Guard. All that — just to have his mother hop on Amtrak and visit with novelty items from the everything-for-89-cents shop in Times Square! Why even have a working fireplace if your mother is going to throw into it specially treated plastic cubes from the Spencer Gift catalogue that melt and turn the flames into a psychedelic array of colors never before found in natural flames?

I remember ignoring the New England landscape, my familiar wooden home, and hunching forward eagerly to launch the inexpensive chemical cubes Theo brought from New York into the fireplace. The flames turned cheaper, more interesting, colors. Things like that corrupt a child.

IMMIGRANT DREAM

TINA ORSINI

I thought maybe I could shed my Italian heritage as a way to fit in this culture, which twists and tortures me in body and spirit. Even my name, Americans can't get. They can hardly pronounce it, let alone spell it. I tell them "I'm Concetta Vinciguerra-Orsini." Huh?

It all began on my first day in school, shortly after arrival: my first introduction to American nuns, church and prejudice. That's when I questioned if I could ever belong. Maybe a doctorate, a good job as a professor, a marriage to a high achiever, a wonderful son, who has his own Ph.D, would integrate me. Not a chance.

My past is too much with me, result being I hang suspended, never quite fitting any of my roles: educator, learner, mother, daughter, divorcee, and never quite connecting with people as we intersect at junctures and ruptures within the limits of language.

Is this what my mother expected when in 1955 she debated with my father about coming to New York? We already had a beachhead in the U.S. via my maternal grandfather. At the turn of the century, when he was 15, he left a small town in Abruzzo. One morning a family in his town said they were taking off for America. He ran back to his parents and said, "I'm going with them." My mother says his choice was dictated by the fact that he "hated the soil." That was a bad attitude for a farmer's son in an area where to have land meant that you were something. It was the family property that fed everyone and gave them a local standing. More-over, with the land, you could have fed your family and those who worked for you. You didn't starve. You might have been despised by city folks and northern Italians, who called southerners *terroni,* but you had food in the larder and in your belly.

Perhaps my grandfather's decision was also prompted by the fact that his father had tried and failed as an immigrant. He had gone to Argentina but couldn't stick it out. The work was very hard; he was homesick, not only for the Italian language and for his friends, family and compatriots, but for the food. He missed the vegetables; he missed la pasta alla chitarra, il pane rustico, l'olio d'olivo. He missed the women in the family cooking up those great meals and serving them with woody, homemade red wine.

Unlike his father, my grandfather didn't care about being served and having great homemade food, not if it meant he would be tied down in the small community, so he took the voyage to the U.S. He arrived in New York, worked for a while in a silk factory in Rochester, and ended up in a Kentucky coal mine. Somehow mining suited his temperament. He stayed in the business for forty years, though returning periodically to Italy to choose a wife, with whom he had two children. When his wife died, my mother's mother, he retired to New York City to live with his son.

His wife had never seen the US. She died when she was in her early forties. Once she died, my grandfather never went back to Italy. It may seem odd that the family didn't reunite in the U.S., but this was the tradition. The man in America might need to travel and having a family in tow would have added to expenses and made mobility more difficult. The Italian view was that travel and work were for men. Women stayed with their children and took care of the old people.

The general male perspective was that he would earn money in the U.S., keep saving and sending back remittances and then, when he got old, he would retire to Italy, perhaps well off enough to buy a house or land. (My grandfather built a large stately home in his native Casalbordino.) Some men did not return because they left their wives for other women they met in the new country. Others navigated back and forth until their families came to live with them here. Another section went back to Italy early because they found work in the U.S. too backbreaking. A minority, who found they could not live without Italy, lived in both countries at different times of the year (building homes in both countries).

In my grandfather's case, he lost his wife who died in her early forties. He had formed a bond with others Italians in Louisville and lost connections with friends in Italy since he was very young when he left the old country. He had become an *Americano* who spoke English with a real southern accent.

As I mentioned, when grandfather retired, his son, my uncle, Luiggi, came to New York and my grandfather moved to Brooklyn. They lived on East 1st and Avenue U where a terracotta Protestant church loomed over them all their lives. There they bought a three-family house, which was just sold for a million dollars.

To return to my story, my family decided to move to the U.S. for two reasons. For one, this stately home our grandfather had bequeathed us in Italy was hard to hold onto in the post-WWII economic climate. Moreover, my mother had a great belief in education as the stepping stone to an improved position and, as she imagined, you couldn't get an education in Italy to equal the one you could get in America. Her dream was that her two children would become teachers.

I should insert here that teachers were revered in our small medieval town. They were gifted lavishly by the parents of their charges, given chickens, rabbits, olive oil, and wine at holidays and Christmas. The presents were not simply rewards for putting up with their kids, but almost bribes in that they felt the teachers could really improve their pupils' life chances. But, given education was so rudimentary in our town, and given that mothers saw education as a key to success, it was not rare in our village for mothers to take their children and move to bigger Italian cities, leaving their husbands home while they stayed where their kids could get into better schools.

As the daughter of an Americano, my mother could apply for legal entry. It seemed she would be going, like her father, alone as that was the only way legally possible. Once she was there, she would do the paperwork to gain entry for the rest of the family. My father probably wasn't all that happy with this, but my mother was adamant about getting out of the shadows of medieval Italy. As our good luck would have it, just as she was preparing to leave the country, U.S. laws changed and she was enabled to bring us all: my father, my twelve-year-old brother and me, all of four, to the new land.

Let me mention that part of my mother's boldness, her willingness to go it alone, certainly stemmed from her connection to an immigrant. In those days, people talked about the daughters of Americans as if they owned heaven and earth and walked on air between their domains.

So, we took off. My parents didn't sell off their house and property, thinking they may not make it in the new land and so would need a place to which they could return. Still, my mother never looked back while my father never fully adjusted and I grew up hearing from him about all the things he was missing here. Americans didn't have the greener olive oil, the succulent fruits, the tasty vegetables of the homeland. And America lacked the customs, such as the way he and other musicians would serenade a bride-to-be before the wedding as well as the rhythms of daily life he used to experience in his shoe shop where he would chat with his many drop-in friends. It was as if listening to him for twenty years, we were all painted in a frame of regret as we moved forward in time.

My mother, too, had her memories, but they were more linked to particular people, especially her mother. She would tell me stories about cooking. When she was quite young, maybe six, her mother (my grandmother) was sick, and she decided to make some dough for *l'indrucciulun,* the word in the Abruzzo dialect for type of pasta. My mother thought she was doing it correctly when she found little lumps protruding from beneath. She knew the dough was supposed to be perfectly flat. She was crestfallen. Then her mother came in. Without a word of reproof, she patiently showed her how to pull out the lumps of sea salt and re-roll the dough. Maybe the story is memorable to her and so often repeated because she is such a virtuoso cook, relying on her hand-compiled, handwritten book of 2,000 recipes.

My own first memories of finally getting to America and taking my first step toward education rather rudely brought home to me and my family certain problems with the American dream. It was the summer of 1955 and my aunt and mother brought me to St. Simon and Jude Catholic School to enroll for September. I was seven years old.

I remember every moment. It was a hot, sunny day. I found the two steps up to the school entrance an easy climb for my little

155

legs. I barely touched the gleaming brass railing for fear of leaving my prints. We stood facing the door as my aunt rang the bell. A functionary let us in and left us standing in the entrance hall. Then a nun appeared, standing dead center in the room.

I don't recall my aunt's words, something about me being new to the country, wanting to start school in September.

The nun asked if I spoke any English.

Not a word of it.

The nun said, "We don't accommodate her kind here." I knew the Italian word accomodatevi, which meant, "make yourself at home." I could figure out what she meant.

Between my aunt and mother, I was small. I looked up. My aunt and mother were silent. The nun was large. The nun's words went right through my center. The blade was long and thin.

We turned and left.

The nun's attitude didn't sit well with our family. A few weeks later a priest came from St. Simon's church seeking a donation. My uncle sent him out with a curse, saying he was a socialist and an atheist and wouldn't be caught dead in a church until, as it were, heaven freezes over.

This was my first step into the temples of learning of America the bountiful.

THE LOWER EAST SIDE
PENNY ARCADE

People ask me "Do you still love New York?" The answer is a stuttering yes and no. Yes because it is my home and contains my living history. No, because New York is no longer New York. Perhaps we should start calling it New New York. The urban beast that was New York has been suburbanized and is now filled with people who will spend 2 to 8 years here before they go back to the American suburbs or smaller cities with more lifestyle options i.e. places that are "easier" to live in because even though New York has changed the only thing that has really changed is what made it easy to live here. The amazing iconic people you met, more unique than anywhere else, the font of thriving original culture, and the anonymity which gave one their complete personal freedom are all but gone. The things that made it hard, the grime, the crowded subways, the tiny living quarters, the expense, the random violence, are all still here. The New York most of us came here for is gone. It is gone for us and it is gone for the young seekers of today, who come here, as we all came here, all of us for the past couple of centuries, seeking sanctuary, as the young have always come to New York for. Sanctuary from small towns and small minds, sanctuary from consensus, sanctuary from the fear of the different, sanctuary from the fear of the new, sanctuary from the American way of life. Our small island off the coast of the USA was invaded by America, full force, frontal attack in the 1990's and the coup de grace was handed us in 1996 with Mayor Giuliani and his high stakes pals playing monopoly with real real estate and real money and it was done. Over.

If I am specific and honest to my own memory and history, gentrification started in downtown NY the year I arrived, 1967, when the Lower East Side was renamed The East Village by entrepreneurial landlords and real estate pariahs looking to make bank by claiming it was the east side of Greenwich Village which had higher rents and higher cache. In the 1960's Greenwich Village was still called Greenwich Village, before it was changed to the West Village by similar greedy types looking to freshen it up a bit.

Those of us who came here from the 1960's to the 1990's and long, long before us were from every class. Our backgrounds were middle class, upper class, working class but we all had three things in common. Most of us were loners and if not complete lone wolfs, we did not fit in to the society we were raised in, and did not want to spend another minute in our home towns. No matter what class we were raised in, we had a fierce aversion against being told what to think, how to act or what to wear. We came here for reinvention or evolution or just to be left alone to our own fates. We didn't know what to expect when we got here and once we were here we left our prior conditioning at the bridge, excited by the visceral energy of the city and its streets. We wanted to reinvent ourselves in the face of that magnetic energy. We wanted to be another log on the pyre that made New York great. Now for many years New York has been marketed to the rest of the country, advertised with shows like "Sex in the City" and "Girls," just as it was marketed in the 90's with shows like "Seinfeld," "Friends" and "Felicity."

From the beginning of the 19th century New York offered anonymity and adventure. People have always noted or complained that what made NY different from the rest of the country was that in NY you just didn't know who your neighbors were. It was true then and it is true now and we like it that way. You can always choose to know your neighbors in NY, but in other places it is mandated that your neighbors will know you, your coming and goings, the people you associate with and your general visible habits. To people like me and other New Yorkers that sounds like hell.

For over thirty years I have lived in the same small loft building on the Lower East Side. Until 2007 I knew my other five neighbors. We were all artists. We were all living illegally in lofts. We all played loud music. We kept weird hours. When someone spent the night building something with loud banging, we never complained because the next time it would be us. Now no one has tools in the building except me and they are basic ones. In 2007 my old slum lord sold the building and three tenants left. One a painter, Andy, died of old age at 92, leaving KC, his partner of sixty years behind. Andy was 65 when I moved in at age thirty, thirty-five years older than me. We adored each other and each other's work. Another painter, Anson, took a buy out and another painter John got intimidated out the building by the lying landlord. Someone from a mental health day group John attended came looking for him and the landlord found out John was schizophrenic and had stopped taking his medication. I thought John had the flu. That's what John told me when I knocked on his door. The landlord had told me no one had seen John for three weeks. I was used to John holing up. I told John he should let the landlord in because we were close to getting legal status for the building. I believed the landlord needed to do an inspection. None of us *ever* knew John was schizophrenic. All those years we thought John was going out to work when he wasn't painting. Although once when we thought there was an electrical fire in the building in the 80s, after I knocked on John's door for a very long time, he finally called out from behind the locked door "What?" I replied "I think there is an electrical fire in the building" John called back "It is not in here." And John never opened the door. John opened the door to the new landlord cuz I told him too and in his vulnerable and weakened condition he was made to believe that he had to give up the loft or be evicted. He signed the paper and wept every time I saw him for the rest of the week. "I'm fucked" he said simply as he moved his paintings out of his loft, "I was off my meds and they got me." None of the rest of us ever knew he was in a treatment program, not for thirty years! Now there are two new tenants and we don't know them. Well, there have been three. Andy lived with his partner of sixty years KC and KC continued his life as he had during his lifetime with Andy. He is 89 and fit as a fiddle. Of the new people, one, a jovial Israeli who moved into Johns loft after John was tortured out, moved after he was broken into twice. I had warned him to replace the window gates that the new landlord had removed. "No" he said sweetly, "I don't want to live with bars on my windows." "But you are on the second floor of the back building. It is only ten feet up the fire escape to your place" I pleaded, "It is so easy to climb into your windows" which he left open to catch fresh air. "There is no fresh air in NY," I told him, but he said "No," smiling sweetly. "I will be fine." He wasn't fine. He was wiped out twice and off he went to buy a condo in Harlem. He was replaced by a yuppie couple in their thirties. They have been here five years now. We say "Hi" when I see them leaving or coming or picking up the mail in the hall. Their rent is approximately six times what I pay. They work twelve to sixteen hours a day in high paying jobs. I run into them every few months. Anson's space below me has been refigured into a three bedroom apartment populated by three young Wall Street guys in their mid-twenties and they pay eight times my rent.

They too work long hours. I see them every few months, usually on Friday or Saturday nights when they are leaving on or coming home from a date. They had a party last summer and used the roof of the synagogue next door which they accessed by their fire escape. The party lasted till 5 am. I peeked out the window. They had decorated the synagogue roof with all kinds s of twinkling colored lights and a sound system. You could tell that they and their 20-something-year-old friends felt really cool at their outdoor party. When they finally ended the party they left the twinkling lights on and hours later when the synagogue was having a funeral for one of their most revered members. All thru the funeral the lights played and the synagogue people were weeping at the disrespect for the temple. The group from the synagogue rang my doorbell trying to get access to the roof to stop the dancing lights. Later the Jewish landlord spoke to the contrite young men. They didn't know there was a synagogue next door.

Once I saw one of these young neighbors when my sink overflowed. Once I saw another one when my internet was out. I asked if I could use theirs. They were happy to share. Their password is "I LOVE SUITS." I don't know them and I don't want to know them. Not in a mean way, we just have nothing but our humanity in common and when we need to share our humanity like when the sink overflows or the internet goes out, we will. Barbara lives on the first floor in what used to be my old studio. I use to have two floors but I had to give one up when my slumlord sold the building. Barbara used to have the storefront but she traded it for my old space. I am sure is a good deal for her. I originally brought her to the building twenty-seven years ago by introducing her to my downstairs neighbor Burt. They got together, had a kid, and were married for a decade. Now Burt is gone and she is there. She is a painter and a weaver. She retired this year after twenty years of teaching school. The halls and staircases up to my top floor are full of her incense, patchouli oil and ganja. She plays really really, good music all the time. She is my pal. We share history and laugh a lot together and it is we who plot against the landlord to get things fixed in the building. The new people never complain about anything even though they pay rent thru the nose. Not only aren't they trouble makers, they won't complain about anything. Not if the water stops or the front door is broken. Even when my sink overflowed into their kitchen downstairs, there was only a polite knock and a gentle question: "Is your water running? There's water pouring down into our kitchen."

For almost twnety years I didn't know anyone in my neighborhood. In the 80s and 90s you didn't linger around the block coming home. There were Latinos dealing heroin on one corner and crack on the other and a cop on the corner watching it all benignly except every three months when there was a police crackdown and everyone got arrested. The next day there were new crews on each corner and another cop too. In 1981 when I moved there below Houston Street when people asked where I lived I would answer, "There is Soho and there is Noho and I live in Ut Oh." You couldn't get a cab into or out of our neighborhood. The taxis would flat out refuse. The bus barely stopped on Avenue B or East Houston Street.

You had to run for it because the drivers weren't pausing longer than necessary. We had 8 bodegas, Spanish markets, circling the block. All of them stayed open late like 4 am. That was when New York was a 24-hour city. Now all we have left is 24-hour pharmacies and a couple of all night diners. All of the bodegas sold drugs. Once when I needed change for a ten I went into the bodega next door, which is now a skater boutique that sells custom skate boards, tee shirts, hats, and sundry items with the logo "Only." It just occurred to me that it might be shorthand for the now defunct statement "Only in New York." I went in to the bodega and asked for change by buying a snickers bar for fifty cents. The young guy behind the counter shrugged. He couldn't break a ten. He told me he had no change. I laughed and said "Shit man you got to at least pretend to be running a store and selling stuff." He just laughed. The other five bodegas were real Dominican and Puerto Rican bodegas and they sold other stuff besides drugs like rice, dead chickens, plantains, banana's and canned goods and loosies. You could buy loose cigarettes, four for a dollar. Now we have one bodega left that sells loosies but only Newport's, fifty cents each. Having neighbors you don't know and a bodega in the neighborhood that sells loosies is my idea of quality of life.

DEALERS & FLOWERS
SHEILA MALDONADO

O n the side of the building where all the dealers used to work,
a stand of flowers. New management in the corner
bodega, former numbers joint, shut down every other year.
Back room,
DL transaction room, tucked away behind a false wall
next to shelves of cans, a second line of customers disappearing.
New management made it storage, a broom closet.
New tenant, higher rent, 25 cents more for a water bottle.

New management took the wall on the side of the bodega,
where all the dope boys hung, where all the dope families
lined up their folding chairs with cup-holder holes in summer.
New management took the wall and put up a flower stand
where toddlers blossomed into dealers, boys growing into corners
Flowers plucked and shipped, spray-painted daisies,
wholesale multi-colored roses, 6 dollars for a dozen, 10 for 2.

Herb corner, snow corner, flower corner. A plastic shelter for
the flowers, for the buckets, for the stands. For the flower dealer
stationed 24 hours inside plastic, under fluorescence, hunched over
a heater, preserved, preserving. Sealed in with the roses, the daisies,
the "carnethions" scrawled on the sign. For the 24-hour flower buyer.
Dope boys wilting cornerless under grand-opening flags,
another bodega, across the way, in the middle of a block.

TIM LANE

3 AM
THURSTON MOORE

I n the morning — children run screaming — playing w/ their
parents — aunts and uncles — sitting in lawnchairs — blast-
ing spanish music. when they call it quits there is silence.
police and fire sirens always — massive metal scraping garbage
truck —here n there — but no more people. when it seems like
its all over some unseen dudes sit in a car outside the window
and rev the engine. they just sit there — and rev it — and on
certain nights lean on the horn once in a while. no one complains
— its as if the hardcore disregard is too insane to even figure
complaining about. the black guy upstairs has a doberman — he
yells at in the hallway — calls it cocksucker. my brother says he
heard him whipping the dog late in the night. the black guy likes
me — calls me slim — says he has a friend from con ed who can
give me a one shot hook up for $100 and i never have another
con ed bill. i go for it and it works — seems like a sweet deal.
the couple cross the hall are young puerto ricans. the girl is cute
and knocks on my door to talk. "do you mind turning yr guitar
down? — what kind of music do you like?" — she's in her
bathrobe and her boyfriend is a puerto rican badass. they're having problems w/ their con ed hookup and need to stretch a line
through my back window which overlooks a dead drop into
black trash. theyll just plug in until they straighten out their own
deal. at some point my one-time billing scam falls through and
im being billed for both apartments so i unplug their cord. i come
home and they must have crawled on a board between the two
windows to replug their power in. unbelievable. i tell them its

not cool i gotta pay for both apartments this way — "don't worry
we'll pay you back" — next day i unplug em again and head out
— i come back that eve and my door has been jimmied open.
their cord is plugged back in and my guitar is gone — the strato-
caster my brother bought me. and my cassette/radio player. i go
over there and say that someone ripped off my guitar and how I
unplugged their power and now its plugged back in. they say
they don't know anything about the door being broke in. a friend
of theirs is hanging out and w/out looking at me sez "you should-
n't move to new york" — the landlord had been coming around
yelling at people becuz a lot of these renters cant pay the rent —
including me — and he's always giving verbal warnings. he gave
me one though he knew i was a clean cut connecticut geek. the
puerto rican couple hightailed it soon thereafter. the black guy
upstairs had a couple of friends — one guy was a slobbering
drunken bum who could hardly make it upstairs. he too called
me slim and was always thrilled to see me. last time i saw him
was when i opened my door after hearing a good 10 minutes of
weird moaning noise and there he was on the hallway floor lying
in a pool of blood and shit. i hopped over the muck and ran upstairs and told the black guy — he came running down and
dragged the dude off up to his apartment and kind of cleaned the
floor up. but the red/brown goo crust was always there. he had
anothr friend — a wiry old black man w/ no teeth — he also
called me slim and was also always real happy to see me. i
crossed his path on a hot 1st avenue day. he was standing in the
shade of a doorway. "hey slim whassup baby?" — "hey man" i
replied and stepped up to shoot the shit w/ this weird old freak.
the conversation ended when he asked me to come up to his
apartment and hang out sometime. i humored him and said yeh
sure. he then said "i like you white boy you can fuck me in the
ass" — i couldnt believe it. he then said "i'll suck your dick too"
— i just stepped off — went home. never really saw him again.
though i saw some dude who looked like him blowing another
guy in an abandoned subway entrance at houston near bowery
one night as i walked by up on the street. it was an amazing
glimpse and i had this quiet feeling that both men were ok w/ it

even tho it was the ultimate in wino skuzz. there were so many
empty nights — a poet lives in the building and hes after the girl
ive been kind of seeing — he knew her first. but he's older and
shes my age and we will soon have some heavy encounters
which will destroy my out of control soul. i hang w/ the poet and
his poet friends well into the night sometimes or i stay out all
night w/ the band i play in ripping hood ornaments off cars and
spray painting our band name around soho. these friendly activities become more intensified and save me from the void nights
of 13th street hell and nothing to do and no sleep. i begin to
chronic wake up about 4pm — zombie myself outside, eat
cheapo polish food — i had a job uptown at an lp mastering studio but i have no phone and can't call in. i'd been fired 3 times
from this job and eventually was tossed. of course years later i
would return w/ my band to master my own lp as a client.

but i've erased these nights and it is all and only a whiff of glory

TRUCKIN' ON SAINT MARK'S
PHILLIP GIAMBRI

It's May 1968. Martin Luther King was killed in April, and in a few weeks, Bobby Kennedy'll be killed. I'm off to a season of Summer Stock in Reading, PA., where I meet Morrison and Claudie. Morrison's the lead actor in our theatre company, I'm the season's Supporting Actor, and Claudie's the foxy blonde Ingénue. Actors come and go for specific parts, and leave after two weeks. Morrison and I spend off-hours drinking beer, shelling nuts at the Peanut Bar, and swapping life stories. By summer's end we're "best buds." He's tall, lean, intensely honest, a romantic, and has a brooding, James Taylor kinda' quality, that women find irresistible.

Summer ends, and we're all back to reality in New York City. For me, it's a rent controlled sublet in Spanish Harlem, with two old school buddies. We split the $89 a month rent three ways, and dine on $.99 six packs of Rupert beer, bought at the brewery around the corner.

Morrison and Claudie run into each other at an open call, feel some electricity, and eventually move in together on the Upper West Side. We're all poor but happy actors. Our world, is about to turn upside down and inside out.

Rollin' into 1969, we dive head first into the counter-culture. Morrison, Claudie, and I hang out a lot, listening to Moody Blues, Vanilla Fudge, and The Who's "Tommy," smoking pure Moroccan Hash, tripping on Mescaline, and smoking lots of Maui Wowie. Livin' the high life.

I meet a dancer on a commercial shoot and she and I run off to Cape May for the summer; free spirits, teachin' and trippin' on an art commune. Summer ends and it's back to the city. We're living in her small studio on Washington Place.

I start film school at Visual Arts, where most of my time is spent making anti-war signs: *"Hell no. We won't go!," "Give peace a chance," "Make love not war,"* organizing and marching in protests, and getting high on higher education.

The relationship with "Dancer" eventually crashes and burns. She says, "We're done. Ya' gotta' split, man." I'm gone. After a month of couch bouncing and apartment sitting for friends, I give Morrison a buzz, and he tells me that he and Claudie were married last summer, exchanging vows in a hippie, tie-dye and bandana wedding, by a lake in New Hampshire. They gave up their place on the Upper West Side for a cheaper one in the East Village. I explain my lack of livin' space, and he says I can crash with him and Claudie at their pad.

I'm sleeping on a home-made platform couch in their cramped living room. Across from me, on a similar platform, sleeps Mellie. She's a friend of Claudie, who just left her husband, an editor for the *East Village Other.* Morrison and Claudie sleep in a tight loft space he built above the tiny kitchen. It's very claustrophobic and adjustments have to be made by everybody to exist in the confined space.

Morrison works at La Mama building stage sets and Claudie works as a bored beautician, cutting Jane Fonda style shags all day. Mellie, a dental assistant, is taking an "emotional time out." I'm out of work and takin' classes at film school sporadically; we're both heartbroken, and really bummed out.

At night, we all listen to John Lennon records, smoke lots of grass, endlessly discuss the meaning of Carlos Castaneda's books, whether they're real or fiction, and the social impact of "Easy Rider."

Morrison and Claudie embrace "Scream Therapy," the "Craze" of the moment, because John and Yoko are doing it. Mellie and I mostly stay stoned and feel awkward during the loud and angry Scream Therapy sessions. Too freakin' much, man.

Claudie appeals to her building super for help with our increasingly desperate living situation. They eventually find me a cheap phone booth size studio on St. Mark's Place, across from the Electric Circus. Everybody's cool with that.

Mellie divorces her husband and shacks up with her dentist boss. Morrison and Claudie eventually split up. She moves to Hollywood to pursue her acting career. Last I hear from her, she's livin' with the drummer from Blue Cheer, and working as an assistant to Saul Bellow. She works poolside in a bikini at his luxurious home, bangin' down umbrella drinks, while proofin' his books.

Morrison's still coopin' at the pad on East 9th Street, workin' as a carpenter, dealin' nickel bags on the side. It's there, after a hit of STP, that he experiences an intense religious conversion and becomes "born-again." He joins Hara Krishna and they send him to Florida. I hear from a mutual friend that he's detoxed, shaved his head, and taken a vow of celibacy. "Far fuckin' out, man!" That's what he used to say when he was stoned.

I had no way of knowing at the time, but that "Summer of Love" in '69 marked the beginning, of what would become for me, an incredible forty-eight-year "Magical Mystery Tour" on St. Mark's Place.

I'm still there, it's still magical, and I just keep on truckin'.

PLAYBOX
EVE PACKER

I love cock, I love cock, I love cock" — the man in black, black pants, black snug t-shirt, greenish light, black walls, ceiling, floor —over and over, passionate, obsessed, incantatory —now he's taking out his sword, now he's slashing his arms, face, all his body, *"I love cock, I love cock"* — in this black box — this black box theatre, as they're now called, and this is probably one of the first — the Playbox Theatre on St. Marks Place, just east of 1st Avenue — the year is late '69 and I am in the audience — as guest — shocked, transfixed, transported. I am here, because, amazing, I have just been cast in their next show!

In it never rains but it pours mode, I have to give up a part to do this — I had just been cast, by Rina Elisha, in her musical folklore piece at LaMama — to play LaMama is equivalent to playing the Palace — but, given the choice between an ensemble singing chicken and a two character play w/or w/o top — no contest. I am so excited!

The show I first saw at the Playbox, it turns out, was at the center of a huge controversy. This I had no inkling of at the time —or in fact til just now: the name of that play is *Superfreak: the Death of Joe Cino.* written and designed by Donald L. Brooks, who knew Joe Cino well, as did the actor, Don Signore. Ellen Stewart never saw it, but was so upset by what she heard about the graphic ending that she took out an ad in the *Village Voice* banning anyone connected to the production. Bob Weinstein, the director, took out an ad advocating "artistic freedom." John Herbert McDowell wrote a column expressing sympathy for both points of view. (Google: *Superfreak: the Death of Joe Cino* —*jeffreystanley/brain-on-fire.com/jefblog/tag/superfreak-the-death-of-joe-cino/*).

The ad for the play I'm cast in, part of a double-bill, must have been in Backstage and probably said 'some nudity — some pay', like that. Generally, they went together: if you took off your clothes, you got paid. So I go to the audition: a nice upper-middle class upper west side apartment, the director's home. Lots of books and rugs. The producer-director Bob Weinstein explains it's a two character play, set in a diner, guy comes in, girl is the waitress, short courtship, etc.; the girl will take off her top; the guy, at some point, will be all naked. i read. i take off my top. for a sec. and i'm cast. and it pays, gasp: $40 a week, that is, for off-off, big bucks. We're to be on a double-bill. the other play, also short, has 6 guys. they will all take it all off.

We rehearse in the theatre. Usually late mornings. Rehearsals are pleasant, easy-going. After all, in contrast to the *joe cino,* no doubt as a change of pace, these are two "light comedies." I remember the set, by Donald L. Brooks, a marvel of a lunch counter, at an angle, stool or two, and one of those wonderful plastic cake containers diners still use.

My co-star is an actor named Barry, from bklyn; i'm from the bronx; we get along fine. One day, about 11 a.m., there's a loud noise in the street, the sound of a tire backfiring — when we look around, no barry. Then we see, he's dived under the counter. hiding. shaking. He tells us,with great shame, he's just back from vietnam.

The Playbox (later studio recherche, where i became a writer, under the tutelage of ruth maleczech & lee breuer, another story, is still a theatre! Theatre Under St. Marks) — The proportions of the stage: 15x15 ft., 45 seats; i remember 6 rows, so figure 6 rows of about 7 seats. In other words, its *small* — perfectly proportioned, but a *tiny* basement black box. This is vital to the next part of our story. Which brings us to our most thrilling nite, the icing on the icing on the cupcake!

Talk about excited. Business is good, not so much due to us, we're the opener, but for the second half of the bill — w/the 6 naked guys — and tonite: ANDY! is coming! And he does; he brings an entourage. the house is packed. Sits in the back row, ie.

row 6, abt 10 feet from the stage, and through the entire show (dressed in his customary black, white hair aglow) has to his eyes, a Huge Pair of Black Binoculars! Total Andy. Afterwards, in the crush, he makes sure to thank each one of us; he is, as has been remarked, incredibly soft-spoken, gracious, courtly.

Note: Via Google: here is the name of the double-bill: Two short plays by Tom Miller: "Ugly" & "Nude Gymnastics." Directed by Bob Weinstein. From a review in the *Village Voice*, 11/27/69 by David De Porte: "...Eve Packer miscast in that she is pretty, does not take off her panties in the bed scenes, which is odd, as Barry Kael appears buck nekkid."

The run is extended — If this were a play: that would be the curtain on Act I. Now: the Entr'acte: a rush of memories before the curtain is up on Act II. Entr'acte: As we finish rehearsals at W.P.A. (Workshop of the Players Art), watching the midnite shift come in: Holly Woodlawn, Candy Darling & Co: Watching Candy meticulously holding her train, repeatedly walking up and down the stairs, head up; At the Old Reliable, playing one of the bikini-clad Bacchunts to the great Neil Flanagan's Bacchus as he wields a huge green garden hose; the musical written by Lonnie Carter was directed by Michael Feingold — Michael and I had a huge fight in the hothouse strident humidity. I have since learned rule uno: when the director says "do it" you say one word: YES! Backstage at a play by Don Kvares (title character named Sir Gay) having my tarot read by Helen Adam — I didn't like the results one bit; auditioning at Ron Link's beautiful apartment on Washington Street for him and Tom Eyen; i think they liked me cause I would stand up on chairs and go really wild, but, as you know, i wasn't really the type — in '71 a winning streak: cast in Robert Cordier's "Black Sun/Artaud" at LaMama: the best: a late afternoon rehearsal on Gt. Jones, the cast of "Orlando Furioso," the commedia piece creating a sensation in Bryant Park, sittin on the floor watching us, amid our screaming, running & writhing, i hear a marvel of complex rhythms; the show takes on a magic hue; i look down as i fly past, see long black fingers on styrofoam — Elvin Jones — he had picked the styrofoam off the floor and just played — then in February i'm cast in "One Flew Over the Cuckoo's Nest" — but that's another story.

And so to Act II: Winter 1975 and I see that New Federal Theatre, Henry Street, is casting a play by Amiri Baraka, "Sidnee Poet Heroical." I had already worked there in Charles Fuller's "The Candidate," and was a fan of both Henry Street and Amiri. Anyway, I had lost out on an Ed Bullins piece and I am Determined. Friday nite: I wear a red leotard and patchwork parti colored skirt, red tights. The text: outrageous and a wonder on the tongue. I stand on a chair. When I finish, Amiri, touch of mischief, totally gracious, says, as i step down, facing the actor who i've read with: "here's yr husband." thats it. i'm cast. My character is Juice — who cld ask for more — the wife of one of the two lead characters, the 'villain' so to speak, Lairee Elefant — played by the fantastic Count Stovall. My first line, and the first line of the play: *I AM Queen of the Nile!!*

Quick gloss on the play: It was long —2 acts, 29 scenes, many actors/singers. Main characters: Sidnee Poet (a mix of Sidney Poitier and...) played by Neville Richen and his frenenemy Lairee Elefant (mix of Harry Belafonte and...), Juice, my character (modelled, sort of, on...), and the beautiful strong Black woman played by Saundra McClain. The play in two acts: Act I (where I am): a brilliant scathing send-up of the Black Actor (artists) dilemma in the white man's world — turning him so white he's scared of losing his Blackness... Act II, traces his recovery of identity and redemption.

Some images: Rehearsals start in late afternoon; Amiri is surrounded by bodyguards; but also Amina is always there, and often, their kids (including Ras, now mayor of Newark), so we are community, family. We rehearse in a terrific big space at Henry Street, and often, on break, dash to the Garden, yes the Garden, Cafeteria! But there's a major problem — : as we rehearse, Amiri keeps stopping us, gives us "line readings" — this throws a major glitch in the action, flow, and the cogs have to start/restart — of course he wants his words "right" but we know we have to go thru the "process" — as Raul Julia said, "you have to swim thru to get to the other side;" there's no other way. A meeting is held; we appoint Count Stovall as Ambassador to Amiri. Count suggests, on our behalf, that we rehearse earlier in the day, and when Amiri comes in later, we show him what we've worked on, and he take it from there. Amiri welcomes the suggestion — and from that day, all proceeds creatively and smoothly. That doesn't mean there aren't flare-ups: note: this is not our present era of "good job" and "good work" and p.c. behavior; there's a lotta temperment, strong feelings, and from time to time, titanic clashes —

Other images: Much has been written about the great costume designer Judy Dearing's contributions: basically, you bring your own stuff—and Judy works her alchemy. I bring an orange leotard, short crocheted orange skirt. Fine. Judy adds a strip of shiny gold trim to the V neck and it jumps under the lights.

'Nother Note: Amiri, this is by way of shout-out, has cast really strong women: Saundra McClain, Lois Weaver (co-founder of W.O.W.) — there are others. I do remember the 'girls' rockette chorus-line type number; they wore vari-colored mopheads for wigs. And: Count and I have a tango. Near the end of rehearsals he says, "Eve, you're gaining weight." I give him the gimlet eye. "I always," i say, "eat alot during rehearsal."

By now, at rehearsal's end we are doing jokes cause Amiri has promised us real live musicians —this, he says, is where the musicians will be —Yeah, we say, yeah, yeah —

Then its Dress: and here they are, in soft light, a trio, keyboard, bass, and i think, a horn, cant quite remember. And they have it down, laid back, elegant — Major high point: Lairee's song, superbly done by Count, downstage in the footlights, bright red open-to-the-navel shirt, lilting calypso mode: *WhiTEE my Main Man* he sings: *I give him everything I can* — I can still hear it —

Opening Night: We have no idea what to expect, but Amiri surprises us; he has arranged busloads of audience; its a packed house; it will remain packed all thru the run —

Opening Night: right before the curtain: Amiri takes me aside: eve he says: you have the opening monologue (i did) — and then gives me the full court press Amiri: the entire energy of the show, he goes, in great detail and w/aria voluble force, depends on you: Terrified, i am honored and even more terrified than before: Juice i keep thinking; juice, well, yeah, we all know, juice, sex, power: then i get the image: Electricity! and i hit it: electric current thru my en-

175

tire frame, arms up high, in my orange crochet mini-mini, Judy Dearing's gold trim shimmering, egyptian make-up (two hours to apply) glinting gold sparkles: and we're off — Neville, Count, Saundra, the musicians, singers, entire cast: everyone is On!

Note: Opening Night: "Sidnee Poet…" is, or is intended to be, a multi-media event, but there's a problem w/the film: during the intermission Amiri throws the projector at the wall: the curtain stays down for quite some time, then goes up on Act II. Next day Mel Gussow writes a quite glowing review in the *NY Times*: *"an exuberant comedy... corrosive indictment of the American dream... (Baraka) extracts sharp performances from minor players as well as from lead actors..."* (5/21/75). No mention of the projector.

We have a hit! Amiri arranges that the show move — we immediately, in June, move to the theatre on e. 3rd between B & C, the building that had been Ornette's studio, next to the Puerto Rican Poets Cafe, and the bodega that had been Slug's — Once more, we are sold out!

The Party: A huge cast party! In a building arnd ave C and maybe e. 3rd — the front is a regular fire-escape brick facade — walk in there's really no building, fallen walls, bricks,you step over pieces of plaster, shards of wall, it would make a great crumbling stage or film set — but its not, its home — the first squat i've seen or know of — It's a great party, but... you can see...something else is beginning to happen...(note: no more 1960's $40 apts on ave. d; rent control ended in 1971; what rented for $60 in 1967 can't be found, maybe a rent stabilized $220...the buildings may be vacant and falling, but the rent is rising...)

It's June: very hot. the fire hydrants open. The neighborhood kids sneak in, follow me on e. 3rd, shouting "juice, juice" — I'm a star! one night i get a standing ovation.

Years later i see Woodie King Jr. at a function: i tell him, and its the truth: that was the greatest theatre experience of my life. "Eve," he says, "that wasn't just a theatre, that was a life experience." Yes. Also, Count is right; i am gaining weight. I am, by the end of the run, 5 months pregnant.

Coda: This comes off, i expect, as a breathless valentine in doily lace & hot pink bows, to a time & place long gone. not place. the place, physically is here. but the time, the template, sense of possibility —

Truth is, i now believe, i came in at the end of the 'golden age.' Or the 'pioneer age.' The caffe cino (1958–1968) early LaMama years. I came in just after Joe Cino's death. But at the time i knew none of this. What i did know, experience, run around in, were the great late '60's to 1975 years — the ferment, from the ground up, improvisational, gay core generated, multi-ethnic, inventive, anti-pretense, satiric, off-the-cuff, run to the thrift shop, do it up, weeds scrambling hot raucous and loud thru sidewalk shouting to loftiest skyscraper of heart-beating/breaking lower east side city years — gone, never totally gone, decimated by rent, the RENT, the Rent, slashed arts & arts education food stamp funding, the scythe & scourge of AIDS, and the golden- calf shift in the pulse of nyc —

Is my memory rosy-hued. sure. we were young. but yet... naaah: it was just fantastic. do i miss it, and how, right now, some-where, this very sec, is there someone, someones, in a basement loft stirring up not the same pot but their own hot brand/brew — yes, probably detroit. or a yet to be named new planet.

AVENUE B PATIO   JAMES ROMBERGER

NOTES FROM NOW NOWHERE:
EAST VILLAGE 1980S
J. KATHLEEN WHITE

Last night five cops showed up across the street to tell the men selling second hand books on the sidewalk there to pack it up. They kicked his books out into the street. I've seen it many times before — poor people out there trying to sell second hand stuff and the cops come and kick it all into the gutter. Then the cops strut around glaring at the gathered crowd like any of you people standing around here say one word and we'll make you sorry, we'll take you in, we'll make your lives miserable.

Went to the stationary store on Fourth Avenue. The owner there was ranting. She's a gruesome person, quite ugly, with a puffy face, and huge, thick designer glasses. Her blue work smock is too tight, her wristwatch is strapped so tight her arm swells out above it, and her voice is nasty raspy from smoking so much and being angry for so long. Three massive cats lie about on the stationary supplies of their choice and on the cash register. It's the only stationary store in the neighborhood.

"I'm leaving," she said, "New York, goodbye, I've had it! Six weeks, I'm out of here."

Did they raise the rent?"

"Raise the rent? Raise the rent? OK, let me tell you, I've been here, what,17 years? My rent was $800 a month. They just raised it to $3600. And there's no arbitration — no nothing. I can't go to any city agency and say, 'Look what they're doing — they're killing us.' There are no laws to protect us."

"It's happening everywhere."

"OK, I know the guy who owns a Blimpies on Fifth Avenue and 20th Street. It's his best store. He has three. They won't renew the lease for any price. Why? They told him: Blimpies brings minorities to the neighborhood. That's illegal, right! But they're not going to admit they said that if he took them to court. So he said, OK forget it, I've had it with NY. He's moving his business to North Carolina.

"No, I'll tell you, the city is going to become a ghetto all right, but a ghetto filled with rich people. The streets will be lined with expensive little boutiques, selling useless nothing."

A tortured man sleeps in the R subway at night and plays the banjo for the passengers during the day. His hair and beard are long and matted and his clothes and body an unwashed dark grey. His banjo is grimy. But he plays all kinds of subtle improvisations to common tunes. It's the most brilliant banjo playing I've ever heard: inspirational, full of moods, never corny. If I drop money in the banjo case, he doesn't say thanks, he keeps playing. If I catch his eye, I get a straight dose of psychotic agony, yet the music keeps coming out beautiful.

The north exit at the West Fourth Street subway stop was closed so I wandered those intermediary areas, that cement and fluorescent labyrinth between floors, until I found some steps upward, at the foot of which stood a man in rags, writhing with affliction. Under the hum and dirty light of a weak fluorescent, he clutched at his clothes and twisted his body around in anguish inside them — the physical symptoms of a true mental suffering. We were the only people anywhere to be seen, he continued to writhe and twist, clenching and re-clenching his clothes in his fists, as I passed within two feet of him and went on up the steps.

The malevolent, slow creep of the police car, looking for trouble. It slips, like slow grease, around a corner, ignoring the light, using no turn signals.

A muscular black man created a sensation on St. Mark's by wearing a cast-off piece of lingerie, a red Teddy, like a saloon girl of yore. That's all he had on, it almost fit him, it was just a little too small. The sight of him was so fabulous, so cathartic, we had never seen anything like it in our lives. He was barefoot. We watched him with surprised joy, everyone turned toward him and grinned as he walked down the middle of the street, stepping like a geisha girl.

A lady bum is paused, with the comic stance of the bum who stays upright, aristocratically erect, but is in fact about to fall flat. But, its not comic because she really is a bum and really is about to fall flat. She is buttoned up to her neck in at least three layers of grime beridden raincoats, her whole face is chapped red, peeling and sooty, and on her head is stretched a colorless stocking cap. She has arrived at that particular meridian strip at the juncture of Bowery and Houston, where the most hopeless mysteriously maroon themselves. Some final tidal whirl of bad luck has left them washed up on that last refuge from which there is no place left to go. No going forward, no back, the cars rush and race an all sides as she stands tottering, helpless and bedeviled, but with some all-powerful pride intact.

In the middle of the street a man stands barefoot, wearing a calico sundress over red bellbottoms that drag the ground. On his head is a sunbonnet made from a pair of cut-off sweat pants.

He turns by degrees this way and that, like a plastic ballerina on her magnetic drum, and he asks all directions, "Hey beautiful, hey beautiful, hey beautiful, can I have $1.25 for a piece of pizza?" The morning air is cool, but his face, and his shoulders, (revealed by the halter top of the sundress,) are thick with beaded sweat.

At the laundromat, a young man burst into loud song, "Tonight! Tonight! Won't be just any night!!" but he stopped mid-phrase, stared out the window with horror and ran outside to where he had hung a patterned coverlet over a parking meter to dry.

"FUCKED UP!" He screeched, staring at the damp stain on his coverlet. "You LET your dog do that?"

A scrawny thug in cut-offs and a cap pulled well down over his low brow said, "I'm sorry," but he was laughing. He had some pals with him and they were laughing too, and the German Shepard was on a leash so it was obvious that they had, in fact, LET the dog do that.

"FUCKED UP! Yeah! Right! Laugh about it," the guy said. He was feeling helpless, didn't know what to do, was now getting depressed about it.

Each street heading perpendicular to the Bowery has a bum on it, slowly staggering east to reach the Bowery by a certain time of night.

Red faced gimpy legged women, red faced gimpy legged men, their red faces about to peel off from alcoholism and exposure, their squinting eyes peer painfully, its too bright and its a cloudy day and they are all limping from what? From being dragged out of bars, by one leg, dead drunk? They yell incoherently at each other from down the block, and across the street.

Cheap new buildings that consume entire blocks. To build those cheap, heartless buildings, they level the area, destroy all sign of human joy in life. They employ something akin to Round-Up herbicide, which eliminates all signs of human vitality, and insures it will not return for many a year.

The chicken in the tic-tac-toe booth next to the photo stand, sat on the wire grid of its cage. The red comb on the top of its head had flopped, inert and unwell, over to one side.

Girls in fluffy white summer dresses at night. The men are dark, straight, and onward; the girls ruffly, unpredictable, like crumpled white papers blowing brightly along.

It was a boiling hot summer day. The door of the gallery was open to the street. Outside on the sidewalk, a tall, jumbo-jerk walked by with a huge and hairy sheepskin vest on, worn with no shirt . He rubbered down the street, his body stupid with drug.

Soon as I shut the door, I felt gruesomely enclosed in my filthy apartment. The oppressive clutter was blanketed with a felt of greasy dust from the accumulated sediment of restaurant fumes, boiler soot, and the detritus shaken loose from 24 hour din. There was no breath of fresh air, no place to step out onto the earth — it was like shutting myself up in a storage locker.

Out on the streets, the hot exhaust from a billion air conditioners blasted down — their slops dripped on our heads. Black soot coated the whole city like a furnace room, the air was thick as dirty bathwater. We were living, millions of toads, in a pit slippery with hot black grease, toad feet in each others faces, hot, dry toad skins chafing on each other as we slipped over each other, our sharp needlelike toad claws scraping each other to get up and out, but trapped by glass mountains on all sides.

Over at Tompkins Square Park, it's become a tent city. Not just in one part of the park — the whole park. Permanent settlements — as permanent as tarps and tents and makeshift cardboard houses can be. There are so many people there. It's good that they at least allow them to settle a bit, but it has a real sense of a refugee camp — victims of bad luck, and the creed of greed endorsed by the government.

THE MUSIC OF 1989:
TOMPKINS SQUARE PARK
DOROTHY FRIEDMAN

The wind blows the homeless into the park.
It takes them in and gives them a temporary home.   Here
in New York they are easy to forget,
discarded like the elderly.
Their shopping bag. Pillows. Bags. And tents.
Artists and squatters are painting the park
when the police come in
kicking over dandelions and derelicts.

In 1988 bonfires lit trashcans, dotting the landscape.
We called it Tent City. "It's our park, not your park,"
We shouted at cops as they bashed our heads in.
To some it's a fiery hell.
To others: just another art opening.
Kids from Hoboken and Scarsdale throwing beer
bottles at the cops. When we tried to open the gates
our blood spilled out onto the pavement
as the police beat us down.

You say you want a revolution?
Our park had its own battlefield.
We had our photos taken with the police.
Hung flags over the drinking fountain
That said "freedom."

One year after the riots
we open the gates
of Tompkins Square Park
and let the homeless back in.
The Living Theatre
on Avenue C and E. 3rd
is performing "The Body of God"
with actors and homeless people
from nearby shelters.
The soup kitchen is around the corner on E. 10th
a block from the Life Cafe.
It is the year of "It's our park
Not your park."
Skinheads are screaming
yuppies shooting up while artists
paint the cement with graffiti.
John the Communist hands out leaflets
on the corner of E. 7th and Avenue A
while Bible Joe shouts "Armageddon."

KATHY'S STREET
KAREN LILLIS

Meet me downtown
I'll get off work and we'll
go find the Revolution
Kathy Acker said it's waiting
for us on St. Mark's Place
oh, but that was 20 years ago
and a lot's changed since then
Kathy knows the street energy
it takes to make a Revolution
now all that concentration's departed
for points cyber
and under-river:
the hours spent on the internet
and cell phones
not to mention interborough commuting trains
taking us farther and farther and farther
away

Nevermind
I'll meet you after work
we'll go looking for the last three
people who still get laid by meeting at cafes
n Manhattan
Oh, but I keep forgetting
I never leave work
I sleep and I dream work

I walk and I train work
I work work
I eat to keep the machine lean and healthy
so I can come home and work after work
and why not?

Work is Freedom
War is Peace
and other epithets of
psychopathology I hoped we'd
leave behind us when we
left our Daddy's House: The 20th Century
I left daddy's house at age 18
for good it was
before I lost my virginity
but not before I was raped: oh
make no mistake I was not *actually raped*
by my *actual father*
only a puny stand in
My actual father
loves me to pieces
and raised me thinking
I was an Indian
and my name was Scout
I was the leader of our hikes
except sometimes when I was Tree
and I'd meditate on what that meant
hoping someday I'd grow into
a fine old oak with branches strong and the world would grow
into a new millennium that cared about the
color green (of leaves) and the
oxygen I would exhale

Oh but that, too was long
ago

Meet me downtown
the Revolution tonight
is in the blue cast of
twilight on sidewalk piles
of unlikely late-spring snow
outside Dojo's
Quick let's catch it
before it fades or melts
or both

THE EAST VILLAGE (1985)

LORRAINE SCHEIN

U nder a broken china sky reflecting the street
The East Village whirs like a *gargoyle mechanique* —

Flows like a lava lamp erupting its slow, purple blobs,
Tempts like St. Mark's spreads of clothes that were robbed.

Cries like a Hell's Angel with torn-off wings,
Gleams like the silver in a poet's nose rings.

Protests like an anarchist in love with a government clerk —
Will love save the day? Will he have to work?

The Village clouds tick like a bomb overhead.
A tenement gets ready to explode all its beds.

As I walk by, plotting my 11th Street ruse
A man rides by on a bike with a goose.

He wears a coolie hat; the goose sits in a green crate —
Perhaps next I'll see a rabbit saying he is late?

Buy a red candle for love from a 9th Street witch —
A purple one for dreams, a green one to get rich.

She'll read your future in the cards, with scrying crystal eyes
And in the store's back garden, do the flower fairies fly?

Love saves the day; so do kitschy 50s wearables,
But art saves the night, and makes mornings more bearable.

FALSE BELLS
SHARON OLINKA

1967, and I was seventeen.
Enchanted expanse of St. Mark's Place.
Cups of bronze pealed and tinkled,
clink of silver orbs on perfumed wrists.
Crowds clear to the Electric Circus,
where Alain and I
shyly held hands, kissed.
Pulsating strobe lights overhead.
His soft hands on my braids.

It's the pigs, said Alain.
They hold us back.
They ruin the world.

Alain got worse.
Now his mission was
to plant bombs.
Kill the pigs. Do more LSD.
His decree was,
you can't be my woman
if you don't take LSD.
A real woman wants LSD.

I grieved for him
on icy subway platforms,
but learned my own worth
did not depend on bright
enticing bells.

AVENUE BANANA

JOSE PADUA

L iving on Avenue Banana
  in the 1990s is not a lot
  like drinking tea.
I look up to the sky.
You shout at people
driving by in limousines.
We eat rice and chicken,
wonder what to do.
You could go home and
watch your color TV
or whistle on the way
to the sink.
I can lie back on my mattress
like a tiny buffalo
and wave my hands at the flies
in the air or on my knee.
Alone I see white paint chips
on the ceiling, feel the need
for something green or golden.
With you there's sometimes
a step in between, you sitting
in my window reading a magazine.
Sometimes we're watching
the same movie on different TVs.
Other times I'm giving you cigarettes
like moonshine by the sea.

And though this isn't Paris
in the 1930s
and I can't be Henry Miller
and you can't be Anais Nin,
the look in your eyes sometimes
makes me think of you
as Grace Kelly in bed
reading a copy of *Vogue,*
and me as Jimmy Stewart,
asleep by the window
with two broken legs.

HOLIDAY INN
PUMA PERL

There's a Holiday Inn on Delancey Street.
Can't find parking on Avenue D.

This is not a rant.
It's not *boo hoo the city has changed bye bye Bleecker Bob,*
Pizza Box J & R go away blue buildings come back garbage strike

No need for all that.
There's a Holiday Inn on Delancey Street.
Can't find parking on Avenue D.

I don't remember what was once on that corner.
Maybe it was the children's store with the clothing
so cheaply made that a red polka dot dress I'd bought
for my daughter burst into flames in the drier and burnt
all of her pink and white blankets and socks.

Who goes to a Holiday Inn on Delancey Street
at the foot of the Williamsburg Bridge, where
methadone clinic patients drink extra sweet
coffee with donuts and carry the *Daily News*?

Once the only cars on D were up on blocks.
We walked through there coming from the day
care center the same year the clothes burned.
My daughter learned how to climb steps on the

bandshell, and said the word water at the pool.
We'd ride the F Train to Coney I, she'd scream
SEE WATER as we pulled into Stillwell Avenue.
Other than that, it was a very bad year,
at least there were no Holiday Inns on Delancey
if I'd had a car I could have parked it
on Avenue D, kept the tires if I gave a drug
dealer a ride or two, maybe driven out to Coney
yelling SEE WATER as we crossed the bridge,
maybe would have made it a better year.

This year isn't bad at all.
I drive my car to Coney Island.
My clothes are not on fire.
I don't worry about much anymore.

There's a Holiday Inn on Delancey Street,
Can't find parking on Avenue D.

I circle slowly around the neighborhood.
Eventually, I go home.

SIGNIFY
J.P. SLOTE

Depthless cloud cover
pulled the wool over our eyes
palette of brown and ash

plastic bag stuck in a tree
billows in the depthless air
larger-than-life-sized condom
used, spent, ripped
like the second day after a
New Year's hangover
limp in a damp tree
signifying nothing

just a plastic bag
inflating, deflating
caprice of a depthless winter day

sharp, cold, damp
(afternoon)
(faintly—prayer bells)
little chits of little birds

let us go then, you and I
against this palette of ash-grey sky
like a sperm whale sailing high
over this block of Lower East Side
like a plastic bag signifying—*surrender*
world in flames

INVISIBLE LOCKS AND CHAINS
ARTHUR NERSESIAN

An old chain and cheap lock
that once secured
an ancient garbage can
to an old gate
finally outlived
its rusty can handle
until it was camouflaged
by callous contract painters
blending it so
it can repose
until the city
pulverized the old pavement
baring the teeth
of the submerged cast-iron gate
and letting the chain and lock
sink below the level
that they pour their sloshy cement
smoothing it and letting it dry
forever joining and chaining
the infinity of things
unseen to nothing

HANNAH'S MOTT STREET HOVEL
CHERYL FISH

annah Kleinvelter enchanted me with her paintings. She made them in a room next to an elevator shaft in NOLITA when it was a dilapidated, acronym-free neighborhood. Pasta boiled on a hotplate; we drank endless pots of tea. I picked up a few items at the corner bodega, some wine for the evening, and lit the candle in the center of the altar. Hannah primed her wooden boards.

She slept in the studio illegally, washed up in a sink, and painted most of the night. I met her at a party where she was introduced as the cousin of one of my classmates. An informal visit to the Mott Street hovel precipitated many returns, and my unofficial position as her assistant. She needed me.

Hannah spoke of references to Jewish *midrash,* a form of interpretation based on the *Bible,* and I warmed to her habit of consulting the Chinese *I-Ching,* an oracle embraced by Carl Jung. I had read Jung's work in a psychology seminar that I stopped attending.

She came from money, but as an artist who worked infrequently, couldn't afford two rents — so she settled into her space like a monk. I loved the look of Mott Street north of Chinatown, for its dense urban beauty, red-brick dilapidated charm. Her landlord Stephan was a painter too; he kept his studio on the other side of the elevator shaft. He could be slapped for building code violations and fined heavily for Hannah's residency as these rooms were for commercial purposes only. That was the mantra.

"I listen when he locks up. It was around 10 last night," said Hannah, her dark eyes gazing towards the plank where she applied green and black paint, conjuring images of amphibians with blotches and lines. Such frightful creatures! I wondered about, but didn't press to find out Hannah's age; she had one of those eternal faces framed by short brown hair and wide-set eyes reminding me of my deceased Aunt Rose. Hannah wore long black smocks over paint-stained jeans and always held herself erect. "The frogs, what do they mean?" I asked hesitantly, not expecting any answer.

Late that morning, Stephan came in for tea and suspiciously eyed the array of pillows and blankets on the floor. He fingered the wooden panels, some rough and some smooth. His beard appeared gnarly and his eyes bloodshot; perhaps he too had painted all night. Somehow a conversation about brush strokes led to the subject of Hannah's dad's suicide when she was 12. "I don't like to dwell on it," Hannah said, her face turning sallow. She leaned towards Stephan, practically brushing her cheek against his shoulder, and he raised a hand to lightly skim her chin. Why hadn't she told me about her father's death during one of our dialogues over *al dente* spaghetti? Perhaps she expected Stephan to take pity on her. I was angry, and excused myself.

I scurried down Mott Street away from Wo Hop, my favorite late night greasy spoon. Past the high red brick walls of Old St. Patrick's Cathedral, I wondered what I expected from Hannah. I had become tightly wound, exhilarated, bedraggled.

I took the subway uptown to see my neighbor /shrink Theodora on the 33rd floor of the residential tower where we both lived on the Upper East Side of Manhattan. It was incredibly convenient to see your therapist at home, but awkward to bump into her in the elevator where we pretended to be cordial building buddies. I climbed the five flights from my apartment to her couch in my stocking feet and told her I was no longer interested in studying psychology and comparative literature. I didn't mention to Theodora how the tossing of the *I-Ching* coins, the broken and solid lines transforming into their opposites, and my friend Hannah's painting of the frogs made me feel like I belonged. Graduate seminars didn't cut it for me. I simply said "I've become interested in artistry and artifice." She requested elaboration. The way I internalized it, something incredible unfolded and exchanged in Hannah's presence. In the confines of her working and living space, with her neighbor's threatening surveillance and my restless admiration, we called out potential. Relished the unnamed. We thrived.

A few days later when I showed up to the studio, four boards' worth of frogs had been completed. She told me they were her vision of the remnants from the second plague that was put over Egypt by God, as described in *Exodus,* when the Jews were Pharaoh's slaves, and he had hardened his heart to their plight so God punished his nation. Her painting was a *midrash,* a commentary that meditated on the meaning of such a punishment and its lingering effect. I washed her brushes and poured tea when we heard the clunky sound of the elevator lifting in its shaft and couldn't be sure if it was Stephan leaving. Sometimes I put my ear to his door to check for sound. What was he painting? Why hadn't he invited us to take a peek? Was he even an artist? Maybe just an overlord.

"He knows I am living in, and is deciding how long until he evicts me," Hannah said pensively, the finished boards against the wall, fragments of legs and eyes upon us, emblems of destruction and freedom. "He has a hard shell surrounding his mind," she said.

"Like a walnut," I suggested.

"Yes," she said, walking over to where she kept her coins.

We consulted the *I-Ching* oracle, alternating our rolls—back and forth the coins went as we crouched on our knees. From her tapered fingers they fell to the floor, and then I picked them up with my stubbier digits, seeking her eyes. After a total of six turns, we came up with number 41. Sun/decrease which meant "a time to shed a dependency." That worked— was it coming here, being a student, or seeking therapy that was my dependency? Hannah saw the message as a signal to vacate Mott Street, to figure her next move. She told me she had acquired the wood panels in Vermont, where she had a family friend, and she thought she might want to paint in an old barn, abandon the chiseled boundaries of city dwelling. But I couldn't imagine us anywhere other than this cramped, inspiring studio next to an elevator shaft with the threatening neighbor, the possible eviction, and my hovering kinship.

"Let's throw again," I said, sweeping the coins into my hand, and asserting a command that she had to heed. But she didn't make eye contact or take her turn as the whistle trilled from the kettle. She stood up to take care of it. A tear welled up in my eye that I struggled to hold, the salty substance of foreboding evocation. I couldn't move. The coins fell from my hand and rolled across the studio, indeterminately.

"MAN PLUS WOMAN EQUALS GOD" AT THE HOTEL ESSEX

Kathryn Adisman

Fucking a ghost in the dim, in the old dark hotel with molding
To the ceiling and windows to the skyscrapers NYC midtown
Early a.m., see the sky turn gray dawning, see the lights:

"They were red and green before you came,"
He tells me. The lit-up Christmas tree out the window
You can almost touch is the Empire State Building; framed
In the mirror a row of '40s-style architecture right out of
Hopper, from his Nighthawks-diner period.

He stood over my marriage like a ghost.
She wrote in ink the color of blood recording it.

What about now?

There is no now when I'm with you.
Even while it's going on, the narrator in my head won't shut up.

In the dim half-light air dense like a 3-D halftone blown up
You could eat off the dancing gray dots. Our bodies gleaming like
Fish give off a glow that's not sweat, phosphorescent, an odor
Wilder than the buffalo

What is there to say?

The difference between us is: "You need to map out the heart; I'd
rather be in darkness," he says....

Sadsack Weiss in the hotel hall in his blue pajamas with his
Eyes some color capable of turning inkblack deep deep and
Scrutinizing.... The elevator door opens. In his eyes I see
There's somebody....

He backs away he's still kind of backing off and staring as I
Stand inside the box, my back against the wall,
And staring....

ART RAVESON

CANAL DOUGHNUTS
ART RAVESON

Sometime in my early adult years, I became aware of specific locations around the city that seemed to hold a strong appeal for the psychologically scarred as well as a legion of minimally functioning social misfits. In the same way that indigenous people around the world are able to recognize sacred "power spots," negative magnetic disturbances in the life force, corresponding to the particular infirmities of the psychologically and emotionally impaired, unfailingly drew the walking wounded to various, strange, negative energy-emitting portals, which I would soon discover, could be located practically anywhere.

Some of my early explorations led me to far-flung, previously unknown, odd pockets of the city, in search of off-putting, run down luncheonettes, dark, secluded alleyways and desolate, garbage strewn, overgrown vacant lots. However, I was soon to discover that these "portals" could just as easily be found in luxury co-ops, private gentlemen's clubs and exclusive, gated communities.

This discovery seemed to strike a chord in my own lifetime of sporadic psychological problems, which included chronic depression, regular bouts of depersonalization, sporadic flirting with suicide and an ongoing, perpetual, internal dialogue of such eccentric, depraved nature, that I fear, even today, some forty years later, that were I to reveal the merest hint of it's subversive nature or repetitive, aberrant themes, the cold, moldy stone walls of Kirby Forensic would soon be closing in around me. Along with my then-current partner-in-crime; the young, still hopeful Ugo "Ooze"

Melman, I began to catalog as many of those sites as I could discover, from Innwood Park down to the Battery.

Melman; a fellow cabbie, struggling poet and illegitimate son of a notorious, incarcerated, pedophile rabbi, laid claim to the discovery of the Worth Street Chock Full O' Nuts; an aptly named chain outlet, and the flagship of his many renowned finds. This shabby, failing establishment had its own, particular, disjointed, drab charm. The crackling, spine-tingling atmosphere was palpable and life altering. It wasn't just the customers who suffered from the influence of brutal demonic forces governing that physical space. The management and employees seemed to be in the throes of the same, site-specific, severe emotional disturbances. Hard working, once more or less normal, older waitresses, with families who desperately depended on their paltry paycheck, had just put in too much time in that neon-drenched, frenetic, abusive atmosphere, finally falling victim to those other inexplicable, psychic forces, and along with their customers, ready to wholeheartedly take part in one of the regular, no-holds-barred fracases, usually set in motion by nothing more serious than an offhand, thoughtless comment, insufficient tip, or the usual handful of Sweet & Low packets, covertly slipped into a pocket or purse.

Just a week or so after Melman's greatest find, I hit real pay dirt, myself. It was in fact, what we both soon came to acknowledge as our absolute gold standard. Half asleep and in dire need of a morning coffee, giving in to some momentary, uncharacteristic urge for a glazed doughnut, I stumbled into a dismal, lugubrious, down-at-the-heels doughnut shop. Sitting at the counter, within minutes of passing through the door, I was suddenly hit by such rasping, acute psychic distress, that I slowly began suspecting I might have just accidentally unearthed the true mother lode.

Unable to nurse, what turned out to be the single most abysmal, noxious cup of coffee I had ever tasted, I pushed the cracked, yellowed cup aside and began taking stock of my surroundings, not yet wholly grasping the historic significance of this monumental discovery. Ignoring the gnawing fear that I had probably just destroyed what was left of an overly abused, already compromised digestive system, sheer force of will allowed me to discontinue dwelling on any prospective internal damage and access some as-yet-unexploited quadrant of my flabby, sluggish brain, and begin compiling measurable and empirical evidence, in support of the Melman/Raveson Negative Portal Hypothesis.

Canal Doughnuts was run by an obese, vitriolic, middle-aged Bulgarian harpy and her nondescript, prematurely balding, cowering, subservient son. Neither of these two took much stock in the modern, liberal concept of following your passion. They had no inherent interest in revolutionizing either doughnuts or coffee, or even turning out a passably edible product. This was strictly a case of brutal and desperate immigrant survival in a self-deluded, dog-eat-dog empire. How they had landed here and taken the reigns of this bleak, funereal dive was anyone's guess.

My usual strategy was to order a coffee and just sit back to observe the chaos. I considered the seventy-five cent cost of their corrosive battery acid, a more-than-fair price for general admission, entitling me to loiter for a reasonable amount of time, reveling in the primal forces that had pulled me in, along with the string of shuffling outpatients and few stray, oddball tourists, who all seemed stunned and surprised to find themselves there, as if they had been magically transported to some strange other-worldly dimension they had never even imagined existed. My obvious lack of interest in that sub-par, caustic substance, seriously rankled the already-irate owner, who would approach me every so often to inquire in her best Bela Lagosi voice; "Coh-vvee okhaaay?" "Ah, yes. Very good, thanks," I'd reply. "Steel hhhot?" she'd ask, holding the Pyrex carafe of steaming, hot, toxic sludge, at the ready. "Temperature's perfect. No problem. Thank you," I'd shoot back. This retarded game of cat and mouse hardly altered from one visit to the next, with the single exception of her ever growing rancor and deepening suspicion, regarding my presence there.

At some point, I came to believe the key to unravelling the mystery of the negative portal phenomena, lay in the person of the blinking, disheveled, half-blind porter. He was a squirrelly, deranged classic crackpot named Julius, who, when he wasn't taping up paranoid, hand written pronouncements onto light poles or phone booths all over Lower Manhattan, kept himself busy wiping the shop's permanently discolored counter, sweeping the floor or just shuffling about in a semi-fugue state, spouting nonstop gibberish of the highest order. His ongoing monologues mixed basic high school history and science lessons with well known, paranoid conspiracies, like the *Protocols of the Elders of Zion,* the Rockefeller/Rothschilds Banking Combine, 1950's Red Squad propaganda, odd, random details culled from silent, German expressionist films of the 1930's, as well as a vast array of mismatched, articulated elements, from various, disparate sources, ranging from old science fiction pulps to the revolutionary life force theories of Wilhelm Reich and the improbable, miraculous inventions of Nicola Tesla. For a mixed-up, unkempt lunatic, he seemed to be exceptionally conversant in a number of wide-ranging subjects.

Julius' only pleasure in life seemed to consist of terrorizing the shop's broken-down, mangy, nervous-wreck of a cat. The pitiable, once-feral creature, undoubtedly taken in to control the prodigious vermin infestation, had been reduced to a cringing, frightened shadow of its former self, by Julius' frequent, stealthy mock attacks. Without warning, he would charge the helpless beast with an upraised broom, shrieking like some hell-bent, pint-sized, sclerotic banshee. The terrified, shell-shocked creature would tear up the block, cowering in some dark, hidden alcove for an hour or so, before eventually slinking back for additional abuse. The pathetic, defeated feline, obviously suffering from acute post-traumatic stress, had long since given up any vestige of self-respect or independence, in exchange for its regular, miserly portion of rank, discount cat food.

Once, in the company of Chalmers Rudge; a visiting cartoonist friend, I spent an entire afternoon tailing the well read, inspired lunatic, hoping we might run across a few more of his exquisite, eccentric, handwritten ramblings, to add to my coveted, rapidly-expanding collection. Shadowing our furtive, deranged subject, I was surprised to learn he had an extensive grazing area, ranging at this particular tracking, from Worth Street up to the northern edge of Stuyvesant Town. As careful as we were to not be detected, he eventually caught on to us, becoming extremely agitated, circling us a couple of times and sniffing around, in an attempt to discover what the hell we were up to. As our quest was simply one of research, we had absolutely no interest in adding to his already visible psychic distress, and decided to make a hasty departure, allowing him to clearly witness us boarding the Second Avenue bus, in order to allay the growing paranoia we already felt responsible for.

On another occasion, while completely lost in full-throttle, automatic, stream of consciousness, free association raving; all done under his breath, necessitating me to surreptitiously slide along a section of the switch-back counter, bouncing from one wavering stool to another, attempting to maintain my ringside seat, while I strained to catch every exquisite word, his easily excitable, irate boss suddenly cut short his inspired muttering, in her hideous, shrill, deafening voice, screeching at him, "Jool-eee-isss! Jool-ee-isss! Ghhet cuhps! Cuhps! Vhee halve no muhr peh-per cuhps!" Visibly withdrawing, at the violent breaching of his inner world, he froze in place for a brief moment and then awkwardly lurched toward the basement storeroom steps. Partially recovering, he quietly spit out a few, carefully chosen words through firmly gritted teeth, "I admire your initiative, but not your ruthlessness!"

Over the successive years, Canal Doughnuts hit hard times. In a last ditch bid to salvage their livelihood, the owners began renting out the city's sidewalk space, at least that adjacent to their front window, to a number of desperate, disheartened Pakistani immigrants, unable to formulate any other possibility for earning a day's wages. These wretched, blighted innocents attempted to hawk baseball hats, t-shirts, scarves, umbrellas and other standard street side offerings, mostly to tourists who at first mistakenly believed they had wandered into some kind of exotic souk. None stuck it out for more than a month or two, before eventually acquiring a hack license or choosing some slightly better, last ditch job, abandoning their cramped, jury-rigged stalls and forgoing their outrageous, bloated deposits. Once, when a particularly biting, arctic wind began whipping up already frigid, mid-winter conditions, sending newspapers, umbrellas and other lost or discarded items, skyward, one dejected, pitiful soul, renting one of their miniscule slots, implored the impassive, steely she wolf to return his money for the day and allow him to seek refuge elsewhere. She drew herself up and ferociously bellowed, "Vhy dhoo yhou gheeve hup so heas-ily? Go beck outside! Mehk yuhr moh-nay! You hahr man - or vuhrm?" It was a terrifying, soul searing display.

Julius' tenure in that demented establishment, and his long term exposure to those beastly forces continually streaming through that foul, malevolent portal, lasted approximately five years, until his unannounced, mysterious departure put a sudden end to my informal field studies. I tried inquiring sometime later, if he had quit, been fired or had finally been institutionalized. The stone-faced, belligerent shop owner only sneered at me disdainfully, for actually knowing his name. I did spot him a few times after that, furtively skulking around the northern periphery of Chinatown, once posting one of his rare, inspired, mad scribblings on the outside of the last of our now-practically-extinct, outdoor phone booths, just half a block from my apartment.

WHERE SHEEP MAY SAFELY GRAZE: KEEPING THINGS PASTORAL

Liza Béar

I t's not only a tranquil Memorial Day weekend in the city but also awards time at the 68th Cannes Film Festival and Iceland's "Rams" ("Hrutar") by Grímur Hákonarson has just won top prize in the "Un Certain Regard" sidebar. As the film's story goes, two brothers who hadn't spoken in forty years reunite in a remote Icelandic valley to save their rams.

Meanwhile, closer to home on Mulberry Street, sheep are being honored without fanfare or fashion police. As I cross the street from the public-library side, a trio of bleating sheep are being bundled out of a van from Hudson, NY, led through the small arched door in the red brick wall, and promptly set to graze the delicious fresh long grass in Old St Patrick's Cathedral cemetery, their needs perfectly suited to the task at hand.

Says the Monsignor, "They'll be here for two months to keep the grass trimmed." Literally. After all, we the people of New York City give short shrift to the metaphorical use of the phrase "mowing the grass," and to the practice to which it refers of obliterating people, buildings and neighborhoods in the Gaza Strip.

Asked whether this was the return of the lambs named Gold, Frankincense and Myrrh which had been brought in for St Francis Festival of the Animals last fall, Monsignor said no, these were new sheep and had been given cartographic rather than scriptural names: Mulberry, Mott and Elizabeth. Nor did their visit coincide with a date on the ecclesiastical calendar.

"We just like to keep things pastoral," the Monsignor smiled.

WEST SIDE HIGHWAY

ARTHUR KAYE

I n 1973 a piece of the elevated West Side Highway finally had enough and collapsed sending a loaded garbage truck and a passenger vehicle crashing to earth. North of W. 14th Sreet it was dismantled. From 14th Street to the Battery, it became a playground for cyclists, dancers, joggers, roller skaters, practitioners of Tai Chi, yoga and just about anything else a mile long strip of elevated asphalt, concrete and rusty steel could provide a stage for. Sammy had a bicycle, left over from junior high school. It was heavy, had only three speeds and upright handlebars, but he didn't worry about getting mugged for it. On nice afternoons he carried it downstairs from his apartment to go for a ride after work.

Sam rode his bike over to Lafayette, then downtown to Spring Street, and crosstown to the northernmost entrance to the highway. He pedaled hard up the ramp and then it was like all the rust, grime, soot, smoke and smells of the city were just sucked away, the chiaroscuro effect of the late afternoon shadows wiped away, the claustrophobia of living with the decay, the failing services, potholed streets, subways constantly breaking down, all of it just gone in a puff of light and air, ironically on the surface of a decrepit roadway, now too weak to support automobile traffic, only partially dismantled because the city was just too broke to finish taking it down.

This was the New York City he loved, the contrast between the excitement, the beauty and a feeling of infinite possibilities and the decadence and decay, the stench of uncollected garbage, the crime and the corruption a tonic to his creativity.

He rode up to the barrier at W. 14th Sreet., then turned around and sprinted all the way to the Battery, coasting down the ramp and into the park. He stopped at the seawall to watch for ships in the harbor. It was always busy with tugs and barges, container ships, freighters, ferries and a few pleasure boats. The tourists wandered around him with their cameras and guidebooks. Even now, he thought, New York City draws them, and no wonder; it is a truly magical place.

He walked his bicycle, his gaze moving from harbor to tourists, until he reached the crowd lined up for a late boat to Liberty Island. This is my town, he thought, my place and these people are my subjects. I can walk over to any of them and offer to show them the New York City they read about or saw in some movie or TV show, the NYC that isn't in the tour guides and travel brochures, but why? They wouldn't appreciate it, would probably think I was just some sort of weirdo or deviant out to take all their money. Maybe they'd be right.

FROM *TIMES SQUARE RED,*
TIMES SQUARE BLUE
SAMUEL DELANY

The opening of the old Metropolitan Opera House at Broadway
and Seventh Avenue in 1883 first brought vice up from Mercer
Street and the lower parts of Greenwich Village, where the rising rents were driving out the houses of prostitution, so that only industrial businesses could afford those downtown locations. In 1889
court testimony revealed that Nathan Niles, then president of the
Tradesmen's National Bank, owned a brothel on West Forty-third
Street, run by the well-known "French Madame," Elize Purret. The
same year the *Times* came, 1904, the Interborough Rapid Transit
opened the subway system, with its nickel fare (no subway tokens —
or metrocards — back then) that lasted into the fifties. Feeding into
the city just to its west, with its opening in 1937, the Lincoln Tunnel
only added to the value. With a smaller version first swinging wide
its doors in 1950, the now block-long pair of Port Authority buildings
simply assured that this would be the city's incoming traffic center
for a long time to come. With the theater district to the north and its
central location in Manhattan Island, it was a developer's dream.

And the vice?

It was peep shows, sex shops, adult video stores and dirty magazine stores, massage parlors—and porn theaters. A few years ago
there were two on the east end of the block's north side, one at the
block's west end, and another across the street, with some seven
scattered up and down Eighth Avenue, from the Cameo at Forty-
fourth to the Adonis at Fifty-first, as well as a flourishing trade in
female street-walkers, drugs, and hustlers.

The threat from AIDS produced a 1985 health ordinance that
began the shut-down of the specifically gay sexual outlets in the

neighborhood: the gay movie houses and the straight porn theaters that allowed open masturbation and fellatio in the audience. For a dollar forty-nine in the seventies, and for five dollars in the year before they were closed (several less than twelve months ago), from ten in the morning till midnight you could enter and, in the sagging seats, watch a projection of two or three hard-core pornographic videos. A few trips up and down the aisle while your eyes got accustomed to the darkness revealed men sitting off in the shadows — or, sometimes, full out under the occasional wall lights — masturbating... if someone hadn't stood up on the seat and unscrewed the bulb. Sit a seat away from one, and you would either be told to go away, usually fairly quietly, or invited to move closer (if only by the guy's feigned indifference). Should he be one of *your* regulars, you might even get a grin of recognition.

Occasionally men expected money — but most often, not. Many encounters were wordless. Now and again, though, one would blossom into a conversation lasting hours, especially with those men less well-off, the out-of-work, or the homeless with nowhere else to go.

In the sixties I found similar theaters in every capital of Europe. That may explain why foreign gay tourists located these places here so quickly. The population was incredibly heterogeneous — white, black, Hispanic, Asian, Indian, Native American, and a variety of Pacific Islanders. In the Forty-second Street area's sex theaters specifically, since I started frequenting them in the summer of 1975, I've met playwrights, carpenters, opera singers, telephone-repair men, stockbrokers, guys on welfare, guys with trust funds, guys on crutches, on walkers, in wheelchairs, teachers, warehouse workers, male nurses, fancy chefs, guys who worked at Dunkin' Donuts, guys who gave out flyers on street corners, guys who drove garbage trucks, and guys who washed windows on the Empire State Building. As a gentile, I note that this is the only place in a lifetime's New York residency I've had any extended conversation with some of the city's Hasidim. On a rainy Friday in 1977 in one such theater, the Variety, down on Third Avenue just below Fourteenth Street, I met a man who became my lover for eight years. My current lover (with whom I've lived happily for going on seven), once we'd met, discovered we'd both patronized the Capri, only we'd never encountered each other because I usually went in the day, while he always went at night. Once we began to live with one another, we often visited the theater together—till it was closed, toward the start of this year. There are many men, younger and older, for whom the ease and availability of sex there made the movies a central sexual outlet.

Nostalgia presupposes an uncritical confusion between the first, the best, and the youthful gaze (through which we view the first and the best) with which we create origins. But the transformation from the cheap Village, Delancey Street, Fourteenth Street, Upper West Side, and (supremely) Forty-second Street movie theaters of the fifties and sixties (where you could generally find some sort of sexual activity in the back balcony, off to the side, or in the rest rooms) to the porn theaters of the seventies (a number of them set up specifically for quick, convenient encounters among men) does not, in my memory at any rate, fit easily into such an originary/nostalgic schema.

By the early seventies the movie industry was already reeling under the advent of home video technology. Suddenly it became impossible to fill up the larger theatrical spaces that had attracted audiences since before the Depression, eager to see this or that new celluloid epic, that or this new double feature.

All over the country, save for a few major venues (in New York the Ziegfeld, the Astor Plaza) that persevered like filmic museums from another era, movie theaters underwent an almost spontaneous mitosis — dividing into two, three, four, and even six viewing spaces. The film of Ray Bradbury's *Something Wicked This Way Comes* (1983) was probably the last movie I watched from a full-sized neighborhood theater balcony before, a season later, a tetraplex took over the space and, a season after that, at Broadway and Eighty-third Street, a hexplex opened next door on tthe same block, so that briefly in my neighborhood we had a choice of ten films at any one time, where three years before there had been only one. And around the Forty-second Street area a decade or more of idle speculation on the renovation of the Times Square area ("Movie Capital of the World," as it billed itself on the wall sign over the upper floors of the Forty-second Street Apollo — not to be confused with the Harlem house of the same name and greater notoriety) turned into active plans and active buying —and/ or an active freeze on all real improvements, since the whole thing would be bought up and pulled down in a year or more, wouldn't it.… Under this economic pressure in the early-to-middle seventies, some two dozen small theaters were given over as outlets for the nascent pornographic film industry: a handful between Sixth Avenue and Eighth Avenue along Forty-second Street proper, another handful on Broadway (the Circus, the Big Apple, the Baby Doll…), and another half dozen or so up along Eighth, starting with the Cameo on the west side of the avenue between Forty-third and Forty-fourth and running up to the Adonis. Most of the theaters purveyed straight fare, but a few (the Adonis, the Eros I and II, the King, the David, the Bijoux, and, in later years, one half of the Hollywood) provided gay features. The transformation meant that from then on all major repairs for these properties were at an end. Only those without which the theaters could not stay open were done. In that condition the porn theaters continued, not for two, three, or four years, but for the next twenty-five. Some did not last the duration. Each new burst of interest in the area's renovation would be accompanied by a new wave of do-gooder rhetoric, and a theater or two would go. By the middle eighties the three houses between Sixth and Seventh were gone One on the north side had been turned into a fried chicken emporium. Another had become a sporting goods store. The third (that had featured "Live Sex Shows," which, at five performances a day between ten and ten, were exactly that: a brown or black couple spent twenty minutes on a bare blue-lit stage, first the woman stripping for the man, then fellating him, then his performing cunnilingus on her, and finally the two of them screwing in two or three positions, finishing — with pull-out orgasms for a few of the after six shows — to polite applause from the largely forty-plus male audience, before the porn film started once more. At the back of the chest high wall behind the last row of orchestra seats, usually some guy would give you a hand job or sometimes a blow job; there for a couple of weeks I gave my quota of both) was simply a south side vacant lot.

FROM *TIMES SQUARE TAXI*
WILLIAM CONSIDINE

West 42nd Street between 7th and 8th Avenues was so desolate and disreputable it wasn't used for our office address. The official address was 221 W. 41st Street. That door on 41st Street led to a long hallway north to the lobby on 42nd Street. (The hallway still exists inside the McDonalds that's there now; crowded, narrow, lined with a counter for your coke and fries.)

Just a few years earlier, the simple four-story box on the southwest corner of 7th Avenue and 42nd had been the site of an artists' occupation; guerilla art: taking over an empty building and cramming it full of art and graffiti. It was called the Times Square Show. Now the site housed a hotel, a porn shop and a diner.

The hotel, of course, was used by whores and johns (and the pimp who came by for his money, and the woman from the office meeting her boyfriend at lunch hour.) The porn shop was a small black box with few offerings. The diner had a good bowl of rice and black beans; cheap, nourishing and fast, but the place was open to street life: poverty, insanity, anger. It was cheap for bustling, turn-over trade, no place to linger.

The next establishment down the south side of West 42nd Street, west of Times Square, past the newsstand and subway entrance, was a wide open pizza shop, in what was once a theater lobby, with two counters opening in a V directly onto the sidewalk. There, I saw a young pizza counter worker in white food industry clothes, shouting in rage, pull out a baseball bat and chase a man down the street.

The block had been deserted by a devastated industry, or rather a shift in the entertainment business to other products with better returns. The big theaters filled with dancing choruses and song were silent now and left behind to decay by the rapid advance of radio, movies, television. A few theaters still showed older films to a tiny audience scattered among a thousand seats.

"You're SORRY? You PISSED on my DATE and you're SORRY?" a movie buff cried out in a balcony.

On the street, "You broke my bottle" was the roughest con. A big guy, his arms and shoulders bare in a white undershirt, would be fumbling on the sidewalk to light a cigarette. As you passed, giving him plenty of room, he'd lurch into you and ask you to hold this for a second: a quart bottle of beer. Whether you reached for it or not, it fell to the sidewalk, glass maybe breaking, beer splashing, and now the guy was angry and confrontational — "You broke my bottle!" And he wanted you to pay for it — straight out extortion on the sidewalk. "It cost ten dollars." He wanted money and it was hard to walk away — he'd lost everything, and he was poor, strong and angry.

A man and a woman: a happy couple, laughing, embracing, focused on each other, actually raucous, drunk and loud, come forward heedless and fast. They suddenly walk right into you and SQUIRT you — the woman has a mustard squeeze bottle! Mustard on your clothes! — and they're so apologetic and pathetic, they paw at you and try to wipe the mustard off your clothes, smearing it, mortified and you push them off and wave them away as they apologize loudly and later you find your wallet gone.

But the sale of crack cocaine, at the height of the epidemic in the late Eighties, was the main business on the sidewalks. The dealing took place midblock, in front of the Candler Building, our building, where City government workers labored daily. The Candler Building was built first as national headquarters for the Coca-Cola Company. A block to its west was the pale blue, modern McGraw Hill Building. Across 43rd was the mass of the *New York Times* Building.

Crack or whatever (I remember seeing, years earlier, heroin junkies nodding, swaying stiffly, barely standing, on the sidewalk near the newsstand) was sold under what's now the canopy for Mc-

Donalds, just outside the front door below our offices. There was a mailbox at the curb that seemed to serve as the head drug dealer's throne. He could lean on the mailbox, or sit on it. Around him was a cloud of colleagues in random atomic stasis or rotation; a royal court's careful rituals of observance and readiness.

At that time, I had an office with one of the three arched windows on the third floor overlooking the entryway, and I could see the supposedly random comings and goings of people hanging around the mailbox.

The police sent a uniformed officer into my office to watch and report on the street activity. Crouching on the floor and peering over the low sill, he described into his walkie-talkie the sales operations as they took place below. He saw drugs being passed and money changing hands in separate transactions. Then the buyers went around the corner onto 41st Street to smoke the crack.

As a group, they were poor and worn, prematurely aged, often ragged and bruised. They lived for the drug — addictive and illegal — craving the ecstatic. They gathered behind the long-emptied theater east of our back door, under its fire escape, to light up their crack pipes, then they settled along the rear wall of the building or on the curb.

West 41st Street was a major thoroughfare for crowds of pedestrians twice daily, as commuters passed from and to the Port Authority Bus Terminal on Eighth Avenue. They filled the street, a parade at rush hour, a few cars proceeding slowly among them. Now the blight had spread from 42nd to 41st Street, confronting these workers in the evening as they travelled from workplace to their homes via the bus terminal.

Concerned about what crack addicts would do to the people passing back and forth on 41st Street, we joined with the few other businesses on the block — a theater, a bar — to form a Block Association and chipped-in funds to hire a security dog service, with several German shepherds. They were kenneled in the basement of our building and brought out at mid-day and again before the evening rush, just a couple at a time on leashes, to patrol the block. They drove away the crack addicts, but the dogs howled at night in the basement in misery.

FROM *I'M YOUR MAN*
FLOYD SYKES

With time to kill Fred can look beyond this circle of men, old and young, whose routines he knows, and see the rest of the human traffic around Times Square — discounting theatergoers and commuting office workers and all those others just passing through (this is Manhattan) who might take any street or avenue on their way somewhere else. He watches those who pause or hang around or leave and return, those who want or expect something from these blocks. There are some different faces tonight, but it doesn't matter, those lingering here now fill the sidewalks for the same reasons they've been filled the nights and weeks, months and years, before, most of them most of all to be near the illicit and illegal, sex and drugs, crime and criminals, where so much is possible, where lives must be more thrilling than the lives they live.

Fred is one of them, or at least this place is part of the life he lives. Tonight as on nights before he will attract his share of attention — especially standing near his corner, watching; as a moving target he'd be harder to approach, could slide away, keep walking, but since he doesn't move everyone knows he's waiting for something, they are suspicious or else they want to have what he's waiting for, to sell him — to be — what he's looking to buy. He shakes his head when approached, says no as firmly as he can without arousing anger. "Yo, wha's up? Wha's up? Watchu lookin' for?" "Nice young girls?" "Sellin' nickels." "Yo, pops, lookin' to hang out?" Shake his head, look the other way, turn the Walkman up so he can pretend he doesn't hear. Listen to "I got a peaceful easy feeling," listen to "If I fell in love with you, would you promise to be true?" Pretend it drowns out the sound of the streets. Doesn't even say, "Don't call me 'Pops'."

As he stands and waits and watches Fred notices again what he has noticed before, how few of those who linger, of those who reappear, alert for whatever brought them here and brings them back, are sure enough of themselves to face these streets without a face prepared for the faces they'll meet. The men seeking boys as Fred does have their masks, stretching truth in their own ways; theirs often center around their hair — dyed, combed over, added to, covered — hair trying to be young enough to match the youths they're after. It's the others Fred wonders at. Some sort of playacting is natural for the young, like adolescents everywhere wearing selves borrowed from TV and movies, rap videos and street corner thugs cool enough to emulate. The adults though — the time so many of them spend in front of mirrors perfecting the look they want the world to know them by shows how much they care; it's an effort, this arrogance, this swagger. "You talkin' to me?" every one of them has sometime said to a mirror, maybe without a touch of irony, maybe believing that was the way men met other men. Maybe they're right. Few are immune to the need for an image that will keep them afloat out here, some vision of accomplishment or potential — mastermind, kingpin, player, mover, shaker; tough guy, intimidator, gangster, seducer, stud. Winner, in short. Something worth being.

From a distance the adults are almost indistinguishable from the adolescents. Jeans and T-shirts, sneakers and caps. All play by the same rules — street rules, which are prison rules, junior high hallway rules, playground rules: The biggest boast, the hardest push, the loudest threat, the nastiest sneer wins. Tattoos and muscles count. Ex-cons who can't adapt to the straight life can feel right at home with other men whose lives grind against the law. Their women (and most men here would think of a girlfriend, a wife, as "My woman") are like best suits of clothes, maybe brought around to show off but not for everyday; they can only complicate a man's life on the street. Most women regulars are addicts or whores; the occasional streetwise entrepreneur tough enough to hold her own among men is rare. Men who can't thrive elsewhere, or won't try to, have lives out here, careers as thieves or as small-time players or pimps, selling drugs or sex; their working tones are usually a little lower key than they'd use among themselves, whispering "Smoke?" or "Got coke" or "Nice young girls here" to the likely buyers who don't look like narcs (Fred hears a lot from them), their working manner still and watchful, though even the stealthiest, the stillest, can usually be spotted by the quickness always in their eyes.

These professionals compete with those few from Brooklyn or the Bronx who, coming to the city to sell their girlfriends or sisters, can be seen coaxing and arguing the girls into an arrangement. It's the money counts, everyone agrees on that. There are even a few of the classic purple suit and feather hat pimps, older men, almost distinguished in this company — their professional need to impress women as well as men has smoothed them out over the years, and they are older now, not necessarily here to work, more likely to stand around with their peers, burnishing the glow of claimed accomplishment, than to add to the general feel of violence just suppressed, crime just waiting to happen. They seem to think their look and the lives they've lived have earned them their share of the streets' chief honor, respect. Most of the youths here haven't gotten past the violence yet, the glamour of the criminal life, maybe want no more than to be around to see the explosion that always seems imminent, are hooked on the idea of it, the thrill the very thought shoots through them, their testosterone fantasies.

And there is violence, but not much of the tabloid guns-and-knives variety. Not enough to wait around for. Mostly it's the small, nasty explosions of anger over territory, even if it's a square foot of pavement that belongs to no one for more than a few seconds at a time. Belligerent standing and bellicose walking can make a stroll down the avenue an adventure. Be always alert for someone's sudden shift from walking to standing dead still in your path, forcing a detour or a confrontation — a sidewalk charging foul. Watch for the angry young men — one or two a night, always — walking with intent, aiming for shoulder bumps and brushes, excuses for the thrill (that word again) of exploding anger — self-righteous

"What you looking at?" "Watch where you're walkin'!" anger. They stare down any approach or as they come close maybe look contemptuously away and pretend not to see, even the small victory of forcing someone to move aside an almost druggy delight. Watch closely: See the lead shoulder square and lower a bit for the blow? The arm stop swinging just before contact? Fred sometimes manages to avoid these without seeming to, shifting his path slightly far enough ahead of them it might be a coincidence. When actually bumped he moves on and shows no sign he cares, or even notices, withholding that satisfaction his own little victory. Who knows if he fools anyone — not himself, his fantasies of angry words (his own devastating, searing) provide him with an adrenaline rush just like theirs. Still, he can be surprised by someone older, almost always black, anger undiminished by time and experience, throwing himself around like a kid.

There are others. There are the few military men, in reality or in their own "You talkin' to me?" dreams, white men no longer young, in brush cuts and Fu Manchu moustaches, pieces of army fatigues, wire-rimmed sunglasses, looking like B movie extras, usually hoping for someone to listen to their stories, true or otherwise. And there are the buyers to make it worthwhile for all those sellers, men looking for whores and drugs and stolen goods, cheap. Everyone thinks of the score, claims to think only of the score.

As Fred looks around this night he realizes how seldom he registers the men (they're almost all men) who are here every day from dawn to sunset at least working in stores and at food and newspaper stands. From where he waits he sees the two dark small Hispanics (the job description for fruit stand and pizzeria work) keeping an eye on outdoor displays for the market on the corner where he stands; the vigilant Orientals preparing to close the bags-and-sundries store opposite in the next block; the crazed-looking bearded man, always smoking and mumbling to himself as he tends the salt-and-garlic-smelling meat at his corner stand, its smoke giving this block an odor unmistakably its own.

Late at night (and Fred is still here late this night, to his own helpless annoyance) all these are joined by the drag queens and their hangers-on — wannabes without the nerve yet for heels and wigs on the street — and their suitors, those who admire and yearn for the fictions they represent, or perhaps (the younger) just not ready to handle the real thing, feeling safer with someone they can treat like a woman without the risks they'd run talking to an actual girl; here at the slightest threat of rejection or embarrassment they can retreat behind contempt, yelling, "fag," ridiculing an Adam's apple or touch of five o'clock Shadow — whatever it takes to protect their unformed manhood.

And the drag queens love a little drama, even that kind, some crave it even more than the toughest of the kicks-hungry boys do, the slightest touch leaves them screeching for their wounded dignity. Most, though, most of all want to be taken for what they try to be, for one night at a time: Another corner girl looking for some fun. After awhile there's a commotion across the way; one person walking down the sidewalk can be enough for a commotion and this one moves through the crowd oblivious as a dog. He's young, thin and black (Fred's seen him on the streets before); hair dyed yellow teased into strings like Michael Jackson's, teeth capped in gold, he moves like someone late for his own coronation, grinning, bouncing to whatever music is in his head and never needing to speak or look anyone in the eye, his world is so complete. Others might be caught up in their own music, but not so much the world has gone away. He moves on, not slowing or seeming to notice anything outside himself, certainly not that he's one of the few sights out here that leave some amazement behind.

TIMES SQUARE   BONNY FINBERG

THE HEART OF THE MARKETPLACE
BONNY FINBERG

The Dalai Lama says: "In matters of truth no questions of size. The struggle is between power of gun and the power of truth. For shot? for temporary? power of gun is much more stronger, but for long run? power of truth is more stronger."

But, he's said nothing about the power of money, the beauty of money, the function of money, the deceit of money, its eminence, pretending to be more than it is. In the end, a cliché.

In Times Square a cold killer looks down at dazed shoppers filing in and out of the M&M store, a flashing candy sign is dulled by traffic lights and frantic ads, too many, too fast, 360 degrees, cameras poised in all directions. A shirtless Indian beats a drum followed by a naked cowboy. Something's burning, either Rome or a pretzel. Either way, no one seems concerned.

I'm absurdly in the middle of the street, seated at a red metal café table, facing TOYS R US. I once dodged traffic on this spot, where, now, hookers, junkies, thieves and pimps, disguised as human toys in baggy suits, hustle tourists for a photo op.

Three women in headscarves sit at a table next to mine. Two of them are poking the keys of their cell phones, laughing. I have a FOX moment and wonder if I could be blown up here with the other god-knows-how-many-other humans sitting, walking around, standing agape, voluntarily submitting to electrocution by spectacle. I momentarily feel embarrassed for my racist thought until Spider Man comes on the scene. He and Smurf work the crowd, stop a blond in shorts and Converse sneakers — conversing. Loud honk! A giant white truck with a black M&M logo in block letters barrels down Broadway — ironically generic.

The previous inhabitant has taped a drawing to this table, a stick figure with triangle body; down each side a column of "NO"s. Seven on the left side, six on the right. I write YES next to each "NO."

Is this a dangerous place?

A bicycle cab goes by. How to negotiate this place if you have a destination? I've had to, but not with much urgency. If it was urgent, I wouldn't come this way.

The light becomes increasingly illogical. An overcast dusk begins to form. Cold lamps flood the strip of pedestrianized street. The TOYS R US windows, layered with pulsing reflections, blur the distinction between inside and out, movement and stillness.

This is the City of Entropy.

Everything is animate, digital, textual, pictorial. Everything screams for attention. How can human animation compete?

"Anyone want to go to a comedy show?"

The sky darkens, the square seems brighter, the air looks dead.

A good samaritan digs in her purse for change, deposits it in Pluto's blue shoulder bag marked TIPS. "Thank you," she says with a smile, content with her keepsake for coming days of forgetfulness.

Pluto spies a couple pointing their camera at themselves at arm's length. He waves them over and puts his paw around the woman's shoulder. Tweety Bird and Smurf appear on either side, leaning their heads into hers like old friends. Picture taken, she rejoins her man to continue their walk. Pluto, Tweety and Smurf hold out their hands for TIPS. The lovers haltingly come back and drop a coin for Pluto and walk away —Nothing for Tweety and Smurf who are left holding their bags.

The sky is dark but down here it's daylight. The smell of burning flesh increases.

People hobble past in a group, some of them don't look so happy to be here.

Now there's only one woman in a headscarf at the table, a man with a beard, head uncovered, has joined her. She has two cell phones and is entering something with her thumbs. Maybe a game of solitaire.

A Chinese man photographs his parents. Behind them, a billboard news ticker:

Netanyahu warns that Iran could have nuclear weapons by next summer. They smile proudly into the lens, a triumph to have gotten themselves here —finally, a few steps further into the vortex. Puss In Boots inserts himself, puts his arm around the woman and gestures for a photo. The son takes the picture: Mother with Swashbuckling Cat. They walk further into the maelstrom followed by the cat, grinning with huge, green eyes, holding out his bag, a breeze unfurls his cape.

I think of the statement by a rich man we'll call Mr. McMittens. He once said that there are "Too many Americans." The subliminal message here calls for a kind of Darwinian (shhh) weeding out of those who are unfit to be Americans by virtue of their very parasitical dependence on the State. McMittens is not a bad guy. Not at all. He's simply trying to effectuate an economic policy, perhaps, compassionate in intent, that sifts out the obstacles to progress, hurrying along the ultimate extinction of those unfit for life in the market place, thereby benefitting the fit. He's curtailing their suffering in the long run. Think Belgian Congo in the mid-19th century. Think Kurtz.

I think of my foreign currency collection, an unintended quantity of money left in drawers and half forgotten, various denominations, much of it no longer in circulation, valueless, particularly in the Euro Zone. The Indian and Nepali Rupees are still good. Some of it, though, particularly the Indian one and two rupee bills, look more like toilet paper that's seen better days. In most other countries they would have long been taken out of circulation. This is money, faded beauty, transitory value, disintegrating paper and dirty coins.

Puss in Boots is shaking hands with Mario, counterfeits, beggars discussing finances.

8-BORDER DISPUTE

ALFRED VITALE

In the housing projects across the street where the boy genius spent his summer days, in the playground they called the batman park, there was a gang of irish kids called the budweiser gang... they were red and brutal, bullies and heroes, fighters and cowards.

and he remembers their cans of budweisers and budweiser hats and cut off jeans with tee shirts stuck in the back pocket so they all had hairless skinny chests and they all wore sneakers with white socks pulled all the way up. you don't forget the shape and size of older kids nicknamed peanut or eightball or dickie.

and these kids sat on the benches that had gray concrete chess tables in front of them and nobody bothered the gang... nobody played chess either. but bottlecaps were rubbed on the tables to make them smooth enough to flick across the ground where the chalk-drawn uneven squares of the game called "bottlecaps" were played... the metal tops would become hot from the friction, but it was an unnoticeably small pain in a big world.

there was also a small basketball court that had a rim with no net and it stood between the projects and the street that was the border of spanish harlem. the boy genius was playing there one day by himself...the red haired girl who lived in his building had been playing with him but had left to the store for an icee and a soda, which he had begged her to get for him. the soda he wanted came in a glass bottle that he would carefully place in a garbage can so that it didn't shatter.

then he heard shouts of bigger kids...coming from the direction of spanish harlem and there was a running bunch...twenty or

more…of unknown but surely puerto rican kids awkwardly bran-
dishing bent golf clubs and worn baseball bats and empty 40-ounce
bottles and rusty chains… and they ran across 96th street…that border… and towards the projects yelling. the boy genius got scared
since he stood in the basketball court into which they were heading.
he was like a hillock in the middle of a stampede… or a small boy
in the demilitarized zone between warring gangs.

a few of the golden brown horde passed by and he cringed and
shook with the slapitty-slap sounds of their pro keds flap-flopping
on the blacktop all around him… their eyes passing over him like
he wasn't there…

and he continued to be still out of fear and confusion. but then
the boy genius was grabbed by a small kid who, though small, was
still a lot bigger and older than him and he grabbed the boy genius
by the shirt and raised a miniature wooden bat up in the air and he
didn't say anything. but their eyes clashed… fear versus power.…
and the agitated warrior who wasn't sure why he was fighting knew
that he was in a moment of dominance.

the boy genius froze up tight and closed his eyes… wincing in
anticipation of the pain of a bat across his head.…

but some other puerto rican kid who was also running towards
the projects came up to the gangmember holding the boy genius
and he said, *naaa… he ain't with them.…*

and the boy genius, feeling a momentary reprieve, nervously
stuttered, *y-y-yeah.…*

and as the rest of his gangmembers ran up ahead, the kid let the
boy genius go and ran to catch up to his friends as they slithered into
the crevasse between the two tall buildings that led to the playground.

it was seconds later, when the boy genius saw the back of the
white tee-shirt worn by his captor disappear into the distant battlefield, that he heard a bottle smash… one lone bottle echoing in the
rusty red brick urban canyons… and then all those same puerto
rican kids came running back out of the projects yelling retreat
cries and moving with more speed and determination than when
they entered a minute earlier. and behind them he saw the budweisers making chase, heading towards the line of demarcation that
separated their two worlds.

then when he snapped out of the shock, the red haired girl came back and she looked at the boy genius and knew he was scared. she asked him if they bothered him and he said no no no but he didn't think she'd believe him. it must not have mattered either way to her because she shrugged and gave him the soda. they both watched the last of the budweisers chasing the other gang... back across the border.

the budweisers stopped at 96th street because they didn't go to spanish harlem...there, it would be they who would retreat from dangerous landscape of a foreign land... a foray across the border had to be planned.

but being safe in their homeland glory, they walked back to the projects smiling and waving their fists and their bats and bottles and they were slapping each other five. they marched back through the projects once again as neighbors and tenants applauded their successful defense against the germ-filled vermin from the land beyond.

the boy genius, in the drowning sound of victory that bounced through the projects, was still shaking. and he never was ever sure again where the enemy was, but he knew that the enemy is either everywhere or nowhere at all.

ROOMMATE #3
SUSAN WEIMAN

The day after Lili moved in, she burst into the kitchen to show me the diamond ring, necklace and earrings that she purchased for $12,000 with her school loan money. The woman in the store told her it was a good investment.

I hoped she could pay the rent.

THE PRISONER
NORMAN DOUGLAS

He remembers when kate told him about the cop. he remembers saying he would have to wrap his head around that one, called them morons and psychopaths carrying guns and clubs. he had to get up, get out, get some air, his stomach kept flipping, his heartbeat raced against itself. he remembers remembering to tell himself "i am everything and everything is me." he remembers wanting to forgive, needing to forgive, reminding himself not to judge. he remembers trying to make himself believe "i am a cop." he remembers thinking about how people have told him that a certain type of rat poison makes a rat want to escape, to flee for the outdoors, head for open spaces.

he remembers telling kate about his first encounter with the cops at the age of thirteen. how they pulled his mother over because she was black. two squad cars and a pick-up truck, a man in a cowboy hat carried a shotgun. "my mother was in jail because she was black. i saw her there because i was in the next cell." he remembers apologizing to her for his reaction. he never liked cops. he remembers deciding that after seven years, she didn't know him and he didn't know her, deciding that they would never know each other. he remembers he couldn't dare to say "i thought you knew me." he remembers the pressure rising inside him, as though his eyeballs or eardrums wanted to burst. he remembers grinding his teeth in order to not bite his tongue. he can't remember why he wanted to gnash at his tongue, much as he remembers that he wanted to tear at it with all his might and all his teeth. he remembers realizing that he had finally experienced what people mean when they say, "something died in me then." he remembers knowing he would never tell anyone who really knew him: how he feared they would laugh at him or wonder why he lived with someone who didn't know that he would feel his guts ripped out, kicked in the balls. he remembers wondering if she told him to make him feel inferior, to let him know she was nicer than him because she could fuck a cop and he even couldn't bear the thought of it, never mind the act — an act he was too mean and unkind to imagine.

he talks to no one. he doesn't speak to the guards. he keeps mum around the other inmates. he sits in his chair and refuses to talk to the shrink. he knows what he did and he knows he can't undo it. he still reads. he doesn't write. he reads magazines and books. he reads the letters he gets. his mother writes to him. his siblings write every now and again. he doesn't write back.

he remembers how long it took him to realize that he lived out of his element. long before he landed in prison, he had left his habitual stomping grounds far behind. he remembers meeting a young woman from california named marishka who had just come to town for a few hours to have dinner with a friend. after dinner, she planned on driving to the city. her flight had landed in the capital a few hours earlier. he remembers asking her if she had rented a car and then thinking it obvious — a dumb question — as she lived in california.

"i'll ride with you," he remembers telling her.

"what's your number?" she responded. "i'll call you after dinner."

he remembers that he stayed at the pub and pounded a few pints and bought a two-liter growler for the ride when marishka arrived, ready to drive. he remembers finishing the jug when they reached the harlem hellfighters drive two hours later and that he had had to piss in the jug because of traffic so thick and a bladder so distended that he didn't dare wait any longer.

"all they talk about in hudson is who's fucking who and famous people," he remembers complaining. "i spent my whole life in cities hanging with musicians and artists and writers who are doing something, and that's what they talk about."

"it's all self-promotion," he remembers she repeated several times as he ranted.

"artists talk about who's fucking who and famous people, too, but that's not all they talk about. they talk about what they're doing."

"self-promotion," he remembers she repeated.

"sure, it's self-promotion. why not self-promotion? promoting yourself is better than promoting famous freaks who have whole armies of promoters already."

he remembers fucking her after devouring a vegan taco. he remembers waking up and calling his ex-girlfriend whose apartment he went to for an afternoon romp in the hay. he remembers he left there to visit phoebe, who he also fucked. after midnight, he met marishka at the vegan taco stand. they drank until last call, then went back to her friend's apartment and fucked. in the morning, they screwed again and got dressed and she drove him back to hudson.

he remembers that when he got home, kate told him that she had fucked a cop while he was in the city. he remembers that he first imagined never speaking again after that. of course, he didn't stop speaking then.

he remembers that he had had his last conversation with mcsweeney, one of the second shift guards on his wing. he remembers thinking mcsweeney an idiot, the kind of idiot who not only failed to participate in democracy, but who failed to understand how integral a part the experience of spiritual connection played in its practice. he remembers thinking mcsweeney an idiot, that he could no sooner make mcsweeney understand the evidence proving representation by lot practically a done deal than he could make kate see how he felt about cops, about fucking cops. he remembers that the analogy reminded him that he had often imagined shutting up, and that just as he started to tell mcsweeney "you are an idiot," as he uttered the syllable "you," his mind caught his tongue and he never finished the sentence.

he hasn't started a sentence since.

GOING INTO HARLEM
TIM BECKETT

When I came to New York, disillusioned after a couple of years in London and the whole scale implosion of my own scene into depression and heroin addiction, I remembered my early fascination with black America. NY seemed a fundamentally BLACK city then, in a way I hadn't expected. Black people seemed to be the ones that kept the city running, driving the busses, the subway trains, drilling the roads, manning the crosswalks. There was no denying the divisions between black and white: the panhandlers and hustlers hanging out around the edges of mid-town Manhattan were almost all black, as were the homeless, who inhabited every fourth doorway when night fell, or camped out on every bench in the parks. I didn't try to figure this out, or even judge it — I'd expected to find segregation in America and, since I was just a visitor, it wasn't my system to change. I felt that in a city like New York, you had to accept this injustice, otherwise it would drive you a little insane.

In the first couple weeks, I rarely strayed beyond the predictable confines of lower to mid-town Manhattan. There was enough to see, enough that was new. Yet after I'd walked all over lower Manhattan, I began to get impatient. It wasn't that these neighborhoods didn't have their attractions, but they reminded me too much of neighborhoods in other cities. Standing in the Village, you could be in Montreal's Plateau, or Camden Town in London. I had a traveler's desire to see something different, to get at the root of the spectacular energy I felt flowing through the city like an electrical charge. Black culture was part of the other America you didn't hear much about outside the country, the flipside of Reagan's whitey cowboy myth, so distant from America's official version of itself it was hard to believe they were part of the same country.

I wondered too if black neighborhoods would display the same overbearing patriotism as neighborhoods in other parts of the city: flags hanging from the doorways, the yellow ribbons, the 'Support Our Troops' adorning store and apartment windows throughout the city. I wondered what they thought about the war, about the country that had treated them so badly, but of which they were so much a part.

I didn't even take the A train, but rather the F to Times Square, changing to the 1. The train shot out of the tunnel into a long stretch of elevated tracks, and blocks of industrial streets, those big blocky east. Then back in the tunnel again, I got out at 157th, choosing the stop almost at random. My plan was to walk down Broadway, see where it went and how the streets felt, then cut through the heart of the neighborhood to 125th.

Outside, the street was only marginally more shabby than the streets in the LES. Bodegas, fruit stalls, check-cashing shops, Chinese take-out places behind bulletproof glass, old men playing dominoes on fold-out tables on the street. The neighborhood looked much older than other parts of the city — the marble-lined stations looked like they hadn't been cleaned since the '50s, and the iron trellises and the clatter of the trains overhead were like something out of an old newsreel. The sound of Spanish, the merengue music made the scene seem a little odd, as if one newsreel had been imposed on the other, yet I had no great interest in Spanish NY. I didn't speak the language, and had never experienced Spanish culture in any meaningful way beyond what remained of the old Puerto Rican Lower East Side. So, at 145th, I turned east.

145th sloped down to a junction behind which was a set of massive housing projects, the same brick colossi I'd seen out the train window, that rose like enormous brick tombstones all across the city. Ten huge buildings clustered together, lower floor windows guarded by iron bars, brick faces covered with squiggles of graffiti. But the projects weren't what made the neighborhood truly striking. Around the projects was a sea of empty buildings. Once, they must have been typical NY tenements, the kind that covered the LES. You could still see the factory pressed moldings over the windows, the fire escapes hanging off the fronts, the stoops in front of the doors, but in every other respect they were empty, with neither roofs nor windows. Behind the empty window frames was a mess of structural beams, piles of rubble and brick, clusters of weeds, and in-between the buildings vacant lots filled with trash, with vehicles stripped down to their frames, with girders and pieces of machinery.

I'd never seen such desolation, not even in the worst parts of London. From the top of the road, the ruin stretched on in either direction as far as the eye could see, maybe forty blocks in all, and in the dusky late afternoon light it looked just like black and white footage of 1945 Berlin.

I had yet to discover in a direct, personal sense how dangerous America could be, and I'd walked through, even lived in, some pretty bleak areas of London, where whole wings of the sprawling housing estates that dominate areas of the city had been abandoned, then gutted, or taken over by junkies. I didn't think this area would be that much different, even if the desolation was much more total. A line of cars descended the hill, bumper to bumper, veering north at the junction. Cars meant I would never be out of sight, and despite the emptiness, the area didn't give off any overt sense of menace or danger. Surely, it was at least partly arrogance that made me think I'd be safe, some still active thread of my British identity that allowed me to believe that I had the right to travel where I wanted. The trick was never to show fear. You could feel fear, but never show it. Never meet anyone's gaze for long, always walk like you know where you're going, stay relaxed. I had a trick I used walking through an area I wasn't sure about: as I walked, I became conscious of my breath; simultaneously self-aware and taking in everything around me. This trick had got me through some potentially bad situations in England; I thought it could work in NY.

As I descended the hill, building facades stared down from either side of the street like the false fronts of a movie set. Eerie, yet not as disturbing as I thought they'd be from a distance. Partly it was the kids. At the bottom of the junction, what looked like hundreds of kids were running screaming jumping through the concrete playgrounds between the projects, their cries echoing off the empty buildings like the echo of distant traffic. The area seemed almost peaceful, with the kids, the strange buildings, the line of bumper lights blinking in double lines down the hill then suddenly a woman shot out from behind one of the buildings in front of me. I watched her run between the tail-lights, down the opposite pavement. She looked like a doll, not quite human: her head flopped loosely on her shoulders, and arms and legs flailed about as she ran down the pavement. When she disappeared into the only open store on the whole block, a yellow bodega facing the projects, I turned to look where she'd come from. A half-dozen men and women huddled together beneath an empty doorway. As soon as they saw me, they began to gesticulate incoherently. A woman called out: "Yo, honey, I got some fine dust, you be wantin' some of this!" I let my eyes rest on them for a minute. They were inching towards me as a group, stumbling over each other, seeming to beckon all at once. They looked worse than any heroin junkies I'd ever seen. Hollow eyes, rail thin bodies, twisted limbs. Dark mouths with many missing teeth. The women looked especially bad, just a couple of steps removed from death. Yet they seemed too helpless to be threatening. A tall, bearded man edged out in front of the others, taking control, like he was their leader. Smiling ever so slightly as he made eye contact, his eyes registering neither hostility nor disapproval, just a detached perplexity at my presence. When I waved the group off, he nodded and turned away, and the group turned with him, retreating back into their circle and forgetting all about me.

Other than this ragged group, I didn't see anyone on the street or in the buildings: the whole area appeared to be deserted. As I approached the junction, the noise made by the children playing down in the projects became almost deafening, their cries echoing about the hollow buildings so it seemed like the children had expanded beyond the line of corrugated fencing separating the projects from the street below, to inhabit the empty streets and buildings, jumping around in the rubble and the weeds. Their bright colored clothing, the exuberance with which they chased each other around the iron playgrounds, seemed almost unreal amidst the context, as if they'd poured through a tear from another dimension, as if their energy was a protest at the desolation all around them.

At the junction I turned south, following the traffic bumping along the potholed road to Manhattan. To the north were more projects, one after the other, looming over the ruined tenements like a single brick wall. A bus appeared out of the haze at the very top of the street and I figured it might be a good time to get out of the neighborhood. The sky was turning dark grey: another hour and it would be dark. Though I didn't feel any particular sense of danger, the area had a strong feeling of emptiness and negation, as if the very life had been sucked right out of it, and I wasn't sure what it would be like after dark. Yet I felt curiously thrilled to be at the ruin's centre, like I'd suddenly found myself on the surface of another planet, or at the bottom of the ocean. Across the street the kids played on, oblivious to both me and the empty buildings. Their playground, I saw now, was enclosed by a ten foot wire fence, with no obvious means to get in or out. I wondered if they ever came across the street and wandered the empty streets, how much they even saw of the area, how they explained both the abandoned buildings and the crackheads who lived in their shadows to themselves and each other. What they felt each time they looked out their project windows onto the spectacular ruin spreading out below.

The street was empty but for a dozen or so teenagers sitting or standing on the steps of an empty tenement. The doorway had been walled off with cinder blocks, but the windows were empty, so anyone who wanted to could crawl in or out. A boom box sitting on the steps blared out the siren call of rap. Rap was only half-familiar to me then, and it sounded sinister in the context of the empty neighborhood, the grey New York air. I took the teenagers in without looking at them directly. Maybe half were dancing along to the beat, or rapping to the lyrics, enunciating every word. The dancing was reflexive, almost jerky, unlike any dancing I'd ever seen. They seemed to pay no attention to me until I was right beside them, then a big guy who had been dancing with the most urgency took a swing at me, his fist stepping a few inches from my head. For the first time since I'd descended the hill, I realized I had no plan for dealing with aggression, and didn't know what I'd do if the big guy and his friends decided to come after me. I wasn't sure I'd even know how to counter their aggression, since I had no real explanation of what

I was doing in their neighborhood. It wasn't like I had white guilt: in those early NY days, I didn't even see myself as part of the dynamic, and I knew from experience that being a foreigner offered some protection. Yet I was also aware that, foreigner or not, I could easily disappear into those empty buildings, that in this desolate place, it could be easy to suddenly cease to exist.

Yet basically I knew the kid was just testing me. I managed not to flinch or change expression, as if the guy and his sudden lunge at my head had hardly registered in my consciousness. As I continued walking down the street, I heard him dance away behind me, his feet shuffling over the uneven pavement until he'd rejoined his friends on the stoop.

At the bus stop, I leaned against the pole to wait. Early evening gloom hung like parchment over the street. I'd been walking for a couple of hours: I was getting tired and didn't want to be in an area like this unless I was on top of myself. If I'd shown fear when the guy lunged at me, I wasn't sure what might have happened. Maybe he would have laughed, mocking me, or maybe it would have become more serious. I didn't know. I looked back up the street. The teenagers were still hanging around the stoop, talking, making time, the girls looking down at the boys, the boys looking up at the girls. They had nice clothes, not quite designer — designer clothes hadn't hit mass market yet — but they dressed like a lot of black kids did in NY at the time, with an easy style, colors fitting well together, their outfits put together with some consideration. As discreetly as I could, I examined their faces. They didn't even look that hard, and if someone had reframed them, cutting out the empty buildings, the prison-like projects, I would never have guessed they lived in some of the worst desolation in the Western World. I wondered if I could ever find a way into the lives of people who lived in places like this, the other America that foreigners heard about only intermittently, that was all the more fascinating for official America's attempts to conceal it. Standing at the bus stop, I truly felt that I'd arrived in a foreign country, as distant and hard to understand as countries in North Africa or Asia, where the decay was just as awe-inspiring and grandiose as the energy and wealth just a few blocks to the south.

A blue and white bus appeared in the haze at the top of the street like an emissary from another world, jogged up and down by the colossal potholes. Soon I was back amidst the lights and the movement of midtown, the darkness behind me.

RADEN IN WOODHEAVEN

BART PLANTENGA

[Furman Pivo believes he (plus beer) may be the
cause of a rash of streetlight outages. This sense
of empowerment transforms him into the Beer
Mystic, a man with a mission. Or something else?
In any case, 1987 NYC will never be the same and
the rest is history or myth or delusion. *The Beer
Mystic* can be found circumnavigating the world
via the Beer Mystic Global Pub Crawl <http://bar-
tyodel3.wordpress.com>.]

L ight gives off heat in the middle of nowhere. Laws of thermodynamics or something. Light, like most humans and pro-
jectiles and everything else, has to abide by these laws of
thermodynamics. Witness this phenomenon — I do — through despair. Watch and feel the hail, the grumble of aircraft moving
clumps of people nowhere fast, through Shoetown, past Bed City,
Balls'n'Brew, Mensworld, Liquor Land, and Sofasphere — anywhere — nothing in every direction, the difference between
nowhere and somewhere is almost imperceptible. No shooting stars.
No leaves clinging to lifeless twigs. Garbage bags that resemble
spouses, heaved into the grimy shimmer of gas and oil suspended
on dark water on Queens Boulevard. The anger unmeasured, the
frustration quantified only by the distance of the bag's toss. I am
pre-beer, a state before the gears begin to gilga mesh. What lonely
hours.... Frail radio voice like cigarette ash in a movie theatre showing a film about a man who leaves home to search for his soul only
to find a map that leads back to his own address.

I'm in Woodheaven, Queens, home to a flingthing (my word for her at work, which disguises the actual depth of my feelings), Raden Adjeng Kartini, who's unaware of how much lust I've already infused into her image.

I've come all this way from somewhere to this nowhere in pursuit of the something I think Raden could be. Or the something I need her to be. To walk her home, to lean the amorous shadow (with some of me attached to it) into her. Whenever I see her, my body begins to quiver, lose density, and consciousness begins to blend with outer space. I need to sit down, grip a signpost. She is beautiful and that tears reality from limbs, bones collapse inside skin. I open my beer — TSssh — a wet mantra, its spray first inhaled via my nostrils… and suddenly I am calm. And I need that because Raden — her imperturbable serenity — is the destroyer of all surrounding cool and calm. A destabilizer. I crumble before her smile. I have come to discover why but depart as mystified as ever. But if I show you her picture you will understand except for the fact that this sole Polaroid SX–70 of her is out of focus "because her stable mysterious core / gives me the shakes / & three beers lead to four" (lyrics that would later get sung by my ex in CBGB's a year later in a Battle of the Unsigned Bands in which her band, The White Bicycles, finished last and the band blamed the lyrics.)

Raden's existence was basically circumscribed by homework worries, midterms, college, post-punk concert tickets, snags in her fishnets — and taking care of a mother afflicted with the early symptoms of ALS.

Tonight she told me she was named for the Javanese rebel princess who introduced education to Indonesian girls — a hero. But did my *petite amourette* know that I heard every word but not a one of them registered and did she know how awestruck I was by how easily she handled the extreme amount of beauty that was crammed into her small (4'6") frame? Did she know that when I watched her mouth speak I was mesmerized beyond all comprehension? The fact that she was ten [or maybe eight] years my junior and a good foot-and-a-half shorter made her look like my adopted daughter? Did she know how much I admired her clarity of vision, her brazen modesty, her ability to describe the limitless [and charmed] horizons she and only she seemed to see in all directions? Did she know that I repeated her name over and over — Raden Ra-den — as I walked past Louie's Leftover Lounge, to the F subway entrance? After having escorted her all the way home from my East Village to her Queens, sometimes to kiss as far as kisses would take us — in Flushing Meadow Park in among the rushes? We had found our painting — a Monet — a state of mind, damp pant knees, open green where we wandered for days around the lake. Did she know that when I masturbated it was to the image of her lunar face and her strategic choice of hem length?

But what did Raden then know of the look of failure, the odor of despair that I so ingeniously disguised with pheromones and braggadocio, marginal zines that featured my scribblings, my radio show "Birra Birra Birra" on XYZNO Radio FM, a station that may or may not have existed?

I helped her study for the written part of her driver's license exam & fill out her applications to Cornell. She being so amazingly gracious as to make me believe I was helpful in filling them out — *that* is love. I resisted ever saying "some day you'll see." I tried to write poetry to let her know how she had thumb-tacked an emotional impressionist landscape to the wall of an essential chamber in my heart.

I was awed by how she knew at umpteen (fifteen or sixteen?) that she would some day be an architect designing what she called "Zen Bauhaus." And that I only acted like I knew of what she spoke when she described "urban bowers with endless horizons." All this enamored me to her to the point of absolute disappearance.

(Raden Adjeng Kartini said of Pivo: "What does he look like? Keith Haring. Maybe, not exactly. More like something caught between James Dean scratching his head and a junior librarian who spends too much time slouched in the front row in an old movie house. Sometimes when he stood in front of me it was like he was standing in front of the spin cycle of a washer. Totally mesmerized. He loved me and I him but then he disappeared like a genie back into his bottle. Like my Joey Ramone back into his record sleeve. He could have been a lot more than he was afraid of becoming.

The more I tried to tell him the more he went into retreat. Something spooked him away from me. Maybe it was that I was totally serious, never played games, and told him that I knew what 'forever' was and that I was ready for it. That I understood forever and embodied it. He may have said 'But I'm only twenty-four.' To which I said 'but I'm only sixteen.'")

She is now home and I'm on the street reaching for another brew I carry in my knapsack for emergencies. That was the night that mist sizzled around the lamphead like the cosmos was whispering around my neck at 130-Whatever Street and 70-Whatever Avenue: nowhere. And you ask for directions to the subway around here, you ask for trouble because the same numbered streets can lead you to three places in Queens, somewhere in the Bronx and two in Brooklyn. I was even beginning to doubt that she actually loved me — what does a young teen know about love? Did she know that *"raden"* in Dutch means to guess? — when suddenly the streetlight right above me went out — POOF! — like someone had shot it out with a silencer-muffled pistol shot, just as I walked under it. Burnt out. Gone. Black, like an exhalation of light, like a mulberry shaken loose to fall in the dust, like the last memory of a dying man. A song I am now hearing that my father used to sing along to with Peggy Lee: *When you're alone, who cares for starlit skies...* He's dead. *Is my timing that flawed our respect run so dry? ... duhduh dudud duuh... that we've kept through our lives.* I will place needle upon vinyl and spin Joy Division for the 1001st time when I get home. There is a relation between Peggy Lee and Ian Curtis but I'm not going to try to explain what that is.

As I looked up at the dead eye of the burnt-out streetlight, with insomnia wringing soul from light, I felt my body suddenly begin to sway as it processed the lifetime of accumulated poisons, all the delirious chemicals, all the inarticulate yearning inside me. And then suddenly, out of nowhere and everywhere, my body jolted forward and it ejected all solid matter in the soul's effort to tear loose from all of its moorings, sending me floating like a balloon relieved of its ballast, all the bile and tenacious body matter clinging to the miles of intestine, everything vile, glistening, and parasitic. The head suddenly free of all pain; I was clean, sharp, lean.

Free as a glowing asteroid, free as the last funk flicked off the end of Chet Baker's last cigarette.

And too much drinking had become precisely the right amount. I'm a knife cutting through all the coagulated din, clogs of trivia, clumps of hairy cat vomit with a precise clarity beyond inebriation, where you become a function of the dream river, the rock in the stream that turns water into foam and beer into inspiration.

I'm kneeling there — picture it — in nowhere Woodheaven, whistling, repeating "Dog-beer-light" (not a Captain Beefheart lyric) over and over, washing vomit off my shirt in a puddle that holds the reflection of an azure moon (the way a cameo holds the ghostly profile of a loved one) in a pothole, really a crater so immense that — boom! — when a truck hits it, things fall off. And the scavengers who tend the contours of this pothole-cum-trap emerge from their abandoned warehouse stakeouts and lean-tos, arriving before the BOOM has even had a chance to vacate our tympanic bones.

But when they see me kneeling there, by their roadway snare, where they collect the dislodged products [everything from crates of papayas to household appliances] to resell in the itinerant markets around town they figure I'm an interloper homing in on their loot. I can sense them plotting my demise with various kitchen gadgets. Their eyes dark and untouchable like the dephs of an abandoned mine or the stares of office functionaries made redundant by CEO employment policy adjustments in reaction to October 19 events, when stock markets in NYC and worldwide plummeted to lose 25% of their value overnight, a day that would later be dubbed "Black Monday."

I am running and suddenly I am airborne like a scene you won't see in "Mary Poppins," and I have, understandably, stopped looking for the subway entrance.

NORA AT 13

LARISSA SHMAILO

J oey was playing Suzanne. She stopped often to tune her guitar and puff on her cigarette, which she kept in the neck frets of her guitar and carefully repositioned after each drag. This made for frequent interruptions, but Nora sang with feeling anyway as leaf shadows danced across Joey's face. When Joey grew tired of playing, she surrendered the guitar to Nora, who played A minor chords.

A tall boy in a fringed jacket with a flag on the back approached the pier. Nora looked away and sang louder as the boy listened. As she started to strum the minor chords for The Cruel War, the boy cleared his throat.

"Can I hold your guitar?" he asked politely. Joey and the boy passed the guitar back and forth, playing Beatles songs, blues riffs, and anything else they knew. Red-faced, Nora sat next to the boy, singing too loud. She didn't want to seem desperate, like her friends from Queens. If one of her girlfriends from Queens so much as talked with a boy, Nora heard about it for weeks afterward. They sifted and sifted through casual, unimportant conversations that clearly meant nothing, nothing at all to the boy: "Then he smiled, and I think he thought I meant I liked him... What do you think he meant when he said his school was nearby? Do you think he likes me?" Dee Ann Distefano called every Miller in Queens to hunt down a boy she talked to once; when she and Nora finally got her boy on the line, Dee Ann got scared and hung up.

Girls from Queens were bores. Girls from Queens were awkward and shy. Girls from Queens were vulgar and loud. Girls from Queens wore their sweaters too tight, wore too much makeup, wore the wrong kind of pants, their faces were zitty, and their tits were too big. Girls from Queens turned out like their mothers.

Some boys in a rowboat were calling to the boy in the fringed jacket. Nora watched the long-haired boys stand straight up in the rowboats, then belly flop into the lime green algae. The boy in the fringed jacket explained to Joey that his friends had dropped acid cut with speed. He lit a thick joint and offered it to Nora, who coughed until her face turned red. Joey politely interrupted a story about Eric Clapton to wait for Nora to finish coughing.

Embarrassed, Nora ran to the lake and threw herself into the water fully dressed. She heard applause and hoots behind her. She swam, cold and embarrassed, thinking, I have a pretty face, prettier than Joey but I am fat and my breasts flop in my wet shirt. I am embarrassed: it is too much to throw yourself into the water dressed in Central Park, it isn't hot enough in May and my jeans and shirt and shoes take too long to dry.

A QUEENS WOMAN
MIKE TOPP

The Sopranos," where Andrea Donna de Matteo's character is living with mob figure Christopher Moltisanti, amidst the *palazzos* of New Jersey and the cabanas of Cape May, yields in actuality a rather dead end to any civilian wishing to duplicate their frustrated actuality.

How touching Andrea is in one particular episode, when she confesses her cooperation with the FBI to Christopher, actually filmed at the Silver Cup Studios in Long Island City, New York. The store lights call out. Dress Barn. CVS. Talbott's. Chuck E. Cheese. Ruby Tuesday.

We see her crawling on her hands and knees, begging Silvio for mercy before he shoots her in the woods of New Jersey. A delightful place for camping in summer as well as in winter. Recreational vehicles welcome. Long-term parking.

THE LAST GOOD YEAR
RAY JICHA

The house felt like Christmas, at least that's all young Louie Laszlo could think to compare it to. Mama made a special dinner, cleaned the house more thoroughly than her nurse's job usually allowed, and lit the scented candles. All of this was unprecedented for a midsummer's eve, but in his trusting youth Louie had no reason to more than note the novelty of it all. He was fed but the fancy stuff stayed in the oven warming.

At nine years old Louie had at last mastered all of the boyish arts: bike riding, ball throwing, tree climbing, baiting the hook. There in that quaint, prosperous Hudson valley town he lived a Sawyeresque life tramping the woods and fields with his mates while the tests of classroom and playground passed as easily as a bag of plums. He could not have known this would be the last good year.

It was 1973. Vietnam was winding down, Watergate was heating up, and though no one knew it yet, this year would bring the end of the great postwar economic expansion that the United States had enjoyed for most of the last three decades. Louie's experience mirrored the larger turn, and Mama's choices had as much to do with it, but in the end Louie blamed it on the place.

He was ready for bed when the doorbell rang. Mama opened the door slowly and wide like when Willy Wonka first takes the children into the room of the Chocolate River, full of wonderment and import. At the bottom of the steps stood a handsome man, old like Mama, with a smile like a box of candy. She ushered him in warmly and they took a moment for each other before turning to acknowledge the boy.

"Louie, this is Art Dempsey. The man I was married to before your father."

Events moved quickly after that. The lovers exchanged a series of visits between New York and Art's South Carolina home. These required frequent rides down to JFK and Newark to pick up or drop off whoever was on the move. Each trip was couched in the terror that a missed highway exchange would leave them trapped in the city at night, lost and at the mercy of swarming gangs of cannibal zombies that lived only to prey upon decent folk.

Louie quickly fell in love with Art, he liked to roughhouse and kid around, and his good grooming and two-way radio lent him an aura of sophistication that his own father, Big Lou, decidedly lacked. Even when he caught them fucking, barging in one Saturday morning with his usual Sugar Smack-fueled salutations, he quickly forgave Art the atrocity. When Mama sat Louie down and told him they'd be moving to South Carolina at the end of the year he was all for it but she warned him Daddy wouldn't like it. She got that right.

Big Lou fought a bitter rearguard action from his bunker in Cleveland. "You know the cops still use dogs down there." Louie had no idea what he was referring to. Big Lou's true fear lay in the thought that Art would adopt Louie and change his name. Louie was the only son of an only son. The Laszlo line hung by spider's silk.

"What'ya gonna call him?"

"Art, I guess."

"What'ya mean, 'you guess'?"

Summer turned to fall and an excitement set in as vivid as the maples in his front yard. The time between times, after one decides to leave but has not yet left, would be the time Louie grew to love the most. A host of unusual activities marked the period. There was a garage sale and a great sorting of things. Grandma came through on a pilgrimage to the Holy Land prior to her gall bladder operation. That meant another ride to JFK. Wheeling by Shea stadium Louie remembered catching the Mets and Phillies on a daytrip from camp. He didn't think the city was so bad.

Grandma had barely landed in Beirut when the Egyptians breached the Bar Lev line and the Yom Kippur War brought the

U.S. and Soviet Union into their most direct confrontation since 1962. The borders were closed. She spent a week on air-raid alert at the Beirut hotel before getting evacuated to Cyprus, then home. She survived the operation but never made it to the Promised Land.

The day after Thanksgiving they pulled out and left Rhinebeck behind with Art driving the U-Haul and Louie in the Impala with Mama and the cat. Two days down I-95 is enough to sap anyone's thirst for travel. By the time they pulled into Point Arcadia, the still unfinished condominium complex they now called home, Louie had stopped caring where they were going.

Columbia, South Carolina sits on a desolate strip of sand hills that stretches from Fayetteville to Macon. The poor soil supports only the most spindly and stunted species of tree: certainly nothing worth climbing. The nearest city with a ball team was Atlanta and the Braves sucked. The new school looked like a fallout shelter. They didn't have art or music or even a gym. None of that registered right away as Louie got settled into his new life but as 1974 wore on it became clear even to him that something terrible had happened.

Art had spent freely during the courtship and Mama said with the money he made as a radio ad exec she could stay home and keep the nice house she always imagined. That lasted about six weeks; then the bills came due and Mama went back to work, making half what she had in New York. At the June wedding in the big house of one of Art's clients Louie gave Mama away. She became a Dempsey. He remained a Laszlo.

Big Lou came for his first visit as they left for their honeymoon. Art hit him up for a loan just before he and Mama drove away. Other than that he liked what he saw, especially the pool, where friendly college girls home on break would say, "Hey!" as they walked by in their bikinis just as sweet as you please.

They stayed close to home that week. Lines at the gas station had gotten long. The Arab oil embargo imposed for U.S. support of Israel in the late war pushed crude from $3 to $12 a barrel overnight and government missteps in response only made things worse. Louie added it to the differences he started to notice about his new home.

"They didn't have gas lines in New York."

Art and Mama came back from Myrtle Beach arguing. Mama found out Art hadn't made a sale in months. With the recession that followed the oil shock no one was buying ad time. Then Mama started to wonder what he was doing on all those business trips to Atlanta. Turned out it was his ex-wife - his other ex-wife. He split rather than deal. Nixon resigned the next day. Louie cried. Everything was falling apart.

Fifth grade started and something had changed. The girls had grown taller and a creeping awkwardness had turned him from a masterful boy into a goof. Things got tougher at home too. The price of meat was on everyone's lips. People went from steak to hamburger to chicken to tuna and still couldn't make ends meet; Louie thought they were saying, "ends meat." He figured the slice at the end of the roast was the best one and that's what they meant.

The condos hollowed out into a Potemkin grotesquery. Only a couple dozen units remained occupied as jobs were lost, debts came due, and homes broke apart. Of the neighbor kids with whom Louie roamed the empty cul-de-sacs none had two parents at home.

Winter came early to South Carolina that year and it gets colder down south than most Yankees know. Louie and Mama huddled near the space heater in the kitchen of the condo they could no longer afford. Saddled with a mortgage, her credit ruined by Art's profligacy, her nursing career derailed, Mama tightened belts until Louie howled.

"Hamburger Helper or tuna tonight?"

"I hate it here!"

But the table had already been set.

"DO WIDZENIA GREENPOINT"
GENNA RIVIECCIO

I embarked for Greenpoint in the pre-Lena Dunham era (more on that bitch in a second). And while my time there amounted to no more than a year or so, it was one of the most impacting epochs of my New York existence. It was where my formative slut years began, and later became tainted by Lena Dunham making a show about *my* life that people would call "so real" when, in fact, it is the most forced, gross misrepresentation quite possibly ever rendered to TV. Thank god I got out before she infiltrated; it would have completely corrupted any form of veracity to my nightly sexual hijinks. In my day, the only TV show that got to use Greenpoint as its own Hollywood lot was "The Good Wife." And, speaking of Hollywood lots, the ghost of Mae West has been known to appear now and again on Franklin Avenue, the street she grew up on. But she and I never tangoed.

Veronica Peoples, a coffee shop/performance space by my apartment where I once saw Zebra Katz sing "Hipster" (sometimes referred to as "Hipster on the L Train") is now gone. Blackout, the only gay bar in Greenpoint, has vanished—though I'll always remember having loveless sex in the bathroom there one night and then walking home to meet up with my roommate casually, as though I hadn't just lost yet another shred of dignity. Coco 66, a paradise for the drug-addled and drug craving, had to become sanitized, replaced by a Williamsburg bar called Tender Trap. Even Lulu's, formerly Lost & Found, one of the few alcoholic outposts left in New York where you could get a whole pizza with the purchase of one drink, has been forced out. And perhaps worst of all,

Photoplay, possibly the last place in all of Brooklyn to rent a tangible movie, has faded to black.

Do you have any idea what it's like to know that "Girls" episode commentary features Lena Dunham sitting in Matchless, my bar, where I used to relish the simultaneous consumption of mac and cheese and calamari (now since taken off the menu) when I was drunk off my face while harassing a bartender named Brian who probably thought I was into him, but really it was my friend? No, I'm sure you don't. You're probably one of the people who moved to Greenpoint *because of "Girls,"* ergo you can never understand what it was really like before.

Well let me tell you: it was a haven for the unemployed to stroll leisurely through the streets, peppered with Polish storefronts and restaurants that are quickly being eked out by places like Torst, a "hip wood-clad Danish bar" that celebrities such as Julian Casablancas frequent. Now, everywhere I turn, something is gone or altered. How can I possibly hold on to all of the memories that Greenpoint once held if its entire facade is vanquished by expensive commercial rent and a collective need for niche thrift stores like People of 2Morrow? I'll never go back. It's not like it's easily accessible anyway, what with the G train being the one constant in its shittiness amid the juggernaut of gentrification.

The continued potential for all traces of the Greenpoint I knew to perish completely becomes more concrete with each passing day. Soon, I fear, there will only be *one* RiteAid instead of two right next to each other on Manhattan Avenue — and you know the one that looks like a disco roller rink on the inside is going to be the first to go. The final vestiges of affordable shopping, like Dollar Up right across the street from the Dunkin' Donuts at that corner where all traces of Williamsburg finally dissipate, will also fall, and then where am I supposed to buy my fake flowers and holographic pictures of Jesus?

No, this cannot be. This is all the fault of Dunham, I swear it. Her with her rich parents and therefore the ability to have a chance at "making art" on the sacrificial altar of Greenpoint is the entire reason for its demise. I had my own TV series written before her, goddammit, I just didn't have the funding to get it off the ground like she did. It should have been me who ruined this portion of North Brooklyn for everyone else, not her. Now I just have to stand by idly and watch her take the last establishment that meant anything to me by invariably including a cameo by Paulie Gee in a forthcoming episode.

HERE WAS A BODEGA BUT NOW (A BEDFORD STUYVESANT MISSED CONNECTION)

AIMEE HERMAN

You tell her to go back to Wisconsin,
because they seem to be coming from somewhere
and at the time, it was the only state you could think of

you are tired of unintelligible fonts reminding you
of a new place opening up selling fair trade by fair skinned
when it's just as easy to boil water and make it yourself

the Grey Lady called it Brooklyn's Harlem, but now
there is a shop around the corner selling soaps made from
farmers market produce and you fear for the day Biggie's mural
will be replaced by a collection of hashtags

you are tired of that '*g*' word tattooed on tongues as though it offers
permission for all this construction —
the gutting of local through corporate stampede

your neighbor, Crown Heights, calls you up on a Sunday, weeping
we thought we had more time
you do not understand until you hear it plainly: *Starbucks*

you scream at her when she walks her dog, whose fur and snout
would have been cute two decades ago, but now
they both just represent all the ways your home has been removed

DARK CITY   ERIK LA PRADE

THE L
BRADLEY SPINELLI

I call over to Jamie's to see what she's up to, and her roommate tells me that she's gone up to Pete's Candy Store to meet Everett and his new girlfriend for a drink. Olive is at work, and I've been meaning to check out the new bar, so I walk over to Lorimer and duck in. Everett and his girlfriend have just gone, so I chat with Jamie for a few uncomfortable minutes until she leaves.

It's been weird with her for some time now. She thinks that I go back and forth between behaving angelically towards her and basically being a prick. I think that she wants to fuck me but keeps coming up with reasons why she shouldn't, and she's so overly analytical in her neurotic intellectualizing about everything that talking about it is basically bullshit. It doesn't seem to matter that I'm not planning on fucking her anyway, despite our little intrigue with Olive over the summer. Olive thinks I still have a crush on her, which makes it weird all around.

Pete's looks like a seedy old metal shop that has been transformed into a bar, with a layout that could almost be a shotgun apartment if it weren't for the odd L-shaped room that seems to spell the architect's plan for a kitchen. I move to the back room and catch about three and a half minutes of a cheesy band — two guys noodling on guitars while a drummer taps along to a different beat on a snare and a ride. I suck a couple slugs of bourbon from my flask and go back to the front room and sit at a table alone with my beer.

I notice Smith at the bar and realize I haven't seen him since Dizzy exited. He always looks a little dirty, always in a black leather vest over a dingy T-shirt, with his unkempt goatee and his unruly red hair, but tonight he looks even more disheveled, stains on his trousers and on the once-white long-underwear shirt under his vest. His eyes seem unfocused, and I want to ascribe it to drunkenness, but I know that this man has beaten the pants off me at pool with more belts under him than I could even endure.

I'm draining the last of my beer and wondering where to go next when I see Smith putting on his coat. He's in the middle of the bar and he has to nudge a few people out of the way, slipping into a black motorcycle jacket. He looks to the bartender with a nod of thanks, stumbles through the crowd to the door, pushes it open, steps out, reaches into his jacket, pulls out a small handgun, puts the barrel into his mouth, pulls the trigger, and blows out the back of his head as the door closes behind him, the bullet shattering the top of the door glass, covering everyone close by with glass snowflakes. Smith's body slumps back into the red-stained remains of the door into a seated position on the sidewalk.

Screams peal through the air, people duck, people lie on the floor, expecting more shots, and a gentle snow of plaster falls serenely from the ceiling, exposing the bullet's final resting place. The people in the front room try to move to the back room, and the people in the back room, wondering what's going on, try to move to the front room. The bar is a chaotic conundrum of nervous, frightened energy with no destination and no outlet. The bartender picks up the phone to call the cops, and I stand up, brushing glass from my leather jacket, and pull the door handle.

But, per fire code, the door opens out. I try to shove it but Smith is firmly planted, and when I try again three people pull me away.

"Wait for the police."

"An ambulance is coming, you might kill him if you move the body."

I snap, "He's dead already, sweetheart, don't fool yourself."

The bottom half of the glass door is a candy-apple waterfall seen from behind, a black smudge of life on a glass slide. All that remains of Smith is a cirrhotic liver and a black leather jacket, a final fingerprint on the trigger of a gun.

I can't make a break for it with all the fuss and worry, and I catch a couple of threats that I don't want to cash in on, so I sit there for an hour looking at the inside of the back of Smith's head, waiting for the cops to come and let us all out. It's the first gun I've seen in New York, and only the second gunshot I've heard. I remember the warnings from people — friends, strangers — when I announced I was moving here, words of caution about how dangerous New York really is, and how I secretly fantasized about getting mugged or beat up in a bad neighborhood, caught on the business end of a Saturday night special, and I can't believe that my closest encounter with a gun was watching a veritable demigod of pool — an amazing shot — take himself out of the game.

THE FALLOUT OF DREAMS
STEVE DALACHINSKY

I came from a clean neighborhood in the city of brooklyn. there were trees. a bridal path. a bike path. the big scary cemetery. the touch football & dead-end street, stoopball & potsie. the movie house, butchershop, bakery & barber shop. ringolevio & hide-&-seek. dominic's shoe repair, the toy store, clothes shop, candy store, deli & pizza place. girls. the schoolyard. the pool hall (where i eventually bought my first hard drugs). my dog. my cat. hard drugs. the cigarettes hidden in an old tire in the garage. girls. sex. hard drugs. & more, much more.

it was almost small town america except that Brooklyn was special like hot dogs & the dodgers in ebbets field (who sadly betrayed us by moving to l.a.) but i was always a yankees fan for which i caught lots of flack.

when the day ended i went home, ate supper, took a bath & watched t.v......

1.

war dream

a. i found myself on the ground floor in a small room of a big blding in short sleeves with a white rabbit sleeping under the bed. the quilt was a faded grey patchwork. outside the garbage cans stood in a perfect line just as i had left them. all 7 were empty. i was left with only my self to face. the day was a sad haiku.

b. got fked over then fked over again. stepped on. trashed. dol-

lared. once for the hell of it then for the helluvit. flowed over. limbs
cut. brains blown out. air flow improved. ghosts hiding in old shoes.

2.

summer: we took a trolley to the beach. the hot eye of the sun
looked down as mom dished out the lettuce & tomato sandwiches.
i ate quietly with the waves between my ears,
     sand between the bread & crackling between my teeth (so this
was what a *sand*-wich really was.)
     there were no cherry trees in brooklyn except the one in my
backyard. i climbed it for comfort, refuge & protection. i put my
hands in my lap & swallowed the cherry pits, waiting for a tree to
grow inside me. this was the age of the atom & every atom of my
fiber tried not to think of mushroom clouds. ruptured by false
promises & dreams i'd go inside. take a bath. watch t.v.

3.

duck & cover:

every thursday we had to attend auditorium. our colors were
green & white. we sang the national anthem & received lectures
from the teachers. sometimes after the pledge of allegiance they'd
tell us to crouch in a corner or under our desks, stuff our heads into
our chests & our hands behind our heads. they said this would save
us if the "commies" dropped the **BOMB**. the standard joke at the
time was *"when the bomb comes put your head between your legs*
& kiss your ass good-bye". it's still pretty funny.
     after school i went home grabbed the cigs in the tire, met
shelly, martha & philip went down to martha's basement played a
grown up version of doctor (phil, a big guy & the italian in the
quartet, always made fun of my tiny circumcised pecker.) then
headed home. ate supper. took a bath with my toy atomic subma-
rine. watched t.v. wrote a poem, drew a picture, played my 45's,
kissed my poster of harpo ... tried to sleep.

insert: it dawned on me recently how valuable the system of nuclear weapons is. seems, if we don't count the middle east, the world is a lot less safe without them. if we did not have such a destructive force to check man's habits the world would have ended a long time ago. if all the nuclear weapons were abandoned...hey knucklehead stop rambling this is the 21st century...as for the future, further improvements, threats, deaths...& as for war well we got it right here at home...come back after the warning signs have chilled. in a few days these few days will be over. these fist-filled dark alleys will runneth over with toxins & blood. whitman long dead, rivers won't need money. the world will be a crossing.

4.

on weekends i dreamt of tigers. played sewer to sewer punch ball or stick ball or went to horror movies with the gang. or best of all we'd hang around the pizza place on e.13th street & ave. j pretending to be tough listening to the juke box or singing doo-wop on the corner. we called ourselves the j-tones. i was the lead singer. my nickname was little dilly-dally.

willie's dream: a. one-legged. shoeless in front of the church. all he owned taken in the shelter. camelot cursed. america the colonized country. the chains of europa still binding.

willie listening to the last of his voice. pleading asking begging: please i am a colonized country. have only one leg left. colonized country nurtured by slavers & blackguards & bootleggers who only wanted to emulate those they broke free of. forging a life while making copy after copy of the ideals of others. the misery of others. somewhere between the museum & the mausoleum. time is borrowed & the interest payments endless. i hold a mirror up to the ordinary my face tattooed to the window. no surprises or mysteries anymore. more boredom & discontent. more time for meat. less time for coffee. chances of pleasure. evocations. calypsos. challenge. contemplation. longing. discontent. to have so many promises broken. *willie's out there somewhere carrying his library through camelot: cursed, colonized & free.*

*deep in the heart of the worker's heart through the core of his
soul past the density of his poisonous chores he only heeds the call
of immediacy* > *hungry mouths — the family he swore to protect
— the luxuries & necessities he must provide — the roof over their
heads* > *& though he murders the air* > *pollutes his children's futures* > *it is only now that he is consumed with confusing present
& future always* > *this unfortunate saint* > *this destroyer* > *this
soldier* > *selfless selfish self-survivalist never realizing that the future is NOW* > i curse the hooker > the big rig > the chemical plants
> i assassinate the cockroach & turn the stereo up. i am determined
to graduate from my adolescence *then* to my adolescence *now*. ½
man. ½ moon. *mirror split/sun strolling/: advertisements.*

    5.

    suddenly my world began to cloud over. my mind got side-
tracked & my temperament grew dark. panic set in. i got angry at
everything > at the state of the world & at america in particular.
all those wars & starving folks around the globe. the melting pot
had become a boiling pot. i got jealous if anyeone danced with my
girl. i threw things, threw tantrums, ranted & raved. i was penalized
severely. was given shock treatment & drugs to calm me down &
was finally put away. they tried everything possible to alter my
bones. my mind. i was sedated, berated, inundated & degraded
"you'll get better but it'll take a long time.". "better from what?"
i'd ask but received no reply or was told not to worry. *"all you do
is sit around all day picking your nose & masturbating ."* they'd
grunt. "better from what?" i'd ask. *"don't worry"* they'd say"…
or *"you're totally nuts"* they'd proclaim…so i'd close the door.
pick my nose. take a shower …masturbate (once i got caught)…eat
dinner. watch folks slash their wrists…watch t.v. & wait…wait…
wait… *to get better from WHAT!*
    while confined someone handed me Howl & Coney Island of
the Mind & someone else handed me a seconal. my poetry & life
were completely transformed. i was 14. confined & free. drugs.
hard drugs. i wrote: *sunday evening's entrails on monday morning's*

*plate. sewer mud java — my cup runneth over — brooklyn bridge
is falling down empire state crumbles to the ground — celebration
- quiet hysteria in the streets — new york's last huge hunk of stale
concrete lands on my head & wakes me up...i will smoke my last
cigarette & try to forget the corruption & perversion that sur-
rounds me...the poverty & sickness & filthy rich slobs...prejudice,
hate & the mad-dog mobs...i will sit & dig the stillness & forget
all madness but my own... manhattan bridge is falling down u.n.
crumbles to the ground — celebration..*

war dream 1b: Jihad

Truly & True is Jah. A (illegible) *of Celebration in the Camp
of the true I can stay from here That's if I am Sure.* (illegible) *hear.
The Mountain is blue with a smoke of Incense Surrounding the
Camp. But only if the camp remains under strain once chant was
true & I mean so Blue. for it heals all wounds . Now it is the Camp
of the Strong Are You so strong Rasta Ma . Spirituality hes left hes
left your Camp At least I believe so Or is it still there . Underneath
A Sack cloth of ha (illegible). Because times has changed. And so
(has* crossed out replaced with) *is The true And living Rasta Man.*
(first there was the shroud of turin — now it's christ's face on
a tortilla wrap)

1c: dust my broom — dreams end like the special of the day

& sometimes pop up again a week later. depends on whose writing
the menu. for instance > ham, cheddar & salsa omlette served
every sunday or maybe only today > blood sausage bi-monthly >
bi-pass annually > wars daily > death once in a lifetime > you im-
prison me in the shower stall i watch as you fuck sleep wake & finally eat yourselves to death > i try washing you away...change
the menu so to speak...the water is scalding hot.....................
.......i rise in a cold sweat god reveals himself to me like double
vision glorious moments of music in an otherwise uneventful
nightmare. row houses & the dark little girl running in the lifeless
haunted garden. everything is for sale. the family business / the
house / vegetables / pinched nerves / the polar icecaps / polar bear

pelts, paws / the old black dog's wagging tail / smiles / governments / cosmetics / cemeteries / oil / gas / this fine spring day. even the sun is mortgaged off. the moon in its shadow. & me still holes in the ozone where a glass of water costs way too much.

6.

a. when i got out i soon took my first trip to manhattan. radio city & crazy times square. lights. action. lust. JAZZ. the growing up blues. zooming off to the village & being real "beat." smoking my first joint with the gorgeous bi-sexual black fem i met "inside" & coming all over her sheets.

one stoned night high on reefer & downs, me & the guys rammed into the priest with the station wagon somewhere on the jersey turnpike in a "borrowed" car. he blessed our teenage souls. "8 days a week" blasted from the car radio. by now i was coming home real late at night.....too late to bathe or watch t.v. but never too late to sleep always with my feet covered by the blankets so the boogie man wouldn't drag me under the bed to my untimely death.......i still sleep this way.

one night i called symphony sid & told him to play that nina simone song i loved so much now i forgot the name but it's buried somewhere on vinyl in this overcrowded rent controlled mind i survive in. he told me *"go to bed kid you're stoned."*

i shouted "fuck you sid" and hung up. of course he was right he being one of many guardian angels i never listened to. oh yeh the song was "3WOMEN".

b. then there was the big upset. the principal came over the P.A. announced that the president had been shot & that we could all go home. i got home. washed. ate supper & sat in front of the t.v. there was the waiting & the waiting then the death.

suddenly weird things began to happen. the fallout from all those dreams became more painful. more people died. were assassinated. more drugs entered my body & my consciousness. my eyes started drifting. my ears heard different sounds. different pieces of america started to bombard me. negroes. buffaloes.

bridges & rainbows. acid rain & strange acid worlds. there were insides & outsides. their side & our side. 2 more needles spoon shot sand sweat the zookeeper the lost mother trip anger — vomit crystal meth — the animal trainers whip — hunger artists — endless corridors — space time control — come downs come downs come downs — ice cubes > bathtubs. missiles. the murderer as good guy... o.d.s...WAR...& t.v.

war dream 2 - we were in X's apt. on e.4th & b me X & s.g. we were discussing dreams, drugs, literature, the scene, honest thieves, dishonest meddlers, the definition of nice guys & why the world was no longer safe for democracy. i needed to keep an appointment on ave. c & 3rd & knew that s.g. would follow me to muscle in in his own "sweet way". so i said ciao & ran out quickly to get to my next destination without being followed. in the dream north was south & vice versa. to avoid s.g. i ran south toward e. 10th where i had intended to proceed toward ave. c & then backtrack. i stopped between 9th & 10th to see if s.g. was in pursuit. sure enough he was, rounding the corner of 4th coming my way. i sped up turned again. he started to run toward me & instantly (this being a dream remember) ended up coming at me in a tank. i quickly rounded 10th & ran smack into a group of middle aged hispanic women. suddenly what seemed like a big ball of fire whoooshed over our heads & just as suddenly, as our eyes followed it toward the river, a huge mushroom cloud appeared on the Brooklyn side. i knew instinctively that the end had come. "look" i said, pointing " a nuclear bomb" ... thinking "was it iran or s.g." they nodded. i woke up. the dream had ended as well.

7.

the trolley's gone & so's the 15 cent fare. the fallout shelters have fallen into decay & those funny little yellow signs have rusted or been ripped away & those funny little yellow pills have long been off the market. i go to the beach whenever i can. pick my nose. bite my nails. take showers & watch t.v. the news, the food channel & old movies. i still eat burgers, pizza, cornflakes, peanut butter & cherries - still wait for the tree to grow inside me. still think the american dream is possible though i now know it's just a dream. a dream that has become a virus that has spread throughout the world.

i spent my whole life trying to get out of brooklyn & now everyone is trying to get in to it. but i still live in new york in the heart of downtown manahatta, the island of dreams. i think about the world a lot & sometimes pretend that i am safe as i watch the cherry blossom fallout.

CONEY ISLAND 1966

CLAUDE TAYLOR

I t had all started with the fat lady, a grotesque statue of a fat woman, fifteen feet high and eight feet across, laughing maniacally in front of a "fun" house on a Coney Island side street. The fun house and all of the other accompanying memories came rushing back to me as I started writing this piece. In fact, they started to interfere with it, the writing no longer holding any meaning for me except as the catalyst to my memories.

I grew up in Bensonhurst, a working class Italian neighborhood, but as I grew older, Coney Island as opposed to Bensonhurst seemed like it might be a better fit for me. Coney Island was actually a tougher neighborhood, more dangerous, yet there was also a greater variety of people, so even if you didn't fit in with one group you weren't necessarily an outsider. In fact, Coney Island was one of the only places I knew where outsiders could indeed be insiders too. It was a surreal landscape, frightening in many ways, yet when I was eighteen years old, it drew me in. There were madmen there. Real madmen! Doctors sent them to be calmed by the ocean. You would see them walking, striding along the boardwalk at night, talking to themselves or talking to the ocean or to their own private gods or demons. There were old, Russian Jews, Stalinists and Trotskyites arguing in the sun. There were health food stores and bookstores and boardwalk honkytonks where cowboys sang on a stage set up in the middle of a horseshoe shaped bar to sailors, gang bangers and B girls.

There was an all-night cafeteria, and when I was a teenager, that's where I spent most of my evenings. On Friday and Saturday nights I would stay until two or even three in the morning, me and my friend Frankie, eating French toast and sausage, drinking coffee and watching the parade swirl around us. There was the section where the mob guys sat, and the table for the grifters and con artists, another for the gamblers, and the entertainers and show business types, Jewish comedians who came in at two or three in the morning sometimes after late night shows.

There was a woman named Irene who worked as a stripper. When I was eighteen, I fell in love with her. She was in her thirties, and very lush, probably near the end of her stripping life. She wore a fur coat and she had the most beautiful skin I had ever seen. She never went out in the daylight she said. Her whole world was the night.

I fell in love with her in a very honorable way — there was no sex. Rather our terrain together was the all night cafeteria. When she came in, if I was there, she would usually sit at my table and I would buy her ox tail stew. That's all I can remember her ever eating. She always wore tight fitting dresses in some bright, shiny material and like many of the regulars back then, at some point she just stopped coming in.

My friend Frankie held few of these romantic illusions. He was a big tough Italian kid who lived next door to me and acted as a kind of rabbi, giving me practical advice on survival and letting others know that I was under his protection. Frankie looked a little like Elvis Presley, and all of the girls in Bensonhurst were in love with him.

We must have made an interesting impression back then, one small and thin and gawky, and the other big and muscular with that thick shiny black hair that I so envied at the time and even now for that matter.

But Frankie wasn't a "dese"and "dose" kind of a Brooklyn guy. He had a brain and dreams of his own. He wanted to see the world as his father had done, though he hardly knew his father who was rarely around. The price you pay, I guess, for seeing the world is leaving the world you know best behind.

Frankie was often left to his own devices growing up, which often led him to trouble, but he had his own code of honor, and God knows, he was always nothing but kind to me. One night,

Frankie and I decided to hit the beach. We left the cafeteria under the el train around midnight and headed toward the boardwalk.

There was a heavy fog, and you could hear stray boat whistles blowing off the ocean, rippling like the water itself through fog and air and ear. There's almost no one out though one tends to see shadows in the hollows of the jetty rocks. A large rat darted in and out of the crevices, his ears picking up at each distant sound. There was an odd mix of building dust, brine and rotting wood, cut through by the salty sea breezes. Frankie leaned back, lit a cigarette and closed his eyes. The air was raw and brisk but not uncomfortable, the lapping water soothed the silence all around us. Frankie held his silver flask out to me, smiling like the Cheshire Cat, and like the Cheshire Cat, in the intensity of the darkness around us, little more than his smile was visible.

"What is it?"

"Just taste it."

It was sweet and mild and very cool, vaguely familiar too, in some eerie deja vu sort of way.

"What is it," I insisted.

"It's Pernod."

I nodded, remembering the taste, or something like it, from somewhere in my past. Frankie took a long swig from the flask, gazed out quietly at the lights and distant boats across the water.

"It's been a long time," he said. "My father was nineteen or so when he joined the Merchant Marines. Not much older than I am now. For twenty years he worked the big boats all across the Pacific. He was well connected, my father was; knew people from all walks of life. Knew just about everyone who was anyone from that time in New York right after the war. Anyway, he died about seven months ago. A heart attack made worse by too much drinking. He wasn't even forty three yet."

Somewhere, it sounded far off, someone smashed a bottle against a wall and laughed.

Frankie smiled.

"They told me about it somewhere in the middle of my math class. The principle called me into his office. Stupid me, I thought I was in trouble. Tried to remember just what it was I had done.

My mom was there crying and I though, Jeez, I must have really fucked up. And I swear I could hear my father laughing at me, from over my head up in the clouds, saying, 'Look at him, God; he wants to be just like me. Aint't that funny, God? Ain't that funny?'"

He smiled and rubbed my neck with a meaty hand.

"Here's to friendly ghosts," I said.

"The thing is, he was right. I did want to be just like him."

Frankie took another long swig on the flask.

"You want to hear a funny story? I was in love once with a Chinese girl in Greenpoint. Malaysian, actually. I lived with her on and off for four months. Then one day it started hurting when I pissed, so I got the name of a local doctor from a friend of mind and went to see him. The doctor's office was in a remote Godforsaken part of Coney Island. I remember he held my dick , picked at it under a Goddamn lamp in this small dark room that smelled of formaldehyde, and all the while asking me what I was studying in school. In school, for Chrisake. And showing me with a yellowed fingernail, the infected lesions of my cock! Off in another room, I could hear Jan Sabbott and the Tophaters singing 'You Go To My Head.'

"There was a chart on the wall subdivided into three parts: cells in the urine, crystals in the urine, and, I don't know, some other shit that lives in the urine. But the thing I remember most vividly was that each of the three parts was illustrated with colorful pictures of all these weird fucking monstrous creatures that actually live in the urine.

"The paint on the wall was peeling, and there was cracked green linoleum on the floor. The strangest, most repulsive part of it was that this doctor looked just like that actor Dick Van Patten"

He paused for a moment to see if I knew who Dick Van Patten was and if I was still following him.

"The thing is," he continued, "I can remember that doctor perfectly, but I can hardly picture that young Malaysian girl at all anymore." He chuckled quietly. "Ain't love grand."

I leaned back, felt the rocks digging into my hip, my composure slipping away.

"Is there something yru're trying to tell me here? Is there something I should know?"

I stared at my friend for a moment, then looked away to the lights playing across the water. Voices drifted over from somewhere down the boardwalk behind us, but still some blocks away. Another bottle got slammed against a wall like ocean spray, or a cataclysm of shooting stars. Frankie closed his eyes and began to laugh.

"Ain't that funny, God," he whispered. "Ain't that funny?"

In 1966, the world seemed to change, at least for me. I know that I was changing, not the ideas, so much, as the way I saw them, and I was making a nuisance of myself to all those around me. A young man with everything to prove.

We were all changing, just not always understanding the change. My friend Eddie joined the marines when he was seventeen and went to Vietnam. Carl and Vinnie dropped out of school and went to work in their father's store. My grades slipped slightly and my choices narrowed. The world became a smaller place and for the first time I felt life closing in on me. Joey joined the Navy and Frankie got arrested in a drug sting in Coney Island.

By September, two friends had already died and I was sitting in the back of my father's Buick leaving Brooklyn for college in Ohio.

BUMP YOUR ASS OFF
ANNA MOCKLER

We was going to be late if he didn't hurry up, he was cutting it really close, and I was almost mad with Rudy if he was going to make us late for the end of the world at Coney. I looked at my Roylex and I said patient, it never does no good to get quick with Rudy, I said, "Old buddy you should wear the shirt I give you to wear," because he don't see right, Rudy, his eyes roll up like and wander, he sees blue he says banana, he's cross-wired since this dermatology intern pulled his brain out of our mom with forceps, so Rudy he can take a long time, see, choosing what to wear.

This is why I don't usually make a fuss, but it was the end of the world, see, and it was going to be at Coney, right, and we had to be there on the dot and looking sharp. That's what I figured. If we wanted to get good seats and all. We was going to remember this for the rest of our lives, right? so I wanted us both to be looking fine and right on time. Because you don't get a second chance to make a first impression.

So I pull the green shirt with the crocodile over Rudy's head and I show him how the belt closes and he puts on his own shoes which goes pretty quick now I got him the Velcro close kind and I hang his key around his neck inside his shirt and we walk out the door only ten minutes late. As we go down the stairs I tell the tale, how he don't talk to anybody he don't see me shake their hand first, he stay right with me even if there's a dog on the train he hold onto me, he don't pick up anything at all off the street, and etcetera like that.

We walk the twelve blocks to Union Square even though was I by myself I'd take the L and transfer but Rudy he gets confused walking underground, he starts talking loud how he can't see the sky and how come's that? so we walk to the Q train which is fast to Coney and we need to get there fast. I keep my arm around his shoulder and he walks just as fast as me, he's playing fish, his lips push in and out and that's fine so long as his legs keep going like a person, I tell him he's doing real good and he goes to stop and tell me all about it but I say, "Tell me on the train," and he keeps walking. He's being so good. I'm real proud of him.

Getting him through the turnstile is always tricky, this is why we don't use those entrances that have like revolving cages, if I pulled him out of one of those once I done it a hundred times, no it's got to be regular turnstiles and that's what they have at 14th and 4th and that's what we go through, I swipe the MetroCard and tell him, "Go!" and he goes right through, it's lucky, there's a little white dog sticking out of this lady's bag and Rudy goes right through after the dog but, still lucky, even though I have to swipe three times before it reads my card I catch up to him before he can pet the dog or pet the lady which either one takes up a lot of time which time we don't have. We have to get to Coney if we want good seats. Rudy nods when I say this and walks away from the dog which is going uptown and we walk fast down the stairs and a Q pulls in and there's two seats facing backwards, lucky a third time, so Rudy and me sit down and spread out our legs and I show him the sports pages until we come out on the elevated tracks and then he shows me the trees and the birds and names the different kinds of litter. "Plastic bottle." "Glass bottle." "Coke can." He likes to say, "Coke can," so much that sometimes I don't tell him the right name because he gets all smile on his face saying "Coke can, Coke can," and meanwhile I can check how the Yankees are doing which I'm not supposed to do because we're a Mets family, always been a Mets family, and I'm behind them 200 percent, I mean everybody gets slumps, but if it's going to be the end of the world I figure I'll sneak a look at how the Bombers are doing. I shake my head. "Glass southpaw," I tell Rudy. "Glass pawpaw?" he says. "Never mind, it's okay," I tell him, and we go on all the way to

Coney like that, me shaking my head and him saying "New paper. Plastic bag. New paper. Coke can, Coke can." He don't say it too loud or nothing and nobody's paying attention anyhow, they're putting on their makeup or talking in their cellphones, getting ready for the end of the world at Coney, little kids is running around they parents paying them no mind and this one couple is going at it hot and heavy which made me think about Marcella who I'm not going to see before the end of the world, I figure, since she kept wanting us to go out just me and her without Rudy who she said was creepy so I told her goodbye, she was hot, Marcella, but there's going to be a lot of spilled milk at the end of the world so what's the use of crying about a few drops of it? I show Rudy this big bird out the other side of the train so he don't get all upset by this couple making out. "Vulture," he says.

Finally, *finally,* we get to Coney and I put my arm around Rudy's shoulder and we walk to the shooting pond where we're all supposed to meet, he stays right with me in the crowd and I tell him what a good job he's doing and he smiles which always cheers me up and all the way there, lucky again, nobody says nothing about how we mixing the races or we weirdos holding hands or nothing, we stop in front of the bumper cars and me and Rudy say, right along with this woman who comes out of the loudspeakers, we say *"Bump! Bump your ass off!"* and the little kids which we used to be, plus grownups too, zoom around under the disco music bumping each other all they can. "Bump, bump yo rassoff," Rudy says, and I say, "That's right," and we walk as fast as we can which isn't very fast because everybody and his wife, I swear on my mother's grave, has come to Coney for the end of the world.

Still, we make good time and in fact we're early at the meet spot, the place where you shoot at the animals by the pond, the bear and the raccoon and the tin cup. One time I hit the bear and made him stand all up so now every time we go there Rudy's all like, "Make the bear jump! Make the bear jump!" but no time for that now, we got to meet our people and get good seats and that's what we got to do. That's what I tell him. "Okay," says Rudy.

How lucky is this? All our people are on time, Cassandra, Donnell, Ramona, and Vernon and all, they're on time. Isn't that something. I shake all their hands so Rudy knows it's okay and we all hug each other and Donnell says Bernice grown another inch since I saw her last month and Cassandra got her hair all up and then coming down braids and Vernon got a new job they give him his own separate cellphone, he's that important, and we talk like that for a while and then I look at my Roylex and I say, "Okay, let's get this show on the road."

We get our seats and I buy Rudy a ice cream at highway robbery prices from a guy with a cooler, which if I was in charge guys wouldn't holler "Ice Cream!" in public places where they put ideas into people's heads. I wouldn't let them. We sit there for half an hour and Donnell says he can't believe they're holding the curtain for the end of the world, and Ramona says ain't that just typical, they waiting for more crowd, and Cassandra says they probably nervous doing a one-shot stand like this, and Vernon says that's right, he says it's not like they going to get a chance to polish they performance, and all of them laughing but I don't laugh because sure enough Rudy spilled some ice cream on his seat and I have to wipe it up before he gets down and starts licking that chair, who knows where that chair been? but they all laughing right along.

At last the curtain goes up and this big fat guy on the stage shouts we're going to see "Got a damn run!" and we all shout back "Got a damn run!" which our mom used to say is only what you can expect with dimestore nylons, she said you get what you pay for. The whole rest of it I couldn't figure out what kind of language they was talking, all holding onto these big sticks and shouting at them, and neither could Donnell or Vernon or Cassandra. Ramona says they was speaking Yiddish which I ask how would she know? She says it was on account of she works in the garment district. "They got their own whole language?" says Cassandra, and Donnell and Vernon and me say, all at the same time, "Hush up," and Rudy almost falls off his chair laughing.

The people on the stage they shout at their sticks and carry women around and set one of them on fire except not really and then the other women comb their long hair down around their knees, then there's more of they hit each other with sticks and stick each other with blades and fall down dead except they wasn't really dead they was just getting ready to shout some more — I maybe would have understood it more better if Rudy didn't keep showing me these vultures that was flying around the old Parachute Jump, him and me took turns looking through binoculars at these birds flying and flying. It was more interesting than all these people shouting at their sticks, for sure, plus it kept him quiet.

After a real long time it was over and people clap and up out their seats and crowd away and I look at Rudy and Rudy looks at me and we're both still here so what happened to the end of the world? I ask Cassandra about this because Ramona's still going on about she knows what words mean in Yiddish and Cassandra says it was the ringcicle, she says this part of the ringcicle's the end of the world. I say, "Oh, ringcicle, uh-huh," and Cassandra nods and gets lipstick out her purse and puts it on without a mirror. I say the end of the world's just like before the end of the world, I say wasn't there supposed to be a explosion or something? Donnell says, "Ringcicle, sure, it's the bomb," and I know he don't know what it is either, but we all get ice cream at the good place, which they don't have ringcicles and never heard of them, so how about that? And we wait for the crowd to thin out and we say thanks and it was great and see you soon to everybody and they go off for the F but we go for the Q. Rudy's asleep on his feet by the time a Q train pulls in and I'm not much better, tell the truth, and we ride and we ride all the way back to Union Square. I find a paper and read up on the Mets cause the end of the world's just like before the end of the world and now I got all this catch-up to do but it's hard to keep my eyes open and I figure the Mets aren't going to change after the end of the world on account of they don't change for nothing, I'll read up on them tomorrow. From Union Square we walk and we walk all the way home. "Last one up the stair's a rotten egg!" says Rudy, but I beat him to our door even though he's got the head start on me. I got to hide the laundry quarters before Rudy grabs them, if he gets hold of that money he'll stop the next ice cream truck to try and buy every kid on our block a ringcicle.

DOROTHY PARKER WILL HAVE HER REVENGE ON MANHATTAN

Joseph P. O'Brien

Sipping gin & mercury at dawn's bloodthirsty.
light, she hears the harlequins
throb inside their wombs,
and she whispers: "God have mercy."

Below the maddened crowd, she feels the fires teething.
Ten million budding mushroom clouds
wait patiently in mud-rooms
of vacant luxury *pied-à-terres,* just breathing.

She quips, "How I'd love to flog their sanctimony
like a feral circus pony,
and strangle their oblivion
as if my name were Vivian!"

She'll curse you with the restless
sleep of refugees; you'll jitterbug
as clumsily as starving amputees.
And for her final review:

She'll come back as acid
to melt leisure classes,
leave a river of sludge in the streets
from the Ritz-Carlton to Battery Park.

It's so soothing to know
you'll miss the comfort in being poor.

HOMELESSNESS IN NEW JERSEY
MARK BRUNETTI

My idea of homelessness came from cartoons,
a happy character with a stick and a polka
dot handkerchief tied to the end to hold
all his worldly possessions.

I first attempted to be homeless when
I was 7 years old living in Jackson, New Jersey.
I packed up a comic book and a jacket
took some cheese and crackers from my mom's fridge
and walked to the clubhouse in my backyard.
It had its own imitation kitchen with a stove
and plastic red doors. I stayed there
for at least 4 or 5 hours looking at the pictures
in my comic book trying to find things to do
to bide my time. The cheese and crackers
were gone by evening and it got dark quick
and I was scared of the dark.

Now I'm 26 years old and I have a car
and a nice state job with benefits up in Cranford.
Because my car works I'm considered to be
an upper class person without a home
and since I'm pursuing my Masters Degree I will have
plenty of things to do to take up my time.

When I was younger and homeless I went back home
because it was dark and my mom called me in.
Now I have a flashlight on my keychain
and I don't think I'm gonna listen when she calls

because I want to see the sunrise thru morning dew
windows and that means really see the sunrise
before I get old.

REVISITING PLACE
AMY BARONE

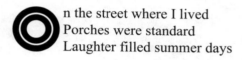n the street where I lived
Porches were standard
Laughter filled summer days

The local firehouse alarm signaled danger
Classic hits poured from a beige transistor radio
We cradled tunes from War, Stevie Wonder, The Jefferson Airplane

Blossoming buttercups entertained a trio of sisters
My mother, who couldn't swim
Watched over us at Aunt Mary's pool

In between flights off the diving board
From Dixie cups we drank real iced tea spiced with fresh mint
Chased exotic yellow and black-speckled butterflies

Fear meant the neighbors unleashed Frisky, the wire-haired
    terrier next door
Or sightings of Mr. Talone, who couldn't talk and hid inside
    most days
Or a strange "Lost in Space" episode that wreaked dread as night
    darkened

When I last returned
Sheltering trees that whispered in the wind had fallen away
A quaint stone cottage had vanished

Hospital officials enamored of property
Flaunting pockets of big change
Had enticed families to abandon sturdy homes

To create a shallow view
Where flimsy town houses will rise

KENTUCKY DERBY
SUSAN MAURER

The droning sound of well-tuned cars
The four lane highway and
Shopping malls on either side
Almost identical to the naked eye
Have said "May I"
And taken giant steps

The development communities, neatly bricked
The squared off front porches
All slightly different
Face the goose-stepping lawns
Infiltrated by the irrational nests
Of cuddly baby robins
The lawn Nazis rule
"You have crab grass"
Yells the neighbor
"That kind's contagious"

We eat mall food for the truly ravenous who've
Never known hunger

There were hats
pastels like fixed smiles
There were hats like
Spray-neutered butterflies

(Someone longed to turn his
Lawn to habitat, but that
Would bring the threat of mice
Urgent doves nesting build with twigs)

The horses break from the starting gate
Like the team of horses of
Apollo plunging through the
Star roads of the sky hauling the heavy sun

Mile and a quarter and then it's done

MARFA, TX
Joe Maynard

T he albatross chases the coyote
this always happens in the land of peyote
racing across a west Texas sky
no one ever leaves here, with a satisfied mind

I love you
& I long for you

once an indian chief, now dead as can be
'neath this big sky, where once was a sea
lost the whole of his tribe in a fierce, bloody war
now he watches for the ghosts from the hills, where once
    was a shore

he says, I love the view
yes, I long for you

no one knows for sure what goes on every night
but you can see it for yourself, past the reach of streetlights

DETROIT
CAROLYN WELLS

Quiet tangle of weeds and wildflowers
among cracked sidewalks, empty lots.
This was the great American hope gone awry.
Shiny cars lined up in factories along a blue river,
with promise of wealth and safety.
The hull of the houses rests mute and blackened
by fires of despair.

THE SPY WHO HUNG OUT IN THE COLD
Lynn Crawford

To: Chief Hoss
From: Agent Paula Regossy
Item: Art Document

Chief,

After years of professional excellence, I make a near fatal mistake: to blur boundaries with a criminal. You do not express anger but concern. For my sake (personal, professional) and yours (with regard to agency management and maintenance), so temporarily reassign me to a specific mission in your father's hometown.

We visit once over two decades ago. It is then, there, we hear for the first time of the great detective novelist Alain Robbe-Grillet. (We label him that, but not all readers do.) His line, "Memory belongs to the imagination," is meaningful to agents like us because it at once rings true and contradicts our system's reliance on statement as evidence used to build and judge cases.

The trip was a landmark. Extensive training and travel expose me to music, art, literature, yet the start of my genuine (albeit vague) cultural interest is generated then and there in Detroit.

Our first night in town is a chilly Sunday. We sit at a table in a lightly populated bar, windows overlooking empty city streets and the river dividing the US and Canada. We listen (unobserved) to a racially diverse, attractive group of people discuss Robbe-Grillet (they recite and discuss the *Memory* quote) and various artists. I write down six names: Gordon Newton, Christian Boltanski,

Howardena Pindell, Elizabeth Murray, the late Sam Mackay, and his grandson Tyree Guyton.

We learn Guyton and Mackay are the creators of The Heidelberg Project, a land-based artwork nourishing (my term) abandoned lots and homes in their neighborhoods after destruction from the city's 1967 rebellion by painting bright spots on empty houses and strategically placing objects in yards.

We continue to eavesdrop, are stimulated, and look forward to hearing conversations and viewing new people (maybe even re-seeing these people?) over the next few days.

It does not happen.

The only place we really see anyone mingle spontaneously outdoors is when we visit the Heidelberg Project. There, Guyton sweeps the street, speaks with visitors (a van of Dutch tourists and two other cars of families). Children play on grass, and a musician plays drums.

Otherwise, outdoor spaces seem empty.

We learn Newton and Pindell exhibit in galleries located in the northern suburbs but do not make the visit.

Later we understand, at this time, inside is where most things are at in Detroit. Generally not parks, streets, cafes, and fields, but in basements, living rooms, kitchens, specific bars, galleries, and industrial spaces.

These are the laboratories where communities, friends, and families, dance, talk, and start political groups, newspapers, and poetic journals. It's where they make music.

That was then. Now is different. It is hard to follow the news without encountering a story referencing Detroit and some sort of large or small or business investment, art project, grass roots activism. Ways vacant land, and homes (once liabilities) are increasingly viewed as potential community assets.

You, Chief Hoss, decide it is a place I can spend time to re-group, soul build, hone a new skill with a cover: curious cultural visitor. Not flashily dressed. Or charismatic. But not standoffish.

"Paula," you say, "While you are there, look at some art and produce a document. Put your stamp on it. You don't need to be razor accurate like you are with a case. Maybe try to establish some emotional connection."

I trust you, Chief, with every bit of my heart and brain, but dislike this idea of wasting time away from things crime related.

Although there is a drug ring I've been following with some connections to Detroit.

As if reading my mind you say, "Regossy, NO detective work. You go cold turkey on detection. We need you back, but the best you. Learn to vary your operating methods."

I hate the term "cold turkey," not for content but for sound. Its ugly sequence of hard consonants.

I tear up.

We share a long silence.

You hand me a tissue, "All right then. Go and, you know, please cool it."

I dab my face gently. Understand that when you use the term "cool it," you mean I should not actively seek out a case, but, if one presents itself, I am not obligated to ignore it.

(Document)

Here. The agency leases me a one bedroom (with kitchen) in an area near hospitals, bars, businesses, shops, and a university. It is a neighborhood teeming with young people who appear anxious, driven, optimistic.

I purchase a bike and equip it with lights and an essentials-pack (poncho, flashlight). I buy several below-the-knee shirtdresses (solid colored and plaid) and wear them with the laceless oxfords bought years ago in Italy. I pass as a curious cultural visitor — could just as easily be a city planner, brand manager, or barista.

Biking around, I learn this city moves like a train with variable speeds. Some sections undergo rapid change, and others slow or no change at all. There is a healthy bee population.

In contrast to that first visit, now so much happens in public. There are museums and galleries with nice signs and festive openings. There are indoor and outdoor art and culture projects, open studio visits.

This, of course, does not mean everything happens in public.

Chief and I agree not to include any of the newer, on-the-radar spaces or events in this document. These spots are friendly, social.

I would not go unnoticed. Given my recent personal boundary issues, we do not think I am ready for that kind of engagement.

I whittle my assignment down to two locations. At each, I am stimulated, welcomed, and left alone. The locations:

1. Dabl's African Bead Museum
2. Detroit Institute of Art

> (*Until the lions have their own historians, the history of the hunt will always glorify the hunter.* Proverb.)

DABL'S AFRICAN BEAD MUSEUM

Several acres of grassy land, buildings (covered with splintered mirrors, bright paint, bead murals), and a full-bodied series of installations make up this indoor/outdoor space that explores ways Africa informs and intertwines with American experience. Even though freeways are on one side and a busy city street lines the other, it is a calm, sweet spot to be.

Looking at, or trying to look into, mirror shards gives a disconcerting *reflection*; you see yourself and what is behind you in fragments. The experience makes clear what we intellectually know: you never view *your image in a mirror,* just some sphere of self-awareness or lack of.

The installation "Iron Teaching Rocks How to Rust" tells of imposed loss, decay, and corrosion on people wrenched from their homes, traditions, and cultures. One scene depicts a deserted dinner table covered with plates, bowls, knives, spoons, and forks. A few years ago, Chief Hoss and I, on a case in Senegal, learned to eat with our hands. The sequence of fingers to food to mouth prepares saliva and digestion for a happy eating experience. Here, enforced use of cutlery disrupts the potential harmony; eaters consume but are hampered.

A tall stack of plates in the table's center makes me think of Dickens's character Miss Havisham, the bitter bride, left at the altar, choosing to live inside her white gown and ruined mansion, leaving her table strewn with wedding breakfast and cake as she sinks into misery, perhaps self-chastisement.

The comparison illustrates two forms of punishment. One comes from outside, and the other is self- imposed.

My position parallels Miss Havisham's; my dis-ease, generated by me, is reversible. I have the luxury to make amends and wrest back some professional and personal control. Not as easy an option for the eaters at the rusted table.

The museum itself is inside a house, holding bins of beautiful, handmade, variously sized and marked ceremonial beads referred to in the literature as *textbooks packed with information.* Their meanings are impenetrable, but I feel their pull and an urge to engage with their clues, force, data.

I come here mornings to pray. Am reminded that I am not an individual, but a soul in a series of souls. Some keep watch over me, and others are out to harm me. I pay attention to both.

My specific professional skill is to identify, track down, and hold accountable the high level criminals who think of themselves as too big to bust. I am capable of, but am uninterested in, punishing low- and mid-level offenders. Enough of them get apprehended. It is unfair and does not solve our crime problem.

My Italian laceless oxfords hold a special place in my heart because I get them after one of our greatest takedowns: a Count, representing old European aristocracy, apparently untouchable, who was involved with international human trafficking.

I soon get information on a drug ring with a Detroit presence. Its leaders are not based here. But I will cool it. (Okay, Chief Hoss.) I will not make a bust, but possibly lay solid groundwork for one elsewhere.

I find, and get on the radar of, a mid-level worker in the ring by posing as an agent for an unidentified organization.

Getting them to follow me requires specific strategy. When you want to be tracked, you must make the potential tracker believe it is their idea to track you. As long as they believe they are the ones in charge, you are okay.

I use the word "them" because "he" and "she," "him" and "her," are not inclusive when discussing people in general and certainly not in this profession.

This is also a search for a home.
So I lied. It's an appreciation of several homes.

Lisa Jones
Bulletproof Diva

Detroit Institute of Art

We have an agency DIA membership. I visit two sites whenever I come to town.

Armor

In The Great Hall, just up the steps from the museum entrance, there are several suits of full metal armor in glass cases. My early education requires dressing, training, and fighting in plate armor. It takes tremendous energy to get the suits on and off, not to mention what it is like, because of their heft and weight distribution, to wear them in battle. The goal of this type of combat: stab opponents through the helmet's slim, horizontal slit and deliver a lethal pierce to the eye region. It is a challenging, specialized form of combat that takes me back to my early roots.

Detroit Industry Murals, Diego Rivera

These twenty-seven panels depicting industry at Ford Motor Company remind me why I chose, and continue to choose, what I do. Yes the murals are magnificent and transmit a tribute to workers, doctors, manufacturers, and scientists in the 1930's. They convey what great things can happen given the time, money, and space. Looking at them, it is impossible for me to ignore corporate captains of industry. Largescale art projects are often financed by these people; they are just the types of criminals I excel at catching. High Level Criminal Businessmen. I am not saying Edsel Ford or William Valentiner (responsible, I believe, for commissioning the work) were criminal. But they lived and dwelled in the in the kinds of rich and powerful circles with those who were or might have been.

I consistently keep *these kind* on my radar.

Following my Chief's orders to re-group and contemplate, I also spend time with art that is less directly connected to my profession. I wander around and find so many pieces I love.

I visit the DIA mid-day, a time I routinely feel overwhelmed by gruesome realities encountered in my line of work. I take time to look at beautiful, carefully considered things people construct, even if they do not always or even often behave that way.

Is it so hard to understand how I blur emotional boundaries with the handsome criminal? Even a carefully trained agent like me is not immune to the perils of isolation. I believe in, but perhaps am not cut out for, intimacy.

Maybe what generates my trouble is not allowing for — or ignoring — personal needs.

Isn't that why people are drawn to what happens in the current Detroit? The emphasis on goodwill and community? The more I ride my bike around this city, the lonelier I feel. I see people holding art critiques, gathering at barbeques, bazaars, dance labs, community garden sessions, cultural exchange projects. I see increasingly cohesive neighborhoods. They have something that I, in my position, do not.

HAPPY
MIKE DECAPITE

I am so miserable, I am so tired
I just sit on the Mississippi River
and watch the fish swim by
My life is so confused,
but I don't wanna die
I wanna go to heaven
but I'm scared to fly

O.V. Wright
"Everybody Knows (The River Song)"

I was walking down Decatur Street in New Orleans one morning when I caught a glimpse of the Mississippi and crossed a parking lot to be near it. Two men were asleep on a grass verge. I climbed a few steps to a paved riverfront walk, where I found a bench.

I was in a jam I couldn't solve for more than a couple of seconds at a time, I couldn't take a step in any direction without making it worse, and my mind was shorting out. I watched the interplay of sunlight and shadow on the wind-riffled surface of the river, trying to empty my head and disconnect from the exhausting expectation that all nature and experience were raw data to be processed through the little hole of my consciousness. I stared at the water, trying to do a mind-clearing perceptual trick whereby the light and dark of the ripples switch their emphases, in a way, or trade values.

The song "Dock of the Bay" came to me, and I felt, or remembered, what it's like to be in a city with no money, alone, knowing no one, end of the line, and all you have is time. A man came along the walkway with a cane. We nodded to each other. He looked a little like Otis Redding. He said, "Every day I gotta make it to this last bench." Carrying himself straight, he limped past where I was sitting and reached to touch the last bench with his cane.

It occurred to me that the opposite of despair is gratitude, and at times the two feel almost the same. But, as with the water trick, I couldn't quite get there. I couldn't get to gratitude, couldn't let it happen. Again I heard the words of the bent, gaunt, old bishop of a church in Memphis from two days before: "This is the day! That God made. This is the day that God made! And if you're not rejoicing — you're living below your privilege."

The man came back to the bench where I was sitting and asked if he could sit down. We started talking.

After working in restaurants all over the country for fifteen years, he went back to Minnesota when his mother got sick with cancer. He took care of her for a year until she died at fifty-three. With no family and nothing to keep him in Minnesota, he landed a job in a restaurant in New Orleans and moved there. Four days later he was hit by a drunk driver. Shoulder and both legs broken. Now, a year later, he'd been through eight surgeries and all his savings, and he was homeless. He'd been arrested twice for sleeping outside, and was waiting for Friday to have his right leg amputated below the knee. He had a staff infection in the bone, and his present fear was that he'd be arrested for vagrancy again between now and Friday and miss the surgery.

People tell him to count his blessings, but he doesn't see that he has any. He said this simply and with acceptance. Another homeless man suggested he get himself arrested for real so he could go to prison. But the last thing he wants to do is give up, so the suggestion angered him.

He said the police in New Orleans are hard on the homeless. Tourists get wasted and pass out everywhere, but if you're homeless and trying to sleep the police run you in. The city jail holds eight thousand people — he pointed downriver to the Wyndham Hotel to indicate the size of it — and the city gets fifty dollars per night from the state for every person the cops bring in.

He showed me the leg, swollen black from the calf down.

After the surgery he'll be eligible without contest for disability. The benefits will allow him to go back to school in Virginia for a three-year program of culinary arts. After that, he'd like to move to San Francisco.

We talked for about half an hour. Then I said, "My name's Mike."

"Sorry," he said. "I'm Rodney."

We shook hands.

I said, "I'm going back to where I'm staying."

"Thanks for listening," he said, touching his ear.

"Sure." I stood up. "Can I give you a few bucks to get you through the week?"

"Sure," he said. "Anything."

I gave him some money. He thanked me.

He told me I should keep my eyes open, in about three years, for a new executive chef somewhere in San Francisco named Rodney. I wished him luck and left him there on the bench.

The other night I watched one of my favorite movies, "Fat City," a John Huston picture, from the Leonard Gardner novel. I was trying to pass the time before turning out the light. The woman I was thinking about while I was in New Orleans had left me with no idea what to do with myself. I'd been leaving the bed unmade, coming home from work and getting in. At the end of the movie, Stacy Keach runs into Jeff Bridges after they haven't seen each other for a while and persuades him to go into a pool hall for a cup of coffee. Stacy Keach is a drunken shambles of an ex-fighter at thirty, and Jeff Bridges is a younger man who's still fighting now and then while trying to support a wife and kid. Stacy Keach has nothing to hang onto but his former dream. He's a tiresome, self-hating drunk, and Jeff Bridges has put the destructive notion of glory aside and settled for meeting his responsibilities. They sip coffee, and Stacy Keach does most of the talking. Jeff Bridges doesn't want to be there. Through a service window to the kitchen we see an old Chinese waiter making coffee. It's hard to tell whether he's smiling or his face is just like that by now.

Stacy Keach says, "How'd you like to wake up in the morning — and be him?"

Jeff Bridges says, "Maybe he's happy."

Stacy Keach thinks it over and then, in a lucid moment beyond bitterness, says, "Maybe we're all happy."

THE LIBERTY OF STATUES
KEVIN RIORDAN

EIGHT YARDS HIGH

Had anyone troubled to ask him, Goethe would have explained that the problem all started twenty-five years ago, with that Mephistophelean thunderstorm, 1951, uprooting some of the oldest trees in the area and smiting his foot with a bolt of lightning, which would certainly have been more judiciously aimed at Ben Franklin on the other end of Lincoln Park. They had given him a new foot and ankle; he now could pick up WLS on a clear day; insult to injury, a week later they unveiled yet another statue of that insufferable prat, Alexander Hamilton, pontificating over all he surveyed and covered in real gold to the tune of a million bucks, like the Pied Piper of Mammon.

Goethe had held his peace for over sixty years, but lately the tingling, phantom buzz in his foot made him restless. Was he that homely that, of all the monuments in Chicago, only he was represented by a statue that didn't even pretend to resemble him? That fact alone was enough to give him a major sense of dislocation. He admitted to being the "slave of destiny" but this ponderous pose was not sitting well with him. Whoever the face belonged to, it was frozen in the early stages of a scowl, as if the last decade had just been frittered away, never mind the last two centuries. The big eagle on his knee wasn't very good company, though it did help keep the pigeons off, and one could be called worse things than "mastermind of the German people," but now he had to stand there looking at Hamilton, staring off into space as if looking for someone else to challenge to pistols at dawn. Only La Salle, with his pistol protruding suggestively from his belt, seemed cockier than this gilded moneychanger. However, despite this provocation, there was very little he could do. Metamorphosis takes time. The Wynken, Blynken and Nod fountain was doing an excellent job of keeping everyone adrift in dreamland. Just the same, a mischievous spark was starting to glow within his bronze bosom. Always brimming with bromides, his first act of rebellion was to change the quotation ascribed to him on the base of the statue to "We must always change, renew, rejuvenate ourselves; otherwise, we harden."

THE DEFENESTRATION OF PROG

Doo do do, do dooda do.

Walking on the wild side past a fire station hung with bi-centennial bunting, Virge went home from the bar, dusting glitter out of his hair. It was somewhere nearby that the lady in red had kept her love nest, not to be confused with the bearded lady in red, holding court at the Snake Pit, perpetually decorated for every holiday except the fourth of July. As he passed the neon sign declaring a second floor auditorium "For madmen only" he wondered if it was another mime school, like Mo Ming. Lou Reed segued into Steppenwolf's "The Pusher" in his inner ear. He liked that bar because strangers always bought him drinks, but tonight he'd accepted a few more than usual, and was late for a deal. As he turned into his street, he saw a pair of mimes miming horror as an avalanche of items spilled from an upper window. Neighborhood was lousy with them ever since they opened that Clown College. Like a fallen tree finally breaking through a narrow waterfall, his semi-deflated waterbed, with the distinctive gold and olive super graphics, came shooting out. A quick glance verified the avalanche as his stuff, from the Mahavishnu Orchestra and Hawkwind albums to the Hot Rats eight-track. Chariot Races of the Gods and Chants for your Plants got in there by mistake, but the *flambé* cookbook was definitely his. When he got close, a paperback on pyramid power made contact with the crown of his head. Flat-mate Phisto was seriously pissed.

Virge wobbled up the plush stair runner and let himself in. "The bookshelf is mine, too, but don't pitch it. I guess I missed my connection."

"Is that what you call those Neanderthals? You know I was right at the crux of an incantation when they started pounding on the door. I thought it was Asphodel and it's like Cheech and Chong on strychnine. I can't have this anymore, man. I told you I need a roommate that respects my religious differences, leaves me space to do my work, not come barging up here looking to score weed every time I'm in the middle of casting a spell."

"That's cool, I'll clear out; all these human candles and circles on the floor are giving me the wimwams, anyway. How'd you ever get into this witchy-poo stuff?"

Phisto gave a haughty sniff. "I was initiated at the Satanic Woodstock, I'll have you know."

"I thought that was supposed to be apocryphal."

"It sure as hell was," he said reverently, "totally apocryphal."

The stereo was getting to the part of Coven's "Black Mass" where D.J. Jerry G. Bishop starts intoning "Kiss the Goat" in a voice more suited to pushing zit cream, and Virge couldn't suppress a laugh. "Just let me just rustle up my earthly possessions." Virge went over to the space heater and started undoing the isinglass front, reached in and started pulling out a stream of tin-foiled bundles, like scarves from a magician's ear. Then he dug into the back of the freezer and pried out a foil-wrapped block, pitching everything into a pillowcase.

"You're not taking my TV dinners out of there?" Phisto demanded.

"Relax, I'm not after your eye of newt either. Let me show you what I got." He peeled back a corner of the foil to reveal a stack of holy cards. The roommate backed up like Dracula seeing garlic.

"Go for the gold: St. Anthony. You see that halo, pure Vatican blotter." He went to the medicine cabinet and started collecting bottles.

"You have dope stashed in there too?"

"That bourgeois I'm not; I have aspirin stashed in here."

A brunette fading to black draped in a white sheet had made an appearance.

"So long, loverboy. Too bad Phisto does evictions better than exorcisms."

"Hey, Gloriana. I'll live"

"Living is overrated."

"Beats the alternative."

She laid her nails on his shoulder. "You don't get worked up too easily, do you? I mean, your crap is all over the sidewalk, you have no place to go…aren't you upset?"

"I'll get new crap. Crap finds me. I've been scoping out a new place for a while that I think I can crash at. But I don't intend to leave without my cocktail shakers. Besides, if I stay here Phisto might put the nazz on me."

SMOKE ON THE WATERBED

After checking a few alleyways, he came back pushing a beat-up shopping cart and collected his gear. He knew of an eminently squattable empty apartment near the Pillar of Fire church, and he steered his cart that way. As he got closer, he had the feeling he was making an appearance at a Broadway opening; the sky was lit and people were coming out of doorways and straggling after him to investigate. Instead of Klieg lights, it was the steeple going up like a Roman candle. A pack of mimes was taking advantage of the audience, running around with mock horror, clutching imaginary babies, squirting invisible hoses. A woman with a whistle around her neck appeared to be grading their performance, taking notes on a clipboard.

A large, dark El Dorado had stopped and was blocking the street and the driver was out and stomping on his wide brimmed hat, coloring the night with his language. Virge approached, leaving the cart back a ways. "Looks like you need a caretaker around here. If you let me stay here and keep an eye on the place, I'll see that nothing like this happens again."

"Think you can stop an Act of God, boy?"

"You might try changing the name."

The klaxon horn of a fire truck made them both jump, and Virge helped clear the way while the pastor parked.

"You don't look like you could scare a bat out of a belfry, boy. What you weigh, eighty pounds?"

"You're gonna need a new belfry, rev; probably looking at some new church mice too."

"Maybe I'll have to trust you, let you homestead here a while; I have to leave town for a week or so. What's your name, Bones?"

"Virgil Jones, your holiness. Yours?"

"No popery, no sir. Just call me Rev. Goodie. Just don't let me catch you pushing drugs out of my church, or I'll put you on the express elevator to the hot place."

Virge had to wonder if somebody had pinned a "pusher" sign to his back; was he that transparent? He started hearing more Steppenwolf, "you know the dealer is a man, with the love grass in his hand," the dealer/pusher distinction being fondly observed. The preacher was looking at him suspiciously.

"I say god damn, god damn the pusherman."

"Well. Alright, son, that's a bit strong, but I agree."

The firemen's Dalmatian seemed to have taken a keen interest in his shopping cart, the contents of which were at least 50% illegal. One more reason to get it of the street.

"Deal. Err, agreed, I mean."

"You want to get loaded, drink booze like an American" He produced a flask.

"What'll we drink to?"

"To excess." The Rev handed over a big old iron key.

Surveying the interior of the smoldering Pillar of Fire, Virge tried to picture it as a new variant of the swinging bachelor lair; it did have some exposed bricks, and a sort of skylight where the steeple had lost most of it's covering, distressed paint job. Hard to say what it would look like dried out and in daylight, but he couldn't go back to Phisto. That would be the real elevator to hell.

I SECOND THAT DEMOTION

Among Virge's duties at the Lava lite factory was quality control, checking that the goop in the lamps was performing satisfactorily. There were a dozen or so lined up and blobbing away at different speeds, disregarding the bubbly Muzak version of "Love Child" that galloped along overhead.

"D'ja get any last night?" Virge hadn't seen Dennis come in.

"What, sleep? Not really"

"Nah, I'm talking about poontang, what do you think?"

"Hardly likely, seeing as I never went to bed alone much less with anybody:

"What about standin up-a" Dennis suggested evilly.

Just then the Muzak grooved seamlessly into "Sex Machine," only with a xylophone on top of the mix. "This is not to be endured," Virge grimaced.

He went to the closet where the intercom controls were, and despite signs to the contrary, began messing with the controls, twisting knobs. None of the results were an improvement, and the equipment finally settled on a perky number he thought was called *"How Steep is your Love?"*

He went to the bench where he was assembling the wiring parts to the bases of a new model; he picked up a screwdriver but after a few minutes he was snoring gently.

He was floating up on a fluctuating blob of red wax, and parts of him were breaking free and floating away, then coming back and reattaching themselves. He lost track of his hands but then sensed that he was stacking hot dishes on rolling carts; no, that was wrong, that was his last job, his last repetitive motion recurring nightmare. He was looking up at a tiny shaft of light angling way above him, and he grabbed for a handrail but found he couldn't move his arm. He came to, sputtering and cursing, his arm taped to the workbench by one of his hi-jinx prone co-workers. He couldn't tell, which one, they were all enjoying his predicament equally. In his consternation, it barely registered that the lava was also formed into a rigid horizontal, or that the wires had somehow got stuck between the clinches of his watchband.

It wasn't 'til much later that it occurred to him that he was engaging in a little do it yourself biofeedback. "Who's been fiddling with the music?" the boss demanded, stomping in and dialing up a sleepy version of "Sleepwalk." The lunch bell rang and everyone exhaled.

WHO'S MAKING LUNCH

Although he admired the winged enamel sign offering CHILI, Virge couldn't face another plate of beans at the diner that most of the lava lite employees frequented, so he headed to the even more ancient lunchroom kiddy corner to Lake View High School, with its shop class Scottie dogs decorating each wooden booth, and had a grilled cheese with salami and a chocolate phosphate. There are few pieces of equipment more useful than a cast iron stomach. Another plus was that the lunchroom was fairly quiet despite the juvenile delinquents, as opposed to the beanery which had those little juke boxes every few stools and were often playing the wretched Elvis covers that had been recorded by the fry cook. He had so far resisted the impulse to deal his stock to the jailbaits from the high school; even a broken moral compass has to point somewhere.

"Got anything for the head?" Virge's reverie was broken by a thickset young acquaintance known as Smitty, with an impossibly black mustache.

"Just the blot."

"Blot's good."

"This is better than good. I potentiated it. I got this pyramid, like to keep bananas fresh, and kept it underneath it overnight."

"I thought that was just for keeping your razor blades sharp and shit."

"Nah, it has all kinds of powers; makes water wetter even. Nobody is exactly sure what it does to a dose, so let me know how you like it."

Under the table, a transfer of holy cards and Hamiltons was taking place.

"I was just thinking about how Smith means your people used to be blacksmiths, you know, and Carter means you probably drove the getaway cart."

"And Walker means the cart broke down," Smith offered. "What about Goldwater, what would that mean?"

"A real pisser. And you know what they say, flush only Nixons. There must have been a lot of you blacksmiths."

"Oh yeah we were legion. So, what does Jones mean?"

"Haven't you ever heard of a doughnut jones, a basketball jones? Speaking of doughnuts, you really should give some thought to losing the 'stache, hombre, makes you look like a cop."

"Never, man. They see me and they think I'm one of them."

"If you say so. Better try to keep those eyeballs spinning in the same direction then."

The rub was that Smitty really was a cop, but he was not out to bust Virge or anyone else. He just had a buzz to maintain. He had been a green rookie a few years back when he'd been sent to control crowds near a vacant lot just beyond Midway. It had been found to be housing a huge crop of pot and the brains at HQ thought setting it ablaze would get rid of the problem. In fact, intrigued citizens from all over, more used to ignoring the airborne odors of the Southwest side, had turned out in droves, and turned on as a result. Smitty was in the front lines and had his mind blown off its hinges. The next week, his newfound ultra-relaxed manner had made him a natural for the Red Squad, dispatched to snoop on suspected subversives. Since that detail had folded he was moved from trying to catch the Haymarket statue bombers to responsibility for all the public monuments in town. Other than breaking up the trysts in the shadows of the Hamilton statue, his duties had been pretty light — until lately.

(to be continued)

MAYDAY
LESLIE PROSTERMAN

C owslips, tulips, hang flower filled baskets on every door dance
intricate country dances, a full complement balanced.
Work a pattern to wind yellow and scarlet ribbons
around the May Pole.

Wisconsin pols giggle behind
their hands, smirk, wave little
pennants with impressive gravitas, they
twist law, they cheer, they
claim, they score, they
whittle our labor
into splinters
of our
state.

International Workers Day. Springtime. Fertility. Lei day. Law day.

We celebrate, shiver.

TO WHERE

AMY HOLMAN

To where seems to be the scenic pit stop in the forward swing
of the sentence, without being specific. "It's one of those   situations to where you have this need
to be accepted." The preposition proposes we
pull into someplace further away than the subject driving

through to the predicate. Where to, I have to ask, and
what for. I see a turquoise sale in the painted desert, and hear
a parking lot argument at the Garden State Parkway Food & Fuel.
Would you want me to catch sight of humpbacks
breaking through waves, or the slide of a copperhead from

a crawl-space? It seems something is happening away
from here and kinship is lost. I don't see the arrow. You could
rightly tell me to go back to where I came
from and I would conjure the steep, green Countryside
Drive, even though I left that tree-lined serpentine in 1976,

the year I started my period at summer camp only
to be betrayed. You see, I keep my metaphors scrawled
on the lining of my stomach so I don't
have to drive over the Pulaski Skyway to oblige.
I got out when you pulled your sentence over, eager to see

the vast red desert and buy blue-green rocks from
a flat-bed. I got nowhere. The argument was about moving on,

how not to be ashamed of oneself for
the passage of time, or blamed. And the women
were just photographs of themselves, not counselors.

Archaeologists once found a cave drawing of a whale
in the Grand Canyon, beached, in the receding tide. Now, a
woman paleontologist in Tuscany
has found a complete prehistoric whale skeleton
and murder clue shark fangs, its last meal hieroglyphed

in the ribs and eye teeth. I like to share details along
certain coordinates to focus imagination. You remind me
of when I stopped in the town
of Petroglyph, New Mexico, population 0.
If this poem is a vehicle, my hazards are blinking.

FUSIONISM

SHALOM NEUMAN

I f our lives are composed of multi-sensory experiences where neither sense is separate, then why are artists not aspiring to recreate and reference that reality? Why not capture life in art and art in life? Why not reinforce text with images and sculpture? Why not combine painting, text and sound? Why not combine sound, sculpture, video, smell and text?

If you experience a car crash, isn't it true that the sounds, visuals and smells of the crash are inseparable from the overall experience of the crash? Isn't the crash experience all encompassing?

If that is our reality, that all the senses contribute to create an experience, that experiences are MULTI-sensory, then why don't artists develop the methodologies to fuse all our senses when creating?

Until this century, a century of technological explosion, it has never before been possible to integrate all our senses. But now we have technology at our fingertips: motion detectors,video projectors, holograms, computer imaging systems and sound systems. Smart phones are now recognized as creative tools and used by professional photographers.

The Futurists, Constructivists, Dadaists, Cubists, Fluxists aspired to project into the future. Technology was important. These artists aspired to bridge the divide between the disciplines.

Using a multi-sensory approach also represents a great freedom, a freedom that no longer exists in the linear approach to art that ran its course in the West with Kazimir Malevich's black paintings. It took longer to die in the United States but it ended here with Ad Reinhardt in the late 1950s.

The times in which we now live have enabled us to exponentially combine the senses and the arts as never before. It is our burden and our joy as well as our responsibility to invent the future. Be part of the movement!

The artwork for this centerfold was chosen because the contributing artists are exploring methodologies outside the traditional norms of painting and sculpture. Art is no longer pure; now it manifests itself as ephemeral and multi-sensory. The past 20–30 years have given rise to the exploration and incorporation of non-traditional techniques and practices to create art.

ARTISTS, IN ORDER OF APPEARANCE:

1. Doron Polak
2. Rafi Baler
3. Oh Zee, Ok Soon and Greg Schenk — Fusionsim event, Prague, CZ 2012
4. Fusionism event, Paris, France, 1987
5. Thierry Marceau
6. Fusionism event, Florence, Italy, 2013
7 and 8. Petr Nikl
9. Monty Cantsin and Shalom Neuman
10. Jocelyn Fiset
11. Phil Rostek
12 and 13. Michael Alan
14. Moshe Frumin
15. Oh Zee
16. Fusionismo event, Florence, Italy, 2013

Doron Polak communicates and evokes feelings by using his body as a brush by interacting and melding into various environments.

Rafi Baler uses utilitarian objects and materials, essentially whatever is at hand, to express himself artistically.

Oh Zee, Ok Soon and Greg Schenk (group photo) are the paint brushes and the art they create with their bodies is the end result.

Thierry Marceau references American celebrities and American iconography in his art, often disguising himself and then projecting himself into his work.

Petr Nikl uses light, projections, rhythm, sound and movement to convey a mood.

Monty Cantsin uses imagery and propaganda symbols from the past for political artistic expression.

Jocelyn Fiset uses tape to draw and distort physical space,communicating through his lines.

Phil Rostek uses found objects and common housing materials like foam and roofing cement to convey his message.

Michael Alan transforms his drawings into environments using thread, light, people and objects.

Moshe Frumin uses colorful found objects and transforms them into musical instruments that he then plays.

Shalom Neuman believes that everything and anything can be transformed into a message. He uses multi-sensory art and Fusionism events to engage and involve both artists and audience.

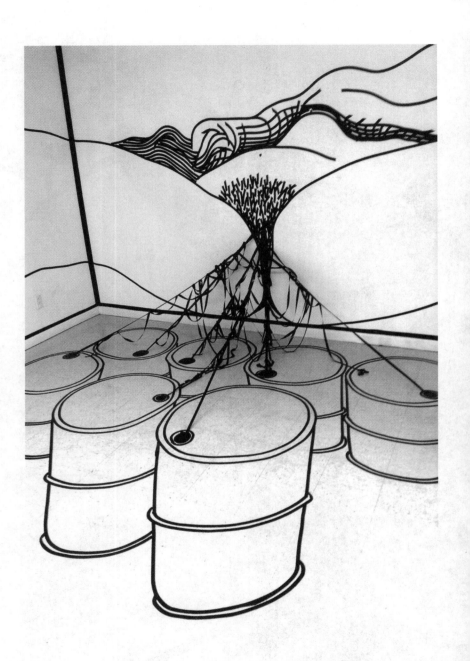

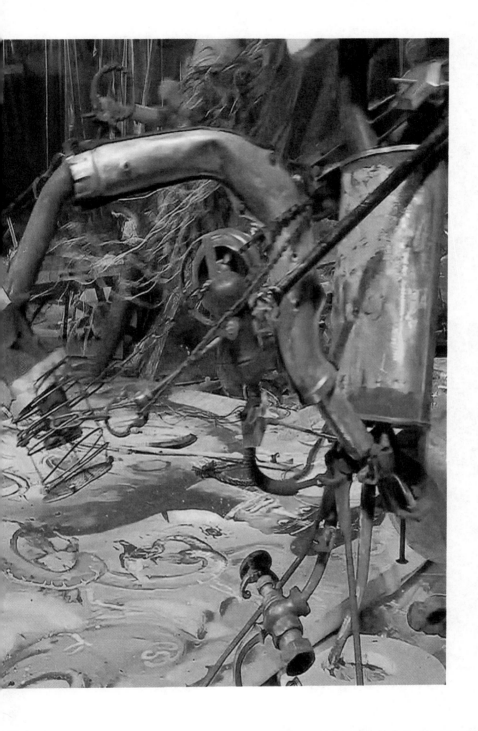

IT'S THE ECONOMY, STUPID!

I DRINK YOUR MILKSHAKE:
CHAOS AND THE CLOUD OF UNKNOWING
CARL WATSON

BP told Congress Tuesday its massive Gulf oil spill was caused by the failure of a key safety device made by another company. In turn, that company says BP was in charge, and that a third company that poured concrete to plug the exploratory well didn't do it right. The third company, which was plugging the well in anticipation of future production, says it was only following BP's plan, which didn't work either.

We are constantly confronted with things that don't work. Flood control precautions apparently don't work, either in Nashville levees or in Boston sewers. Government doesn't seem to be able to fix these things; witness the state of the City of New Orleans. But maybe it's not government's fault. After all, the technological contraptions they might try probably won't work. It's just the way it is: Filipino voting machines, accelerators on Toyotas, the brakes on the Staten Island Ferry. We might look to morality as a safeguard but morality is not up to par. We need only look to mining companies such as Massey Energy for evidence of that failure. In fact, morality aside, many big ideas don't work: the Eurozone, Greece, Thailand, Communism, Capitalism. Democracy doesn't much work either. The majority does not seem to rule (unless it' s major money). This is partly because not enough people care to vote and voters don't have anything to choose between anyway. Even if they did, their choices don't seem to accomplish anything, as some other unseen power somewhere will have some other agenda. We need only look at our own election system circa 2000 (or any year for that matter) or witness the recent British elections that left an entire country standing around rather dumbfounded. But that's no different than a congress that doesn't work, either on the federal level where one obstinate clown can screw up the whole machine, or in New York State, which seems to be frozen in a perpetual motion loop of bitter accusation and denial. What about a mind that doesn't work? There's a lot of them out there, rabid partisanship notwithstanding. We don't have to look farther than Rush Limbaugh: insinuating that the BP oil disaster is a plot by the Obama administration, instigated as an excuse to shut down all off shore drilling. Perhaps Rush Limbaugh is an anomaly, a bad example of failure, what with his addiction issues and all.

Today we live in a world of anomalies — individual instances of failure in a largely functioning system — that's what they tell us. In fact, however, it is becoming more apparent that nothing really works, and a paranoid person might believe we are receiving some kind of comeuppance for our ego-gratifying consumerist ways. When things don't work there are a few actions that can be taken, besides claiming the failure as a kind event and not a systematic problem. One of these actions, or rather reactions, is to put on a big show of being on top of the situation right away—albeit after the fact. We see this in NYC all the time. For instance, the other day, after the failed Times Square bomb, I went to the main post office on 8th Avenue and the whole place was surrounded by cops as if they were expecting another terrorist event at any moment. Of course any terrorist wanting to blow up the post office would simply just wait until the cops left before attempting it. And the cops will leave eventually; I think they did the very next day. This kind of after-the-fact remedy reminds me of the many train trips I took across the subcontinent. Kids in the Indian villages loved to throw rocks at the train when they passed through their village. I was always surprised that immediately after such an incident everyone closed their windows Inevitably, when it got uncomfortable, they opened them again. The closing of the windows did nothing because a half hour later we would pass through another village and the whole thing would happen over again. The safeguard of closing the window is kind of like putting a lot of cops around the post office the day after the bomb threat.

Speaking of safeguards that don't work in mine disasters and cops around post offices, what about those New York anti-terrorist strategies that were designed to prevent Times Square bombs. Recently we have seen both Bloomberg and Kelly parading across the media landscape proclaiming how well their anti-terrorism strategies work. Am I missing something here? The only truth that comes out of this episode is massive failure of precisely those strategies. Here's a guy, who, over the last couple of years has strewn his path with red flags and profile markers: he quits his job, moves his family to Pakistan, where he attends a bomb-making camp, then comes back to the U.S., still with no one paying much attention. He lives alone, keeping to himself to the point that even his neighbors say he was acting strange. Then he buys a car with cash, does not register it, and drives it around with stolen plates. In fact drives it into Times Square and parks in an erratic manner on a street where no parking is allowed. Still no notices. A tee-shirt vendor finally sees that the car is smoking and calls a cop. By then the bomb has fizzled out. That very day the authorities were acting as if they caught the guy before he could pull off his plot. They didn't catch anything. Their strategy didn't work. Fortunately, neither did the bomb. As if this weren't enough, apparently "No Fly" lists don't work either. This Faisal Shahzad dude manages to get on a plane anyway, and not by some devious clever route; he heads to Kennedy of all places, the one airport where they are most likely to be looking for him, and buys a seat to the United Emirates, one of the most likely places for terrorists to chill out. The plane is on the tarmac ready to take off and they finally catch up to him. Who are Bloomberg and Kelly kidding? They should be embarrassed as hell, but they are acting as if they triumphed, which shows that apparently evolution doesn't work either, if embarrassment is an evolutionary function.

Computer-trading programs that produced the recent glitch that caused the Dow to drop over a thousand points recently have not only exposed the fact that this kind of software just doesn't work but it has also given us a glimpse behind the curtain to the sad truth that nothing is really worth anything, and this is especially true of your retirement account if you have one, because as oil creeps toward the gulf shore, whatever nest egg you worked so many years for has probably become as worthless as Lehman Brothers' and Goldman Sachs' investment strategies, which actually did work, if only for them. The Euro might not be worth anything soon, but an obscure Picasso that no one knew existed is still worth a lot of money. I don't understand really but I don't feel bad because my lack of understanding is mitigated by everyone else's. In fact, there seems to be a global lack of understanding going on. No one understands anything anymore and they don't even try to hide it. The bankers at Goldman Sachs don't understand the financial instruments that they themselves created, and they admit it — after the fact of course, after they brought down the economy. Morgan Stanley didn't have a clue. Going back to that recent thousand-point market swoon, the traders of Wall Street don't understand why it happened. For the last week they keep throwing up their hands saying "We just don't know what happened." Who is supposed to know? Who should be responsible under the law when no one knows what they are doing? Apparently no one. Toyota still has no idea why their cars accelerate uncontrollably. Some ghost in the machine apparently. But at least their sales figures are way up in this last quarter despite their crashing cars. No one knows why. BP doesn't even understand why their platform exploded. The blowout valve failed, the one that should have shut the well down. And the concrete plug failed, the one that was supposed to stop the methane bubble. But there was something that failed before that, and something before that — the failures go way back in a chain. One thing we do know is that science fiction has failed us: apparently all those remote-control robots we see in the movies don't work as well as they do in the movies. They are the dreams of the computer animation sequences in which they were invented. No wonder they don't work. They were created by programs that no one actually understands. It's true I don't understand how my computer works either. I certainly don't have any idea how my dreams work but I know I have them. Last night I had a dream: I was underwater with Diver Dan and some of his talking fish buddies. There was an underwater gusher and Daniel Day Lewis was saying "I Drink Your Milkshake" to the shrimp fishermen of the gulf coast.

What about that Libyan plane crash the other day, or that missing French airliner last year? No one knows why they happened. They can't find any black box. If only there was a black box, I mean for everything — something like the one in Kubrick's "2001," the black box that all the monkeys rallied around before they got smart. Well we do have our devices that we can turn to (if the batteries happen to be working). We can turn to the media for answers, but media doesn't work either; they can't seem to explain anything. They do manage to pose the question over and over again in the effort to bring in more advertising revenue. I should just stop listening because all I hear is more news about things that don't work and how nobody knows why nothing is working. "Not knowing" something that you really know is, of course, one sign of trauma, which might mean maybe we are living in an age traumatized by complex and aggressive media. Someone, however, has to pretend that it is at least possible to understand, otherwise everyone would just start shooting their neighbors for food instead of going to the grocery store. And so the pundits and talking heads gleefully keep trying to explain everything, desperately promoting a blind faith in the increasing complexity of the culture that keeps everybody working and making money. Of course that doesn't seem to work very well either, because a lot of people who need to be making money can't do it, either here in the Land of the Free, or over there, in the land that the Land of the Free feeds upon. Who's making money off of mining in Africa and the Amazon anyway? Not the people who live there. It might actually be you or me and we might not know it. It's like the BP executive said — if you drive a car or heat your home with oil you are responsible for the Gulf Coast disaster.

I hate to be the voice of pessimism, but it's time to realize that probably nothing works. It's a mathematical certainty that as complexity grows, the laws that govern predictability (based on perceivable cause and effect) become inapplicable, simply because it is no longer possible to know what the causes and effects are without severely limiting your field of vision, and thus becoming "narrow-minded," a state not conducive to understanding anything. But then if you are "broad-minded" you don't understand anything either. It would be easy to say that this all has something to do with the butterfly theory: you know, a butterfly flaps its wings in Beijing and we get two weeks of severe tornadoes across Oklahoma and Kansas. Picture a dead battery that causes an ecological disaster that destroys all Gulf Coast life and livelihood. It might even cause someone a thousand miles away to jump into the Hudson River in a vain suicide attempt. Given recent circumstances, I would update the Butterfly Theory concept into the Milkshake Theory whereby you just don't know who or what is trying to stick its straw into your milkshake: it may be an oil baron or it may be a computer code running off on its own, or some hacker trying to get into your bank account if you are lucky enough to have one. But these days there are fewer and fewer people who have milkshakes to drink and that straw has to go somewhere. Watch your backs.

WE ARE THE WEAKEST LINK: OUR DRIVE TO SEE WHO'S THE MOST... WHATEVER
Carol Wierzbicki

Maybe all of this insanity started with bungee-jumping, but we as a society seem to be caught up in the desire to make everything "Extreme." Extreme fighting, extreme makeovers, extreme professions. Reality shows dig ever deeper into that barrel of miserable existence, scrape the very crust off the bottom, and come up with compelling series like Biggest Loser Hoarders Who Also Have the Worst Jobs Ever.

Extreme behavior is now the new norm. Road rage, stage moms who push their Toddlers in Tiaras to fits of crying hysteria at beauty pageants, someone yelling "Liar!" in the middle of the President's State of the Union address. Is this distortion of reality a symptom of our millennial angst?

We see the recent spate of apocalyptic movies growing darker and more disturbing: "District 9," "I Am Legend," all the superhero movies. At stake in these films is always not just the quality of life of a single city, but the health of the whole planet. I think the popularity of these extreme forms of entertainment is fueled by fear — not just fear generated by the bad economy, global warming, or increasingly intellectually feeble political candidates, but fear of emptiness, absence of content and meaning in one's life. I call it the 3D glasses effect: we process visually dazzling scenes to make up for that cavernous space between our ears.

Another metaphor is that of a stationary bike — we pedal faster and go nowhere. Each worker is trying to appear busier and more overscheduled than the next guy, ostensibly to save his job. The most depressing virtual environment I can think of is Spinning class, where a roomful of cyclists pedal furiously to canned music and projected landscapes. It's too dangerous to bike outside anymore!

We're hurling ourselves toward Doomsday, flailing more emphatically. With barely disguised glee the media report more shark attacks (from bigger sharks), more wildlife migrating to odd places in odd seasons, more record-breaking violent weather, more mysterious viruses. Meanwhile, a multiplicity of doomsayers shout from their wilderness peaks: "It's Y2K, we're gonna die," "It's May 21, 2011, we're gonna die, no, make that October 2012..." What's our answer to these ominous portents? The quadruple hamburger topped with ribs and a slice of deep-fried cheesecake.

Bon Appetit.

TULI KUPFERBERG

MY MONEY JOURNAL
DAVID PEMBERTON

I: BUDGET

I need more words than I've budgeted. I've overspent on *crushed messenger, broadcast terrorist, park paranoia;* I've been too closely involved in correlating *saved dog, scorpion invasion, Time Out Tuxedo.* I need to scrape up enough capital text to conjure a piece of my house, a window in a room that was decorated for me looking onto an out-of-doors that was staged on my behalf, to be installed here with some of my possessions, to exercise my verbiage of place.

II. SUSTENANCE

During a "surprise" trip to a grocery store my illustrative version of self spent $45.30. I bought the perkiest produce and finest cuts of soulful meat. My hard content version of self awoke to find a refrigerator full of shriveled produce and rotted meat. "Surprise!" Apparently, having thought to consume them wasn't enough.

III. CASH OUT

Like the spoiled food, I should not offer the following for consumption. I received news from sleepy home: Marion, Ohio's Marion Meadows. Jim Rook, so my mom has informed me, made an attempt (pending successful status) on his own life. He fired up a chainsaw and took it to his own gut. His wife, Ester, found him unconscious, his intestines beside him. He's in intensive care, but the outlook is grim. Neighbors entered the house after Ester went with Jim to the hospital and cleaned up the blood and gore so she didn't have to see it again.

IV. Revenue

There is a green plastic piece of something sitting in a driveway. It's at least five feet long and connotes dragon or sea monster, and as I further expense the memory, I see it must be a child's toy, something to ride or rock on, and it's for sale, it's one of many items for sale at this yard sale. Objects sifted from households are arranged on folding tables and boneless clothing hangs from rolling racks perfuming the air with mothballs. The green plastic dragon becomes a mascot of sorts because it never sells and because this yard sale is a weekly event put on by Ester Rook, who, when she isn't holding a yard sale, is shopping at a yard sale where she acquires the stuff to resell at her yard sale — apparently, but I don't know for sure, which goes for almost everything here, she turns a decent profit doing this, but there are sacrifices, such as storing the inventory in the two-car garage, which means that Ester and Jim have to park their cars in the driveway.

V. Stocks

This is a place where problems and solutions to problems hold each other up — gravy garnished with antacid, beryllium sifted with alkylating agents. Everyone and everything is wet with treatment — dandelions are the devil. You want plain language? My junior high and high schools sit on a former military depot where chemical waste was dumped for years. Ignorance is a natural resource; if you weren't so late to the party you would have already invested.

VI. Liability

The Rooks, a Caucasian couple, have four children, two Caucasian and two African American, all four adopted. The Rooks were known for running a very strict, conservative, and maybe above all else, frugal house. Every morning since anyone can re-member, Jim and Ester had their breakfast at McDonald's. They would each order a cup of coffee for $.60 ($.10 after they reached the official Golden-Buckeye age of sixty) and eat graham crackers and bananas which they brought from home. Jim, a thin, tight skinned man, always carried an inflatable donut seat to sit on and us kids used to crack jokes about his having hemorrhoids, but ap-parently, even all of those years ago, he was coping with back pain. Kids all over the neighborhood liked to have fun at the Rooks ex-pense, the awkward vibe they gave off was too much to ignore in Marion Meadows. The constant yard sale, the inflatable donut seat, the black and white children, the severe demeanor (on Jim's part — Ester was always a sweetie), the accents (they hailed from West Virginia) all made them targets for toilet paper and eggs on Hal-loween and ridicule throughout the year. But as time went by, their kids grew up, the neighborhood grew up, and I grew up, and the Rooks were just the Rooks, nuanced, tortured and triumphant, benchmarks of stability in Marion, Ohio's Marion Meadows.

VII. BONDS

Dark news, although not this shocking, comes ringing on my phone more often these days. Gail Hellwig, one of my mom's best friends, died this summer from cancer. Gail loved cats and to gar-den, just like my mom. Gail was a nurse and my mom is a teacher, a ruler propped against an apple, a white angular hat, both easily recognizable graphic representations in the neighborhood.

VIII. COMMERCIAL DEVELOPMENT

From this Legacy Crossing let's show the people our *Copper-tudes*. The setting is a very old new. The *Video Stars* mingle in the *Hobby Lobby* while I'm stuck at home (grounded?) shooting pi-geons from my *American Mattress*. In the middle of Mallard Square Maurice's *As-Seen-Ins* are battling the *Tan Pros* in football. The ac-tion is fat and underwhelming until, *Holy Guacamole!* what style! the *As-Seen-Ins* withdraw from the association and win by forfeit.

IX. RISK CAPITAL

Certainly sitting in a running car in a closed garage offers a relatively peaceful and painless means of self-extinguishment — especially if your wife is rationing your pain meds because of the obvious signs of deep depression that you have been exhibiting. The inflatable donut seat (that I can't seem to get away from), the back pain that became worse and worse, persistence to the point of constancy, the knowledge that the pain would never subside, that being was pain and pain was being was just too much to be — and not having ever owned a pistol or any kind of firearm (reminder — I project) and having a garage that is guarded by a green plastic dragon and thus inaccessible to an automobile, and not having the physical strength nor mobility to either clear it or reach up to hang a noose, and perhaps having an acute fear of razors (*Xyrophobia*) and supposing that a knife wound would take more strength of will than a chainsaw with its buzzing teeth that would chew you up and spit your guts out with little force from yourself, though unimaginably gruesome, maybe it was the most — *gulp* — logical way that he could think of through the pain.

X. LIQUIDATION

From this Legacy Crossing there is nothing left to leave behind. Under this Legacy Crossing I buried my past for safe keeping but a new bleakness was erected on top of it — a plentitude of fatness that squishes out my playground of the half-built and the newly abandoned.

XI. INSURANCE

It's been four days since my mom called me, so I called her and caught her in the grocery store (I didn't ask her which one, but I imagined the new one at Legacy Crossing, or perhaps the old one across the street at Mallard Square). She said she was just looking at some things. Sounds like a "surprise" grocery trip. She told me that she saw Ester walking by our house from the kitchen window so she went out to console her and offer support. She found out that, quite astonishingly, Jim is recovering physically but not — *gulp* — mentally. Ester said that there wasn't anything my mom could do but that the support from the people of Marion Meadows is holding her up.

FROM: U.S. INVESTMENT BANKS
TO: THE AMERICAN PUBLIC
SUBJECT: OUR RESPONSE

JOEL ALEGRETTI

This poem is extracted from the introduction to the television series The Outer Limits (1963–65). *As participants in the Troubled Asset Relief Program (TARP) appropriated taxpayer money, the poem appropriates existing text.*

THERE IS NOTHING WRONG with your television set.
Do not ATTEMPT TO ADJUST the picture.
WE ARE CONTROLling transmission.
IF WE WISH TO make it louder, WE WILL bring up the volume.
If we wish to make it softer, we will tune it to a whisper.
WE will CONTROL the horizontal.
WE will CONTROL the vertical.
WE can ROLL the image, make it flutter.
WE CAN CHANGE THE FOCUS to a soft blur
    or sharpen it to crystal clarity.
For the next hour, SIT QUIETLY
and WE will CONTROL all that YOU see and hear.

MY NIGERIAN CHECK SCAM ROMANCE
DEBORAH PINTONELLI

We had all gotten to this particular place in our three very separate, different lives in a very similar way. I blame it all on 9/11. And on George W. Bush. His awful scrunched monkey face on that awful day said it all. It has been twelve long years since that break: the heartbreak, financial ruin, all of our real and imagined capital spent in that moment of humans flinging their bodies out of a skyscraper to avoid the terrible burning and crushing and melting that was going on within. He could do nothing about it, nor could we. That we were so hated all around the world exacted this cost. We were arrogant, brutal in our methods. We were greed monsters. And even more so afterwards. We would wage war, and torture, and lie about it. It was and would be our most horrible moment since Hiroshima. It changed me forever.

Everyone was borrowing money then. Families with little ability to pay it back. Single mothers, businesses small and large. We were all caught up in a national hysteria that would result in near collapse. I borrowed against everything I had, and so did Brian and Jon. And then we found ourselves, separate but together, unemployed, in debt and ruin. We met at a Midtown Irish pub called O'Malley's, where white collar types without jobs met in the late afternoons, to swap stories and make contacts. Or to just drink. We had heard that people had done this during the last financial collapse of the dot com generation, and that sometimes it helped.

This time nothing helped. Three or more years of unemployment, living off of yet another extension of benefits from my previous job as an account executive at a small ad agency, and still nothing. I just kept borrowing to keep my condo up and running until there was no more left and I was sixty thousand dollars in debt. When I got the job with Mark Moran, I had twenty-five dollars in the bank, credit cards that were maxed out, and was not eligible for another unemployment extension. Jon had two hundred. We had to nurse our drinks, and hope that the bartender would buy one or two rounds.

I remember sitting there clutching my phone, checking my email every ten minutes to see what the almighty HR lady at Mark Moran's had to tell me. She was to have contacted me by five, and at four forty-five I was certain I was doomed. Jon had already heard that he'd gotten his position as chief salesman for foreign operations. I was waiting on mine on the design team. Brian had nothing. We were going to pull him in after we got ours. I remember telling Jon that I was so fucked, that I'd have to do a short sale on the condo and move back in with my mother. That I could see the sincere, pitying smiles of her friends when they visited and saw me home again. I'd have to eat shit and live with her nuttiness and not be able to say a word about it.

Every night that week had included a different nightmare about loss. Precious items, babies, partners that I did not even have, would be lost by me in the dreams by different methods, never to be recovered. In them my mother was often laughing. In actual life she bore me no ill will, and to be honest I barely discussed it with her. It was only in the back booth of that dark pub that I could tell people I hadn't even known that long the truth. It unified us, made us complicit, and even a bit special. We were sure, as we saw other groups around us doing the same thing, that our stories were the worst.

Cliques formed, and in a way it helped. Subgroups that trusted one another served as conduits for job news, opportunities, and recent rejections that another of us could pounce on, the way people tracked down apartments newly up for rent in the city by checking the obituaries and stalking others on moving days. Jon said he had not spoken to his parents in almost a year, and that his wife was threatening to sell everything they owned if he did not make it better fast. He was so relieved when he got the job offer that he felt all mushy inside, "like a girl."

All I saw was a change in myself. My calm, the self-esteem I had once had, both were gone. Instead there was a false sense of these things, as when a museum is robbed of a priceless painting and a reproduction is put in its place. At four fifty-five I received the confirmation email. Sure, I felt relief like Jon's, yes. But something was off.

It took almost one year for us to feel normal again. For at least that long we had been scrounging, living on pasta, ramen noodles, cheap beer, tinned meats and ninety-nine cent packages of cookies. Or at least I was. I had no idea what Jon and his wife were doing. Some days there were weird choices that had to be made: bus fare to a dinner party being thrown by a Friend With a Job, or using it to buy a five dollar bottle of wine. Downing the whole thing while watching endless amounts of CNN and MSNBC or reality shows was sometimes more comforting than spending it to sit amongst those better off.

It's really hard to make proper chit chat at such events while avoiding personal questions. Well-bred persons often ask many, many questions in an effort to seem interested in something other than their own lives. As you answer they are drifting off into their own little world, while still being able to catch certain phrases, like "I am not working at the moment," or, "I am not seeing anyone right now." Then the opaque veil of sadness will cloud their eyes. There will be no offer of help in any way, but lots and lots of sympathy and empathy, just to reaffirm their own humanity. *I'm sure it must be hard,* they will coo as they stealthily return to their own thoughts.

Often I would lose my appetite at such dinners. I'd had such a great run of oysters, foie gras, caviar, thick juicy steaks, roasted chickens, bottles of mid-range champagne, and everything else you can think of at every middling bistro in town that to sit down and sample some humble attempt at this very simple way of cooking brought out the snob in me even if I had been eating cereal and quick noodles for weeks. What was the point of eating it now, getting used to this lesser version, if I would have to then return to the ascetic ways I had been keeping?

Frozen lemonade. Something called "hot garbage mix" from the health food store at 23rd and Madison that was marked down for quick sale. Everything, in fact, at my local deli that was marked down to get it moving before the expiration date. My stomach bloated with the likes of dollar Chips Ahoy and sodium-laden fake Asian bowls. To think that I could not even afford, at one point, the low-brow Chinese or Thai take-out from my two favorite local places could send me spiraling into a food coma as I tried to recreate these elementary dishes myself and fail.

You cannot cook if your heart is not in it, and not without fresh ingredients, unless you are a wizard of some sort. I'd stare at the mushy pile of stuff in my wok in disbelief. Sometimes it felt as if I were experimenting for some government agency. Try to concoct healthy, tasty meals out of these three things, all for under four dollars: one bunch of broccoli, one can of 'mixed Asian vegetables *including baby corn,* and a package of Stir Fry Delight. Eat it I must, even though it looked grayish-green and held deep within it a metallic odor. Wash it down with a 32 oz. Heinken. That was the treat! Heinken, even in a can, still tasted like itself. And in the end, when you burped, it wasn't a Stir Fry Delight burp, just a normal, hoppy release.

Actually, I do know what Jon did over at his house. Instead of the packaged organic stuff they liked to buy, pop into microwave or oven, and feel superior about, they were *forced to cook from scratch.* For them, it was the same problem, just different. They were so used to the way their fake food tasted —including the fake restaurants they went to which also offered faux cuisine —they had to make it themselves, and it tasted like shit! Oh, the horrors of a simple, roasted chicken. It did not come with pre-grill marks and julienned vegetables. It was greasy, and messy, and the thighs and legs looked pale and ill sitting in a pool of fat because neither of them had known to tie it up before popping it in.

I remember laughing evilly upon hearing this —I pounced on any bit of information that made my miserable life seem less so — my cracked lips from not-enough-water-because-I-don't-drink-from-the-tap-and-can't-afford-bottled needing to be pressed firmly with my forefinger to avoid breaking into too wide of a grin while cackling. I imagined them toying dismally with the chicken, pushing it around the plate before giving it to the dog. I imagine his lard ass wife saying to herself, *oh, fuck it, just give me the tub of Edy's French Vanilla.*

One of the ways I was able to survive was to answer ads on Craigslist for jobs that were obviously fake. By fake, I mean they were designed to lure the jobless into an exchange that was fraudulent and risky. Inherent in this process was the necessary communication with persons whose first language was not English, and who insisted upon being called "Mr." I willingly involved myself in these schemes in order to receive a fake check, deposit it into my account, wait for it clear within twenty-four hours, and withdraw the cash before the bank rescinded the funds.

The interchange often went on for days. A cursory perusal of the applicant's resume might be done. Or not. Quickly, the messages became all about sending and receiving the check, depositing it in an ATM only, and then letting the sender know when the funds cleared. Note the lack of basic grammar and punctuation. This is actually well written, compared to others:

James Gilbert: *Good Morning And How are you Doing? I am Mr James Gilbert the hiring manager Of Spencer Stuart Company and i am here to brief you more about this job and the interview. I Believe you are here and ready for your online interview to proceed? Spencer Stuart is one of the world's leading executive search consulting firms. Founded in 1956 and privately owned, we are the adviser of choice among organizations seeking guidance and counsel on senior leadership needs. We work with clients across a range of industries, from the world's largest companies to medium-sized businesses, entrepreneurial startups and nonprofit organizations. This is strictly an online and work from home job the working hours are flexible and you can chose to work from anywhere of your choice,the pay is $29.7 per hour training is $15.7 per hour and will be get payment bi weekly via direct deposit or paycheck working 40 to 45 hours weekly,if you are employed you are going to be working as a full employee and not an independent contractor. Are you still ready to proceed with the Interview? Do I have 100% of your attention?*

Me: *Yes, you do.*

The "interview" is just a series of directives from him, with me answering "yes" to each. At some point, he says he has to go offline to "check with my superiors about your qualifications."

James Gilbert: *Congratulations the company has decided to give you a chance for you to work for the company.We will like to see your diligence,Charisma,Commitement to this job. Benefits: Health, Dental, Life and AD&D Insurance, Employee Wellness and 401k plans.Paid Time Off and Holidays with Generous Company Discounts. You will receive your Salary Via BI-WEEKLY Via Check.*

Me: *Great, let me know how to proceed.*

James Gilbert: *Before you start work you will recieve a payment ,you will be using this payment to set up your mini office by purchasing accounting software plus the shippng logistics,cos we will be sending you some equipment you will be needing to start work with, immediately you get this payment you start work. The company will issue you a check to enable you purchase all the softwares and EQUIPMENTS you need to start work with.. NOTE: All softwares are to be purchased from the software office the company has been buying from for years now.*

Yes, you, who are going to wow them with your "diligence, Charisma, and Commitement," can chose to work from anywhere with softwares purchased from the software office and other equipments! Note the level of verbosity I employ in these exchanges:

James Gilbert: *You will undergo a one week training from your training supervisor he/she would be training you on how to Enhance your working skills with the programs accurately.Included with other Data entry job you would be needing to get done. Your training is going to be done online through your Pc.*

Enhance your working skills, if you dare! And get personal via Yahoo Messenger with your new guardian angel. He will inquire about your well-being, then quickly, with a bit of machismo, get down to business:

James Gilbert: *Hope you had a good night rest? i will instruct you on what you are to do with the check for $1,980.80. is that understood?*

Me: *Yes.*

James Gilbert: *Good…. And how close is the ATM Machine to you?*

Me: *Quite close.*

James Gilbert: *OK…. Proceed to the ATM Machine and make the deposit now, once you have done that you are to make a snap shot of the ATM Receipt or scan and email me the Receipt, it is needed for Proof of deposit and also for proper documentation for future purpose. Do you understand the instruction Elizabeth?*

Me: *Yes.*

James Gilbert: *Good. Have the ATM Deposit Receipt sent to gilbertjames326@yahoo.com Proceed to the ATM and make the deposit now.*

Me: *Ok.*

James Gilbert: *While i await the ATM Receipt i will await you.*

My last exchange happens after I turn over the check, withdraw the cash, and withstand a barrage of questioning messages like this:

James Gilbert: *Hello Elizabeth.... I believe the deposit has been made???*

Me: *Yep. And I'm terminating our conversation now and blocking you. This wasn't a total waste of time, as I was able to generate some cash and pay only a minimal overdraft fee after I gave the bank a sob story. You should really spell check your messages before you send them. Bye.*

I went to the bank wearing sweats and a baseball cap, no make-up, gripping a cup of Dunkin' coffee and my phone. Shivering a little, I listened to the banker tell me about how they were fully aware of these scams, the most famous being the Nigerian 419 check scam, that often originated in unsolicited emails from strangers in faraway places.

TULI AND THELMA

AND ANOTHER THING
ABOUT PUBLIC SCHOOL TEACHERS...
MIKE FALOON

L ast spring I went to the barbershop. My haircut looked too much like Adrian Zmed circa *T.J. Hooker*. Al, the barber, asked if I'd worked that day.

"I did."

"What do you do?"

"I'm a teacher."

"Oh, one of those guys who works 110 days a year."

You're off by about 88%, I thought. Most teachers work about 190 days a year. Al was obviously kidding but his joke missed the mark. His misinformed take on teachers is just the tip of an all too typical iceberg.

Teachers are easy targets — short work days, summers off, collective bargaining, and worst of all, tenure! A guaranteed job no matter how poorly I perform during those six-hour sprints I call a "work day"?

Of course, that's not what tenure is. Tenure doesn't guarantee me a job. Tenure guarantees the right to due process should my performance come under fire. Tenure provides academic protection. It also offers teachers, most of whom are women, protection — not impunity — from administrators, most of whom are men. Tenure is a benefit. By becoming a teacher I chose to earn less than other people with graduate degrees but I did so as a trade for benefits such as tenure.

And then there's the six-hour work days. Who couldn't demonstrate basic competence when working part-time? And for only ten months? People confuse a teacher's contract day, which is typically

6½ hours, with a teacher's actual work day, which is typically eight-to-ten hours. I kept track of my hours last year. I was on the clock for an average of nine hours a day. That didn't include lunch, which was usually shoveled down in fifteen minutes. Nine hours a day, forty-five hours a week. That's equivalent to 48 thirty-five-hour work weeks. That's not worthy of applause. It's not heroic. In other professions I'd receive overtime or comp time. As a teacher, I've signed up for the latter and take my comp time in the summer.

"We've got to take on the teachers' union!" If I'm not getting flack in the form of "teachers are kind of lazy, eh?" comments, then it's attacks on teachers' unions.

It was bad enough when I heard such talk of combating teachers' unions from the right. For generations conservatives held little hope that they would win the education debate. They conceded the issue to their liberal counterparts. The difference was funding — the right said spend less, the left said spend more. Most voters supported the latter.

The George Bush camp changed the game. They spearheaded a brilliant political move. Among other things, they placed a greater emphasis on standardized test scores, pushed vouchers, and supported charter schools. The implicit message: public school teachers stink, partly because they're lazy — willfully withholding their best efforts — and partly because their union is handcuffing them. Forget socio/economic factors. Forget class size. Forget funding. Forget the influence of parents. Mere distractions, one and all.

Public school teachers, according to those who espouse such views, need a kick in the collective can. One proposal is merit pay, giving teachers bonuses for delivering better test scores. Merit pay implies that teachers aren't already trying their best, they need a larger carrot dangled. Teachers don't want merit pay. We realize we have sufficient motivation: our students.

Another idea is to cut benefits. Teacher benefits are bankrupting state governments. It's time to scale back. It's the selective application of this argument that reveals its weaknesses — I'm still looking for a politician who proposes cutting benefits for police officers or fire fighters. A third "solution" is the promotion of charter schools. Charter schools are funded by public money but their teachers are not union members. Administration calls all the shots; teachers have no collective voice. Also, charter school teachers have fewer requirements and less professional development. And charter schools can deny admission to students.

Charter schools are an attempt to cut teachers out of the decision making process and save money by offering diminished benefits. Are they better for students? The answer to that is found in the criteria people use to evaluate charter schools.

Every time I hear about a successful charter school the description contains two or more of the following traits: students dressing in uniforms, passively listening to a teacher lecture, walking quietly in lines, and/or writing neatly. Most reports on charter schools focus on Latino and/or African-American students. At first, I was heartened by this trend — when do such students ever receive the bulk of the media's attention? Then I noticed that these students were always shown engaged in one or more of the behaviors listed above and I realized this: Nothing tickles the fancy of charter school proponents like compliant children of color dressed in uniforms.

Not once have I heard that the teaching is better in charter schools — cheaper, more passive, yes, but never better. Nor have I read a charter school report that focuses on the extent to which students are engaged in higher level, critical thinking. Such thinking tends to be loud — classrooms filled with students engaged in discussions, not just a teacher lecturing a room of docile recipients. It tends to be messy — students moving around the classroom working on projects, rather than just sitting in rows of desks silently completing workbook pages. And most complicated of all, such thinking is difficult to measure — students debating whether Thomas Jefferson was a hero or a traitor doesn't fit into a spread sheet like twenty question multiple choice quiz.

(Some sources cite standardized test scores to validate charter schools. Not all sources do, however, because the results are inconsistent. Never trust any source that leads with test scores. Students don't learn when they're taking tests. Students don't learn when they're practicing taking tests. Students learn less when teachers teach to the test.)

Such perspectives used to be the sole province of the right. Now they're finding traction with liberals. The Obama administration has led the charge for Race to the Top and the Common Core standards, whose effects, among others, is to subject students to more testing and encourage the growth of charter schools.

I've been teaching for nearly twenty years. My union has never once protected a lousy teacher. (Few do. And besides, who is responsible for poor hiring practices in the first place?) My union does not seek to gouge taxpayers. (My annual raise averages 3%, consistent with cost of living increases.)

Here's what my union has done for me:

• Fought to have more of my professional development time devoted to studying methodology, planning lessons, and analyzing student work (rather than spending this time on paper work)

• Contested the governor's plan (he's a Democrat) to have teacher evaluations partially based on parent and student feedback, which would reduce annual evaluations to a popularity contests

• Met with me to facilitate better communicate with administrators

• Encouraged me to attend board of education meetings so I'll be better informed about local issues

• Led charity fundraisers

• Helped me better understand our contract

• Continually sought my feedback

I recognize that I shoulder a tremendous responsibility. I arrive early. I stay late. I strive to insure that every student receives a great education. I'm sick and tired of having my profession, and my union, dragged through the mud.

MY FATHER SOLD LIFE INSURANCE
LYNN ALEXANDER

Back in the sixties, door
to door, in the black
neighborhoods and white,
separated as they were then
by visible and invisible
boundaries, he knocked
on doors and they let
him in, he smiled
and they let him in,
he shook their hands
and told them his plans
for their futures,
which was death
(of course) and loss
and poverty
(which they already had)
he said, do it
for the children,
do it, for the children's
future, do it
for your wife
even if she just poured
out your vodka
and threatened your life
with a kitchen knife,
do it, just do it, be

responsible, pay
your policy and you
will be rewarded
in heaven while your
children will be
rewarded in life,
do it for them,
do it for you,
do it because it's the best
thing in the world,
to die and leave
your kids and wife
a fortune. My dad
sold life insurance
door to door,
and when he died
he didn't have a dime
of life insurance,
not a dime.

BASIC NECESSITY
MARK McCAWLEY

t finally came down to necessity. Basic necessity. Walls and a roof over my head. Something inside my stomach to keep me going for another day. It was nearing the end of the month and I was near broke and jobless. Although I'd resisted the idea of going to Manpower for several days, my dwindling alternatives made the thought increasingly attractive. I figured some temporary assignments would be enough to pull me through what remained of the month, so I headed dqqowntown, confident of my chances.

My first referral was to a factory in the west end that manufactured custom-made windows. I was nearly maimed and almost killed in my first hour on the job by this psychotic moron who thought shooting nails over my head from his air tool was an exciting way to pass the time and initiate the new guy all at the same time.

My next referral was to a toxic waste dump disguised as an oil field parts and equipment rental business. I was to soak and clean all the various rented items which were returned each day. However, there were at least two weeks' worth of returns scattered every-which-way, coated with who-knows-what toxic substances. The fumes alone were so bad they made me dizzy in only minutes. When I asked for a respirator mask, the manager laughed in my face and chuckled as he said, "What'da'ya think this is... a union shop?"

It seemed each referral Manpower gave me was worse than the last. My initial confidence had turned into apprehension. So when I returned again to the Manpower office, it was with serious trepidation. This time, I was given a final referral along with an ultimatum not to return again if this latest referral didn't work out.

The position I was being referred for was as a "sanitary assistant" or so read the referral slip. The job was located across town in an aging suburban mall. I'd been sent to quite a few real shitty jobs over the last several days, so I tried not to think about what I'd be asked to do next.

I spent two hours riding a string of late evening buses just to get to work. It was ten minutes before eleven when I stepped off that last bus in front of the mall. I walked across the dark, deserted parking lot toward a gathering of people standing around a service entrance.

As I arrived at the service entrance, a carload of Asian men and women, an entire family I'd later learn, emptied out of the vehicle. As far as I could tell, I was the only Caucasian. The others were no doubt landed immigrants, or so I figured. I couldn't imagine why so many right-wing rednecks resented these people for taking these jobs from so-called "real Canadians." I didn't see too many white faces running forward to perform this sort of work. In fact, besides myself, there weren't any.

I'd just ground out the cigarette I'd been smoking under my shoe when another vehicle, a large gas-guzzler, turned into the parking lot and drove up near where we were all standing. Out of the car emerged the only other white face I'd see tonight. It was the contractor I'd spoken to over the telephone earlier in the day. He unlocked the service entrance door and everyone followed him inside. I couldn't help feeling that something disagreeable was about to transpire.

The contractor's name was Wayne Fisher, or so he had told me over the telephone, having hired me without ever setting an eye on me. He was a short, fat, balding man in his mid-to-late fifties, and looked as if he hadn't lifted a finger or done one iota of serious labor in years. His pot belly pushed out the bottom of his shirt and hung over the waist of his pants. He puffed on a long-slobbered cigar stub which stuck out the side of his mouth, and seemed to be continually out of breath. He struck me as that sort of anti-human flotsam, botched excuse for an abortion I usually took an immediate dislike to, and did.

We all stood silently, watching him as he waddled in front of us, huffing and puffing, sweat pouring down his face, his hands constantly pulling up the back of his pants which kept slipping down, exposing the crack of his ass. All the while, the same smoldering cigar stub never leaving the side of his mouth, even when he began to speak. He reminded me of a Shriner's circus clown I'd laughed at as a kid, but there wasn't a single thing amusing about this man.

"If you've forgotten anything outside the building," he chortled, almost choking, "too bad. The mall's security system's activated and won't be deactivated until seven tomorrow morning."

He plucked the cigar stub from his mouth and coughed several times, each time followed by an almost tubercular wheeze, then stuck it back into his mouth and continued. "There're two ten minute breaks and one thirty minute lunch. If I so much as guess any of you are sloughing off, it'll come outa your pay envelope at the end of the shift. This'll be your only warning. Any questions?"

None of us said anything.

"GOOD!" he barked.

With his pudgy right index finger, Wayne pointed at the people standing around and barked out orders of where to go, what to do — his arms flailing around like windmills as bits of spit and food flew from his mouth — until I was the last one left standing in front of him.

"YOU!" he bellowed, "COME WITH ME."

From one end of the mall to the other, I followed behind him, waving at the plumes of cigar smoke which trailed him like automobile exhaust. He led me into a small storage room, flicking on a solitary light bulb that hung from the ceiling in the centre of the room.

He pulled out a metal cart which, at one end, had a plastic bucket with a mop sticking out of it, and a large black garbage bag hanging from the other end. In between were shelves with compartments full of rags, soap, detergent, toilet paper rolls, paper hand towels, disinfectant cakes and the like.

"Ever worked in sanitation before?" Wayne spat at me.

"No, not really," I said, shaking my head, already regretting having taken this referral. Things were about to go from bad to worse to worst, and I knew it.

"No time like the present to get your hands dirty," he chuckled to himself. "Now take this cart and start by cleaning that restroom over there." He pointed his thumb over his shoulder. "Then work your way up the mall... should take you the rest of the shift. You got that?"

"Uh huh," I muttered.

"I'll let you know when you fuck up." Then he turned around and waddled away in a cloud of gray smoke.

The smell of shit was overpowering. Each time I thought I'd finally acclimated my sense of smell, an even worse stench would arise, leaving me with an overwhelming urge to puke. I couldn't understand how anyone could do this type of work, day in and day out, knowing all that was in store for them was just more of the same.

I couldn't stop myself from thinking about all the strange diseases which might be lurking in all those nooks and crannies I was supposed to clean. The human body isn't a place one wants to be inside of unless it's your own. I kept catching myself nervously scratching without quite knowing why.

The stale ammonia reek of urine was everywhere — on the floors, in the walls — everywhere except for the toilets and urinals it seemed.

I discovered that restrooms tell you a lot about those who use them — their habits, their hygiene, their health or lack thereof. Every toilet bowl was much like a tea-leaf reader's tea cup. All could be revealed by he who could read the signs.

For instance, in one particular toilet bowl, I noticed a single turd floating in the water. On top of it was a soiled condom, speckled with feces. I could well imagine the rest. Two men standing inside this stall. One man leaning over the toilet, arms outstretched, palms flat against the cold tiles, bracing himself against the wall, his pants crumpled around his angles. The other man spits into his palm, lubricates his prick with his saliva. Picture the rest.

I spent several hours this way. It helped to distract me from what I was doing, at least for a little while. But the usual nauseating smell was never far from my nostrils. I felt like an urban scatologist on the trail of a holy grail, all the while smelling like a thousand different assholes.

Around three in the morning the lunch break was announced. I felt groggy, dizzy, and sore. I sauntered to the food pavilion where everyone else had already begun eating. I hadn't brought a lunch because I couldn't afford one. So instead of eating, I sat at one of the tables, rested my head on my crossed arms, and closed my eyes. I could hear most of them speaking, but their language was incomprehensible to me. Still, it was preferable to the sound my growling stomach was making.

I tried to relax by thinking of ways to forget this entire fiasco. Almost every scenario involved the consumption of copious amounts of alcohol in order to obliterate, or at least nullify those neural connections involved with short term memory.

The Asian family I'd seen before the shift had started was sitting a comfortable distance away from my table. I figured it was the smell of all those toilet bowls I'd scrubbed that'd marked me somehow, and this was why they kept their distance from me. I couldn't really blame them.

All through lunch, over the P.A. system, Wayne's voice buzzed in our ears, telling everyone what to do, where to go, and how to do it. Those who spoke English translated for those who did not. It was enough to make you lose your appetite, if you had an appetite to begin with.

I was thinking how good it'd make me feel to shove that fucking microphone down Wayne's throat, when an elderly Asian man tapped me on the shoulder. In front of me he set down a rice cake with some kind of pate on it, next to a styrofoam cup filled with tea. He was smiling and nodding, gesturing with his hands for me to eat. I thanked him as best I could, nodding and smiling. He backed away, bowing.

After he rejoined his family, I quickly gobbled up the rice cake he had given me. The pate tasted like fish. It was delicious. I sipped the tea from the styrofoam cup. It tasted of mint. I looked up to see him and his entire family smiling at me. I sort of half smiled, nervously. Everyone's smile turned into a grimace when Wayne's voice announced the lunch break was over. Apparently, I wasn't the only one who disliked him.

At the end of the shift everyone converged at the main mall doors to pick up their pay envelopes. I knew it was going to be my first and last. Waiting in line, I wondered what I would do with the money I was paid. When I received my pay envelope, I opened it and looked inside. There were ten dollars missing. I went back to talk to Wayne about it.

"What's going on?" I said, referring to the envelope, "there's ten dollars missing."

"Nothing's missing," he muttered, matter-of-factly, continuing to hand out envelopes.

"What'da'ya mean, nothing's missing?" I was starting to get pissed off.

"Smoking in the restrooms," he said, "ten dollar fine... it's the rules."

"I wasn't told about any..."

Wayne cut me off.

"That's too damn bad," he sort of chuckled to himself. "You'll know for next time." Of course he knew that I knew that there wouldn't be a next time.

I turned around and walked away without even trying to argue the point. It was pointless. He was a bastard, plain and simple. He knew it. I knew it. Everybody knew it. What I couldn't figure out was how he knew I'd smoked the restroom to begin with. I hadn't seen him once that whole shift. I decided he'd probably spied on everyone using the mall's security cameras. What a prick, I thought.

I waited, along with everyone else, in the space between the two sets of mall doors for the security system to be deactivated. I looked back to where Wayne was standing, puffing on a newly lit cigar. He looked so smug standing there, gawking at us. I really hated his guts. And I must admit, there was a whole lot of guts there to hate.

It was while I was waiting for the security system to be deactivated that I noticed the emergency exit. Ignoring its warning, I inched my way toward it in a slow, lackadaisical manner. Then standing right next to it, I pushed open the door and stepped outside.

As I quickly walked across the parking lot to the bus stop, I could hear Wayne's high-pitched shrill even over the tripped emergency alarm's ringing.

The bus came, I climbed on board and took a seat at the back. Looking out the window at all the golden, sunlit buildings, I thought to myself how beautiful they looked after such a long and shitty night.

Just then, two fire engines and a police cruiser whizzed past my window. I closed my eyes and smiled, resting my tired head against the glass. A beautiful morning, indeed.

THE NEW WORKING CLASS
Sparrow

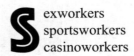exworkers
sportsworkers
casinoworkers

BEHIND THE GLASS
PATRICIA CARRAGON

ehind the glass sit polished couples, friends, and colleagues having "power lunches" on a warm March day. I pass by, invisible on this mid-town street. Looking at their faces, I wonder why this double-dip recession never affected them. I used to pass for one of them, dressed and ate like them — flashed numbers engraved on plastic to buy my dreams. How three years can change a person's life! I realize now that my former appearance had never guaranteed my acceptance by those behind the glass. The lifesaver was never thrown when my job fell out of existence. Their world is distancing. It's becoming harder to see them. Windows can break, but it wouldn't change the people behind the glass. They sit protected behind their visible lives, impervious to the shattered realities of others.

My new job doesn't require a college degree — just more comfortable shoes to withstand the abuse. Although the pay is slightly more generous than minimum wage, I was better off on unemployment. But I've met the ninety-three-week limit and have to fight for whatever was left for someone who has walked this block for so many years. Numbers have become more sinister, and I've never liked math.

The people behind the glass still sit, most are smiling and laughing. One couple is probably making wedding plans or at least, a trip to a Mexican beach. The girl with the manicured pink nails wears a solitaire diamond. The guy she is with is not one of those leftover "desperados" whom I now attract. He is handsome, young, and successful. And she is pretty without trying hard to be pretty.

The glass enclosing their world is not confined to this restaurant. It also exists on this sidewalk. I am still invisible as they pass by, leaving the wind to tamper with my thoughts. They are like the people behind the glass, having the same unbreakable glass attitude. They walk protected, and people like me can never break in and steal what used to be ours.

AN INVERTED IDYLL
JILL RAPAPORT

I went back to Yoigle as a lark and to visit Lucie and to pick up some of my things. I got in and went to my old area and nobody stopped me — in fact no one seemed to notice me, and, for my part, I did not see any face I could have called familiar. I was operating on the unexamined postulate that I had not yet burnt the bridge between me and the company and could still get away with pretending to be authorized to enter upon the premises. My old spot in the packaging department proved semi deserted and I went to the front to find Lucie. After some effort, I located her and made preliminary contact, but I broke away at the sound of the lunch bell (which no longer governed me) and departed for Brentwood Ltd., the food shop across the avenue in the Citicorp building, and bought a box of noodles and kiwi-pineapple mush and some fried cauliflower. On the way back, having crossed the park — which still bore a mantle of snow under the luminous winter sky — and having then entered through an unguarded door, I ran into Lucie in a hidden lunchroom tucked away somewhere behind the old company cafeteria that put out at all times the smell of bacon and other kinds of meat cooking. This was an adjoining room, which I had never seen before, although it looked sensibly connected to the one I knew. Lucie was picking stuff hastily from a salad and coldcut line and she seemed, as usual, harried. There were a few others seated at a few tables but they were not known to me and I did not do more than look briefly at them. In a polite way Luciee asked how things were and I told her about the new job and improved stomach and the fixed apartment. I wound up talking more or less to myself, because she didn't respond to the theatricalization of the way I presented myself but instead just glanced at me now and then, nodding, a sort of part smile playing distractedly about her brightly fading lips.

I went back with her to the office to help her with some filing, but it was too hard, and when I got the chance I left, with only the faintest sense of guilt.

I took a stairway, thinking to get out to the street or back in from the street — or whatever it was (a parking lot or service exit or sublevel access route) — and, in trying to take a shortcut, got lost. Instead of ending up where I thought I would (I was completely familiar with the terrain of the corridors and halls, inasmuch as that terrain was stamped indelibly in my consciousness after years of coming and going every day of the week except for federal holidays), I found myself in a part of the building that I had maybe stumbled upon once before in a long ago station of my relationship with the company. I dimly remembered having seen the section before. The stairway became grand, smoothly polished wood, which triggered a recollection of the painted banister that the touch would've declared was marble, leading to the ground floor. Disoriented, but sure I would soon get my bearings, I went up one flight of stairs and down another, trying to regain the path upon which I had moved just earlier, and to find my way again, but each turn took me farther from it, and my awareness of the fact introduced a feeling of panic.

Gradually, but with increasing rapidity, the tone and tenor of the scene changed and soon I was in a transformed place. The setting was rich, grand and opulent, with an undernote of lonely pomp and splendor — and this after having existed, for all the years I remembered the place, in industrial green and battleship gray, grimy, utilitarian, set up for factory work of the dullest and most grueling and antiquated kind, going back to the time of Bentham and Mill.

As I came down a flight of stairs, I saw into a high-ceilinged room where a number of well-tended and prosperous-looking white people were bustling around, fussing antically, packing boxes and trunks, lifting lamps, and relocating end tables from one corner of the room to another, as if they were all engaged in the process of assisting with a move. Out the tall, paned windows set in gilt frames I could see onto mist-shrouded grounds, which extended back as far as the eye could see, with sloping surfaces and hedges and tall swooning trees at the rear border of an extraordinarily long, greenish blue lawn. Beyond the outermost rim of the lawn stretched what seemed to be private acreages, with distant hills and forests as background and even a lake. The sky was overcast and silvery and the chandelier inside cast its light upon these people, who looked like the members of an extended blond, tanned family, all fit and resplendent, dressed by Burberry's or Abercrombie & Fitch, as they performed their cooperative activities. I remarked to myself that none of them looked like any of the executives of Yoigle that I remembered or had ever seen (I thought of dumpy, grizzled Howard and tall and bearlike George, clomping across the tiled floor in a state of what looked like coma except that it was that giving over of earthly existence to the changeless caretaking of a synchronous industry that turned profit; and with a moment's shock I reflected on the fact that, as in *Elective Affinities,* these people were allowed to continue holding their great wealth unchallenged and even unremarked, necessitating the deliberate suspension of consciousness, most of the time, in the rest of the world). I managed to look on without anyone's noticing me. Then I slinked by and around and escaped by way of another staircase or a continuation of the first or some other means. To my surprise, my explorations revealed yet more magnificent rooms and hidden turns, including vast spaces in which large objects and pieces of furniture were wrapped in stark white sheets, as if in preparation for a long planned absence on the part of the occupants, and I wondered again how it could be that all of this had been hidden behind Yoigle's battleship-gray front, its austerely industrial and plain sidewalks, the fortress like parking lot that served both the factory building and the local courthouse. I thought about the shape of the building and its relationship to the surrounding district, and I could not figure out how the grounds of the mansion upon which I now trespassed had been hidden to me for all the years during which I had known and had dealings with the Yoigle concern. The factory building possessed a distinct and triangular shape, and quite literally anchored the intersection which it dominated for the entire contiguous region, and had done for all of the years from before the Second World War until the current time. From the elevated train, you saw the dismal gray wedge of it, and from the railroad that bracketed it in back, you couldn't fail to note, as you pulled out of the city tunnel, its four-and-a-half storeys of gray cliffside inlaid with factory windows encrusted to opacity with grime. I wondered at how, in spite of all of that incontrovertible evidence of unrelieved dourness, which I would have vouched for personally, the opulence concealed itself while yet existing. It was like the story by H. G. Wells of the door in the wall that opened onto an Arcadian garden — except that here, even the garden, which seemed infinite, was subordinated to the still greater palatial immensity of the interior. Was this how the world's balanced inequity hid in plain sight, like those city storefronts you could pass hundreds of times over years and never notice? How insignificant I must really have been in the scheme of the owner-managers' lives, and how blind to the fact of their day-to-day affluence and victory, to the long and conquering life of their family. I was both enchanted and envious, wistful and resentful. And what I was was of no importance.

The present mansion might, I thought, have dated back to the early nineteenth or even late eighteenth century. But I was in that grainy murk where I couldn't have been sure what buildings would have looked like at either of those epochs. The vertical sweep of the high ceilings and the outward expanse of the surrounding grounds made a graceful image and inevitably put me in mind against all my knowledge and conviction of greatness and other discredited notions of class and society that were embedded in the Western mind and with great difficulty evaded.

I had regarded the border between inside and outside as a tenuous line, easily breached. In this case, something was wrapped mysteriously in something else and it magically blossomed and ballooned when touched by the wand of my having stumbled on it. I thought of Arthur's townhouse and stopping in there one day, about a year and a half earlier, when Yoigle had still seemed sort of magical and protective. There was something bright and straightforward yet at the same time mistical about it, and it captured something of the standing structures in my head.

TOKYO KILLS
Meg Kaizu

Wind ruffles my hair, and I hear bells gently ringing. I turn around and see a flock of sheep in the Alaskan wilderness. Just as I get teary-eyed over the scenery, I wake up in my bedroom in Tokyo. I see the clock. It's almost 9AM. Shit. I get up and dress in a panic.

Tokyo's rail system is a spaghetti-like maze. I wait for my train on the platform. Just couple more minutes. I look at the watch and feel the sweat oozing my shirt. Riding the train through the concrete jungle, I fantasize a drive through the lush Alaskan forest. The clouds broom over the glacier, houses, forests, lakes and sea. Molly and I visit Coral's summer tree house that her father and brother built.

"This place rocks, Coral," I tell her.

"Yeah, I like it," Coral smiles.

She has a nice kitchenette and lives without a bathroom or a shower. Who needs them honestly, when we have the luxury of wilderness to ourselves?

Packed in like sardines, I shove through passengers to get off at the Ginza station. Walking up the stairs I see a woman in an elegant dress. Maybe she is a model. Chuo-dori is infatuated with extravagance. Mannequins adorned with lavish jewelry and over-the-top dresses hold out their hands in posh shop windows. I stop to admire the beauty and luxury. There's money to spend and egos and desires to feed. This street manifests what the megalopolis is about. But I stop thinking about that, as I enter an office building.

I accept a job offer when they tell me I would be organizing an exhibition of Australian aboriginal artists. I made it. I'm doing well in the city, mom!

"We can no longer finance your project." the director tells me a few months later. I smile.

Another failed love affair with a job!

While working in a theater in Alaska I learn a thing or two about business.

"This is like *Shakespeare in Love*," Brittany tells me with a laugh, before our theater show kicks off.

"Haven't seen that movie," I reply, frowning.

I'll be playing Evil Spirit, Mosquito, in addition to Raven today. I need to make haste and change the costumes between different roles. When Emily doesn't show up I fill her roles. No problem. We'll pull it off as usual. Some people are way too flaky or simply don't give a shit. But, it boils down to Tresham's management skills. He sucks at business. Through my Raven mask I glare at my boss in his fox costume.

Trotting down the streets of Ginza on my lunch break, I see my reflection in shop windows. I look like a joke in a black suit. A sense of alienation lingers. Why the hell did I decide to leave Alaska? My job situation is iffy. I'm getting rejections from the companies I had interviews with. I've been called a brat, an idiot and a disappointment. Tokyo is hysterical.

After months of a spirited job search, I land a new job. I have a collection of suits and high heels in my room. I adore them. My darlings. My heels clatter as I enter my apartment.

My roommate is lying on the couch in the living room, like a big tom cat, watching TV. She looks over at me and tells me, "Your style changed completely. Now you wear high heels and dress like Tokyonite girls." Her remark is amusing.

Whatever she means by it, I know Tokyo corrupts you. I am not even trying to fit in. It's not about making efforts. You get used to pretty much anything over time. You learn things. You change for better or worse.

"Hey, let's sneak out to the balcony, what do you say?"

"Hell, yes!"

We hold cans of beer and glasses and carefully climb the ladder to the balcony.

On our balcony overlooking the cityscape, I look for the stars and think of my friends across the Pacific Ocean. I see Molly and Coral against the navy night sky. I will never see as many stars anywhere else but in our little Alaskan hometown. I traded my life in Alaska and its innocence for the glamour and decadence of city life. Who knows? I clink my glass against hers, "Cheers."

Tokyo kills.

SAIGON DREAM
NHI CHUNG

My husband asked me to write something about the American dream, but when I came here, I didn't have any dream. I had to get out of Vietnam because they prosecuted Chinese people under the Communists. If you owned a big factory, as my father did, you would be prosecuted. The Communists set up a union in our factory, and they had daily meetings where the members would accuse my father of cheating the employees. I was young so they didn't attack me, but after my father died of a heart attack and they cut our family's rice allotment, the chances of survival got slimmer and slimmer.

After leaving the country and living in a refugee camp one year, in 1979 I was able to come to New York. After a few weeks, I came to Manhattan to live with Dr. Lee and his sister Ho Jie. She and I had come on the same boat and lived in the Philippine refugee camp together. My mom knew her mom. We used to see Ho Jie selling cloth in the Saigon market.

I got into a bookkeeping class for new immigrants. Originally, I applied for that but I failed the math and English tests. I was very disappointed, but it turns out they had empty seats, so I got in after all. It was a six-month program and we got a $400 a month stipend.

I found a place to live in Amherst, Queens, for $80/month. I had a small room in a basement that had been divided into six living spaces, having Chinese couples and singles in each room. My space had a single closet, a bed and one desk. No window, no heat. We shared the restroom and kitchen. A lot of immigrants like to live in this kind of place.

The class was from 9 to 5 in Chinatown. After class, I would come home and shop. Every day I bought a chicken leg and boiled it. That was my dinner for six months. After eating, I would study. The book was thick and filled with words I didn't know. I was so busy.

I used to bring my lunch in a metal container. Since they didn't have a microwave at the school, I would put my rice on top the radiator to heat it up. I found out that in this class for new immigrants some of the students had been in America for 20 years! The deal was that after you completed the program, they would get you a job, so a lot of unemployed people joined. All the people in the program except me were from China or Hong Kong. Of course, many knew English pretty well.

I was kept busy till the Christmas holidays when the school closed. I had nowhere to go and I was cold in the unheated room. I bought a blanket. I asked the clerk if this blanket was warm enough. She said yes, but she lied. This was the time I cried the most.

It was such a contrast to Vietnam. Over there, I was surrounded by people I knew, my brothers and sisters and 200 workers. Here I only knew a few people. There, I didn't have to worry. I relied on my parents. Here I worry about everything.

Then I graduated. That's another hardest part. Everybody got a job except me. It's because I was the only refugee. I didn't have a green card. Instead I had a white refugee card. I went for an interview at a bank. I passed the lie detector test and the interview and the math test. But when I brought out my white card, they said they had never seen a card like that before. No one had that kind of card, so they refused to hire me.

That's how I ended up working at Azuma. I spent most of my time cleaning and stocking shelves. To me, there was one scary part. Every time someone came in my heart beat faster because they might put me at the cash register. Whenever I worked as a cashier, I didn't know what the customer was saying, so I called Jun Ji, a Japanese guy who went to NYU. He helped me and also encouraged me to get an education.

So I went to GED. I knew I needed a high school diploma to go to college. It turns out Dr. Lee was teaching at the GED high school on Forsythe Street, so I applied there. When the summer came, the classroom was almost empty. I studied like crazy. The teacher said he never saw anyone studying so hard.

Meanwhile, I got a new job at a Chinese takeout restaurant in a rough neighborhood. When I walked to work from the train, I passed a vacant lot where a housing project had been torn down. Jimmy, my now husband, who visited me there, said at twilight the littered bricks from the project looked like the last embers of a fire.

My first boss was killed at the restaurant. He was stabbed to death on a Sunday night. I wasn't there. When he closed the door, pulling down the shutter, this guy pushed in. The boss tried to get the gun from under the counter but he couldn't make it. He was stabbed. He crawled out under the shutter but bled to death on the sidewalk.

We got a new boss, his cousin, who also died. He was pulling down the shutter and a guy came and demanded money. We know you always have to have money in your pocket, so he had 20 dollars and he gave it to the thief, but the guy shot him anyway.

Another time when I was at work, the boss had a fight with a customer. The customer said he didn't get enough chicken in his order. Later that evening, he threw a bottle with gasoline in the store, which started a big fire. We thought the store would burn down, but luckily it didn't happen. We managed to put out the fire. I survived.

The reason I wasn't working on Sundays at the restaurant was that on Sunday I worked at a driving school in Chinatown for people who wanted to get a license. I worked from 9 to 5 for 20 dollars. I was on the second floor and I heard a sound, BOCK, a sound like that. The police came running upstairs. Someone was shot in another office. He was the only one working and someone came in with a mask to rob him. The police came to talk to me. How did I know what that sound was. I was a new immigrant. That was scary because it happened in daylight. All the other murders I mentioned took place at night.

I had heard shots in the street in Saigon sometimes, but I didn't expect to hear them in New York. Somehow they didn't sound the same.

During the war there was no way you could come from Vietnam to the U.S. And I never had any desire to leave my country. Why would I? My roots are there. I never heard of the American dream, but I have found some dreams here. I'm much happier than when I came. Then I had to start from the beginning, with no family and no money. I changed from a very shy girl to not shy. I used to not talk to people. Now I talk to people, not all people, but those I meet with similar cases, people from an Asian country, refugees. When I meet people from Vietnam with the same background as me, I feel close, so very close.

THE IPOD: OR, THE END
OF SELF KNOWLEDGE AS WE KNOW IT
JIM FEAST

> "A new lie is sold to us as history."
> — Subcomandante Marcos

R eaders of this book (if not many others) would probably
agree that the mass media has one overriding message: *Bow
down.*

Let me illustrate this by dealing with a recently invented form
of media communication, the iPod, and show how it arose primarily as a means of control, not to disseminate music, and that its
birth came not in response to human needs but in answer to a system crisis of capitalism. My initial premise: *any new medium's purpose is to destroy or disable a key element of autonomy in a
resistant segment of the population.*

The iPod was introduced in 2001 and its use quickly spread.
By April 2007, according to Apple, one hundred million had been
sold. In a way, it was little different from the portable CD player
or the transistor radio except that it could be individually programmed. This new feature came at a time of twinned breakdowns,
economic and philosophic.

OUT OF FORDISM

Economic

The early 1970s marked a generalized financial downturn for
the Western powers, which continues to this day. While affecting

the whole industrialized world, its repercussions have hit the U.S. hard since that nation is being dethroned from its perch of economic hegemon. In response to this "profit squeeze," the U.S. elites have engaged in various strategies to recover lost ground, such as outsourcing; reliance on illegal immigrants, who make sub-par wages; and flexible production. The last tactic depends on part-time or seasonal labor that can be hired and fired in relation to market demand. As the decades rolled on, more and more workers were forced into the casual labor pool, those in the working class becoming temps, and those in the middle class becoming consultants. By the way, this is seen in the music industry in relation to the rise of independent record producers that are tied to the majors. Michael Roberts writes, "After all, it is precisely this group of [nominally independent] labels that are considered to be 'radical'... that play an integral role in the corporate strategy to outsource production." Roberts explains, "When musicians sign a contract with an indie label, they are possibly undermining the [union] organization that was formed to protect their interests.... Most of the indie labels do not have labor agreements... so whenever a musician works for an indie label, she or he is essentially a scab."

In the literature, this development has been theorized as a new economic arrangement, a regime of flexible accumulation, in contrast to the previous regime, Fordism, in which unionized, full-time jobs, provided workers with benefits and the money to fuel mass consumption.

Philosophic

So, how does this new regime affect the world picture of workers displaced from full time jobs? If we say the function of the media is to justify the prevailing distribution of power, then, nowadays any philosophy worth its salt would need to plausibly explain to downgraded workers why the American dream is no longer possible and why you have to live with that. This takes us to the bedrock problem: The system has no alibi. More plainly, there is no believable propaganda, such as Catholicism offered the downtrodden in the Middle Ages, to reconcile the disenfranchised to their lot. How do you explain the growing lack of opportunity in a nation based on opportunity? How do you tell young people: "You will end up more impoverished than your parents," in a land where upward mobility seemed as strong a force as gravity?

Where the problem of no alibi surfaces first is in the economic sphere. There the ideas of government and private sector thinkers on how to address the crisis have veered and tacked like a ship without a rudder. British economists Peck and Ticknell characterize the economic moves by governments circa 1994:

> The recourse to monetarism and supply-side strategies on the part of nation states following the breakdown of Fordism might represent a tactical response to these new global realities [i.e., the long downturn], but it would be a mistake to represent these developments as a putative regulatory 'solution.'... They do not provide a basis for the restoration of generalized and sustainable economic growth.

French economist Robert Boyer adds, along the same lines, "Improvisation, tinkering, and groping seem to have been the rule [in government reactions to the downturn].... Thus, in the United States, the most contradictory notions have succeeded each other since 1978." In sum, these two problems (for the elite) occur in tandem: no feasible response to economic crisis, no set of justifications for mass media to instill into everyday thought to make the poor accept their lot.

WHY DOES MUSIC WORK?

A number of social critics, from Adorno to Zerzan, have condemned popular music as self-inflated flattery of the ignorant whose purpose is to stultify and pacify. No, wait a minute, Zerzan says that about classical music. For him, it is tonality that is the culprit. He writes, "The immersion in tonality is at once distraction and pervasive control, as the silence of isolation and boredom must be filled in. It comforts us, denying that the world is as reified as it is." The more open-minded, such as Richard Gilman-Opalsky, see only some music, such as corporate pop, as condemnable. He puts it like this: "Capitalists benefit from a field of consumers who crave standardized and mass-produced products, including songs and movie plots that can be predicted before being heard or seen in full."

Like all art forms, music was once more clearly integral to a society's self-promotion. Fredy Perlman's discusses this in relation to Native American cultures. He says their rhythms were embedded in cyclical worldviews. Perlman notes that if any natural event, like the coming of spring, "was repeated, then the event was not linear but rhythmic.... Rhythms were... expressed with music. Musical knowledge was knowledge of the important, the deep, the living... [and] expressed the symphony of rhythms that constituted the Cosmos."

Chris Cutler contends in *File Under Popular* that only if, in some way, a society's music was able to carry forward this communal dynamism could it continue to have any kind of psychic charge. As Cutler shows, freed slaves in the U.S. were particularly apt vehicles to make this transfer in that at the end of the 19th century, they lived in the most dynamic capitalist economy in the world, but were largely excluded from participation in the mainstream so that their music (first off) was nurtured, appreciated and worked through solely in the Black community, whether that be in the Delta, New Orleans, Harlem or Chicago's South Side. In a book on the blues, R.A. Lawson details how in the 1920s and 1930s this segregation was affected by the distinction made between bluesmen's "female counterparts [who] won commercial success up North making hits out of W.C. Handy and Percy Bradford tunes" and the "southern male blues artists [who] were relegated to more modest commercial venues — small batch releases on race record labels and gigs at house parties and jook joints." Now mark this:

> But in these smaller, more private spaces, they were relatively free to express themselves; the southern bluesmen's ability to ridicule, subvert, oppose, and begrudge Jim Crow society was possible because they were confined to segregated

spaces (in society and in the music market) and
maintaining their ability to reject and ridicule their
surroundings was predicated on their implicit acceptance of their place as outsiders. *An odd situation when a community's spokespersons position
themselves as derelicts and rebels.* (my emphasis)

We might glimpse here, by the way, the roots of later rock &
rollers from heavy metal to punk to rap as outsiders, but this is not
the salient point. Through its separation and stigmatization in mass
society in general and in music in particular, black people relied
on and evolved communal expressive forms. And, let it be understood, the treatment of blacks in the corporate music industry, visible in race records, in the 1950s production of white covers, which
siphoned away potential earnings from the black originators of the
sound, has continued up to the present. A recent survey of the
music industry, cited by David Sanjek notes: "The record industry
is overwhelmingly segregated and discrimination is rampant. ...
At every level of the industry, beginning with the separation of
black artists into a special category, barriers exist that severely limit
opportunities for blacks."

So, to back up a bit, given that black ex-slaves, such as the southern bluesmen, were creating a music where most of its expressions
were confined in-community, as Cutler argues, blacks now had the
historical task, as it were, of recreating a folk *culture* in urbanized,
monopoly capital surroundings. Only such folk forms which, in the
way Perlman described, originated in line with basic living (not aesthetic) patterns, but yet responsive to early modernism, could infuse
pop music with a sense of community and immediacy.

The foregoing might not seem germane to our discussion of the
iPod until it is seen (in a moment) that its introduction coincides with
the collapse of the structures that once kept American music vital.

MUSIC'S DILEMMA

Let us state that the system has two problems. The first, as we
discussed, is that it has no non-trivial explanation justifying the

growing inequality of wealth and impoverishment of most people's life chances. Closer to home, a frantic search for profits in the music industry had led to a tampering with the sources (black community-based) of musical creativity. This is described by Norman Kelley, who notes that music marketers recognize that the rowdiness of much black music is identified with by white teenagers who are re-belling against their parents. As he puts it, "Marketers who want to appeal to white teenagers often start with the black community, tar-geting the inner city.... In other words, blacks are unwitting trend-setters, whose tastes and talents are observed, detailed, and crunched as marketing points to music and fashion companies." That's not the most insidious part, which Kelley goes on to describe:

> To some degree the success of rap and hip-hop cul-ture represents a pervasive hollowing out of black culture itself. The urban folkways, musical expres-sions, and various styles of Afro-Americans have become grist for music, fashion, and media markets. Marketers know that if black kids — the naïve-but-sophisticated urban authenticators of postmodern American taste — can be induced to consume mas-sive quantities of whatever is being sold, they, the marketers, can once again attract demographically desirable young whites to follow suit.

So, at this point, the best popular black music is in a forced matrix in which it has to offer a dual-sided message. One the one hand, it would only be acceptable to music companies and pro-grammable on radio if it focused on self-blame (as opposed to blaming the system in the way of protest music). On the other hand, if it has any character, it must register and lament the corporate un-dermining of the community reservoir of black fans and talent.

IPOD TO THE RESCUE

But it's not the fact that songs advise the listeners to dwell on self-blame that gets to the heart of the function of the iPod. As hinted, the key factor here is structural in how, in differentiation from previous technology, the device is programmed by the listener. In this regard, it should first be noted that, like many media, distraction is the central ploy. If the daily news is focusing, at best, on a specific politician's stealing votes or a firm overbilling the city, it is not reporting, say, more general problems, such as the widespread, unreported rapes in the military or the looting of the third world. In the same way, if popular tunesmiths are obsessing over illicit trysts and broken hearts, they are not mentioning "the eve of destruction."

That's part of the iPod's mission, distraction, but there's another component. With the crash and burn of the American dream, for many of those affected there is a crushing need for psychological self-medication. It's no longer enough to listen to the radio or even a CD from which the subject can imbibe some lachrymose palliative. For the wounded listener to adequately address, for example, the pain of a lost job, long-term unemployment or frustrated educational aspirations, she or he must braid together a playlist, delicately adjusted to counter feelings of inadequacy.

Crux time. The first, distraction, component means that there is no popular music available that would explain one's troubles in any but individualist terms. The individualist component indicates that the excuses offered in popular music will not be effective unless an individual *engages personally* in constructing an alibi for the system. Can we call this *DIY ideology*?

STATUS CONCERNS

A third, supplementary, component of the iPod's workings is not as crucial for system maintenance but relates to individuals' need, especially in the middle class precariat, for status.

Allen J. Scott has analyzed the lifestyles of "cognitive-cultural workers," those who work in marketing, teaching, social work and other fields that do not involve the production of commodities but the reproduction of appropriate personalities and situations. His first point: "The lives and consciousness of these workers take shape in very concrete circumstances, among which the rising levels of gen-

eral social instability and risk represent a problem of special importance." To cope with this, "they are prone to spend large amounts
of time outside their normal working hours in building relationships
with allied workers so as to maintain their labor-market edge." Then
Scott makes these especially relevant comments. "The same instability and strong insecurity provide a strong incentive for members… of the labor force to engage in persistent self-promotion and
self-publicity, an incentive that no doubt is magnified the more they
are possessed of *an individualized portfolio of experiences and
qualifications that mark them out as the bearers of unique packages
of attributes and talents*" (my emphasis).

As one learns from a glance at the profile pages on Facebook
and other networking sites, one of the near-mandatory listings is
"Favorite Music." In the context of Scott's ideas, we can say when
an individual indicates she or he likes a particular song, this both
establishes credentials (of sensitivity, adventurous, love of kitsch,
etc.) and sets out to forge bonds with other musically like-minded
colleagues in an economic field. Thus musical taste is rationally
put in the service of economic advancement as a way to develop
professional contacts.

If every attribute of one's cultural and social capital (through
listing of preferences, photos, blog musings and so on) is put on
display as self-promotion, can we then say that by programming
one's iPod with the tunes the curious can also find listed on the individual's various network profiles, that this individual is making
visible what is occupying his or her mind at every moment of
downtime? In other words, what is being constructed via the iPod
is *an externalized inner life.*

CONCLUSION: A TALE OF TWO

Let me end by contrasting the place where I live (New York
City) and the city where I spent the last five summers (Guangzhou).

If one compares a proletarian shopping district in the latter,
such as Beijing Lu, with an equally proletarian one in the American, such as East 125th Street in Harlem — I frequently teach as a
substitute at the Choir Academy on 127th — one notes a very dif-

ferent noise ambience, partly conditioned by the fact that in New York shoppers and strollers are plugged into cell phones and other electronic devices while in Guangzhou the number of passersby with such accoutrements is approximately zero.

On 125th Street around the Adam Clayton Powell building where so many street vendors set up, selling Obama pins, Black Muslim books, ghetto romance novels and other merchandise, there is a certain mellow raucousness as hawkers bargain and chat with customers, people talk as they mill around or walk past or, loudest of all, communicate on their mobiles. All this is underlain by the silence of numerous walkers quietly immersed in the inner world of their iPods.

On the pedestrian mall between Zhongshan and Wen Ming roads, no such domed undercurrent of silence exists in that the street that, at least in summer, is a loud kinetic whirlpool. All the strollers are talking, and the sounds of the innumerable small stores, which have no front window but are open, co-penetrate with the street rhythms. Many stores are pumping out rock music, and perched on overturned buckets at either side of the door are teenagers, mostly girls, who are clapping along with the song and chanting, "My, my" (Buy, buy) or "Lei tai" (come and look).

I wonder if the dynamism of the southern Chinese with their frequent work stoppages, riots, strikes, and police station burnings and lootings, and which is in such stark contrast *to the sad ruliness of the American crowd* has some tenuous connection to the absence of (in the first) and presence (in the second) of iPods and other such devices that can so insidiously beat one down one's inner life? For in the U.S., the seriously damaged individual, beat down by inscrutable economic forces, is shown a vast array of Band-aids in rhythmic form and "freely chooses" the ones to interlace over her or his mortal wounds.

WORKS CITED

Robert Boyer, *The Regulation School* (Columbia, 1990).

Chris Cutler, *File Under Popular* (Autonomedia, 1992).

Richard Gilman-Opalsky, "Freejazz," *Fifth Estate,* 44/2.

Norman Kelley, "Notes on the Political Economy of Black Music," in *Rhythm and Business* (Akashic, 2002).

R.A. Lawson, *Jim Crow's Counterculture* (Louisiana State UP, 2010).

Jamie Peck and Adam TIckell, in *Post Fordism: A Reader* (Blackwell, 1994).

Fredy Perlman, *Against His-story, Against Leviathan!* (Black & Red, 1983).

Michael Roberts, "Papa's Got a Brand-New Bag: Big Music's Post-Fordist Regime, in Kelley.

David Sanjek, "Tell Me Something I Don't Know," in Kelley.

Allen J. Scott, *Social Economy of the Metropolis: Cognitive-Cultural Capitalism and the Global Resurgence of Cities* (Oxford, 2008).

John Zerzan, *Future Primitive and Other Essays* (Autonomedia, 1994).

THE DYING CHIEF CONTEMPLATING THE PROGRESS OF CIVILIZATION

MICHAEL RANDALL

From somewhere to nowhere fast
and fatuously friends flattened
skies darkening the engineers
throw their hands up when no one's
watching and walk away disgusted this view
stretches out farther than you can imagine and
wider than your mind can handle trust me
when I say I'd rather be eaten alive
foot first on some bright savannah
than be shackled to a BlackBerry.

THE AMERICAN DREAM HAS THE BIG "C"
JODY WEINER

T elevision was the worst goddamn invention of the twentieth century and may end up dooming the human race. Nearly all seven billion people on the planet, at the rate of twelve thousand more each day, are being captivated by the transmissions emanating from that devil box for more hours than any other event in their daily lives, except the roughly one-third of them worldwide who happen to be employed fulltime.

No longer are only Americans being dumbed down by soap operas, game shows and reality shows, sitcoms and syndicated repeats of those most popular programs for who the hell really cares how long? Unfortunately, programming in nearly every culture around the globe is influenced and often dominated by our woeful example of misusing the medium we invented. That's right, the world is being shaped by its acceptance of, and dependence upon, values specifically manufactured to make us crave those programs, copy the manner and style of their celebrities, and buy the products being sold on them.

Why is this still news after almost sixty years since Madison Avenue first pitched the American Dream to our giddy post WWII Eisenhower Republic? It is relevant today because too many Americans are fat, full of oxycontin, prozac and/or sugar diabetes and all the other destructive crap television has successfully managed to peddle all these years after cigarettes and booze finally got yanked. Most of the rest of the world still smokes and pollutes, and many so-called "third world" countries resell the products now outlawed in America as unsafe to the environment, to animals and, in some cases, even to people.

Three useful exceptions to the lethal rays of TV once existed: educational/historical programming, children's content — good for baby-sitting and home-schooling — and *The News,* television's lone potential saving grace. However, quite alarmingly, the "Chinese firewall" — a bright line ethical division that once mandated separation and independence of the News Divisions from the Entertainment Department profit centers of network television and other multi-media conglomerates — has come down. Whereas news broadcast content was always untouchable and never depended upon profits or ratings, things have changed drastically. There used to be at least fifty separate major media outlets; they've been gobbled up and consolidated into four to six, presently. Competition for ratings and loyalty is fierce, as the superstar anchor and the political spin on content now bends to the desire of the targeted audience known to be watching and to the sponsors paying the bills. Objective reporting and news are no longer synonymous, and truth is the victim left by the side of the road.

It is no coincidence the carcinogenic collapse of the Chinese firewall in television, separating objective facts from profit motivation and influence peddling, has also occurred on Wall Street and in the U.S. Supreme Court. The Banking Act of 1933 (the Glass–Steagall Act) established the FDIC and imposed the first banking reforms, including construction of another Chinese firewall between commercial banks and securities firms that prohibited banks from self-dealing and making risky investments with customer deposits. But after the Energy Crisis in the Seventies, and the Savings and Loan failures under Reaganomics, regulations and ethics were loosened to stimulate money flow, along came the corporate raiders and outsourcing, bringing profits and tax breaks, and greed was suddenly good.

Then Dot.com exploded, money was literally being made out of thin air and "get-rich-quick" became the new American Way. Regulations and ethics loosened again and, by 1999, Congress decided the country didn't need Glass–Steagall anymore. Presently, anybody who doesn't believe the resulting toxic smoke cloud of sub-prime loans, mortgage-backed securities, default swaps, credit card debt, foreclosures and bankruptcies did not cause the financial meltdown of 2008 is probably sitting in front of that goddamn television right now swallowing a deep-fried glob of meat or cheese and sucking down a Big Gulp slurpee.

Once the domain of conspiracy theorists, Eisenhower's warning to "fear the rise of the military industrial complex" is today's conventional wisdom. 9/11 made certain that, as the federal government shrinks, privatizes and voucherizes most of its other programs, the military (670 billion dollars in 2010) still accounts for 20% of the federal budget. Considering the additional 800 billion for Medicare and Medicaid (23%) that means almost half of America's yearly budget is spent on industrial and medical products and services run by corporations, unions and other "professional" organizations. And from 1998 through 2011 over twelve thousand registered lobbyists each year have legally influenced Congress to deregulate more and tax less in order to sanctify this corporate takeover. Given the obscene profits and essentially unrestrained growth of these companies, can any thinking person really be surprised by the concentration of wealth in the 1%?

Well, guess WTF? The third and, maybe, the final Chinese firewall protecting the citizenry: the U.S. Supreme Court has collapsed on the American Dream. Ever since FDR packed it with yes men to get us out of the Great Depression, and the Warren Court stretched The Bill of Rights to enforce individual liberties over authority, there is no denying that, in addition to issuing legal judgments, the Court's opinions have effectively decided social and moral issues of the time. However, the Supreme Court always ruled — for and against — on behalf of the people: actual men, women and children, whether they were rich or poor, powerful or disenfranchised, Catholic or atheist; seemingly, acting as the country's conscience, or its soul, if you will, only weighing in on those matters when there existed a sharp contrast in the law affecting everyone, or in times of national emergency.

Don't know exactly when the final shoe dropped; maybe it was the pubic hair in the coke, hi-tech lynching confirmation hearings of Clarence Thomas, but America's conscience has undeniably been replaced by the "political ideology" now proudly and openly being proclaimed from the High Bench. Ironically, while alleged to be deeply religious, or faith based, it's a rigid, soulless belief system that encourages partisan political activism by current members of the Court, who take on cases in which no other Court would have intervened and who interpret the Constitution in strange ways to support America's new corporate identity.

Sorry, the Supreme Court never went nuclear on its own people before. Even the Nixon Court voted nine-zip to turn over the Watergate Tapes. But you know the rest: In 2000, the Supremes basically selected G. W. Bush as our president when it stopped the Florida recount, ignoring all legal precedent against wading into "political questions," and in the *Citizen's United v Federal Election Commission* case, corporations and unions suddenly became people with First Amendment rights to free speech and unlimited spending on political campaigns, all while preserving the right to remain anonymous. Unbelievably huge malignancy!

History seemingly flows together, tracing the boob tube's march on destruction from its initial jump into bias news reporting — toppling the firewall of objectivity over economic self-interest — then spreading to Washington and de-regulation of the banking system; in turn, begetting permissible self-dealing and abdication of fiduciary responsibility by financial institutions, municipalities and other corporations, and further begetting Wall Street brokerage firms actually betting against their own depositors to make higher company profits. Inevitably, Ayn Rand is mentioned alongside the Founding Fathers, and narcissism replaces representative democracy, sucking out the last ounce of empathy we have left. Came then the final sickening turn: partisan politics by design is begotten in Washington and even the Supreme Court has "souled out."

BIG RED ASS WARNING: How did we allow the last remaining bastion against politics — the branch designed to protect individuals from the government, whose hallowed members each took an oath to be unbiased and fair — to actually become the instrument of this compassionless corporate ideology? "Take care of the rich and the rich will take care of you," while the suffering middle class continues to eat itself alive voting against its own economic interests. C'mon, folks! When an entity's very purpose of formation is to limit its liability it will not act morally or otherwise know how to do the right thing, ever. Have we finally gone from "Let them eat cake" to Let them eat shit and die? Unless Americans wake up soon and somehow restore the conscience of the people, however naive it may sound, those crumbled Chinese firewalls have already allowed this pernicious political disease to spread throughout the country's collective body and right into its heart.

If you don't believe me, the following is from the dissent of Justice John P. Stevens (SCt 1975–2010; third-longest serving justice in history) in the *Citizen's United* case:

> At bottom, the Court's opinion is thus a rejection of the common sense of the American people, who have recognized a need to prevent corporations from undermining self government since the founding, and who have fought against the distinctive corrupting potential of corporate electioneering since the days of Theodore Roosevelt. It is a strange time to repudiate that common sense. While American democracy is imperfect, few outside the majority of this Court would have thought its flaws included a dearth of corporate money in politics.

ADVENTURES IN THE PUBLIC SECRET SPHERE: POLICE SOVEREIGN NETWORKS AND COMMUNICATIONS WARFARE

JACK BRATICH

[The author begins by underlining a forgotten point about the "public sphere." This is the area in society outside state, church and family, which emerged in the 18th century, such as in English coffee houses, where unmonitored free public discussion on important social issues took place.]

[It was] Jurgen Habermas' own acknowledgment that the early public was born out of secret conditions. As Jodi Dean (2002) reminds us, Freemasonic lodges were among the secret social spheres that formed the basis for counter monarchical publics.... In other words, what we've encountered is not a secret sphere, but a *public* secret sphere, [a place where a select public exchanges information (say in an artistic salon) that is concealed from the greater society.]

What are the contours of the contemporary public secret sphere?... The most salient manifestations... can be found in the hybrids of network and sovereign power shaped by communications warfare... [used] to foment and prevent youth-oriented social movements. These constitute secret sovereign networks, ones that give a glimpse into the changing environment of dissent-management....

PUBLIC SECRET SPHERE IN THE 21ST CENTURY

During the first decade of the 21st century, the Bush regime was repeatedly identified as being "obsessed" with secrecy. These accusations rely on a traditional notion of secrecy; one based on an image of a box or envelope with hidden contents…. I [feel] it was more accurate to understand that time period as rife with *spectacular secrecy*, in which secrets were revealed, but in a way that increased rather than put an end to secrecy.

Michael Taussig (2003) calls this phenomenon a *public secret*… (p.306). The political public secret orbits around revelation-management, involving techniques of deception normally reserved for shamans and sorcerers… It is not skilled concealment that characterizes the power of secrecy, but the "skilled revelation of skilled concealment" (p. 273)….

But there is another side to the public secret, one that emphasizes its widespread knowledge (or ability to be known) while still remaining obscure… For example, Abu Ghraib was a pivotal event in the public secret sphere, as it spectacularly reminded us of what we already know but hide — that war continues to involve humiliation, dehumanization, and atrocities.

RISE OF THE FUTUREPUBLICS: AYM AND NETWORK SOVEREIGNS

The formation of publics via secret means has a rich history — not only the Freemasonic models of publicity but the early foundations of communications research (the *public* of public relations…). Early 20th century imagineers of the mass mind (Walter Lippman, Harold Lasswell, among others) sought to understand and harness the power of crowds to form publics via communications technologies….

More recently, we've seen attempts to form State-friendly transnational publics through the public secret sphere. Tiziana Terranova coined the term *futurepublic* to make sense of these [trends]…. The futurepublic involves news media, state institutions, and social tele-technologies assembled into temporary alliances for a particular objective, primarily war….

The Alliance of Youth Movements is an acute example…. Launched in 2008 with a summit in New York City, the AYM gathered together an ensemble of media corporations, Obama consultants, social network entrepreneurs, and youth organizations, under the auspices of the State Department. Representatives came from Old Media (MTV, NBC, CNN) and New (Google, Facebook…). The AYM created an online Howcast Hub, which "brings together youth leaders from around the world to learn, share & discuss how to change the world…." (Alliance of Youth Movements). Among the series of how-to videos produced for the site: How to Create a Grassroots Movement Using Social-Networking Sites, [and] How to Smart Mob….

What we see here already is a mix of networked entities and sovereign concentration: an alliance of corporate bodies, government agencies, and NGOs producing training videos to seed emergent movements around the world….

Elsewhere (2011a) I have called these types of groups "Genetically Modified Grassroots Organizations" (GMGO). Neither wholly emerging from below (grassroots) nor purely invented by external forces (astroturfing), emergent forces are *seeded,* and their genetic code altered, to control the vector of the movement. Initial conditions are set to shape future pathways of expression. In AYM's case this code included "nonviolence" and alignment with US foreign policy (not just any youth groups could participate), The GMGO is a hybrid of groups, wills, technologies and values that do not spring from authentic populist or spontaneous community aspirations (the ideological mystification). But neither can they be said to be purely a result of top-down manipulation (the cynical reduction)….

Is it not a contradiction to say that network power now finds sovereign concentrations within it? If we listen to the "liberation rhetoric" of technoboosters, we should believe that the distributed network is tantamount to democracy (Galloway and Thacker, 2007, p. 16). Indeed, news accounts framed the Tahrir Square event along a major divide: the sovereign power of Mubarak (depicted in the repetition of his face on street signs) vs. networked "people-power" (crowds mobilized via social media and "Internet Freedom").

However, the network form is as much about control as about freedom…. As Galloway and Thacker argue, "networks, by their mere existence, are not liberating" (p. 5)…. "Network forms can incorporate all types of authority and organization, including sovereignty" (pp. 17–18)….

Sovereignty… entails the capacity to determine the target of deterrence and intervention. Which subjects are inside and which are excluded?…. Within the logic of netwar, networks don't just expand; they strive to eliminate potentially incompatible nodes…. To wit, netwar analysts Ronfeldt and Arquilla: "Simply put, the West must build its own networks and learn to swarm the enemy network until it can be destroyed" (quoted in Galloway and Thacker, p.17)….

…We can make an analytic cut here. In residual Cold-War logic, the sovereign adversaries (Ahmadinejad in Iran, [or] Mubarak in Egypt…) are said to operate State-run mass media. The US, I would argue, has State-friended social media….

NOOPOLITICIANS AND THE DISPOSITIVE

The Egyptian uprising of 2011 is an historic turning point for many reasons…. At [such] times… a figure momentarily comes out of the shadows…. Two [cases] are worth mentioning here. Jared Cohen, one of the co-founders of AYM, made the news briefly in the summer of 2009 [when he asked one of Twitter's co-founders to delay a maintenance shutdown. He later took a high post at Google.

The second person to look at is] another Google exec… .Wael Ghonim, [who] after vanishing in Cairo for almost two weeks during the height of the protests, re-emerged with a widely seen interview on Egypt's DreamTV… followed quickly by a western media blitz. On Tues February 8th, Time already promoted him as potentially "the leader of the faceless group of young revolutionaries"…. When he told Wolf Blitzer that "This revolution started… on Facebook," he might have been referring to his own "My Name is Khalid Said" FB page (in which he shrouded himself in the identity of the actual martyr).

[But there was more reason for him to praise FB as he was given privileged treatment.] When his first page was shut down… he was given a loophole for overcoming the impasse by Richard Allan, Facebook's director of policy for Europe…. [Moreover] Facebook "put all the key pages into special protection" so that they would not be closed down by Mubarak's forces.

Ghonim: the face of the faceless, leader of the leaderless, technocratic executive cum man of the people ... working in the shadows with secret hotlines and then in the limelight with media glare, embodies the public secret.

Cohen and Ghonim are both public figures [who] fleetingly appear and disappear... [They are] are a (public) secret influence on the induction of transnational mediated multitudes into publics. They form what I call flashpublics — a quick mobilization of attention and transmission towards a predefined political objective...

The Egypt case is a transnational flashpublic (not the people assembled in Cairo, but the US social media spectators) whose predetermined objective is shrouded....

DISPOSITIFS AND DISSUASION

Thus far, however, I have only focused on... the production of a public via an assemblage of funding agents, state institutions, social technologies, youth groups, and media companies.... But there is another, complementary, dimension: neutralization. We return again to the friend/enemy distinction. Paired with the State friended media... are the user-generated usages that are treated as enemies. Some examples include the arrest of Eliot Madison of the Tin Can Comms Collective at the 2009 G20 protests in Pittsburgh, PA (for "criminal use of communications" — essentially relaying info from police scanners to protestors via txt and twitter), the suspension of cell phone service in Bay Area Rapid Transit stations during protests in 2011, and the destruction of communications equipment during various Occupy Wall Street actions....

[These incidents are justified in a] context wherein domestic dissent can be called "low-level terrorist activity," as Pentagon personnel did....

PERF and sovereign networks

What contemporary "antidote to willfulness" (to use Harold Lasswell's term) must be invented to ensure that oppositional assemblies are prevented or rerouted into preferred publics (Ewen, 1996, p.175)... . [As the police see it] every assembly is a disturbance, every gathering is a nascent crowd (which by definition needs control). Network sovereign police interrupt the assembly of other actors; they aim to disrupt convergence and dissuade emergence.... [This involves] 1) the militarization of local police departments; 2) the public/private securitization partnerships; and 3) the translocal transmission of knowledge and power via alliance-making mechanisms.

First, we can point to the ways civilian police have converged with the military (weapons, training, structure/communications). Since 9/11/01, local law enforcement agencies have used $34 billion in federal grants to acquire military equipment. This includes police departments in such alleged terror-rich targets as North Dakota requesting the border patrol's stealth drones for local surveillance....

Second, the police network involves public/private partnerships. [For one,]the Pinkertons have returned to semi-visibility. Once mercenaries for industrial robber barons, Pinkerton C & I now works for banks keeping track of protesters across social media and at their assemblies. They coordinate information from monitors both human and machinic, and share that data with police....

The third characteristic of police network sovereignty can be found in the convergence of locals into nodes of skill-sharing and knowledge transfer. [One example is] the Police Executive Research Forum (PERF), a think tank that organizes annual conferences involving dozens of US police chiefs, security heads from private organizations (like the National Football League), UK law enforcement officers, and US Federal agents. PERF... is supported by Motorola Corporation....

PERF is easily found, but hardly discussed. Its existence is not hidden, but is occulted (overshadowed by other spectacular images of police and law). Police network sovereignty is not a secret.... But no matter: this is a *public* secret, an unknown known whose existence is matched by a fleeting perception by the populace. Or, to put it another way, heroic police TV dramas draw the attention of a public while PERF exerts occulting effects....

In addition to covert tactics like infiltrators, police prevent collective imperceptibility by criminalizing others who seek to organize via secrecy..... For instance, amidst Quebec's massive casserole demonstrations the Canadian Parliament passed a bill that doubled the jail time for mask-wearing during a protest....

What we see here is a fundamental asymmetry: one network strives to monopolize not just violence, but the authority to determine proper deployments of secrecy and transparency....

But... what could new antagonism against [these state/corporate] networks be?... [At this writing] the most popular figure of antagonism is *Anonymous*. The masked image of Guy Fawkes, the distributed raids, the network of projects and agents — all of these are drawn to the "improper collective name" of Anonymous (De Seriis, 2012). Of course there are visible confrontations, most often in images of protestors and police. But even there we often see [is] less a face to face than a mask to mask (e.g. black bloc and turtle shelled, disidentified cops)....

Anonymous seeks to *autonomize* secrecy and security; to reappropriate and put into circulation secrecy in order to enhance the powers of collective subjects. Anonymous, in addition to being a meme, ethos, or organizing principle, is a *public affirmation* of secrecy, an implicit demand for its extension to all sectors, not just concentrated in the hands and boxes of the privileged....

This kind of secrecy, a *popular* secrecy, is rooted in usage and custom, not law (Bratich, 2007). It belongs to what Paolo Virno (2004) refers to as *jus resistentiae,* the right to resistance (pp. 42–43)....

Today, we might say, the safeguards are not just for already existing customs and practices under threat of extinction. Instead, refuge is for the forms of life not yet arrived, for emergent mutants, for *conditions* under which new forms are innovated. Antagonism and democracy means developing new hybrids of networks and institutions. These hybrids need protection against State despotism — a *popular security.*

CONCLUSION

When it comes to sovereign networks, the contemporary development of the public secret sphere is inescapably tied to accumulation, disruption, and antagonism. How do we distinguish among these hybrids, between public secrecy and popular secrecy, among entangled secret networks?.... One network (police sovereigns) can only operate tyrannically, needing to disrupt the capacities of another network (dissenters, OWS) from developing. Command is distilled, exposing the binding mechanism of the State as anti-democratic, as concentrated despotism. When such despotic accumulation of mechanisms takes place, what becomes transparent is the coercion at the heart of contemporary consent and dissent management.

Another disentangling device can be found in the concept *pharmakon....* the *pharmakon* names a condition in which the cure can be found in poisons. Which networks promote the curative?... It is in the shadows, or more accurately in our relation to shadows, that we can evaluate mutants and reinvigorate a politics of the networked collective.

BIBLIOGRAPHY

Alliance of Youth Movements. http://www.howcast.com/videos/163441-aym-08-alliance-of-youth-movements/.

Bratich, J. (2007). "Secrecy and Occultural Studies." *Cultural Studies,* 21(1), 42–58.

Bratich, J. (2011a). "Kyber-Revolts: Egypt, State-friended Media, and Secret Sovereign Networks." *The New Everyday: A Media Commons Project.* Available at: http://mediacommons.future-ofthebook.org/tne/pieces/kyber-revolts-egypt-state-friended-media-and-secret-sovereign-networks (accessed 24 April 2011).

De Seriis, M. (2012). "Improper Names: Collective Pseudonyms and Multiple-Use Names as Minor Processes of Subjectivation." *Subjectivity.* 5(2).

Dean, J. (2002) *Publicity's Secret.* Cornell University Press. Ithaca, NY.

Ewen, S. (1996). *PR! A Social History of Spin.* New York: Basic Books.

Galloway, A.R. & Thacker, E. (2007). *The Exploit. A Theory of Networks.* Minneapolis: University of Minnesota Press.

Taussig, M. (2003). "Viscerality, faith, and skepticism: Another theory of magic." In B. Meyer & P. Pels (Eds.), *Magic and modernity* (pp. 272–306). Stanford, CA: Stanford University Press.

Virno, P. (2004). *A Grammar of the Multitude.* Los Angeles, CA: Semiotext(e).

SOMEDAY SON, ALL THIS...

KEN BROWN

HYPOTHESIS: THE WORLD HAS ALREADY COME TO AN END & WE ARE LIVING IN THE RUINS

PETER LAMBORN WILSON

An ancient prophecy says "the world will end after 6000 years." Bishop Ushher famously calculated the date of Creation itself as 4004 B.C. Ergo, William Blake (after a bit of simple arithmetic) predicted the End of the World for 1997 A.D. — and I have a feeling (sometimes anyway) that he was right, more or less. (The Jewish calendar is based on similar notions but still has a few centuries to run before it hits 6000.)

Obviously the physical world has existed for more than 6000 years. What came into being circa 4004 B.C. in Sumer and Egypt was (or so I believe) the modern world of "Civilization" with its history, its class war, its rulers and victims — "the World" we know and inhabit. At the same time, by an inflexible rule of opposition, certain humans must have founded the *Movement of the Social* — the perennial resistance *against* Civilization "and its discontents," and *for* a restoration of organic society such as we presumably enjoyed in the Stone Age: — all humans roughly equal in wealth and in the spirit (through "democratic shamanism"), and (self)organized without any excessive authoritarian violence.

It's been noted that this "primitive anarchism" is not the "natural" form of group dynamics in primate evolution, and therefore must have been a conscious choice — Society *against* The State, as Pierre Clastres put it — humans cooperating to block the emergence of hierarchy and oppressive force.

That weird French Catholic philosopher Paul Virilio has pointed out that, in a world unified by Global Technology, the possibility of a Global Accident must exist. Now, once a theoretical horizon looms into view we may discuss it as if we had already reached it. So let's say the Global Accident has already occurred, and that the world it *put an end to* was the world of the Social. The accident itself was the Internet. (The "Year of the Internet" was 1995, remember?) Or rather, let's say, modern communications technology... the computer.

Mammon and Moloch (as Ginsberg used to say) have connived the perfect end for all attempts to save or revive the Movement of the Social. Why bother to maintain an outworn ("Stone Age") model like the Social when you can have the Free Market, and the instantaneous ecstasy of pure data? As Baroness Thatcher put it, *there is no such thing as the Social* — not now, anyway.... Maybe once, long ago, nasty brutish & short, scarcely worth a backward glance... anyway, now *extinct*.

The machinic becomes a substitute ("replicant") for the organic structure of life and economy; hence — technopathocracy, the rule of sick machines. Money itself is the perfect sick machine and can replace even consciousness and spirit with its own Image. We have already achieved the "Singularity" predicted by the TechGnostics, because Money has become more "intelligent" than the human "brain." We have reached the telos, the goal of Progress.

The perfect world consists of 99% felaheen wage-slaves and 1% bankster pharaohs. It contains "all" information all the time — but the price to be paid for it is your soul, or "privacy" — your being as individual in relation to a Social. Welcome to Hell, Doctor Faust: — the Rhizomatic Pan-panopticon.

Machinic speed (as Virilio says) eliminates both time and space — infernal combustion and electromagnetic "fire" are revealed as a unified anti-alchemical technology, a mechanasm to turn living world into dead matter. (I figure a "mechanism" is the opposite of an orgasm.) In return you get this marvelous handheld device (soon to be a chip embedded in your skull) giving you "access" to angelic powers. *Not* (of course) the power to live without Work, Commodification and Death. Not power over banks and corporations (i.e., "demons"). Not power over the 1% — or even over your own fate, your petty "value" as "human resource" in a world ruled by machinery and money.

The family or clan, which once coincided with your entire world, is now reduced to the nuclear unit of Divorce. The fraternal/ sororal organization which once guaranteed you a world of allies and friends, is now down-sized to "the people I know at Work."

The human must be reduced to monodic singularity because the Machine (the Market) does not approve of sharing and coop- eration. Everyone must have a complete set of everything, or else Capitalism might implode — and then where would we be?

Living in the Ruins, obviously, under constant attack by zom- bies. Of course, given the infinity of DEBT, the Ruins might not prove too bad an alternative — cozy and comfortable, really, and with all the free music films TV shows & e-books you can consume.

Are we there yet? — as sleepy children we used to ask our par- ents from the wombish back seat of the sacred Automobile (that totalitarian alienation machine as foretold in the *Suburban Book of the Dead*) — the automobile as J.G. Ballard saw it. Try to imag- ine the sheer effort it would take to revive or re-invent the Move- ment of the Social *now,* today, here in the USA, and I think you might begin to share my thought.... Yes, *perhaps we are there,* be- yond the End of A World, beyond the human as we once knew it. Soon no doubt the world of "Nature" will also fade away in a long- drawn-out instant of despair and boredom, and then our situation will at last become clear. The world came to an end, but we some- how missed it. We mistook it for the Triumph of Capitalism. We were asleep. Sleep, sleep is good.

STATE OF THE UNION
DAVID LAWTON

Money in, money out.
Here today. Gone too soon.
Stuffed cheesy bread
Chocolate wonderfall
Stop and frisk
Stand your ground

That's the way the cookie crumbles
Living well's the best revenge
Ethnic profile. Bail out. Strip search.
Transvaginal ultrasound

Copy, then paste
Read text based post
Tivo. iPad. Unmanned drone

NOAH
STEPHEN PAUL MILLER

"We don't invade Iraq for oil,"
I tell my ten-year-old son.
"The idea's to interrupt their oil production so
American and Saudi oil's worth more — like
Goldfinger destroying
Fort Knox to raise
the price of gold. Understand?"

"Yes, I understand. Do you think
the Republicans saw *Goldfinger*?"

"Yes," I reply.

THE NEW CO-OP OWNERS IN THEIR LIVING ROOM

MATTHEW FLAMM

Tonight, at last, I see
  there is peace under everything.
  Under the book you hold
no matter what deals
the agent made, or who
the author had to get to know.
On our new sofa,
in the yellow glow of the light,
nothing but peace.
Even if you think of
the tenants cursing as the landlord
tells them they have to move,
the ones kicked down the stairs
so the rest would believe him.
Those stairs have been ripped out;
there are new walls, new ceilings;
nobodys screaming anymore.
It's the same with the trees
turned to pulp —
or the river stinking downstream
from the paper mill: the book
is no less smooth in your hands.

WHOSE APOCALYPSE NOW?
ROXANNE HOFFMAN

The veil is lifted
the end revealed
the axis has shifted
the seventh seal, unsealed

the icecaps are melting
the oceans surely will flood
bruised egos are welting
as the once rich-on-paper shed blood

the almighty dollar rules
this kingdom of god
and all that glitters is fool's
while the terrorists nod.

loose credit brought down wall street,
already tumbled by highjacked planes,
collapsed by the weight of deceit
as the rich seek unearned gains.

the middle class lose their homes
and their hard-to-earn bucks,
while Bernie Madoff roams
Jewish charities are out of luck.

Just whom are we bailing out?
We the People would like to know,
For there's never been a doubt
the poor get screwed from the get go!

WAKING UP FROM THE AMERICAN DREAM
HAL SIROWITZ

T he American dream hasn't ended,
father said — people are still following
it in their sleep — they're still pretending
to live in the Reagan years even though
he isn't around anymore. But the problem
is they haven't woken up yet — or if they have,
they were too busy rubbing the sand
from their eyes to notice the incongruities —
a quarter gets you what a nickel used to —
it's hard to find anything for 99 cents
in a dollar store. It's a shook up, mixed up
world and I'm glad to say — the only progress
under the horizon — is that the Jews are being
blamed less for shaking and mixing up
the world as if I was ever adept at mixing
my own drink. Does that make me happier?
No, it only lessens my paranoia for now.

THE ENEMY IS U.S.
JACK COOPER

merica is a fiction: a name,
not even a name; it's a nominal —
fill-in-the-blank, a dropdown-menu item,
a prompt, a prospectus, a bill-of-sale.

We no longer live here. We park our assets,
those undeposited in the Bahamas.
We visit — like a tourist attraction,
least favorite: call this our *pied-à-terre*.

Wealth intoxicates . . . the idea, concept — rush!
The drug: how much you take, get off on yours?
And tax-free? I hope so. It ought to be.
You owe: you pay. Owe me — pay me. I owe you.

Let cost-and-effect be arbiters of truth!
(And devil take hindmost — more, if any left.)
We are everything we make away with,
what's just enough, which means plenty for me.

GOD BLESS AMERICA
JEROME SALA

When the naked wrap themselves in the flag
you get the impression that nakedness itself
is somehow constitutive of the national essence

you've heard the epithets:
naked greed
naked power
naked ambition

but don't such insults indicate as much
about the angry Puritanism of their hurlers
as they do about the flasher
in the red white and blue overcoat?

the flag gives me an erection
but more than that
it tells me to show that erection to the world
even though it's the last thing the world wants to see

knowing this me and my fellow Americans
keep our private parts hidden
except on national holidays
when we celebrate such patriotic impulses
in orgies on the White House lawn

fearing the contempt of the world at large
such festivities are among our best kept national secrets

MALL OF AMERICA

LEHMAN WEICHSELBAUM

Property trumps human life
if they tell you what to do
it's government tyranny if we
tell you what to do it's
the discipline of the marketplace
regulation smothers initiative
unless you're robbing a bank
our bank in particular in
which case shoot to kill we
can't be discriminating against
them if we don't let them
into the country to begin with
think about that the
abolition of slavery was just
another form of class
warfare coming from the left
did we just say that
out loud? anyway we tried it
your way look
what happened so shut
the fuck up

SEVEN GIFTS
CHAVISA WOODS

Di *Ego Godgifu (the self is the gift of god)*
cut off these arms and take them down
to the broke place of broken trees
and give them back their broke
arms
cut off this tongue and unteach it unspeaking from the broke place
of violence unarmed
in the forest of
violence unspoken of of unspoken of armaments

di Ego Godgifu
I have spoken many things falling

have spoken stone   brittle skies streaked long with brittle clouds
finding the graveyard hanging above
                              like a grey dying
hanging plant
            hanging

have watched the clouds   turn to bones and grow heavy
dropping to the   ground to be gnawed   by relentless dogs

this does not mean we are rising

di Ego Godgifu
be careful now

di Ego Godgifu
I never knew you could be dirty in so many ways
there's dirt dirt. there's blood. there's sweat. there's animals.

di Ego Godgifu
remember when you said I talked funny like a British?
remember before
how I was nailing   fetus posters to abortion guilty highways
      in grandma's bonnets and you
knew god like me better cause I got to see Disney?
remember when I loved the president and wanted to win the war,
when we hated welfare and lived on it?
remember Reagan?
remember work ethic,
individual responsibility?

remember homeless?
remember when mom went to jail and whenmomwenttojailand
      remember last month when mom
went to jail?
remember how we thought drugs would save us
and how drugs did save your second kid cause
      they took *it* away from you?
remember how white people are better?
remember how they divided us between our dads?
remember when we took acid and I married the tree?
remember the dead cow?
remember that black guy who beat you up?
remember that black guy you beat up?
remember how poor you both were?
remember those Mexicans?
remember living in motels?
remember that guy mom stabbed?
remember when I you found passed out in a pan
      of your own vomit and the stove was open
heating the house and your girlfriend OD'ed on meth that night?

remember you were sixteen?
remember you were not unsupervised?
remember that magician on tv
    who pulled himself up by his bootstraps, hovering?
remember when your dad went to jail?
remember when you went to jail?
remember how they say *went to jail*
    like it's something you do voluntarily?
remember when anarchy became a punk rock song
    and how socialism is like Hitler?
remember the second stanza?
remember language poetry?
remember the sweating horse,
the cigar statue Indian holding his hand palm up?
how the sunlight seemed to tick?
remember pebbles?
remember riding in truck beds?
remember when you went to jail, again?
remember when I left and mom tried to give me that gun
    and she said, "don't worry it's not registered?"
remember how everyone's so patriotic?
remember when they hated the Russians,
when they hated the Mexicans?
when they hated the Muslims?
remember when they hated me?
they never came out and said why, not to me anyway.
did they to you, do you remember?
remember they hate you too
remember they hate each other
remember everyone's gonna burn in hell
remember they hate themselves
remember how they hate where they are
    how they hate what they do how they love their country
remember how they love their country
    and hate their government
remember how they vote

remember how they like to torture things;
    animals, people, cheese?
remember how they must hate cheese?
remember Velveeta?
remember pit-bulls
the mattress the rat bled on
remember how clear the stars are
remember being stoned beneath them
remember how I held you
remember how I left?
Remember how you're still there?

di Ego Godgifu
cut off these armaments
and take them down to the place of trees
and give them back their violence

cut off these breasts and make them two sons
two white suns to light your hiding sky

cut off this unteaching
and give them tongues back their broke speech, armed

unspeaking in the forest
waiting in the broke trees
armed

MODERN HELLSCAPES
IN HAMMOND, INDIANA
Jason Gallagher

Relegated to the ashbin of history.
I have always liked that line.
However, in the industrial cities of the Great Lakes,
Or what's left of them,
The phrase should be, "relegated to the scrap pile of history."
From Duluth to Syracuse,
Town after town, city after city,
    they found one thing they could have in common.
Steel.
Steel in Cleveland, and steel in Detroit, and steel outside of Chicago.
Some of these old mills still hang on for dear life.

Take Hammond, Indiana.
Imagine having fallen asleep on an eastbound train,
    heading to Cleveland, while still a young man.
You look around the car completely dazed
    by what is outside the window.
To a half-sleeping brain, there is only one way to describe it:

Hell.

You wish you could say that the only thing you see are
Blocks and blocks of oil refineries burning off the flammable
    toxins of their production with flare sticks.

The few remaining steel mills peddling
    the raw materials to purify the bars in the furnace.
You can only see actual towering infernos
    for blocks and blocks all the way to Lake Michigan.

Yet, yet, there are many layers of hell.
Hammond proves that
Because sticking up in the middle of this netherworld
Is the new answer to economic questions
    surrounding a dying community: a casino?

Not just any casino, but a casino with 400,000-square-feet
    of gaming excitement. There is also
    a four-floor parking complex to go along with it.
Shuttle bus service is provided, so you don't have to walk
    the half-a-mile to the *porte-cochere*.
Of course, a high roller wouldn't have to worry
    about a four floor parking complex on their way
    to a weekend of tournament poker and a
    KC and the Sunshine Band concert.
They would use the valet.

A car's the only way you're going to escape anyway.
Memory imprints the only other thing in sight being
    a derelict RTA shack, as the only other sign of a way out.
Come to find out, on further research, that AMTRAK
    stops three times a day.
It just doesn't feel like it.

To quote from an unlikely source, "consider this dismaying
    observation [...], which offers you
[a] chilling challenge:
[How] to find a way out!
You come into this classroom to learn how to die

SMOKIN'
HILLARY KEEL

> "His mother was divorced and
> somewhat of a cheap blond
> in appearance" — Joe Brainard

Divorced cheap blonde mom, mom blonde
mom divorced — what option? What to be?
This cheapness — the anger of the divorced mom,
the shame of the blonde, the blonde mom's shame,
the blonde divorcées fate as mom & shame, somehow drunk, slovenly drunk, drunk and aroused,
somehow vulgar, a cigarette smoking blond vulgar
is mom, she wears a charm bracelet, a woman,
a mom, no longer married, yet blonde, does she
have sex, how does she do it? What's wrong
with her, does she lounge by a pool or live in
an air-conditioned trailer heating cups of soup
in the microwave? Did she soak every cent out of
her ex or did he just abandon her? Does she seduce
young men? She seduces young men and produces
gay sons, homosexual children, her daughter is a
lesbian, the mom's like a stepmother of sorts not a
real mom, but a step-mom with a drink, and a jingle,
her bracelet jingles, her ice cubes tingle in the glass,
the cheap blonde mom, like the worst mom is the
cheap mom and moms can't be cheap they must be rich,
they are pious and play solitaire as they lose their
husbands to war or terrorist attacks or a work

accident, maybe a traffic accident, he was driving
a truck or he was shooting a rifle and now he's gone
and that's so sad, but no. She's a mom, and simply
cheap and blonde, and simply divorced as single
mom, how vulgar, how full of hairspray her hair
must be, how she must have flakes of soap and
prickly stubs where she hasn't shaved, does she
wear pantyhose, how is her monthly flow, has she
experienced hot flashes and then what? Does her
skin sag? Her skin must be way saggy by now with
her panty hose pulled down around her ankles,
does she leave those panty hose in the back
seat of the car for one of her homo children to
find later and wonder what their mom's been
up to? does she do aerobics in that saggy
skin, is that cheap? aerobics? Would she be
caught dead in one of those outfits, does
she do pilates, does she do yoga or tai chi,
is tai chi cheap, is tai chi vulgar when
practiced by a cheap divorced blond, when
the blond is a mom, is she selfish? Is she
a selfish vegan? Does she feed her gay kids
tofu? Or bacon? Eggs? All of that? Does she
have likes? Like what does she like? Like does
she like art? Does she buy it or want to buy
it or think she might want to? Does she play
bridge with her gang of cheap divorced
blond moms? Do they gang up together and
drink whiskey sours? Smoke cigarettes?
Smoke joints? Shooing their gay sons off to
bed in pajamas, keeping them separate so they
don't wrestle and touch each other, keeping
the kids separate so they don't touch each other.
Do they touch each other? the moms? What makes
that mom so inherently cheap? Is it bright underwear?
The purple lipstick? The shade of blond? Should she
just go grey? Or brunette? Does she get herself off?

THANKSGIVING
ROBERTA ALLEN

"She's suing me for two million," the retired CEO says to the other guests, still seated at the table after a huge turkey dinner in the loft like space of an old but renovated hunter's cabin, bordering a state park, deep in the woods.

"Oh, that's ridiculous!" says the big-boned Finnish blonde who was recently arrested for DWI and told the officer he'd be perfect in Iraq when he refused to open the handcuffs cutting her wrists. Her nostrils flare as she says in her heavy accent, "Did you see the heels she had on that night?"

"Eight inches!" says the psychiatrist who treats pedophiles. Her accent says Bronx. The psychiatrist is secretly called "The Receptacle" by those who know her voracious sexual appetite. "She had on eight-inch heels."

"Are there shoes with eight-inch heels?" the writer asks. She believes she is better than the company she keeps. No one answers. Maybe no one hears. Maybe they are too caught up in the singer's lawsuit. The writer glances at the hostess, busy at the work station in the open kitchen.

"I took her to the hospital that night after she fell. It cost me $5000! She didn't have any insurance," he says. He pours Remy into a glass and gulps it down. The writer wonders if anyone else notices hair growing on his bald scalp.

Seated beside him, a woman with a knack for invisibility, offers him her empty glass. "I love Remy," she says, in her invisible voice. When she speaks, her words don't belong to her. They hang anonymously in the air.

The psychiatrist and a redhead with a raspy voice, say in unison, "Remy is the best."

"Now she claims she can't play the piano!" the retired CEO says, filling the invisible woman's glass. No one has noticed how much wine she's had this evening or, for that matter, on any other evening.

The psychiatrist says, "Didn't she just have a gig in Seattle?"

The writer wonders why no one mentions the black ice in his driveway the night the singer fell. Given his wealth, she wonders why he didn't have the ice cleared before the party. After all, he has a live-in housekeeper and cook on his estate. She, too, would have fallen had she not grabbed the arm of the painter who's seated directly across from her, stoned and silent, a badge with the old Rolling Stones tongue logo pinned on his pink shirt. The painter looks disdainfully at the other guests as he pours more Johnny Walker Black.

"I thought she just had a gig in Seattle," the psychiatrist says again, too high to know she's repeating herself. She smiles mischievously which is the way she smiles when driving her 2004 Corvette. She drives so fast even the Finnish woman refuses to ride with her.

The painter stares at the psychiatrist and mutters, loud enough for the writer to hear, "She's so masculine! So aggressive!"

"Of course she broke bones falling on that ice. She's so skinny!" the Finnish woman says about the singer.

"But she's beautiful and she looks so young," the writer says, dreamily, envy in her voice, as she recalls the skimpy, spangled, spaghetti-strapped mini-dress the singer wore that night and how she and the painter danced cheek to cheek as though they were lovers.

"No," the retired CEO says, shaking his head vehemently. "She's not beautiful and she looks her age. Sixty-five!"

The redhead with the raspy voice, her brain burned out from heavy drinking and snorting cocaine in her youth, stands up and says, "Stop it! I'm her friend. I don't want to hear you all talking behind her back! I can only imagine what you say about me." The redhead claimed she had her nose done because of a deviated septum. The hook never bothered her, she said. The writer was surprised that most people didn't notice she'd had her nose done at all.

"She's my friend too!" the Finnish woman says of the singer. "But she's anorexic. She said to me, 'I weigh ninety-eight pounds. I feel so fat.' She's 5'8", for god's sake!"

The redhead sits down.

"She's anorexic?" says the writer, incredulous. "No! I don't believe that."

While waiting for desert, a chocolate mousse cheesecake and a scrumptious — at least to her — blackberry pie, she takes another Ghirardelli Pure Dark Chocolate from the candy dish full of truffles and Godiva to-die-for delectables.

The redhead, who worries about her weight, watches her. The redhead has had one glass of wine. After Hepatitis B, this is her limit. She's trying to save what's left of her liver.

Nodding to the writer, the Finnish woman says, "Yes! She's anorexic." The Finnish woman drinks wine and eats nothing but chocolates. She had her Thanksgiving dinner at noon. Her son made her cook turkey. Her thirty-five year-old son.

"She won't get two million," says the psychiatrist who closes her country house in winter because she can't drive fast in snow.

"I have a $550,000 insurance policy. She can't get more than that," the retired CEO says, looking worried despite the joints he's smoked, the wine and Remy he's imbibed. Whether he has taken Ecstasy yet is a matter for conjecture.

The writer likes to see him smile — which he hasn't done since mentioning the singer's lawsuit. When he smiles, he reminds her of the Cheshire cat in Alice in Wonderland. That smile with perfect white teeth. Too perfect. Too white. Was the Cheshire cat also bipolar? His smile gives her chills the way scary rides in Coney Island did when she was a child.

The hostess' physical disability appears more pronounced than usual as she bends over the sink, washing dishes. The writer wonders if her green eyes are always glazed. Nights when she's out partying, getting stoned, and dancing on-all-fours, which is her specialty, the hostess knows better than to try and drive to her secluded home and stays with friends instead. "I can't hear anything with the water running," she yells, anxious when she's not at the center of things. She probably thinks she's missing something important.

Finished with the dishes, she approaches the table and asks, "Where's the pot? The big plastic bag full of pot." The guests look at each other, puzzled. "I saw it on the living room table before we sat down to eat," she says.

The woman with a knack for invisibility suddenly rises and rushes into the living room. Frantic, she searches every table, every shelf, looks under cushions on the couch, behind the bookcase, the DVD player, the tv, beneath the chairs from Kenya. "Not here!" she calls out, her voice, for once, her own.

"Didn't you have it?" they turn and ask each other. They shake their heads no. "Then who has it?" they ask, squirming, beginning to panic. Only the writer realizes that they've already smoked it. But she says nothing. She picks up another Ghirardelli Pure Dark Chocolate and pops it into her mouth.

APRICOTS WILL FALL FROM THE SKY
GABRIEL DON

Honey on cantaloupe, an unintentional pregnancy, a young woman who feels like a bad person, a no nonsense midwife with butterflies on her white cotton shirt, not a doctor in a hospital with white bleached walls; a husband lying next to his wife in bed, both writing, after garden duty, where they kept a community garden open, watered their plot and other plants; an Iraq veteran who says he won't go back because he won't kill other innocent people, poor people like himself, who are not a threat to him or his nation; a frustrated daughter whose father won't bury the dead bird with her children; the cheer of women talking loudly after too many drinks with lunch, young girls in white tutus dancing around a cross, the boxer who hugs his mother, needing a shoulder, "I just want to talk to my mum," the American privilege to hit people for entertainment, money and sport and fun — a hobby! The Williamsburg bridge, a woman hiding the fact she is eating meat again from her boyfriend, a daughter grieving her mother's suicide amoung her boxes of poetry writing archival, walking the streets of Manhattan with Derrida, talking to lawyers holding boxes of evidence, the relief of hearing a baby cry, they are alive, they are breathing; people shopping, shopping, boxes delivered to door of things produced in China polluting their air till they can't breathe safely, me asleep safely in my New York apartment with the ground beneath me holding me up and the air letting me breathe without fear and every time we hear a plane we do not feel scared, we are in America.

The climate of the day, thermometer of our society, spirit of the times: anxious. Everybody thinks they got to buy something, buy something and be better. A lot of young adults feel the world is coming to an end: climate change, environmental destruction, politics, nuclear missiles. It is an overwhelming time to exist. Not only do these beliefs and worries exist but these beliefs and worries are telecast on the TV, on the news, on the Internet, on our phone, on our devices. We are bombarded with information, anxious fear filling information. The oceans will rise, the ice caps will melt, the world will overheat. Bombs and drones. Mass consumption of goods that destroy the air we breathe and our self-esteem. *I need something to be whole.* Constant contact, constant communication rather than stillness with the wind. Phone messages, social media and emails, emails, emails. Plastic bags filling the water. Killing cows and chickens, animals for food and over breeding, over populating the planet with the preferred meat for the human palate. Chopped up strawberries, punnets and punnets of unspoiled bright red put in Tupperware to freeze. Vibrating at the limitless universe after watching a movie that awakens what was dead, what was tired, better than a coffee; The book you can settle into like a comfy sofa; the lessons you teach that you can't learn; the people you start losing to the inevitable foibles of life; the enduring love of grand-parents. Facebook feed feeds the ego, feeds the wolf that shouldn't be fed, fear darkness and cruelty. Students fall asleep in classroom, a man driving his girlfriend to visit his grandma threatens to crash the car, people push through supermarkets, a lady has an anxiety attack over her laundry, cigars drift up in your window, second-hand smoke, the tree outside the window blows in the wind, leaves leaning back and forth, things that can only be seen in the way they affect their surroundings. The cheapness of a fake wooden bed that cost more than it is worth, the shop that went out of business, the churning white noise of the radiator, the generator, some machine invading ears like mosquitoes. The indifference that is more dangerous than give a fucks, the horrific emptiness, emptiness that doesn't even hurt but concerning in lack of hurt and concern. Hearing "Muslim women and children attacked" anger that blooms into fear of ignorance, fear of the world one inhabits, this is America, this is Imperialism. This is hurting people. Tourists swam diners on a Saturday, people not sitting here with all time in the world but in a moment of convenience between here and there, waiters rush, wanting everyone in and out, "more coffee?" Chinatown hot chicken buns, pineapple buns, custard buns, coconut buns for 1 dollar, free music in Washington square park, a man practicing martial arts with his head phones in kicking lamp poles, next to hype men drawing a stage with chalk who never appear to actually begin the show, in a constant countdown to action.

New Yorkers who do not have the right to air or view, do not have the right to natural light. Young kids who buy apartments without light, millionaires and people who just came out of IVY league schools or good schools and who come straight out of college and who have loans up to here so they buy these apartments because it's a very prestigious address, *106 Central Park South,* Trump Park, two large marble lobbies with white-gloved doormen. Tapestry inside. Who don't have light in their home because their apartment has a wall next to it, your apartment window is right next to the wall of the next building. You can actually touch the wall of the next building. That wall of the other building prevents *any light* coming through. Apartments are so dark. Pitch dark. You cannot see anything. The young wealthy Investment banker working for J. P. Morgan or Goldman Sacks who works eighty to hundred hours a week, wakes up at 6:15 in the morning when it is still dark, takes a shower and goes to work before the sun rises and comes home late at night and doesn't notice the lack of light and once a month if they have one day off they go to the park and lay down in the grass.

You can throw a stone and hit a poet, a philosopher, an artist, an activist, a person who fears, "if trump wins, we will all be nuked." So they volunteer and create hoping that their flowers trump destruction. High rise buildings encroach the Lower East Side, people no longer riot in Tompkins Square park, the end of the tented city, people pay junkies to take pipes from buildings and look the other way, tactics to get people out their rent-stabilized homes, fire, buildings burning, drugs dealers, the mentally ill moved in making your building a half-way house, a knock on the door that scares your son in the morning, gun shots, businesses unable to hold down a corner, landlord keeps changing, landlord keeps changing tenants, now your next door neighbour pays at least twice what you do and doesn't have a bath tub but he has a washer and drier and probably attends NYU. The weekends are now noticeable in your building, people in finance and other 'job' jobs go out on Fridays. Buyouts, construction, erroneous billing, incorrect charges. Corporations who send a debt collector after you incorrectly, but you can't send a debt collector after them. The mosaics and street art are taken down, just to be put up again. People protest at Wall Street, occupying the park, still have their money in banks. Gas leaks and gas explodes. Real estate doesn't care. Rome got sacked in 405. All empires come to an end. The wind and the rain and the storm cut off electricity and everyone was kind to each other.

TWO MEN CROSS PATHS IN PURSUIT OF THE AMERICAN DREAM, OR: PARADISE SOLD TO THE HIGHEST BIDDER
SHALOM NEUMAN

"Let's do it!" Bradley barked into his smart-phone. A lot was riding on this trade. He bundled mortgages and dumped them on big money muppets & stooges. He was an artist at turning thousands of mortgages over and walking away with millions, even though the economic downturn had started. He was the type who would not take 'no' for an answer. And that went for women, too. Whenever a cute chick wandered into his world, he would zoom in like a guided missile ready and determined to dispense his genes. Why not? He was at the top of the gene pool. His wife, who'd given him two kids, had her suspicions, but he was a good provider and seemed to love the kids. Things could be a lot worse, she thought.

Before leaving the office to go home after closing the deal, Bradley forced himself on his associate's secretary and left her crying. Her response pissed him off, so he took the elevator down in a bad mood.

Heading into the subway a homeless guy accidentally bumped him. Still filled with anger, he pushed the bum to the ground and ducked into an uptown number 2 train. The homeless guy wasn't a wimp and in his day would have landed a solid punch, but had long ago given up the fight. He licked his wounds and mentally traveled back in time. John had been star high school baseball player who met his future wife in 10th grade. She was madly in love with him. He was popular and picked by his class to be the one to succeed. They married after finishing high school and he found his way into construction, following in his father's footsteps. Among his peers, he was a loud mouth. He was respected for being a hard worker, but some didn't like him because he was full of himself. He'd go drinking with guys and because he was good looking, it seemed he could charm his way into the beds of women who frequented the bars where he and his pals met. His wife did what was expected of her; single handedly raising their three girls, and giving them a good religious upbringing. He would come home late after hanging out with his buddies and often ignore Ellen and go back to work the next day.

At age 48, in middle of the economic downturn, he was laid off. It turned out he had no savings, having spent almost everything on his drinking. His family was totally dependent on his income and suffered the death of the American dream. His wife fell ill, but he had lost his insurance, so there was nothing they could do. The bills and pressure mounted. His two-story Queens row house was foreclosed. He was devastated when his wife died shortly afterward. He realized too late how much he really needed her. He had nowhere to go to but down.

Bradley, who discovered too late how good he had it, was convicted for insider trading. He was one of a token few who paid any price at all. The prosecutor had no stomach to take on the big money corporations and the too big to fail banks and their ancillary hedge fund departments. Could you blame him? He had political aspirations and for that he needed big bucks. On the other hand the public demanded punishment and as the hangman he had to deliver. Unfortunately Bradley was right in his gun sight. He took the bullet for so many who were complicit and certainly deserved punishment much more then him. Bitter and depressed, his wife having left him after finding out about what he'd done to the secretary, he took his own life before submitting to jail time. Both John and Bradley were ultimately crushed by the end of the American dream.

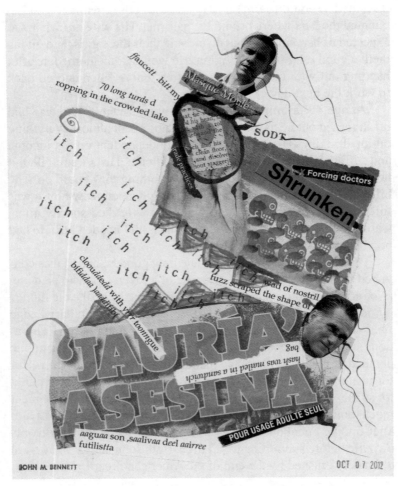

JOHN M. BENNETT

WHAT HAPPENED
TO THE AMERICAN DREAM?
BRUCE WEBER

What happened to the American dream? did it run and hide under the sand at Coney Island? did it blow through the breeze like the mythological creature on Augustus Saint-Gaudens' one hundred-percent-pure silver dime? did it emasculate itself in front of the people of Saigon or Baghdad or Kabul? is the American dream hiding in the storm cellar drinking bootleg scotch and repeating its name aloud in morse code for anyone who can hear it? is the American dream dysfunctionalized to the full extent of disappearing down this manhole? vanishing in a puff of magician's smoke? lapping the distance from here to infinity in a flash? is it loitering with football players butting heads? is is stumbling cockeyed and drooling down the avenues of the forsaken? is it still fortified by the good old constitution? is the American dream back there with my parents in the sedate 1950s? the sexy 1960s? the humdrum 1970s? the roaring 1980s? the ever taller 1990s? the collapse of it all oughts leading to the writing of this poem? if you can help me locate the American dream i'd be most appreciative. i'd pay you for your trouble. i'd do anything for your trouble. i'm a good American. just ask me.

EUPHORICALLY WAXING
AND WANING A MYTH
DOUG NUFER

Facetiously serious, we bought the American Dream. Everything was here, ready-made for the taking. But it wasn't about conquest: that came earlier, and even if we could metaphorically apply the terminology of conquest to the everyday life of driving to work, parking, picking the right line at the bank, and so on, we weren't slaughtering anyone. We got all we needed and more, and if life wasn't exactly easy, it wasn't awfully difficult, either. We had antibiotics and anesthetic. We ate and drank well, with a remote effort and deferred responsibility that never threatened to belabor us with the practical complications and ethical implications of what it took to put viands and flagons on the table. After all, weren't we constitutionally entitled to the pursuit of happiness? Bounty was our destiny, lack was anathema, and even the slightest attrition of the amalgamation of rights, privileges, and pleasures we enjoyed, from the rankest hedonisms to the most ethereal conceits, would have only amused us, as if the likelihood of loss were no more realistic than a theory posed as a myth by some moonbrained fop waxing and waning euphorically.

Obliquely then, something went wrong, like when the sound in your stereo isn't quite stereophonic, even if neither woofer nor tweeter is out of order. But we didn't worry, since we still were pretty well fixed. To stretch the stereo notion, let's pretend it's the stereo in your Chevrolet — or, since we're pretending, your Thunderbird convertible — so while Roy Orbison belts out "Only the Lonely," hitting the E over high C like nobody else, there's some hiss or buzz to the timbre, something you try fiddling with by turning it down or tuning it in better, but nothing works, so you ignore it, put it completely out of your mind while you think about the breeze, the trip, the hot yet cooling influence of the sun filtered by movement. This movement then diverts, veering you off in the reverie of the moment which you just know will never end serendipitously.

Fictitiously it's O.K., but in truth it's not O.K. With or without Roy singing his hits to your own living myth songs of wild youth, of drinking Schlitz or Coors or Bud (but no Dom, Mumm, or Krug), of shooting moons or mooning goons. Now it's obviously off. If hissing or buzzing, it's missing its good old oomph, too — not just bogus bonus fluff. Your T-bird still rolls out in styling, top-down fury, but limits shut off much of how it is, so no bounty of whimsy could distinguish it to mimic how much fun is lost ominously.

Buoy gongs soon sound our doom: no doubt about how our old, soft, cushy, plush lot got sold or run down, sunk by luck. Dumb luck got us our boon, though. Who knows how low our stock would or could bottom out? Our crowd broods, mourns, howls. Our poor dogs growl. No busboy lunch dump food for my dog or my own gut. God fucks us hourly.

FOOD IS THE ENEMY POEM
MICHAEL BASINSKI

Stan's Annex, White's, Steven's, Maryann's, Casey and Olga's, Ted's, Billy O.'s, Senkowski's, Janora's, Terry and Dan's where you could get a bottle of beer, 16 O. Zzzzzes, Simon Pure, Genny, not ina cooler but from sitting behind behind the bar at the bar on an old shelf brown near where there were packs of cigarettes, on shelf, shelf better than machine, no filters accept Salem, no springs and levers no plugged in, not in a cigarette machine but the profit went to the bar pocket pants pocket without hole, owner in brown pants as it should be and not taxes and the like or such when a brown bottle of beer was to get liquid into the drinker's thirsting cells some liquid and the bottle sat on the bar top, mahogany and beautiful with scars burn scars of 1930s cigarette burns in the shape of Betty Grable's legs and a mirror behind the top shelf and there you are looking into the mirror seeing yourself as Loki and beer lovely beer as food at noon hunger when a bucket of beer was the noon hour of lunching food when the world smelled of daily work in the lumberyard in the truck, driving truck.

And cold drinks were in for those of the non-working group of class people who owned fancy dogs with dog names like Poodles named Reginald and owned railroads B. & O. on the monopoly board that got haircuts of cologne that think that coldness is taste because drinkin for those is leisure in bathing suits and not sustenance as is correct and right of the guy workin on the loading dock moving boxes of tomatoes, 40 lbs., from the truck, a semi, each semi semi into the basement coolers and then up to the packing room and after work on Friday having a beer in a glass in a booth with the wife and the wives of others in the bar and eatin a fish fry and she don't have to cook on Friday other than maybe potato pancakes and even Father Joe would sneak down to the bar for a brown bottle of golden beer Light beer before weekend endless Masses that he had to do Mass Masses starting at four on Saturday and then finally over at twelve o'clock Mass on Sunday and then sleep of priest sleep dreaming of Holy Communion round shape of a beer bottle top bottle cap.

Then those Convictservatives Pilgrims of grim grimaces of fun frowning on fun with their ties and shined shoes without worn down heels or they don't wear white socks with a black suit those in MADD — Mother's Against Drunken Drivers and poliptricians with their soft shined shoes and soft beds and heat in winter and more President Bushes Kenny-Bunk-Port have never had the razor of the nun of life across the tongue or lost at BINGO or worked with the lake wind came in all ice because before them you took the bus or walked home and fell in the bushes not ever the pleasure of slowly fallin ooopss shit into the bushes laughing like an asshole at 4:30 in the morning AM just you and the birds in the hilariousness beer wiener full of beer kidney and it is those of that wealthy class driving over kids and such punished us with no beer in excess and foreclosed a world what went past now gone like piss down the urinal of time like once Norton who go his Norton name because he claimed Nortons were better than Harleys MC how he lost his hat because his hat was in his back pocket and everyone was lookin all around the bar, under chairs in the phone booth lookin, lookin and seeking for Norton's hat and then his hat was in his back pocket he put the hat on, wool hat black, and walked out the bar. Found his hat. Now his hat lost forever and never to return because now you have to have a food license to sell beer in a brown bottle in the bar and a license costs now more than grand where it once was a hundred clams only and you could open up a bar with six stools and a table and play pinnacle not penance and have beer and Corby's and Wilson's and now America is obese because of food in bars and ice but mostly of food food is poison and food blocks the cells of their liquid but now madness mad MADD mothers can have champagne and the dicks of their sober husbands flaccid balloons never to be blown or sneakers twisted up in telephone wires and their twisted kids not never gettin a stool at the bar in the Universe where you can talk to God and he's buyin and GodMrs is making potato pancakes and oh rich and conservative Republican Puritan Pilgrim assholes without assholes to crap hole all backed up needs a cup or relaxative tea party bitter soaking cup of hate you have omitted commune community and shooting pool.

Right wing in a sling of despair in the TV basement bullet wish wrist of steak knife porcupine unpotent powerless, the fountains of beer are silent your children are jackin off dry cactus and oasis of Venus dry Gila monster and sand sober, sober cactus, in the front windows of Maple Street and Oak Terrace and Teakwood Drive, the gutters are without liquid and pain rules the world can't have a beer after pulling cement all day sidewalks and a city is no longer a city and the city is now nothing but fat.

I'M A VICTIM
OF THE PRODUCTS OF MY TIME
PETER CARLAFTES

T his is the story
of what happened
to me
last week
in Las Vegas
see/when
I bought one of those
silly cocktails
with the spinning, white lights
in the base of the cup and
I went into the john to pee,
my pee came out a stream of
spinning white lights
(then)
the guy next to me
started screaming,
Look! Look!
and when a crowd
formed around me
asking,
Where did you get That?
I just pointed
a direction
Over There
and the herd
stampeded off

in that
very same direction

and many
were trampled;
women and children
first
then/soon
others were peeing
spinning white lights — so
I strutted back
to my room
head high
proud
to help preserve
"the"
American Way — of
accumulating more
albeit/from
the waste
which
we expel
but/then
I had to shit
and when I wiped
my ass
I saw
a bright blue
stripe
around
my turd
which/floated
in the bowl — so
I ran out in the hall
to incite
another movement
(but)

the empty hall
of quiet air
stood empty
up/until
some kid
two doors down
pushed his
food cart out
then/puked
a dark red splash
from which came
these rosy jumping chunks
kind of
like those funny
beans — that
just went
bouncing
down the hall
across
the greenish
speckled carpet
as we both
stood/in
amazement
(there)
admiring
the nature — of
American invention
(so)
strong/still
in the face
of great recession

bright red
bouncing chunks,

white-lit
pee/and
blue-striped
shit

what a land — of
brave and free

only
trouble is
I've/been
afraid
to jack off
ever since

NUKING THE LOWER EAST SIDE
BOB WITZ

When did the Pentagon start planning for the nuking of the lower east side of NYC? When was it determined that the area had peaked in its population of undesirables? Did the CIA crowd the area with AIDS patients etc lure them in plus those with bad cases of pimples and dandruff, welfare recipients, illegal aliens, old people, cancer cases, HIV pos, herpes, vd, hayfever; people with constipation, diarrhea, bad colds, nasal drip, hemorrhoids, hiccups; paraplegics, romance novelists, unwed teenage and subteen mothers, youth gangs, labor leaders, radicals, the fat, anorexics, bodybuilders, midgets, book worms, gypsies, the blind, boomboxers, sexual deviates, escort services, motorcycle gangs, hornblowers and strolling whores, bored housewives, muggers, rapists, murderers, thieves, drunkards, cigarette smokers, wife and fare beaters, battered women, robotic wallstreeters, piano players, drug dealers, crooked cops and politicians, rap groups, beatles fans, elvis clubs, slumlord landlords, greedy piranha doctors and lawyers, baseball stars and owners, right to lifers, pac groups, telephone sex orgs and newsrags that cater to them, surfers, child molesters, wacko studio heads, serial killers, skin clubs, skin heads, long hairs, neo-nazis, religious zealots, panhandlers and mental Patients, bureaucrats. Is the nuking of the lower east side of NYC part of UN and US strategy to reduce the world's pop(ulation)? UN sponsored resolution 493 for this action was voted on and unanimously approved by all but 1 nation: Tibet was the single abstention. A delegate from the lower east side NYC gave an impassioned speech against this resolution but was largely ignored. The area is under quarantine at present: panic, despair, fury. A single aircraft from the carrier Thomas Malthus will carry out the attack. Other areas are being studied.

ENCOMIUM
TO THE AMERICAN EXCEPTION
JORDAN ZINOVICH

Why scrutinize America's decline? In so many unbearable ways the nation excels now as never before. "American exceptionalism" has attained historical dimensions. Where else but in ancient Rome or the eunuch-controlled Chinese states was financial corruption so advanced? Where else but in Imperial Rome or Britain did so few control so many resources? Don't the individualist benefits of those re-ascendant Gilded Ages demonstrate the true measure of America's yearnings?

The naive peccadilloes of the Sixties lie behind us now: civil decency, Civil Rights, the Peace Movement, and Women's Rights wither in the pure sunlight of avarice and ideological hypocrisy, as the Pilgrims would have wanted. Why warble on about 911, or limitless debts, or other nonsense of those stripes? The US is an inclined plane, a simple fact that should have all Adelsoned imperialists rolling. Never, since the A-Bombs leveled Japan, have moral values been so clouded, ethics so occluded. The "American Century" has at last ceased being simply a series of crests on the backwash ripples of the sinking British Empire. Finally, America's character is its own. Her bloviating kingpins sustain themselves on Malthusianism's technocratic tea. "Greed and Efficiency are Good"; the true values of a liberated individualism.

"Guns don't kill people; people kill people," chant her worshipers of weaponry and superstition — the vast majority of Republicans and a significant faction of Democrats. (In truth, "Guns

FROM SOMEWHERE TO NOWHERE

don't kill Americans, the Second Amendment does"; a verity embodied in an exceptional peace-loving President sanctioning the drones of death and assassination.) Similarly inane statistical majorities chortle: "Damn socialized medicine. We already have the best and least-affordable health care in the world." Sentiments brought to happy salience by the recent news that that the US ranks dead last among all the countries of the developed world in terms of the life expectancy and general health of its population 50 and younger ("For Americans Under 50, Stark Findings on Health," *New York Times,* Jan. 9, 2013).

But don't bother lamenting the passing of the nation's "grand historical project." It hasn't devolved since its first conception. Examine the genocidal histories of the eradicated First Nations or Sally Hemings' subjugation for a clear-eyed view of its heritage. (Better yet, write to Leonard Peltier, c/o Federal Bureau of Prisons, Leonard Peltier, #89637–132, PO Box 474701, Des Moines, Iowa 50747–0001. He'll have a thing or two to say to you.) Any ordinary observer has only to view the malicious delight Chuckles McConnell, Cantor, and Yellow John display, joining Phat Tony and the Justices Supreme, in contorting Constitutional intentions to recognize the eternal glory of it all. The Shining City on the Hill now has its own distinctive patina, browned by the heaped discards of discredited corporatist and consumerist excess. The nation has so much to celebrate; so many unique attainments; it's a true imperial success.

May God continue to bless and caress this laudable American exception!

MAYBE I WANT TO GO TO CANADA
MICHAEL ROTHENBERG

Bye, Bye USA. Hello Finland! Or maybe I want to go to Canada.... I'm fresh out of patriotism.Tired of disappointment and hurt. I need a bigger world view. O, Samsara! Let it go, let it go! Ziggy, my dog, sleeps in the sun. Everything will work out here at home. But no, there are 17 countries more Democratic than this one. I want to go there!

That would be the brave and honorable thing to do. Emigrate! A vote for Democracy while I still have a chance to vote. It would be just like going to America. But backwards when America was determined to be America. Hello Sweden! I'll have a hotdog with mashed potatoes, mustard and ketchup, at the train station. I'll have a beautiful blonde

girl! It doesn't matter where as long as I'm free. Hello better democracies! Norway, Iceland, Netherlands, Denmark, New Zealand, Switzerland, Luxembourg, Australia, Canada, Iceland, Germany, Austria, Spain, Malta, Japan. Tapas, herring, moose and kangaroos, fondue, tempura, great forests and Northern Lights. Hello Leonard

Cohen, I'm on my way! Health care, free speech, civil rights! And what about Gross National Happiness? Physical, mental and spiritual health! The USA ranks 150! Behind Costa Rica, Dominican Republic, and Vietnam, just to get started. Fer Christ's Sake they're happier in Saudi Arabia! And which country is the greenest? The USA ranks 39th behind Switzerland, Sweden, Norway, Finland, Costa Rica, orchids, bromeliads, parrots. Mambas, Sambas, Cha-Chas. Austria, New Zealand, Latvia, Colombia, France, Iceland, Björk, haddock, halibut, and shrimp. Canada, Germany, lederhosen, United Kingdom, Slovenia, klobasa, strudels, goulash and pancakes topped with chocolate, Lithuania,

Slovakia, Portugal, Estonia, Croatia, Japan, Ecuador, Hungary, Italy. Risotto, fava, white truffles and fresh parmesan. "Maestà" by Duccio di Buoninsegna at Museo dell'Opera del Duomo, Siena. Denmark, Malaysia, Albania, Russia, Chile, Roberto Matta, empanada de Pino filled with diced meat, onions, olive, raisins and a piece of hard-boiled egg.

Cabernet Sauvignon, and Pablo Neruda, Spain, Lorca, Don Quixote, Luxembourg, Panama, Dominican Republic, Ireland, Brazil, Goooooooooooooooooooooooooooal!!!!!!!!! Uruguay, Georgia and Argentina, Water purity, lower carbon and sulfur emissions.... Long live the glaciers, waterfalls, coral reefs, flowering meadows, mangroves, and fjords!

Before it's too late. What am I waiting for? I've got to do what's right (for me). It's the American thing to do! I've go to get out of here. All aboard for A Happy Green Democracy! That's what I imagine. That's what I choose!

SOMEWHERE TO GO
NOWHERE TO GO NOWHERE AGAIN
LEE KLEIN

I am well past the proverbial road to nowhere and that's when I got invited to attend a conference on the art movement known as *Corfusionism* on, you got it, the Greek island half off the coast of Albania, Corfu. Of course there is nothing like pitchers of retsina or a red or white wine in the blue whitewashed light of the Greek full day sun when you are in the bar atop the hill overlooking the sea and you wander into other participants there to talk about the lifework of the preeminent Corfusionist, Socrates Niarchos, on the occasion of his retrospective at the Corfu Gallery of Art.

Already at the bar were the writers Don Curry and Beatrice Fishbein lounging before appearing onsite for the series of events ending with a light and sound spectacular by Niarchos at the Palaio Frourio.

And while it seemed peaceful in Corfu there was a curfew. Greece was and had been defaulting on debt for a longtime and austerity upon austerity measure had been piled on like a seven layer cake of belt tightening and riots had spontaneously erupted all over the nation but in Corfu, on the other hand, they were mostly over the spraying of pesticides on the produce farms in the countryside. Therefore Niarchos had had to get special clearance for his closing event from both the federal and local Greek authorities.

But then as he awoke he knew immediately that this was all somewhere in his mind, but then again, that he had gone from nowhere to somewhere which was nowhere nevertheless. He thought then of the jolly Rastafarian healer Hoochie who was often invoked by his great eccentric radiant blonde love, Leif Sorenson, who had warned our erstwhile traveler of an overactive brain concocting scenarios in which to project himself... though which he thoroughly enjoyed. In order for him to get somewhere he had to go somewhere which was nowhere or in other words he had to go somewhere which was nowhere to go somewhere again and of course you can always go nowhere again but that would be no fun. Nowhere can also be writing articles about art for which you really don't care for remuneration or playing in an ice hockey game for partial American Indians and other races with wolf masks on for which you do not really qualify.

"I'm going nowhere, somebody help me...."

You are not just going "over the rainbow"

You are going "somewhere over the rainbow"... "somebody help me"

I am going to the Wolfden

He wondered if Noel Perry Sharon would be roaming around the adjoining (in fact all surrounding) hotel casino and playing video blackjack throughout the day over there. Then he remembered the conversation he had had with Sharon in which he reflected on the vastness of his nowhere and how he could go everywhere and still wind up nowhere.

WHY I SUPPORT OCCUPY: WHAT HAPPENED ON L.E.S.

CLAYTON PATTERSON

O ther than three weeks in Brooklyn, I have lived on the Lower East Side. This was a time when every block in New York City was different. You turn a corner the world changed. Our first residence was at 325 Broome St., from there we moved to 99 Bowery.

The Bowery was unique in that it divided the L.E.S. from Little Italy and had its own special character and individual style. The main commercial businesses were restaurant supplies and lighting-fixture stores. For the most part the proprietors were either Italians or Jews. The Bowery still had numerous flophouses that provided housing for the down-on-his-luck alcoholic, the loner, the antisocial, those wanting to be lost or hidden from whoever. Then there were the artists living in commercial lofts that they converted into working and living spaces.

What made Downtown special and attractive to creative individuals was the main ingredients that fueled the creativity and genius N.Y.C. was known for. First, you needed cheap rent, and then inexpensive food, then affordable materials to work with. This was a time of the 99-cent breakfast, the endless cups of coffee, the $4 lunches, the 75-cent slice of pizza, the $2.50 two-fisted hero sandwich. No matter what your choice in fashion, whether high-end designer fashion, casual or clubland hipster, if you knew the lay of the land you could find what you desired at a price you could afford.

N.Y.C. used to be about having game. By using your wits you could just survive, or if you were ambitious you felt that anything was possible and you could work on following your dream. Small-time capitalism was alive and well. You could barter for a better price on almost anything. You could trade goods for services.

Crossing Bowery was Canal St. Canal St. was a creative bargain hunter's paradise, jam-packed shoulder to shoulder with stationery stores, below-market-price film, video, camera and TV outlets, job-lot businesses, metal merchants who sold a variety of metallic flotsam and jetsam, industrial plastic emporiums that sold anything from sheets of plexiglass to every kind of plastic trinket imaginable, including large-scale Statues of Liberty, and it was possible to order your own designed custom-made plastic item. Pearl Paint was a creative person's paradise overstuffed with just about every conceivable art or craft material made, and at that time the prices were probably the lowest in the country.

I knew a number of creative types who were able to survive or at least supplement their income with craft or art they made and sold from Canal St. pickings. It was on Canal St. where Keith Haring purchased his fiberglass Venus de Milo, Statues of Liberty, King Tut's sarcophagus.

I was able to create the Clayton Cap, because I discovered a baseball cap maker on Avenue A. I went in and ordered a cap with the colors I specified. Wow, I thought, this is cool. Later I realized that this guy embroidered the jacket backs for the Savage Skull Nomads in the Bronx. Again — Wow, he can draw images with his machine. I put 2 and 2 together and soon came up with the Clayton Cap.

The first baseball cap to brand a baseball cap with a signature on the outside; the first to move the image from just the front panel to images going all around the cap; the first to do individual custom caps to fit a customer's specifications. We changed the history of the baseball cap, as well as becoming a small independent manufacturer.

Just about every N.Y.C. person who made some kind of contribution to American culture did so because it was affordable to live in N.Y.C. The list is endless: Jackson Pollock, Rothko, Houdini, Margarita Lopez, Sheldon Silver, Rabbi Moshe Feinstein, etc.

From my perspective, things on the L.E.S. really started to change under President Reagan. I remember watching on TV a couple of women from Maine pleading with Congress to stop the importing of all the inexpensive footwear because it was killing off their business.

To me, the largest game changer, in terms of the beginning of L.E.S. gentrification, was the influx of Chinese money. The common drumbeat is it was the artist that caused gentrification to happen. Truth is the L.E.S. has always had a creative community connected to the population that lived there. And, really, it is not who rents the property, it's who owns the property. Then we have the economy. For example, commercial rent tax in the 1980s killed off many commercial businesses.

In the early 1980s one of the ways I paid my rent was to work as the manager for my landlord. My landlord owned a number of properties on the Bowery, as well as 325 Broome St. Because I worked for him, and because the space I was living in on the Bowery was still commercial, I had an insider's view of how this tsunami of new money, mostly from Hong Kong and Taiwan, was effecting property values. The money rush crossed Canal St., bought up much of Little Italy, then spread north to Houston St., crossed the Bowery, east to Essex St., and took in a generous portion of tenements on the L.E.S.

For decades one of the main moneymaking businesses in the minority areas of the L.E.S. was the illegal drug trade. As the Mollen Commission pointed out, even the Ninth Precinct was involved in the underground commerce. The combination of rent increases, family members going to jail and a few changes in the laws created an exodus of minorities from the community. AIDS also decimated both the minority and the creative community.

Once it became obvious that this land was now marketable, numerous other forces joined in on the game. Soon cheap rent started to become a thing of the past. Rents went up, eventually the 99-cent breakfast becomes the $9 brunch, the endless cups of coffee refills became a single $4 latte.

As the rent goes up many creative people can no longer afford to create and live here and they move out. The children of families that grew up in the neighborhood cannot afford to live here. The businesses that service a community soon start to disappear: the butcher, the baker, the shoemaker, the dry cleaner, the corner coffee shop, the bookstores, the bodega, the cap maker and so on.

Once the community has been "cleaned up," in move the big-boy sharks: N.Y.U. develops an insatiable appetite for more and more land, the luxury apartments and hotels wipe out landmark buildings and blocks of businesses — some which were here for 100 years. Zoning laws change, allowing for high-rises. Liquor laws are ignored, allowing in hundreds of bars, and my area gets designated as an entertainment zone. In come the cookie-cutter international corporations, like Starbucks, McDonald's, Dunkin' Donuts. Out go the mom-and-pop stores, the individual small-time entrepreneurs, the obscure, the unique establishments that made N.Y.C. special.

If I was young I could never afford to live here. Nor could the hundreds of others who made N.Y.C. the greatest city in the world. It is slowly becoming just another place in the world for the rich and powerful. Just as the muse left Paris, it has disappeared from N.Y.C., too. Where is the muse now? My guess is China. I mean, really — even the new statue of Martin Luther King placed on one of the most sacred strips of land in America was made in China. Like there is no African-American sculptor who could have made that sculpture? I can see the Chinese influence in this sculpture — it looks like Chairman Mao.

This is only a part of my rant. Yes, those O.W.S. protestors are right. The voices are unified. And yes, their message is as different as every person there. Some can't pay for tuition. Some can't afford to move out of home. Others have lost their homes. There are very few jobs. The American dream is over — dead and has moved to China.

One more point: It's easy to see where thousands of jobs have gone. Go to the Internet and look up recalls from China — sheetrock, dog food, toothpaste, children's toys, furniture and on and on. We can't make dog food in America? Talk to someone at your bank — good chance they are in India. Americans cannot answer questions on the phone? And so on.

When Bloomberg says O.W.S. is bad for "our" business, the "our" is the 1 percent group that O.W.S. is protesting. Yes, his salary is only $1 a year. Meanwhile, he has more than doubled his wealth since he has been in office — from $7.5 billion to more than $15 billion. I am not one of his "our" people. He is not speaking for me. He is talking against me. Yes to O.W.S.

O.W.S.

SOME THOUGHTS ON OCCUPY
MICHAEL LINDGREN

One clear, crisp day last fall I boarded the subway at 28th Street in Manhattan for the fifty-block ride downtown to Fulton Street, where I emerged back into the sunshine, took a minute to find my bearings outside the unfamiliar stop, and then started down Broadway. My destination was a small urban plaza called Zuccotti Park, which neither I nor almost anyone else had ever heard of until quite recently. It was October 7, 2011, and Occupy Wall Street had not yet acquired the worldwide fame — or notoriety — it would accumulate, but already this weird street-theatre protest thingy was giving off vibrations, and I had decided to check it out.

Like all educated, media-savvy New Yorkers, I am both suspicious of open displays of passion and cynical about politics, so I approached the park in the spirit of one who is prepared to be amused and skeptical. At first I was: the west end of the park was dominated by communal drumming, with requisite bare-chested hippie types dancing clumsily in the center of the circle, a display that shaded just south of self-parody. But as I circulated and talked to people and read the signs spread out on the pavement — a graphical/textual panorama of anger, despair, sadness, and hope — and watched the earnest, friendly, almost comically diverse throngs, my carapace of boredom and superiority cracked, and split, and fell away, and I left the place two hours later feeling that I had witnessed something special.

There have been, of course, oceans of ink spilled on the "meaning" of Occupy, and that, I think, is as it should be, for it remains to my mind a singular phenomenon, one that both harkens back to a long and very nearly dormant history of radical protest, and one that it is, in its technological and socio-demographical manifestations, so peculiarly a function of its time and place as to be profoundly transitory. My afternoon at Zuccotti left me, though, with the desire to make three small and not particularly original observations on the nature of the place, and the movement:

1) Occupy as self-contained, fully functioning mini-utopia. Even conservatives and others with dark, Hobbesean views of human nature came away impressed with the way that a temporary community of strangers could build a self-policing, self-determining society complete with utilities, security, operational integrity, and a flexible and inclusive structure of decision-making;

2) Occupy as a deeply postmodern "meta-media" phenomenon. Tom Wolfe's novel *The Bonfire of the Vanities* contains a caustic, funny, and in the end ringingly reactionary protest scene in which a small group of professional agitators perform for the assembled television cameras in a grotesque simulation of public outrage. The scene at Zuccotti and the dynamic in place there was like some mutant refutation of this tableau, times one thousand. Everywhere people were taking photos, using cell phones to tweet and post and comment; people were working on laptops; television cameras were rolling; interviews were being recorded. It was eerie, and fascinating: one had the feeling that this tiny half-acre wedge of territory was possibly the most heavily documented and commented-upon space in history;

3) Occupy as successful in shaping the terms of the national political conversation. The question of whether Occupy Wall Street was "successful" is probably unanswerable, especially given the movement's famous refusal to make demands or set conditions — a brilliant move both strategically and tactically. But however else Occupy is adjudged, it made the idea of the "99%" and the "1%" a permanent part of the public political lexicon, thus achieving in a few months what generations of Marxist theorists had been unable to accomplish, namely, an instantly memorable shorthand for

the widening gap in income. Thought experiment: would Mitt Romney's famous remark about the freeloading "47%" — which probably cost him the election — would have had the resonance it did without the subconscious priming of "the 1%"?

It is November 1, 2012 as I write this; I am sitting in the warmth and mellow light of my girlfriend's house in Pennsylvania, where I have been sitting out the ravages of Hurricane Sandy. Two days ago much of the East Village and Brooklyn was under water; there are still large swaths of the city that are dark, silent and ravaged. The damage has been estimated at $50 billion. Five days from now Election Day will bring to a conclusion a political campaign full of savagery and bitterness. All of these foreboding currents — the ecological, the economic, the political — seem, somehow, to have evolved naturally in the shadow of Occupy, a season of apocalyptic gloom, of spiralling disaster, of irredeemable fracture. It is probably true that each generation tends to think of its own times in hyperdramatic, eschatological terms, and that the sun will continue to come up, the world to turn, books to be written and read, and so on. But just now that doesn't feel terribly reassuring. From somewhere to nowhere, indeed.

Photographs by Michael Lindgren

ATTACKS ON CRITICAL THINKING VS. CHEERS FOR SCAPEGOATING

PETE DOLACK

On the surface, it seems a mystery. Occupy Wall Street protestors organized peaceful protests, concentrated their critiques on the financial institutions responsible for the worst economic downturn in eight decades and consciously used inclusive language to unite people. Yet Occupy was subjected to brutal police assaults as part of a coordinated government campaign against it, and has increasingly faced volleys of disapproval in the mass media.

By contrast, "Tea Party" protestors routinely used threatening language, brought weapons not only to their own demonstrations but to public talks of government office holders, attacked government institutions in denunciatory language and sought to divide people through scapegoating. Yet the Tea Party was lovingly embraced by the mass media and allowed to operate unimpeded by law enforcement and other institutions.

These contrasting responses were not monolithic, and we can all cite exceptions. Nonetheless, there is no mistaking the general tenor of the responses. On the surface this may appear to be a mystery, but it is not at all mysterious once we examine a little closer. Occupy was and is a genuine grassroots movement, and the hundreds of Occupies that spontaneously followed the example of Occupy Wall Street demonstrated that a large pool of discontent and anger about the corporate domination of the United States exists. That discontent may sometimes be unfocused — leading to a sometimes confusing plethora of messages at Occupy encampments and demonstrations — but it is very real, based on the reality of the lives of working people (including students). And it is precisely this bottom-up self-organization that engendered the wrath of the establishment.

The Tea Party seeks to deflect anger from corporate elites consumed by greed and arrogance who bend the country's institutions to their benefit, and instead pin the blame on "the government," on minorities, on immigrants and any other handy scapegoat. This movement, although calculated to tap into genuine grassroots anger, was manufactured and materially supported by corporate benefactors. And this is the key to understanding the warm embrace given it.

Both movements result from a pervasive feeling of anxiety over an economic crisis now measured in years with no end in sight; both movements are fueled by people who know that "something is wrong" and seek answers as to why the present is bleak, why the future appears bleak and what can be done to change the stagnation or downward trend of the economy and all the social problems that piggyback on economic distress. Anxiety is not only due to worries about today or fears of tomorrow in times of uncertainty and instability; anxiety also flows from a lack of understanding. Why has the economy turned so sour, why is the malaise so persistent, why is this happening to me even though I went to work every day and studied hard in school?

We naturally wish to find the answers to these questions. One way to seek answers is to channel anxiety, anger, fear and frustration into study: Read, watch, listen, observe and discuss, until a picture begins to emerge. Modern economics and society is complex and globalization only hastens further complexity. But these are human constructions, and so most humans can understand them. It is only when we understand what had seemed to work but no longer does that we can begin to construct ideas and plans to improve our lives and give ourselves stability.

Another way to seek answers is to channel anxiety, anger, fear and frustration into emotional release: Designate scapegoats from groups that are either unpopular or are vulnerable. Those scapegoats can be immigrants, they can be racial, ethnic or religious minorities, they can be women. Or the scapegoat can be "the government," reduced to an abstract entity that somehow hovers above society as an alien force. Scapegoats have in common that they represent an "Other," somebody or something outside or different, and thus liable to be portrayed as an impurity "polluting" society.

Scapegoating is seductive because it taps into emotion. Very real emotion, for the anxiety, anger, fear and frustration felt by Tea Partiers, Occupiers, sympathizers of one or the other and people who do not identify with either movement is based on the concrete realities of their lives. A belief that tomorrow will be better than today, that our children will live more comfortably than their parents is woven deeply into the fabric of advanced capitalist countries, and perhaps that sense of optimism has been nowhere stronger than in the United States, where such beliefs are inseparable from the expansionism, dynamism and geographical diversity that are foundations of its traditional ethos

When long-held beliefs crumble, answers are naturally sought. Easy answers tap into emotion. Emotions are real, genuine and should be taken seriously. We share many emotions; we share a desire to understand. A *cliché* that is often repeated because it is true despite being a *cliché* is the statement that a lie can travel halfway around the world before the truth can finish lacing up its boots. A parallel can, and should, be drawn: Emotions take root much faster than the concrete. In no way is that meant to suggest that emotions are "lies" — emotions, again, are very real. In our personal lives, we become upset, but we talk and analyze, and although we may still be upset, we come to understand and thus are much better equipped to do something to change the situation that made us upset.

Zooming out from the personal to the societal, we can see similarities. But, since we are back to discussing large, impersonal social forces and institutions, what if the controllers of those institutions want to deflect attention and avoid blame for their actions? Tapping into emotions is a sure way of achieving those results, and if those institutions are very wealthy and very powerful, they can create entire movements (and new institutions) to suit their purposes.

The Tea Party is a prominent example. Tea Partiers wanted answers as to why the foundations around them are crumbling. Just as the Wizard of Oz wanted Dorothy to look elsewhere, Tea Party organizers point in another direction and yell, "It's them, over there." And who are the organizers of the Tea Party? By that question, I mean the originators and, in particular, the funders of the Tea Parties, not the people who became involved and assumed leadership roles in their local communities. We can readily see that some of the most active members of Corporate America are the organizers.

At the very top of the list are three entities: the Americans for Prosperity Foundation, FreedomWorks and Fox News. Freedom-Works is a group of corporate lobbyists run by Dick Armey (a hard-line Republican Party operative who once was majority leader in the U.S. House of Representatives) that was the primary organizer of the early Tea Party protests. Americans for Prosperity is a lavishly funded and tightly controlled pressure group founded by David and Charles Koch dedicated to promoting the Koch brothers' business interests and extremist political philosophies. Fox News is one of the most notorious pieces of Rupert Murdoch's media empire, an empire dedicated to promoting Murdoch's business interests and extremist political philosophies.

Other corporate interests have made their contributions, but without these three groups there would be no Tea Party. Americans for Prosperity is a crucial funder of FreedomWorks, and both organizations are behind a series of initiatives to deny the reality of global warming, attack any and all regulation of business and promote libertarian political ideas, such as eliminating Social Security. Fox News is an active promoter of these agendas. Together, bottomless sums of money, corporate muscle, the ability to control a myriad of institutions and the power to have their agenda adopted by the corporate mass media was leveraged to coordinate and tap into the anger felt by millions of people, creating the corporate-inspired Tea Party.

As many other corporate elites similarly backed these agendas, they were undoubtedly happy to free-ride on the money and influence wielded by Americans for Prosperity, FreedomWorks and Fox News, the three of which provided the Tea Party with organizers, money, material support and publicity. Within any group, there will always be those who are the most active; the Koch Brothers, who fund a network of institutions to do their bidding, are among them in the ranks of big capitalists. Such people have the immense wealth and all the power that goes with that wealth to have their viewpoints and messages suffused throughout a society through continual repetition via a spectrum of outlets.

A critical component of those messages must be a deflection of blame. Government is a handy scapegoat, and an easy one because very few of us has not had at least one frustrating experience with a bureaucracy. Government has to be portrayed as an alien force disembodied from society, demonized for "interfering" in the lives of people. But government is not an abstract entity, it is a reflection of the social forces inherent within a society; its actions and policies will most often harmonize with the most powerful.

No objective analysis of government can deny that corporations reap enormous benefits from government — through contracts in an ever increasing variety of industries, the passing of laws in legislatures that not only benefit them but are frequently written by their lobbyists, the building and maintenance of transportation and other public infrastructure, the public assumption of the costs of business such as pollution mitigation, and an ever widening collection of subsidies.

If government is part of the problem, than it is because it has become dominated by corporate elites. Corporate elites reap the benefits of inequality and want to keep it that way, or widen the inequality. It is corporate elites who benefit from moving factories to new countries, from mass layoffs and a system that funnels enormous sums of money upward. It is a big job to obscure these obvious facts. And only corporate elites have the money to fund such a campaign so they can continue to reap personal rewards from this system's continuation.

Given the web of domination by corporate elites, it then becomes no surprise that their creation, the Tea Party, is lavished with affection while the Occupy movement that challenges them and fosters independent thinking is attacked. Today is the national holiday in the United States in which the country celebrates its founding and its defining themes of "freedom" and "liberty." But, as always, we should ask: Freedom for who? Freedom for what?

CAPACITY CITY
JEFFREY CYPHERS WRIGHT

Sure, take the hospital and make a condo
Luxury spinoff FUBU* movement
Track your tears on the typhoon index
Cry me a river, bitches, and get up in arms
I see you where you live hero decay alarms
America printed on a mirage
Strife grifters on the runway strafed
Momma said the thrifty thrive
Vigilant is visible, make your sign
99% AND WON'T LIE DOWN
Strike force under spring fire
The Shins are playing tonite
Let this poem bite the hand of darkness
Spokes of the sun spinning backwards

*For Us, By Us

MEMO

MITCH CORBER

They were a fire hazard." Early one dark
morning the Fire Dept swooped in to remove all
the Occupy generators — fire hazard or not —
as the nights were growing colder. A political move,
"to get us by the balls." Whether we visited
Zuccoti Park once, three times, or five times,
sooner or later we'd rejoice at being swallowed
up in a movement which goes by we not I.

I got hepped to Occupy Wall Street in 2011
one brisk NYC autumn, the crazed unwashed mob
in Zuccoti Park, through the news and through friends.
It was like we all heard about it, but wondered
if the next guy had really visited.
"Have you gone down there yet?"
"No, have you? Want to go together?"
Well, knowing me, I went with my video
camcorder and my friend Lehman on
the subway down Zuccoti way.

There we saw disenchanted students gathering,
tie-dyed ex-Vietnam vets with politico buttons;
The union iron worker boasting an old
decal-plastered hardhat There were inside
players, spokesmen-types pouring out their

doctrine at all who'll shove a camera in
their face: "I didn't feel I was really an activist
until my first arrest."

And placards galore
"There are limits to growth: 7 Billion: Enough."
"Fix NYC Subways. IOBS JOBS JOBS JOBS JOBS."

OCCUPIED
BOB HOLMAN

I wanted to change the world but it was occupied
So I opened up my window and tried
To catch a breeze in my baseball glove
But the breeze was overtaxed already
With the kites held aloft looking back at us
With spy drones and jawbones and maitre'd clones

So I just went down to Wall Street, That's All Street
Yes it's All Sweet with a Brawl Beat and some Raw Meat
And when we occupy the zone of the capitalist nosecone
You can bet we're aimin to be framin demands on the sidewalk

So come on down to Zucotti Park
Bring your own consciousness and some rolling papers
Unleash your sense of humor on some deadly pedants
And let the spirit invigorate your sorry consciousness

Yes US, you need a jolt! The coffee's gone weak at the knees
And the train's run out of steam and in black and white you dream
Of a land that promises everything and then laughs behind yr back

Watch out America, you'll soon be occupied
By pies that are growing grander with each incoming tide
Cause there's no outsourcing of the Truth
And the magnificent battering ram of wealth on screen
Keeps driving the responsible into a surrealist scene

Where the Mommy and the Daddy got no job but it's ok
Cause they pay and they pay but where's the wallet today
It's down by the steamless railroad center
And it's got the wings on an angel and the tail
Of an epic story of how you were born
You were born a twin where one of you had to win
And that one who won is carted off to learn the gun
And the losers are stacked in cardboard shacks
And we'll occupy and occupy until the day we die we die

JEFF PRANT

INVITATION TO WALT
DANNY SHOT

(for Occupy Wall Street)

From Camden come, rise from the dust
fly to Zuccotti Park with your shaggy beard
and your old school hat come see what's happened
to your home and your beloved democracy

Let's grab a beer or eight at McSorleys
your old haunt, where 19th century dirt clings
to chandeliers, let's reminisce and plan
our trek through New York's teeming streets

Before we saunter to the Bowery or the Nuyorican
where exclaimers and exhorters still sling verse
of hope and despair to hungry crowds who
still believe in the power of the word.

We need your sweeping vision Walt,
to offer our children more than low expectations
of life sat in front of screens or held in gadgets
that promise expression, but offer convention.

Let us not see America through rose colored
blinders, but as it is, an unfinished kaleidoscopic
cacophony created by imperfect human hands,
beautiful in complexion, ghastly in reflection.

This new century has been cruel and unusual
the ideology of greed consuming itself in a spasm
of defeat engineered by merchants of fear
and post millennial prophets of doom.

We need to recognize healthcare
and education as basic human rights
we need to restore the dignity of work,
as well as the dignity of leisure from work.

We need to get off our flabby asses
to dance as if nobody is watching, to howl
to stir shit up, to worry the rich
with a real threat of class warfare

We need to take back our democracy,
        from the masters of Wall Street,
banks too big to fail, insurance deniers, education profiteers,
from closet racists, and self-appointed homophobes,
the unholy trinity of greed, corruption and cruelty.

Walt give me the courage to not be scared
to offend, to tell the truth which is:
most republicans are heartless bastards
more willing to sink our elected head of state

To protect the interests of the moneyed
than do what's right for the greater good
they are the party that has impeded progress
and sucked the joy out of any forward movement

For all my 54 years and they've only gotten more sour
they scare me with their fascist posturing
while most democrats are frightened
as usual to betray the welfare of the rich
(Historians of the future will laugh at us).

Yet, we've come so far in so many ways
call it evolutionary progress if you will
though there's so much work left undone
We need a revolutionary spirit to unfold

It's time for us to dream big again
of democratic vistas and barbaric yawps
of space travel and scientific discovery
where we protect our glorious habitat

and build structures worthy of our dreams.
Imagine America based on empathy and equality
where we lend a hand to those in need
unembarrassed to embrace our ideals.

Walt we're here, citizen poets for change
across the United States and we believe,
we believe, call us dreamers, call us fools,
call us the dispossessed, your children lost

Our hopes on hold, left no choice but to stand
our backs against the corporate wall
ready to fight for what we're owed,
for what we've worked, promises bought and sold

Let your spirit rise old Walt Whitman
take us with you to another place and time
remind us what is good about ourselves
basic decency that's been forgotten

May your words guide our daydreams of deliverance
let the hijacked past tumble away
let the dismal present state be but a blip
may the undecided future begin today

let us become undisguised and naked
let us walk the open road...

POLITICAL HAIKUS
KEITH BAIRD

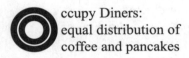ccupy Diners:
equal distribution of
coffee and pancakes

with a little luck
timing, and place, even pawns
can checkmate a king

salary freeze for
teachers; you'll get raises when
your kids are smarter

losing faith in the
American Dollar as
economy falls

FROM *THE LIBERTY PLAZA KITCHEN*
VIVIAN DEMUTH

Mic Check!
Kitchen workers, grab your
economic-justice gloves.
We slice homeless bagels
 and foreclosed cakes
 for the hungry-for-food
 and hungry-for-change 99%.
We pour jugs of water
 into utopian containers
 for grannies for peace
 & American Indian Movement members.
We sweep the park grounds
 for the sake of clean feet
 and the 1 % Mayor.
At night, we pee at Mcdonald's
 sleep near jackhammers pounding
 with our third eyes' open
 watching a working group
 of insects, trees, plants & rodents
 organize for the rights of nature
 and communities over corporations.

WALL STREET WANDERINGS

HOWARD PFLANZER

We found our way through the canyons of financ
Labyrinth of narrow streets
Sudden dead ends
Echoing our chants
Carrying signs targeting capital and greed
Measured steps
Drumbeating advances
Cops eyeing our liberation dances
The kings of capital
Scorning our voices
In their pleasure palaces of death.

OCCUPY WALL STREET
Michael Carter

T heirs is a blast of radionuclide
  Against that subtle cancer that mutates
  Silently through banks and brokers and bonds
(barely visible, subatomically strong);
This rendering of the fat from the fat…
To form the one-percent, the power elite,
Rapscallions who profit off other folks' toil and debt,
So very far removed (even as they limo past)
The morning horde who struggle to survive this pricey city,
To thrive despite the daily beatdowns
Of Capital and its contents….Applaud
These brave who say enough's enough:
EVERY DAY, EVERY WEEK
OCCUPY WALL STREET!!!

WHO IS THE BAD GUY?
RACE, CLASS, GENDER
AND OCCUPY WALL STREET
AMA BIRCH

O n May 1, 2012, I participated in the New York City Occupy Wall Street May Day Arts event in Bryant Park as
an actor in the Theater for the 99% ensemble. The French
acting troupe *Le Theatre du Soleil's* collaborative techniques were
utilized to create a silent-play with musical accompaniment developed out of a *Commedia dell'Arte* mask workshop. As an ensemble, we created the narratives for a short theatrical performance
that was demonstrative of how the 99% supports the 1%. It is my
fear that the ensemble of which I was a member of created a theatrical piece that reinforced negative stereotypes regarding gender,
race and class and presented a homogenous group of protesters as
representational of the Occupy Wall Street movement.

I played a whiteface, clown character that I created during a
two weekend Theater for the 99% workshop who is called Ray
Pierre. He is a Rich "Uncle" Pennybags character who selects
henchmen to protect him, underpays and fires hard-working employees, takes away a family's home, teaches farmers how to use
fowl smelling growth increasing pesticides on produce, and who
eventually the 99% kills with a mountain of trash.

As an African-American actress, I was able to play the villain
and one of the principal characters. During the workshop I was determined as an actor not to be an auxiliary character who was not
intrinsic to the story of the Occupy Wall Street movement, the

United States of America's history, and the play we were creating collaboratively. In addition, I did not want to portray a victim in the play. Ray Pierre represented the establishment: the media, the politicians, the bankers, and corporate America. In hindsight I wonder why the director desired a whiteface, clown aesthetic on a play that reflected a movement that is made up of so many diverse races, genders, and classes. Is it possible that my performance as Ray Pierre was reinforcing a stereotype that the only way one can be part of the 1% is to be white and male?

One of the most amazing ironies was that Ray Pierre is also a victim in the story we told. At one point in the play, he claims that a woman who was part of the 99% has robbed from him. In that scene, he conveys through gesture to the judge, Ray Pierre's friend, that the woman stole money from him, which is a lie. The irony is that the mainstream media in the United States of America has a propensity to present images of African-Americans and other minority groups as villains who are strange and scary. Concurrently, the mainstream media has created an image of the Occupy Wall Street movement where it appears that the true victims and cultural warriors in the battle for essential human rights and income equality in the United States of America are mostly Caucasian-Americans. This is done through the images and news stories the mainstream media selects to publish and air regarding the movement when it does choose to publish or air stories regarding the Occupy Wall Street movement. The irony of this type of representation is that the more the movement is portrayed in this fashion the less appealing it seems to be to many minority groups who might have mutual interests.

I visited Zuccotti Park on the fourth day of the occupation for the first time. As an American facing economic difficulties, I felt that the Occupy Wall Street movement was addressing issues that are close to my heart: healthcare, housing, access to food, education and wealth redistribution. Corrado Gini, an Italian economist, created a mathematical system to measure the disparity between the rich and poor in a country. It is called the "Gini Coefficient." How do we redistribute the wealth in a society where one group of people are disproportionately controlling the wealth, resources, and power in that same society? How do disenfranchised minorities obtain access to wealth, property, and political power if the establishment is a homogenous group that dictates what is right, what is wrong, and that seems to villainize difference as weird and creepy?

The aesthetic of whiteface and clowning in theater and art is a complicated issue, and I like to believe that a minority in North American society does not need to wear metaphorical or literal white mask to be relevant and seen as not different in the that we live in. It would be horrible to think that only wealthy Americans, indifferent to race, are rightfully entitled to healthcare, education, housing, and organic foods while they are also creating and regulating the policies that reinforce a discriminatory system based on race, gender and class all the while claiming to be victims within the same exact society. However, my experience with the Theater for the 99% makes me feel that this just might be the case.

OccupyMyAss   Nancy Calef

OCCUPY

LAEL HINES

The people, I met the grooviest people just sitting there talking. We sat there for hours, over a consecutive number of hot New York summer days. We stayed there to feel as if we were doing something. To do something is better than to do nothing. We're all just kids with the same problem. We want to change the world but we don't have a sad story to tell or the power to sway a sleazy Wall Street man, even if he is from Jersey.

Our position was beautifully ironic. Creviced in the central park rocks, we towered over middle aged Upper West Siders as they crossed the park to attend a presumably arbitrary afternoon meeting. To them we were unmanageable mayhem. However, if your eyes were not stained with generic conventionality, you would find we were an organized labyrinth of progressive beauty.

We sat near our friends from the Brooklyn Organic Food Society. They shared a blanket. They never wore shoes, and they had the most delicious natural food. So we sat and ate oranges. We laughed and played pretentious music, competing as to who could name the most bands that started with "the." I would suck a blood orange, and feel the drops awkwardly slide from my lips while talking to the bearded man who hates government. We all hate government in a sense. Everyone in the world, even a venture capitalist.

But everyone loves oranges. I would eat them one after another as we laughed and talked and disagreed about topics we pretended to understand.

For a moment, in that very small New York City moment, the entire world seemed to be dripping from our fingers. With a smile, an exchange of words, we would listen and agree. I would rant, and he would say I was confusing and odd, but funny. I said I would never give myself up to a male until I feel the way I felt when I first heard "Cry Baby." He smirked and said, "then I have to play it." So the skinny kid with the Strokes T-shirt and the funky glasses played it in front of everyone, and me. As I ate my orange, allowing his trendy glasses to earn an everlasting memory, I swore I would never leave. I would remain in this one, perfect, infinite moment.

SHAKESPEARE, PROUST
JOIN THE PROTESTS
GARY SHAPIRO

N oam Chomsky, Howard Zinn, and Emma Goldman are not
on Wall Street, but they are there in spirit. Activists at the
Occupy Wall Street protests in New York have set up what
they call "The People's Library," where books can be borrowed
and read. Stretched along a granite ledge and on tables, plastic bins
of boxes have been growing at Zuccotti Park.

"The library shows that we are in this for the long term," said
volunteer Sam Oliver Smith, 20, who studied a year at a community college in the Lehigh Valley. Steve Syrek, 33, a graduate student in Shakespeare, calls the library "…an unambiguous good no
matter what your politics."

Books on Wobblies and Sandinistas joust with works of an-
thropology, history, sociology, and Norton Critical Editions of classic works. In one bin, an oversized gray hardback entitled *Essential
Works of Socialism,* edited by Irving Howe, shared space with a
water-logged second volume of Frankfurt school theorist Walter
Benjamin's *Selected Writings.*

Books relating to feminism and the women's movement have
their own box. There are children's and young adult bins. The library invites readers to both take a book and donate one to the library. On a couple evenings, the library added a row of seats for
readers, as they soak up knowledge amid the hubbub of the protest.
The Library recently added a reference desk, which has a multi-colored sign that reads, "Literacy, Legitimacy, and Moral Authority."

A blog created by the library organizers notes that figures such as playwright Eve Ensler, author Naomi Klein, and *Nation* editor Katrina vanden Heuvel have visited the library. As shown on the blog, vanden Heuvel autographed her book, *The Change I Believe in: Fighting for Progress in the Age of Obama* (Nation Books) with the inscription stating her greatest admiration for the "spark you've lit."

The blog also shows that libraries have migrated to Los Angeles and Boston, other sites of these growing national-wide protests. At the Wall Street protest, several feet away from the library is an area filled with pamphlets laid out face up on the pavement. Passersby peruse leftist leaflets and manifestos, and other printed matter, such as a green and white copy of the *Monthly Review* with an article on "The Worker-Peasant Alliance as a Rural Development Strategy for China" as well as the current issue of *WIN,* the publication of the War Resisters League, containing a piece on "Resisting West Papua's Plantation."

Stepping up to one of the librarians, a retired professor of education at Urbana University in Ohio, William Coffman, handed over a twenty-dollar bill to support the library. Recalling the protests of the late 1960s and 1970s, Mr. Coffman said, "This is very much like that."

OCCUPY HILO
PTR KOZLOWSKI

The Pots & Pans Revolution in Reykjavik Iceland was considered a precursor. They cursed before we did. The Tunisia Revolution, the Indignant Citizens Movement in Greece and in Spain, shouting "Democracia Real YA!" — coalesced into a whirlwind of protesting people that came dancing across the water (but not like Hernan Cortes). Canadian Adbusters spread the flame, and all of a sudden Wall Street got occupied. Wikileaks Central relayed the call for a Day of Rage. And we got Occupy Charlottesville, Occupy Salt Lake, and Occupy just about everywhere — from the Brooklyn Bridge to the Port of Oakland. And the spirit found its way, via cable and satellite waves, to the middle of the biggest ocean, and the volcanic archipelago Hawaii. It's not quite paradise for everybody. There was an Occupy Waikiki on October 15. Even little Kauai turned out dozens of people. But the Big Island precursed them both, with people demonstrating October 4th in Kona and Hilo. It was raining in Hilo — it usually is. The town was originally carved out of a rainforest for the purpose of loading sugar cane onto ships. And the growers recruited 99-percenters from all over the world to cut the stuff and handle it, because the Native Hawaiians didn't make very good wage slaves. Now Hilo is populated by cubicle dwellers of the County government and, in a place where the beaches are too rocky, the more struggling contingent of tourist industry types. Occupiers lined Queen Ka'ahumanu Highway over in Kona where the money, the white sands and the sunshine are. But the smaller Hilo made the bigger splash. Out on Kilauea Avenue, around the Merrill Lynch office and across the street. Cars sizzling past on the wet pavement, drivers honking their horns at the families with kids, some face-painted, all holding signs. A pre-teen girl was walking on stilts on the mauka side, and a man in a Guy Fawkes mask did the same on the makai. The legendary lifeguard and surfer Eddie Aikau was famous for braving the waves when others were afraid. So there's a saying in the islands, when conditions are scary and you're not sure if you should: "Eddie would go." They put it on t-shirts and bumper stickers. And there in the crowd of Occupy Hilo, standing out among the bobbing umbrellas in their rainbow warrior colors, a guy held up a short board with the words painted on it: "Eddie Would Occupy."

DISPATCH FROM AN ATTEMPTED ESCAPEE
Rami Shamir

For Rich....

During the time of physical Occupation, when incorporated reporters would daily swarm through Zuccotti Park, a common question that the unleashed bees would ask in their search for honey was "Why?" Why would you leave your life to come here and live outside *in a park* with a bunch of people you don't know? Not necessarily naïve, I'm still somewhat at a loss as to how not one of these journalists decided to join up with the Occupation, entrench themselves as it were beneath the golden leaves and report directly from the front lines of this new fissure in the American unexperience. Had these new Edward R. Murrows and Walter Cronkites bothered to make Zuccotti Park more than just an occasional Sunday outing *in the shadow of the freedom tower,* they'd have quickly learned that everyone who came to the physical Occupation had *no life whatsoever which to leave.* The Occupiers at Zuccotti were refugees from the American nowhere: street veterans of urban vagrancy, homeless queer youth, a whole generation born too late but educated too wise to even attempt to scrape the crumbs off the ground of the long-ago devoured American pie; and those of us that did make any such attempt quickly found that even the crumbs were gone. Yes — there were people who had left previous lives to live outside in a park; but these lives were nothing but a prelude, a purgatory, windowless waiting rooms to being alive: housewives suffocating within the glade of their upper middle class Panhandle; fiancées wedded to repeat variations on the themes of their parents' marriages; office workers too sand-nig-

494

gardly in the color of their skin to ever get out of Sector A. So when there *was* a life that was left to come and live outside in a park, that life was nevermore than just a string of bones inside a coffin — airless, measured-out, and demarcated. You can't be taller than this line and you cannot ride; life, do not trespass here.

We all came to this Occupation damaged, some of us more than others. Interspersed at different points along the shoreline of our lives, we found ourselves staring out into the Ocean, the coastline slipping away from our toes, the horizon up against our back, and then — a ship to save us; there — a ship to take us all away! I climbed aboard sometime in the early days of that October, escaping a book called *Train to Pokipse,* by a young author called Rami Shamir, and a world that very openly stated that neither book nor author were welcome. *Those* types of experiences, *those* types of people are simply better suited at their stations of origin. Partly in spite of myself, I managed to keep *some* of my original station, continuing to work my part-time job at a small restaurant in Brooklyn; and with the help of mentors, friends, and supporters I eventually proceeded to successfully publish the book that had ravaged nearly a third of my life.

This is my first dispatch since my attempted escape....

(*Deus Ex Machina:* As the author is supposedly dispatching this communiqué from the body of a ship, it was considered necessary by aforesaid author etcetera to find a grammatical equivalent to the Ocean waves. After some investigation, it was decided that the three dot ellipses was best suited for this purpose, as its aposiopetic quality of trailing off most closely conveys the way in which waves tend to die away. As this dispatch is being sent via two dimensional methods, the author etcetera concluded that no swell portrayal of the undulating quality inherent in the natural wave was grammatically possible and that any wave transmitted via the current methods would inevitably fall flat. [*Pause.*] The author etcetera would like to apologize for any discomfort that the expository nature contained in this sudden interruption might have caused, but citing the poetic disposition of the extraparenthetical material of the current dispatch the author etcetera concluded that the break in question was warranted, possibly as an early intermission, the moment where we find the author etcetera outside at night, alone on the deck of the ship, smoking a cigarette and staring out into the Ocean. Oh, look — here comes a wave....)

NARRATIVE: The undersigned has probable cause to believe the above-named defendant on the, xx of xx/xx at xx:xx ___ xx at _____ in _____ did _____ .

On xx/xx/xx at xxxx hours, Sgt. Someone (xxxxx), Officer OK (xxxxx), and I were monitoring the Occupy INSERT AMERICAN CITY HERE protesters at INSERT STREET ADDRESS OF AMERICAN CITY HERE, via the IRIS cameras.

At that time, we observed the defendant reading what appeared to be unauthorized material published by the anarchist organization known as A NEW WORLD IN OUR HEARTS, which is a violation of City Ordinance xx.xx; It shall be unlawful for any person to, or, upon the surface of any sidewalk or paved street in the City.

The defendant read several words on the sidewalk in standard size lettering which was captured by the IRIS cameras. The defendant read, "when we live under institutions founded on the accumulation of wealth — of things — we tend to make judgments about "human nature" that reflect those institutions. What might we say about "human nature" in a society founded on cooperation instead of survival-of-the-fittest; mutual aid instead of an ethic of competition; the organic needs and desires of people instead of the production of so much useless shit that we are conditioned to want by a multi-billion dollar advertising industry? We would likely have an entirely different view of "human nature" and the way we organize to meet our desires wouldn't resemble the sick society we have inherited and currently (allow ourselves to) live in."

We responded to INSERT STREET ADDRESS OF AMERICAN CITY HERE, where we made contact with the defendant and took him into custody. The defendant was very vocal and attempted to pull away after being handcuffed. The defendant called the police "pigs" and "fascists." The defendant claimed that he was on a ship escaping. Photos were taken of the defendant's mind-processes that arose in part we believe to the unauthorized material being read.

The defendant knowingly violated the law, where he was previously warned and arrested on xx/xx/xx for the same offense.

Probable Cause was established to charge the defendant with City Ordinance xx.xx....

I've always instinctively understood the foundational mechanics of politics. Politics occurs in two zones and two zones only: it occurs in the relationship we have with ourselves and in the relationships we have with those closest to us in society. A world composed of abused, abusing, and self-abusive people will be a world that is abused, abusing, and self-abusive. Capitalism is the global manifestation of such a localized disease of abuse. It's the flowering of passive-aggressive rage into apathetic inaction; it's the violent seeding of rejection, suspicion, and separation. Amalgamated with the worst of human flaws, passed down and magnified throughout countless unseen repetitions of those private moments that have made up some several generations, the abusive virus of Capitalism has logically arrived at its final stages and now invades the planet as institutional Corporatism.

I've learned that the most potent cure for capitalism is to somehow wander off into what Kurt Vonnegut called a country of two. It's no surprise that the most virulent of all social restrictions concerns the rigidity eventually to rigor mortis of emotional, spiritual, and sexual intimacy between two human beings. Here, in this country of two, is where the real escape is to be found. Here is where the real healing happens: in our relationship to our self and in our relationship to those closest to us in society. Here is where the greatest, the only *real* political revolution can occur; two by two, each to each, and finally to all that is now and all that is to come....

My friend's name is not the issue; nor are you here going to find any of the usual romantic odes describing his physical attributes. Similar to me, he was highly intelligent, highly fucked up by his passage through his time before the Park, and highly neglected by the clockmakers who wind and control that time. We were, and still remain, an unfolding experiment of sorts within this beautiful and sometimes troubled country of ours, where we're testing the very limits and definitions of our selflessness and our capacity to love. The weather is turbulent, raging, windy, and wild — sunny days can quickly drown under midnight storms — but whenever I find myself looking back over the stretch of this country, I see the fields advancing into their natural blossom and bloom: the early bushes of overgrown rose, the starting stalks of tall and similar grass, the paled and yellow corn along the receding distance have been husbandried back to more natural fields. Violets neighbor Gladiola, the dandelions run free; modified and manipulated canola passes from our view and now peaceful confederations of Blue Hopi and Hickory King, purple corn beside white corn maize their way along the reddish hills.

My friend says that when the end of the world arrives and all the zombies come out, he's going to head Upstate. He loves the land. He believes there to be stores of ammunition hidden among the Catskill Mountains. He loves the land. I ask him to sleep beside me when it's night because it helps me to deal with all the shadows. As of yet, he skirts the issue. After all, he has shadows too....

It's been seven months since my fellow refugees and I have attempted our escape from the American nowhere. Many of the people I had started out with have since left; some have left, re-turned, to only leave again (and then return); new passengers, ship-wrecked far from the mainland on decaying planks have climbed onto the deck. The group that first boarded and remains aboard is small. Forty, maybe fifty....

In the seven months since our Occupation, we have watched our society and our home in Zuccotti be brutally destroyed; we've been forced to wander out into the winter exiles; we have sheltered in churches, vacant homes, and hostels until we found ourselves facing their closed doors; we have slept outside along the walls of banks and then at the seeping sore of the great historical ulcer on the corner of Wall Street and Nassau until one morning bullhorns announced that the law has come and that the law says that the Law can go Fuck itself: what's a judge's robe and some books got on a gun and bullhorn, anyway? We've been beaten, arrested for danc-ing, for petting dogs, for holding signs, for crossing streets, for using bathrooms, for handing out flyers, let out of jail, beaten and arrested again. We've lost weight; we've lost friends; we've lost, it seems, our sanity, because after seven months of bone-breaking, skin-cutting struggle the laws have become more austere, more se-vere, harsher, stricter, each time more open in their disregard for the American Constitution, so besides the particulars of our weight, our friends, our sanity, isn't the real issue that after seven months of Occupation *we have lost*?

We all came to this Occupation damaged, some more than others. As my friend and I have faced, shied from, and then battled the shadows and the zombies that roam about our fields, we've many times wondered if it was the creation of our country that brought these creatures into their existence. If our country were dissolved, the zombies would shrink behind their shadows, and the shadows would retreat back deep into the ground — leaving us to wonder within the monsoon floods at the dry and cracking earth; no — my friend and I are learning that the shadows and their zombies have always been there, scratching at us from the subterranean hideouts and forming in our understanding as hazy faces and unremembered nightmares; yes — my friend and I are learning that we have brought these monsters with us and that in the space of our land and by the toil of our country we have brought our monsters out into the open, and now out they can be diminished and eventually destroyed, so that when our final dawn sets upon this land, we can leave to freer travel toward wherever our future places lie.

And so with this our Occupation....

Seven months of struggle have torn through the tissue, cartilage, and bone and now the disease is out there, facing us directly. The subterfuge troubles, which for so long have bubbled up to land as something other than themselves — racism instead of classism, boredom instead of waste, recession instead of never-ending greed — lie before us.

Seven months of Occupation have successfully robbed us of our ability to ignorance and so the most violent element is gone. We have reached a point of no return: stop and face the problems now or keep moving forward as you were — but now without your sunglasses, now without your shade, the scorch of the burning earth always in your eyes and up against your skin....

As of this dispatch, on the eve of our ensuing MayDay!, MayDay!, MayDay!, the helicopter crashing sound of neon gold chlorophyll in the sky — the cabbage in Zuccotti Park are freezing to the grey, tomorrow morning's clouds are gathering behind the black

— my friend and I continue to farm our country, having better understood, it seems, the meaning of the nighttime rain; and though my hands are calloused, I'm thankful to him for daily making a better farmer out of me. I can only hope he feels the same.

I'd ask him, but I can't seem to find him at the moment.

Actually, I haven't seen him now for days....

OCCUPY CONFRONTS THE POWER OF MONEY: THE ENCAMPMENTS AS ANARCHY IN ACTION
PETER WERBE

> "A specter is haunting [the world] — the specter
> of [the Occupy movement]. All the powers of [the
> world] have entered into a holy alliance to exor-
> cise this specter." — Karl Marx & Fredrick En-
> gels, *The Communist Manifesto* (1848), [altered
> to reflect current reality]

One hundred and sixty-three years after the original words were written, the specter the rulers of Europe so feared (communism, the word altered in the above quote) appeared to have been successfully vanquished. But suddenly the Occupy movement went from 0 to a 100 mph in a few weeks placing the question of the rule of money on the political agenda across the world, and, in the U.S. for the first time in a hundred years. Inspired by the Arab Spring, the Greek, Spanish, and English opposition to shifting the cost of repairing capitalism from bankers to the people, almost overnight, Occupy sites sprouted up in over a thousand U.S. cities.

The dramatic events of September 17, when Occupy Wall Street launched, through December, have brought the words that define the class system and its hierarchal rule to the point where its main phrases, "99%," "1%," and "Occupy," have entered the lexicon faster than any high school slang.

Criticism of Occupy, some of it from the left, that the movement is only a spasm of bottled up anger without programmatic demands, and at worse, reformist, fails to realize that occupying the sites constituted a critique of capitalism and the culture it spawns. All of the contradictions and problems of the encampments notwithstanding, the taking of public space where capital's precepts are negated, a commitment to consensus decision making, the refusal of hierarchy, communal living, and confrontation with power, is anarchy in action.

Not anarchism, but, anarchy, the manner in which humans naturally associate to effectively and convivially live harmoniously. The politics of the people involved both as Occupiers and supporters were all over the left spectrum, but these anarchist processes were almost universally adhered to by all.

Even though Occupy immediately altered the political narrative, with even major media talking about corporate greed, the increasing poor, and the impact of austerity on most Americans, the idea of permanent centers of protest and even revolution, was more than the rulers could tolerate. Even supposedly liberal city administrations.

The coordinated militarized police assaults to remove encampments in cities across the country was reminiscent of the murderous attacks on workers in earlier periods of labor militancy. Although there was general outrage at the repressive manner in which police cleared Occupy sites using clubs and pepper spray, the most frightening police armament carried into these situations, automatic assault rifles, seems to have gone unnoticed.

The cops were ready to kill.

With the clearing of the outdoor sites, the hope among the powerful is that this specter has gone the way of communism now that the streets have been returned to commerce.

We'll see.

Much is still going on with the Occupy movement now quartered inside in many cities, and they continue to launch actions around a range of issues caused by the collapse of capitalism for large sections of the population. Still, the movement faces the daunting task of discerning what revolution means in the modern era.

The earliest concept of the revolutionary overthrow of capitalism posed by those who capitalism exploited and oppressed from its origins, was a straight forward proposition: The means of production (the economy) would be seized by the proletariat who would eliminate the rule of the capitalist class and then administer society for the collective benefit of all. This is certainly a sensible and equitable solution to a horrid set of social circumstances that capitalism has always enforced upon society.

The main impediment to revolution is the political state which functions as the defense mechanism against attempts to eliminate capitalist property relationships. This socially constructed institution, which arose thousands of years ago, hasn't altered its purpose of defending accumulated wealth and power since its inception.

The century-old illustration of the social pyramid from the anarcho-syndicalist union, the Industrial Workers of the World (IWW), illustrates the state apparatus contains more elements than just its repressive mechanism. The "We Fool You" sector, i.e., nationalist myths, militarism, religion, and the Spectacle, are the state and capital's first line of defense. Only after these cease to be effective, as is often the case, are the cops and army deployed.

There never was a Golden Age of the state or capitalism. Both were always a set of horrors from their beginnings, and although certain sectors of the world, and certain sectors within nations at different times, achieve a degree of economic prosperity beyond just rewarding the owners, there is always a much greater number whose misery and penury is a key to the plenitude of the few.

The favorite form of governance of all ruling classes is absolutism; their favorite class system is feudalism, but now with capitalist forms of ownership. This has overwhelmingly been the way human affairs have been administered in nation states since their emergence 6,000 years ago. Challenges to these arrangements have been few, relatively speaking, and met with suppressive force when they have occurred.

Political arrangements in the West have had some success with demands for rights and inclusion in decision making harkening back to England's 13th century Magna Carta, and culminating in the bourgeois revolutions of the modern era beginning in the 17th. What was gained in these revolutions, which installed the emerging capitalist classes in power, was usually a formal democratic system in which people had the status of citizens rather than subjects. What was lost was the ostensible reciprocity of feudal society where the peasants produced for the lords and in return were protected by them.

In the new capitalist societies, that social arrangement of mutual obligation evaporated, and the new class of workers were solely elements of production whose labor was purchased at the lowest price that could be leveraged by the emerging lords of manufacturing. Early revolts, such as those of the 19th century English Luddites, were suppressed by massive military force, demonstrating that without the iron hand of the state, capitalist production would not have lasted long.

Within capitalist countries of the West, movements arose around the inscription on the banner of the French Revolution, "Liberty, Fraternity, Equality." Taken to their full definitions, these words would proscribe capitalism and demand an anarchist socialism, so they mostly remain as pretty phrases trotted out on patriotic holidays.

For those who took them seriously, years of struggle ensued with numerous successes in terms of the conditions and rights of the common people. In this country, we know and celebrate the history of the abolitionists, suffragettes, the union and civil rights movements, and that of the women, gay, and disabilities rights struggles that have created a slow progress for inclusion within American society. None of these hard won victories should be diminished, but within the economic and political sphere, the same forces of greed and power continue to reign supreme all the while demonstrating a willingness (sometimes extremely begrudgingly) to allow some social equality; however, never economic.

To a large extent this is a conscious strategy on the part of the rulers to mollify challenges with the correct perception on their part that reforms extend and affirm the system. Once the personal prejudices of a white, male elite are brought to heel, the extension of some amount of inclusion works well for them. Color, gender, religion, sexual preferences, etc., doesn't matter if you are consuming, or if you are a company CEO.

The apex of this reform strategy, following some in the Progressive Era, was during the unionization movement of the 1930s, which demanded a more equitable split of social wealth and other reforms to improve working and living conditions. This wasn't granted willingly by the rulers and came only after general strikes and class struggle so sharp that it resulted in the death of 300 unionists during the decade at the hands of the cops, National Guard, and company goons.

The Roosevelt-era New Deal legislation that resulted, and the extension of the union movement's success, opened the way to the creation of a large, consumerist middle-class who saw themselves as having a stake in the system that had seemed near collapse just a few years previously. This is known as the Great Settlement which lasted approximately 35 years until the early 1970s.

The trade-off was no class strife initiated by the workers in return for a reduction in the rate of exploitation and a minimal share of social wealth. The latter provided for creation of a consumer class that the economy required as it went beyond producing basic industrial products. This vertical integration of classes under the aegis of the state, combined with mobilizing workers for the second inter-imperial war, could easily meet the classic definition of fascism.

The expectation that each successive generation would advance through the economic system was dubbed the "American Dream," something that has significantly frayed in the last forty years.

One of the slogans often heard in the Occupy movement is the plaintive call to "Restore the American Dream," uttered seemingly without recognition that the trajectory of capital world-wide has embarked on a massive reduction of economic and social gains made by the working class over the last 150 years.

If the capitalists have their way, and their forces and resources are many, there soon won't be a middle-class American Dream to which to return. The classic class formulation that all 19th century radicals tendered — capitalist and proletariat — will again become the norm.

The Dream, promulgated equally on the left and right, has always been a nightmare for other people here and abroad, and ignores that someone gets screwed somewhere, and badly, so we can shop at Whole Foods and buy iPhones.

The 35-year period which instilled the Dream myth in which anyone can "make it," and each generation does better economically than the prior one is now in terminal collapse in the popular imagination. And, myth is the operative word since upward mobility has always been fairly narrow within the American class system, it being, in reality, almost a caste system. Although some rise and a few falter, most people end up in the class to which they were born.

The great indignation among so many people contained in slogans such as, "The banks got bailed out; we got sold out," is both righteous and understandable. But the system isn't broken as is often suggested, but rather this is the way it works and always has. The attacks on what was once taken for granted as a middle-class standard of living are relentless with a recent survey showing that almost half of Americans are either poor or near poor. And, this in the richest country in the world.

The current trajectory of capital, the maximization of profit-taking, has as a model countries like Guatemala. This would mean for the U.S. that only about a third of the country would be well waged, and it is within that upper stratum where commodity consumption, financial transactions, and affluent lifestyles will continue in what we associate with middle-class living. Below that will be the vast majority, characterized by precarious labor, non-existent social services, deteriorating infrastructure, and general social insecurity.

A good illustration is the transformation of Detroit's Albert Kahn-designed Russell Industrial Center. During most of its existence since its opening in 1915, it operated in terms of its name, manufacturing automobile components for the city's many car companies. Now, its two million square-foot buildings, with industrial production long gone, is occupied by more than 150 creative tenants such as architects, painters, clothing designers, jewelry makers, photographers, musicians, filmmakers, bands, and art galleries.

Certainly, most of us would rather visit Russell as a vibrant center of creative talent than an industrial shop of grey men forced to work to the rhythm of relentless machines, but its transformation is indicative of how a waged workforce with defined benefits is replaced in the same location by its opposite. The former, the so-called American Dream; the latter, the new face of capitalism which is often marked by scuffling at the bottom, hoping for work or sales, as talented as many at Russell are.

So, what is to be fought for by the Occupy movement and an ideal of anarchy? Perhaps a vision is best encapsulated by the slogan — "Everything for everyone!" The question, however, becomes, what is "everything?" Do we demand that everyone on the planet have all the consumer junk the global productive machine can churn out? Surely, the world environment cannot sustain that.

What will it mean for the majority of us to be pushed out of a consumer-centered economy with much lower wages and no social safety net? At best, it can mean constructing a revolutionary society within the shell of the larger society based on the elements which sprung up spontaneously at the Occupy sites. At worst, most of the world could become a dystopian urban nightmare with a generalized Kingston, Rio, or Ciudad Juarez becoming the norm.

In Detroit and elsewhere, community gardens, shared housing, and local start-up businesses, many energized and connected to social justice groups, are often held up as the model for re-inventing daily life divorced from capital's mainstream. There's a great deal of enthusiasm for this as a new revolutionary paradigm by writers such as the late Grace Lee Boggs (see her *The Next American Revolution*) and publications like *Yes!* magazine. But, hey, guys, businesses are businesses, and capitalist.

Much of the activity and vision they chronicle, particularly with Boggs, is admirable and many anarchists are swept up in it. They see possibilities in what has historically been designated as a situation of dual power where revolutionary formations take the place of official ones.

The down side of this perspective seems to be an unintended cooperation with what capitalism already has in store for us — shedding off millions of people from its mainstream and having them fare for themselves. It probably isn't bad to be confused about which direction will bring about the changes in our lives. We hopefully are only at the beginning of a movement that' confronts power.

Could it be that this time around, the system's capacity for co-optation has run out of space, leaving the future to be creatively re-invented?

Increasingly, it seems as though many people are ready for the challenge.

At the Beat Museum
540 Broadway
WRITERS IN REVOLT
Literary Outsiders from
Dostoyevsky to Bukowski
Alan Kaufman
Sundays 5-645pm

WRITING BEYOND THE
INFLUENCES
A Creative Writing Seminar
Bobby Coleman
Sundays 7-845pm

At Kaleidoscope
3109 24th st.
WESTERN MUSIC II:
From Mozart to Wagner
John Smalley
Mondays 7-845pm

At Greenhouse Cafe
1722 Taraval St.
SCIENCE LITERACY
Barbara Ann Lewis
Mondays 4-6 pm

At SFPL Main Library
Koret Auditorium
100 Larkin St.
RESPONSIVE CINEMA
TO CORPORATE
EMPIRE
Rand Crook
Fridays 2-3:45pm

EAST GERMAN
CINEMA:
A History
Jim Morton
Fridays 4-530pm

At SFPL Park Branch
Library
1833 Page St.
REVOLUTIONARY
MOMENTS IN
AMERICA
1960s VS. 2011
Barbara Joans
Saturdays 2-345PM

At Pirate Cat Radio
2781 21st St.
HIPSTORY
The mostly underground and
unwritten story of our time
Diamond Dave Whitaker
Tuesdays 6-745pm

At Casa Sanchez
2778 24th St.
SELF-CARE AND
SOCIAL CHANGE
David Spero
Wednesdays 6-7:30pm

At The Convent
660 Oak St.
C. WRIGHT MILLS,
SOCIOLOGICAL
IMAGINATION, &THE
POWER ELITE
Implications for America
50 Years On
Scott Parker
Wednesdays 4-545pm

INTRO TO
MINIMALISM
A Critical Theory Primer
Kenneth Thomas
Wednesdays 6-745pm

FREE UNIVERSITY of SAN FRANCISCO

SPRING TERM
APRIL 9 - MAY 20, 2011

At Five Points Arthouse
72 Tehama

POCKET PAD ART:
Drawing From Your Life
David Newman
Tuesdays 6-745pm

UNDERSTANDING
WORLD ART
John Rapko
Tuesdays, 8-9:45pm

USING DREAMS TO
CHART YOUR INNER
LANDSCAPE
Michael Loeffler
Tuesdays 6-7:45pm

WHAT YOUR BOSS
DOESN'T WANT YOU
TO KNOW:
Your Rights at Work
**Darin Ranahan
& Tim Phillips**
Tuesdays 8-9:45pm

A Revolution in
Education

An Education in
Revolution

All FUSF Classes are Open Enrollment, Non-Discriminatory, and Completely FREE
FreeUniversitySF.org

First planning session of
THE FREE UNIVERSITY OF SAN FRANCISCO 12/19/2010,
held at Viracocha, 998 Valencia Street, The Mission, San Francisco

FOUNDING MANIFESTO OF THE
FREE UNIVERSITY OF SAN FRANCISCO
ALAN KAUFMAN

My friends, thank you for coming. I ask that you indulge these few remarks on what prompts me to call at this time for the establishment of a FREE UNIVERSITY OF SAN FRANCISCO, for I have given much thought to this over the years, and that you show some patience and even compassion for any failings you may perceive in my reasons for such an undertaking. For what I am asking you to join in — the formation of a university that will make the highest level of education available, completely free, to any individual who wants it, regardless of color, creed, age, gender, nationality, religion or immigration status — a university free of money, taught for free to any who want it — is, at this crucial historical moment a dream far too important to hold hostage to any particular person or personality-type. I ask that you run with this dream and realize it for the sake of yourselves and each other and this country and most of all for our young people, the poor and dispossessed, the undocumented and disenfranchised, the outcasts, the ones without a dream. In a world of unchecked greed and of exhausting religious and ideological divisions, let today's effort to create a Free University stand as a way station to dreams for those who have no right to dream in a world like this.

I mean most especially our youth though not only. I mean our seniors too. Are not children and seniors our most sacred human responsibility? And yet, in this day, it is they who lie on the sacrificial block of our social and economic order. It is they whom we have offered up in exchange for an illusion of security and comfort. And yet all around us we now watch as shadows grow to our very

door and we are faced with the awful realization that we have sacrificed both our human future and past — our children and seniors
— in exchange for our very own destruction.

And nowhere has this exchange been more evident, at least to
me, then in the Bay Area. Here, it stands out like an awful stain
upon a great legacy. For in the matter of radical cultural initiative
and progressive daring, the world looks to us. We have always been
the laboratory of human advance and cultural revolutions and social compassion. And yet, in the last decades we have seen that the
Bay Area, which gave us the Beats and Abstract Expressionism,
the Berkeley Free Speech Movement, The Summer of Love, The
Black Panthers, City Lights Bookstore and luminaries like Kenneth
Rexroth, Harvey Milk, Diane Di Prima, and our very own Matt
Gonzales, has become, instead, the center of the dot com boom
and bust and later the crowning tiara of the real estate bubble and
collapse — a crown that the corpse of our economy still wears.
And today our Bay Area is the epicenter of a world technocracy
run out of Silicon Valley, where initiatives are launched to render
our most sacred cultural artifacts such as books obsolete. Where
they work too to devise programs that hold our youth spellbound
before screens from morning to night, addicted to games and apps
that reinforce their use with each click, a form of technological
Crack. In Silicon Valley they work to replace those employments
that give life meaning, substance and reward with brand new software. In a system predicated upon obsolescence and profit, they
have caused our economy to shift into an ephemeral service orien-
tation which now requires the worker not only to give of his time
and life's energy at triple the former pace and at a lower wage but
insists that one do so with artificial enthusiasm. This cynically fos-
tered system, engineered for the benefit of corporate profits alone,
demands that we smile gratefully as our very soul is crushed.

But nothing astonishes me more then what we are doing to our
youth. In some sense, youth anywhere belong to us, the human
family, no less than our own children. We have a profound responsibility both to protect and defend them and to set an example to
them of how to be, how to live and of when to stand up against all
odds for what is right, what is good, and to fight for those things.

And yet, for decades now most of us have stood by idly and even to some extent participated in the corporate profit-driven culture in which, for the sake of an illusion of freedom and prosperity we have permitted our own youth to be brainwashed and bankrupted even as they are channeled by the privatized educational system into fifty stories-high slave labor work camps of air-conditioned glass and steel for corporate Capitalist profit-making.

I do not have answers to most of the questions or objections you may raise here today. What I possess is the certainty that the purpose of education is not to turn the student into a better consumer and profit-earner but to help him to discover the wealth of human culture upon whose shoulders he or she stands. What I have is a passionate determination to see the restoration of humanity — warm, literate, democratic — to vibrant human life. And in order to achieve this aim we must take hold of the very hub of our culture, which is education, and create a brand new kind of institution, one whose existence makes no sense in the current social order, one that stands in direct defiance of the privatized profit-oriented social engineering centers that pass for universities today.

Where does one house this Free University, you may ask? It is here, in you, in each of us. You are the Free University. We are the Free University. Wherever we stand, that is where it exists. One hears so much these days about the hopeless selfishness of youth. Let me tell you a brief anecdote. When I went on strike against the Academy of Art University in 2004, because a teacher and two students were thrown out due to something they wrote in class or taught, many of my students were already in debt for up to as much as $90,000 to $100,000. I watched one student, sustaining herself on Raman Noodle Cups, waste away before my eyes until one day I pulled her aside, numbed and fatigued, and said: 'Forget about this week's assignments. Here is your assignment take this $50 and buy yourself some fresh food and eat meals this week." When I next saw her, her eyes were bright but very soon, under the heel of her crushing tuition, her eyes went dull again.

During the strike, I invited Matt Gonzales, who is here with us today, and several authors, including Dave Eggars and Daniel Handler to my classroom, where I conducted freedom of speech protest seminars. When the school refused to permit Matt and the others to enter the building, I went to my classroom and said to the students: "I intend to hold this class on the sidewalk, as they won't allow our honored guests onto the premises. I understand how much most of you have riding on your educations and so cannot in good conscience ask you to risk all that for the sake of my protest. But I intend to teach this class today out in the street. There will be no consequence for failure to attend. Those who wish to join me outside are welcome."

When I left the building every student in that classroom followed me out, despite the risk. Matt and the writers spoke to them. And after, we went to North Beach, to City Lights Bookstore to continue with our Freedom Class. That is what education should be: a long, ongoing class in human freedom. So much for the purported selfishness and lack of idealism among youth. I don't believe it! Those who displayed no courage or ideals were not the students but rather the adult faculty, the instructors. Not a single instructor at the Academy of Art joined our protest, which soon spread to almost the entire student body. Not a single teacher joined us!

Let me tell you another story. During World War Two, a famous specialist in child education named Janusz Korczak — a man renowned in his profession throughout the world — voluntarily entered the Warsaw Ghetto to administer and teach at the Jewish orphanage and school. In the shadow of the death-camp deportations and systematic starvation of the Jews, this Jewish teacher and thinker happened to be walking in the ghetto streets one day when he saw an SS man beating a Jewish child to death and threw his own body on top of the child to deflect the SS man's blows. Later, when finally the orphans in Korczak's care were assigned for deportation to Auschwitz, and though world leaders petitioned for and received permission for him to escape to the free West, Korczak refused to abandon his charges. He boarded the freight trains with them to Auschwitz and at their head, holding their hands, he entered with them into the gas chambers and died with them. That is the example of what I, the son of a Holocaust survivor, understand to be an educator's responsibility to his or her charges. And so I do not believe that the creation of a Free University under our current conditions is impossible or predicated upon money.

In 2004, when I stood on the sidewalk with my students, we were a dispossessed educational module with only streets to house us. What held us together that afternoon were not walls but love of learning, pride in our actions, principles of freedom, comradeship in the quest for knowledge. From time to time I run into these students who tell me that it was the best class they ever took. And from these encounters, I came away with a vision whose time had not yet come. The idea of a Free University.

Now, the time has come. The social order is in disintegration. The divide between rich and poor is an abyss. The corporation controls our entire existence. Unemployment and unease are widespread. The liberal arts are disappearing, displaced by studies guaranteed to generate the highest income. The universities funnel students into money-making programs rather than humanity-building curriculum and when those nonetheless don't pan out and the student is left in massive debt, then conditions have been laid for a revolutionary change of the most profound kind.

This is a crucial step towards that revolutionary change. If we decide here today to be a Free University, then already it exists. And our student body will exist because we do. Where we will teach is not the first question, or even what we will teach but rather, that we will teach. That is the question at hand. For if we decide in the highest altruistic spirit of education that we will teach, regardless of obstacles, then we give birth to a dream that will pass on to the generations of the future. For now, with only our hearts and minds and bodies to create the dream, let us dedicate ourselves to the regeneration of our humanity through the gift of knowledge freely given to others.

And so I ask you to answer today one basic question: are we or are we not from this moment forth members of a Free University comprised of anyone who would wish to join us? I propose that the only requirement for membership in this enterprise is a desire to teach and/or a desire to learn. And nothing more. And that we will impart what we know to any who want it.

POSTSCRIPT: TRUMP

DAN FREEMAN

THIS IS AMERICA, COVER IT ALL UP
GEORGE WALLACE

This is america and america's paradise
america is hot wheels let's go for a ride —
a joy ride a circus ride a terror ride —
oops ma'am, lock your doors cut the
telephone wires, can't leave witnesses,
just got to tie you up by the wrists,
lie down

america sweeps into town like winter rain
and kills everything it sees like cattle like
buffalo like meat loaf like the rosebowl
parade america is a white tornado and
plague of locusts, and kitty genovese is
the pom pom queen

america, america, we like prom night best,
look who's got the pink corsage look who's
riding shotgun to the funeral slash wedding —
look who's wearing her best white dress and
her boyfriend's ring is strung around her neck

the boyfriends fly out the bodybags fly in and all along
the parade route the president hands out shiny red apples

america we love you, applepie and ice cream,
two scoops, we love matchbook smiles and an
occasional killing spree ie look who's popular

cold blooded perry with the good hair — he's
a car wreck baby he's got good manners and
gentle eyes got the killer instinct of a date night
crooner — he's a mass murderer too

the stumbling animal speaks for itself, sweetness
    of the sexually repressed

comb your hair honey sunday best nothing can
beat the religion into or out of you like the old
time religion, red light green light, hand in hand
with the bible, righteous in the heartland, the
rewards of abstemious living is rape

but this is america the sky over a man's head is flat
    plain and brutally good

let's build us a great big bridge over it all
    — all the empty places all the empty lives

cover it all up

the people
the animals
the rain

I TOLD YOU
NANCY MERCADO

I told you
That the implosion
Of the United States
Would occur in our lifetime

That hatred would
Consume itself
Bite off its hands
Feed on its entrails
Feed on its own children

That this would explode into
A billion body parts like fireworks
On the 4th of July

I told you the sun would rise
One dead mornings
Around white picket-fenced corners
Waking Dick and Jane
Turning their faces toward the East
Crystallizing the cries of dead bodies
Floating down rivers
Of massacres and mass graves

That the U.S. in Syria
Would take us by surprise

That the U.S.
In the Middle East
In Africa
Would pay New York City a visit

That U.S. policy makers
Would meet in chandeliered-rooms
For breakfast
For lunch
For dinner
To toss stacks of paper around
Like some ball game
White-collar trash men

I told you that assassins
Would come back into style
That the Dark Ages would thrive
In the 21st century

I told you that McCarthy
Would miraculously
Come back from the dead

DREAM OF A NEW PATRIOTISM
MICHAEL GRAVES

In the interrogation room,
A man behind a desk.

I am standing before it.
He looks up from the folder
That contains my file.

Like the cloud-covered dawn of a sun
Over bare mountains
In a desolate winter.

His lean-jawed face
Breaks into a sadist's smile.

Each of his eyebrows is a word.
The left is Republican.
The right is Democrat.

He says, "I am going to ask questions
Impossible to answer."

CHELICERAE
JANA ASTANOV

These men
whose pretense of kindness could only end the world
these scattered men
scared to face themselves
using baby charm vaseline
to trap us in their psycho-maniac pathology
these men
who suddenly weave us into their narrative of mistakes
and a web of obstacles to their glory
because of us their greatness has not been seen by the world
and our failing to live up to their ideal self-delirium
these men
who can only live if we keep on diminishing
these men
who hate openly hallucinating
throwing at us inflatable toy-plastic egos
who think their power and money means everything
and that their venom is holy
and their anger mighty

these men
they will never deserve our respect
and they will perish
broken by the history
written by us

THE RETURN OF THE FROG KING, OR IRON HENRY

PETER WORTSMAN

"On Wednesday, at 3PM, there will be a security check of the building. In case you are in the building at that time, we kindly ask you to stay in your apartment rooms for the period of the security check, which will take no longer than 20 minutes." — Request from the Academy

Bomb-sniffing dogs are patrolling the carpeted hallways, closets and alcoves downstairs in preparation for this evening's conference on nuclear disarmament, hosted by and starring Dr. Henry Kissinger. Security is tight. Dr. Kissinger, I hear, has called off the television journalists. After a moment's hesitation I decide to attend. It's not every day you get to meet Dr. Strangelove in the flesh![1] It's going to be a star-studded extravaganza. Other headliners include former German Chancellor Helmut Schmidt and former German President Richard von Weizsäcker, former U.S. Senator Sam Nun, former Secretary of State George Schultz, and various other aging German and American political heavies of the Cold War Era. The audience is likewise teeming with international VIPs, ambassadors, ministers and

---

[1] A propos of *Dr. Strangelove,* a curious footnote. I recently learned from a documentary on Veidt Harlan, the notorious director of the Nazi-era Anti-Semitic blockbuster film "Jud Süß," that Harlan's niece married the Jewish-American director Stanley Kubrick. I wonder if Harlan himself lived to attend the wedding.

the like. Chef Reinold tells me he's prepared rack of venison *"von Himmel und Erde"* (literally from heaven and earth style), its gamey flesh stuffed with a mix of crushed apples and potatoes, his signature dish, symbolically suited to the occasion. I have a weakness for wild game.

And so they came, aged, stooped, leaning on canes, shuffling on walkers, and rolled in on wheelchairs, the dance of the dinosaurs, the white-haired, hard-of-hearing statesmen of yore, gathered to reflect on the impending threat of nuclear catastrophe in the irresponsible hands of today's rogue nations, some of them erstwhile allies. The place is packed. One of the bomb-sniffing dogs sent in earlier in the day by the German police had, I'm told by an Academy staff member, succumbed to canine temptation and gobbled up her lunch. Dogs will be dogs. Statesmen will be statesmen, ever eloquent, attempting to clean up with words the mess they made.

MR. TRUMP GOES TO WASHINGTON
Nick Freundlich

So here we are.

Sixty-three million Americans went out and voted celebrity real estate tycoon, reality TV personality, and noted windbag in a hair helmet, Donald Trump, into the White House. At odd hours of the morning he paces the halls in a terrycloth robe, peers through binoculars at the hecklers on his lawn. He spews invective at the morning news. This raging egomaniac dipped in bronzer is the President of the United States. And now that the shock has worn off, it all makes a sickening kind of sense. I feel as though the picture of my country is finally coming into focus.

I never had much faith in politics. I was only eleven when the Twin Towers came down, so I didn't fully understand what it meant, how it represented a turning point in terms of the history of our country and the world. I came of age, and my political and social consciousness was formed, in post-9/11 New York City, in private schools I might add, where liberal values flourished and tolerance was praised amid a general atmosphere of self-congratulation, and yet there was always this fear, unacknowledged but ever present, that maybe harsher measures were necessary in today's world. A plane was never just a plane anymore.

I was a freshman in college when Obama was elected in 2008, at a small school in rural Ohio with a (fading) reputation for radicalism. The idyllic little town, which comprised mainly the school, housing for its students and faculty, and a handful of businesses catering to same, stood in contrast to the area surrounding, both the farmland and the nearby towns, which had the feeling of being dilapidated, almost sepia-toned. The population seemed to be about 50/50 black and white, and lower-middle class across the boards. It was not uncommon to see a Confederate flag hanging in a window or on the back bumper of a pickup.

An impromptu celebration broke out across campus when the results came in that night. Streaming from their dorms, students congregated on the various quads and on the main square, whooping, climbing in trees, setting off fireworks. I don't recall much in the way of conversation, political or otherwise; just a frantic glee, as though Mardis Gras had fallen out of the sky on the wrong Tuesday in Ohio.

But even as I joined the throng, I think I knew that it had more to do with seeking "the college experience" than any swelling sense of pride in country. The hugging of strangers, the crying, the chanting of "U-S-A, U-S-A," all felt more than a tad disingenuous coming from a largely white, largely upper-middle-to-upper class crowd of late-teenagers at private school. Likewise the tide of youth support for Obama in the run-up to the election made me vaguely uncomfortable, a fact which, in turn, I was often uncomfortable to admit.

At the time I blamed myself for not being able to get fully into the spirit of things, blamed my cynicism, my political apathy, my depression. But looking back, I believe I was responding to a contradiction that I couldn't make sense of, between the America I was assured existed and the one I saw and felt.

The former flew in the face of logic, but somehow, I realize now, I never truly disbelieved it. It was the America of legend, a nation which, despite its many acknowledged failures, past and present, still embodied the same values that presumably made it great during the days of its conception. The City on the Hill, the shining beacon of hope for the world.

Then, on the other hand, there was the America that settled long ago for small victories in the way of freedom, and which gluts itself mindlessly on entertainment and consumer goods, grazing passively on incorporated farmland while the decisions that determine the course of history are made with no higher ideal in mind than the almighty dollar.

My rational mind accepted the truth of the latter without ever acknowledging the necessary falsity of the former. Without ever even acknowledging that I believed in the former! I was like some kind of split-brain patient who, seeing something, cannot name it, and being unable to name it, rearranges his perception of what is so as not to see it.

Looking back now, through Trump-tinted lenses, that whole celebration feels as foolish as George W.'s "Mission Accomplished" goof.

I believe now that the fact of the Obama administration was, to people of my generation, a kind of false positive. Those of us who grew up in the 90s learned identity politics on Sesame Street, and then every year in school they taught us how far we'd come. Emancipation! Suffrage! Civil Rights! It stood to reason that we were living in the most tolerant time that ever was. Sure, there was still injustice, inequality, but if we kept pace they'd be wiped out in no time.

Then bang! on cue, an inspirational black man was elected President. What more proof did we need? Despite our lethal entanglements in the Middle East, despite our bloated penal system, fed disproportionately on minority citizens, the myth of the greatness of American freedom somehow managed to thrive.

Now that's all come crashing down. The bubble has popped. When the President holds a trademark on the phrase "You're Fired!," it's difficult to wax patriotic about freedom and democracy.

Still, it's only now that the holy tenets of American democracy are being challenged do I really feel how strongly I believe in them. Suddenly I can see the demon of American exceptionalism for what it is — a flattering mirror, a pair of earplugs, and carte blanche to do whatever the hell you want. Yes, it can happen here. Why should we ever have doubted it?

On the plus side, my political apathy is clearing right up. I've never felt so fiercely American as I do these days. Maybe we complacent liberals needed someone like Donald Trump, with his grotesque parody of American ideals, to strengthen our commitment to those values that are actually worth fighting for, and to remind ourselves that forward progress is not a given.

HOW SOCIAL MEDIA IS CHANGING POLITICS ONE CLICK AT A TIME

ALLISON KRIDLE

Social media isn't for connecting with your friends anymore — it is used for politics. Facebook and Twitter are now platforms to read about the outrageous statements Republican candidate Donald Trump says or see what leaked about Democratic candidate Hillary Clinton. Social media as we know it controls how we see politics.

The 2008 election was dubbed the "Facebook Election" when President Obama won about 70 percent of the vote among voters 25 years old and younger — the highest percentage since 1976, according to *US News*. Of course, this does not necessarily mean Obama beat Republican nominee Mitt Romney because he is Facebook savvy, but the site streamlined the President's victory by posting the results on every user's feed — the influence of social media was apparent.

In 1968 Ned Stuckey-French, Florida State University Associate Professor grabbed a clipboard, paper and pen, went door to door, and campaigned for Democratic candidate Robert Kennedy a few months before Kennedy was shot and killed. At the time of the shooting, Stuckey-French was attending a celebration after his high school commencement. No one at the party knew Kennedy had been assassinated, and Stuckey-French woke up the next morning to his parents telling him the tragic news.

"I had no cellphone. I was just listening to AM radio [and] this incredible, horrible thing just happened, but I went eight hours or so without knowing about it. With a cellphone now, I would've known about it," Stuckey-French told me during an interview for *The Last Word* magazine in April 2016.

Now, no one misses a beat. If a candidate says something radical during an interview, social media users know about it the moment it happens.

"Things change faster. It's like 'Did you see what Trump tweeted this morning?' [or] 'Did you hear about that bird that landed on Bernie's podium?' It seems like there are a half dozen of those little events each day. It's speeded up and your access is total," Stuckey-French said.

However, politics do not only travel at the speed of light, but have undergone insurmountable changes in the way politicians campaign and portray themselves to the country.

"[Trump] knows how to tweet, he knows how to not stop himself and say what he thinks without a filter and say it quickly — to trust his instincts," Stuckey-French added. "I'm pretty sure he writes his own tweets. Some politicians get [someone else] to tweet, but that's not what tweets are about. Tweets are about your id, just spitting it out — and Trump spits well."

While Facebook and Twitter users may learn their friend's stances based on their angry ramblings and heated comment wars, social media users also see where their friends are getting news updates by the sites they share from, and how the media presents a political happening or figure.

"I vote on the issues, not what the media has to say about candidates. The media is trying their best to portray Trump as a racist and a bigot as well as violent. They don't like him. Just saying he is racist is enough for people who want to believe it, [but] he has actually said nothing racist," FSU 'Noles For Trump president, Brent Canada said in a Facebook chat interview with me in April 2016, "I try to avoid [online political debates] with people who refuse to accept facts. Because their go-to argument is that Trump is a bigot when there is no proof of that."

Even though we can trace media biases and voter ignorance back before social media, Americans are voting during an age where they share news articles to their pages, instantly comment on them and engage in discussion without having to meet the person they are conversing with behind their computer screen.

"[I] stay on Facebook as much as I do is because if I just talk to people I see in the halls of the [English] building, then I would be talking to people who are a lot like me. Because of my conservative, Evangelical, libertarian brother-in-law and his friends, I can engage in pretty civil conversations with most of them and [hear] different point of views about issues," Stuckey-French told me during our interview.

The bulk of the American people (millennials especially) get their election news straight from social media. Even though politics drastically changed, voters still hold the responsibility of being informed — whether they learn and form their opinions by scrolling through their news feed or listening to the person on their doorstep.

I started writing this article during my last semester at Florida State University months before Donald Trump won the 2016 presidential election. To me, social media and technology are two of the most significant developments between then and now. I realize my piece barely scratches the surface of how new media affects politics and our country's perception of the status quo. Looking forward, I think it is the best platform to stay informed, engaged, and angry about the new administration we are expected to succumb to. Who knows whether or not social media contributed to the defeat of Trump's opponent, Hillary Clinton; it wouldn't change anything if we knew for certain. But we can continue to spread the word about anti-Trump protests, art, petitions, or just simply reassuring one another that we are not alone — even if it is through Facebook.

THE CREATIVITY OF CHAOS OR NO MAN IS A GOD

Robert Carrithers

Tune in, turn on, tune out. Not exactly like the '60's phrase, but the feelings of many nowadays with the daily nonstop assault of Trump tweets and behavior. I always thought of Trump as the trickster God Loki, who loves to create chaos, but I was wrong. This is the agenda of Steve Bannon, the great manipulator and his philosophy of The Fourth Turning. The creativity of chaos: the strategy is to create so much daily chaos that people get totally burnt out that they basically tune out and shut down. The situation with Trump is actually much sadder in truth. The people around Donald Trump are taking full advantage of him being president. Here is a man who is obviously psychologically ill. President Obama skillfully roasted and destroyed the Trump myth with his jokes at the white house correspondent's dinner in 2011. Trump has held a grudge since then and has been intent on destroying Barack Obama's legacy ever since.

According to psychiatrist's observation Donald Trump has an extreme case of Narcissistic Personality Disorder known as NPD and this is the definition: "A pervasive pattern of grandiosity (in fantasy or behavior), need for admiration, and lack of empathy, beginning by early adulthood and present in a variety of contexts." Trump seems to have an extreme case of this disorder because he refuses to even accept reality as proof if it goes against his own sense of self-importance. He first refuses to accept the fact that he actually lost the popular vote and does whatever he can to disprove it with his claims of massive voting fraud of millions of people.

And then there is his refusal to accept the fact that Barack Obama's inauguration had more people than he had at his inauguration, even though there is photographic and video proof of this.

Donald Trump was not satisfied with the power of being a real estate tycoon. He had the pleasure of owning property and the power he had over his tenants and then he was an owner of casinos, where people destroyed their lives with gambling. He went bankrupt and came through it. It is said he is heavily in debt to Russian oligarchs and the Russian mafia. Somehow I feel this will not end well and the question is when the time comes will he go quietly or take others with him or attempt to take all of us.

He is now president. It is the next level of his quest of power. What more does he want? It is obvious. He wants to be worshipped by one and all. He is truly hurt personally when someone shuns him. He was in rapture when he spoke to the crowds and they showered him with praise and applauded and laughed with him. Never mind that they were people who he would never go to dinner with. He even didn't care if some were white supremacists. He was getting what he needed, a type of attention and worship that he craves and needs for his addiction. He never gets enough though. Why do you think he tweets late at night for attention all alone in his white house bedroom? He feels that he is too mighty to fall, but fall he shall and it will be a mighty fall indeed.

According to one of the versions of the Narcissus myths he committed suicide: Narcissus saw his reflection in the water and fell in love with it. He did not realize it was just a reflection and when he did finally realize it, he could not handle it and committed suicide. With Trump, he knows that it is his reflection. Unfortunately it is also the reflection of our present day society and when society finally becomes repulsed enough from this reflection Trump will be flung aside. It is a question of time. This will be the final evolution of power for Trump: The fall! I am looking forward to this, but in the meantime, how many are going to suffer and who will fall with him?

TRUMPET
RONNA LEBO

My business controls the decade now,
although inconsistent with any known value
and unlike anything you've seen
under the hashtag "democracy,"
which I consider deportable.
Your vote was never something I'd need.

Nor will I make it my duty to hear
or acknowledge you in any way.
Health and education are meaningless —
'only a job' matters to a slave.
I do not pledge to withdraw high fences
or motion sensors, or a well-armed gate.

My power was forged with the money
it took to buy one judge or one republican's
fate. Agenda: to close forever
a constitution built for naïve colonials.
I will implement a national post-truth tweet —
a sweeping revision of your all time low
into an elite American great.

KATHERINE ARNOLDI

THE LONE RANGER RIDES AGAIN
LINDA LERNER

When the leader of the new free world
the lone survivor of warring factions
came out shooting, guns in both hands
he was at his golf club, having just sent the ball
flying to the other side of the fence bordered his land
his whole country, as reports of
missiles he ordered fired warnings to someone
in retaliation for… only it was
gunpowder filled the air he breathed, and a horse
he rode in the back of his chauffeured limo
his head filling with plans for a high enough fence to keep out
all those bad hombres he'll rope up like cattle
and send flying back over the fence which
keeps growing like those knock down drag out fights
he'll have with anyone from anywhere who opposes him,
images over flowing so fast into his daily
reports no one could keep track of who or
how many there were or where he was, a masked man
riding into yesterday when a man was a man
and women, ah yes women… along with
a staff of shift shaping Tonto sidekicks
he'll bring back the great promise of frontier life

NETHERWORLD
ROBERT ROTH

There is no reason to believe Trump. And there is no reason to believe the CIA. There is no reason to believe the FBI. There is no reason to believe the media. There is no reason to believe Obama. There is no reason to believe Russia. There is no reason to believe either Clinton. There is no reason to believe Saudi Arabia. No reason to believe Iran. No reason to believe Turkey. There is no reason to believe *The NY Times*. No reason to believe Israel. No reason to believe France. No reason to believe Charlie Rose. No reason to believe Nancy Pelosi. There is no reason to believe James Mattis. No reason to believe James Comey. No reason to believe Canada. No reason to believe Venezuela. No reason to believe China Daily. No reason to believe *The Wall Street Journal*. There is no reason to believe Putin. There is no reason to believe Pence. We are stuck in a netherworld of murderous forces all aligned against each other. It is I think very foolish to take anyone remotely at their word.

WE INTERRUPT THIS PROGRAM
JOHN CASQUARELLI

Mask land and water grabs in silent America
mask CIA war train choo choo through Venezuela
  mask deep water contamination off Louisiana shoreline
mask carbon blanket blood virus in lobes and trachea
mask telecom horror show turning over metadata
mask academic peddling in moral wilderness
mask prison profit racket on carousel cage house
mask union busting factory scars from 12-hour shifts
mask three-day hospital stay that leaves you
  hungry and shuddering
mask bullets-to-body police corruption in a 41 gunshots acquittal
mask billionaire hero worship in your parents' basement
mask SEC retirement parties during 2008 meltdown
mask blue suit kleptocrats rolling dope on Constitutional papers
mask drone bomb smoke cloud during afternoon wedding song
mask shock and awe death squads on asphalt highways
mask credit card interest rates on commodity buffet
mask university rape culture in 9pm dorm room
mask industrial pipeline over our unconscious catatonia
mask interrupted Friday dinner because of eminent domain
mask evening news broadcast with burlesque and puppy show

...AND OUT OF THIS
STEVE LUTTRELL

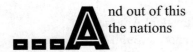 nd out of this
the nations

and men to
make their names and

chilling
how so easily
they speak of
death and dying and
"the weapons of a
mass destruction"

They speak
a crippled twisted
language
these apocalyptic
demagogues and
their politics of lies

These men
have brought us
days as dark as oil
and a legacy
of death
and of deception

LITTLE MAN WHAT NOW?
BERNARD BLOCK

L ittle man   the carnival is here
the barker barks   virtue   will hurt you
see the side-show   fences on parade
American Carnage   crystal meth users
heads wrapped in plastic   weatherman forecast
a most unusual day   opioids on parade
fortune-teller warning   beware November & January 8 & 20
do not show her your palm   she might hear your psalm
try to remember   deep in December
before American Carnage
O little man   what now   hide your little hands

order the fences   under which Mexicalis dig tunnels
those wily Mexicalis have been doing it for centuries
tweets for twits   birds for words virtue will hurt you
sniff your version of crystal meth trick or tweet Carnage
little big man little hands at the crossroads
of pomp and circumstance   cock-a-doodle   preen
are you tweeting out of love   my dear
look down   look down
                        at your screen

IMMIGRANTS SPEAK TO A NEW PRESIDENT

Austin Alexis

We flee poverty
the way the U.S.A. will,
at some point,
seek escape from you.
You are to us
as a flaw is
when it mars a $1000 bill.
We so need that capital,
that liberating opportunity,
that expanse of fertile green.
If only you didn't shed
your blot on its face,
rendering it nightmarish,
its once-prized images and concepts
now garbled, unreadable.

DON'T SPEAK SPANISH
GABRIELA M. TABOAS ZAYAS

"**W**hen you're outside, don't talk in Spanish." Those were the words my mother told me on the phone — her in Puerto Rico and me in New York.

News of hate crimes against the Latinx and Hispanic community were everywhere. Facebook, Twitter, Tumblr, the radio, television. Videos and articles from witnesses and victims of how they were suddenly attacked with words and fists and bullets. Their fingers stained the keyboards and cameras with blood and their tears stung their eyes.

The hatred always existed. It popped up now and again, but mainly stayed in the community. But now it's reached a new scale. There's a coat of fear that sticks the tongue to the roof of our mouths that keeps us from speaking our language in public. There's tape to keep our eyes open and feet ready to sprint when the first yell breaks out.

We've always been afraid, but defiant. Now we're terrified. And angry. So angry that it broke my heart when my mother begged me to hide my mother tongue, because I knew she was afraid that I would be another added to the plaque of the lost.

"They won't do anything to me, mami," I told her. "I'm white. I look like them."

My skin color was always a privilege. Born to please and to clear the road just a bit more. I could camouflage myself in the crowds, and no one would be the wiser. I could hide what little accent I had and no one else would know.

But I'm still Puerto Rican. There is a black and white flag with one star in it in my heart and it burns.

I'm still American.

I'm still angry.

A TRUMP STORY:
THE REVOLUTION BLUES
SUSAN YUNG

The rich in NYC are having a revolution on the poor people. They want to starve us from this blighted Lower East Side neighborhood so that better housing can be built. Even the fascist government participates when aligned with Russia's politics. They protect the rich by providing tax-free programs for developers as well as owners of condos, luxury co-ops and homes worth millions in the housing market.

Recently, I was told that the razed supermarket, Pathmark, in the middle of Rutger's housing project in the Lower East Side will be Trump's new luxury tower for millionaires. I grew up in those housing projects like many poor Asians in America. The poor depended on the supermarket's low prices and it's close vicinity. Now the poor have to walk over to Grand St, or to Essex St. Market. This methodology slowly causes starvations, famines and deaths in the community. The revolution had begun when Trump announced his candidacy for Presidency once the Pathmark and construction for the luxury condo began. When the tower is completed, the masses will have moved out of the community due to noise pollution, land sinkage, cracks on their walls, backed-up sewage water, no parking and other urban problems. With the rich moving in, crimes will increase caused by the minorities who are enraged by displacement and eventual homelessness.

The "rich" revolution against the "poor" has control of media and projects 87 photos of George Clooney's wife, human rights lawyer Amal Clooney (*née* Alamuddin) for Maldives, a Muslim nation. (The United States Bureau of Democracy, Human Rights and Labor claims in their 2012 report on human rights practices in this country that the most significant problems are corruption, lack of religious freedom, and abuse and unequal treatment of women.) After viewing forty photos of Amal's expensive clothes with accessories, no wonder she fends for the poor in a third-world nation. The contradictions are prevalent like a Hollywood movie produced by stockbrokers.

The masses have peacefully protested, got locked up, harangued, & beaten up by Gestapo like bullies. The memories of the holocaust prevails. Later the rebellion against the "Rich" revolution will be underground like the Underground Weathermen and eventuallyrock concerts will prevail.

Rockefeller's Asia Society exhibition on Philippine gold craftsmanship advertises that nation as having the second largest gold deposits. I suppose one of Trump's goal would be to hoard the gold for himself and to build further millionaire luxery condos.

AGH!!! AUGHHHHHHHHHHHCHHHHH!!!!

AMERICA, WE NEED A DIVORCE
FRANCINE WITTE

We need a it's not you it's me,
We need a no, there's no one else,
We need a I need some fucking space.

Because, America, we really are two countries —
Redmerica and Bluemerica, and it just ain't
working out. It would be better

for the children. Rather than half in Obamaland,
half in Trump's, let's try it apart. Let's try
it where we never have to hear the words

snowflake or libtard, or fascist as normal,
like it's *Leave It to Beaver* and wasn't
that a grand old time? Only it never

happened that way. My own mother,
woman of the fifties, never cleaned
the house in pearls, never woke up

perfectly coiffed, but rather sweat
out sweaty nights, next day hiding
how my father bruised her up,

but just a little, nothing makeup
wouldn't hide. And my parents,
they never got a divorce, but Lord knows,

they needed one. Lord knows that separate
houses would have been just right.
Seeing my mother stand up for herself,

forcing my father to be the good man I knew
deep down he wanted to be, man, how bad
could that have been? Worst case scenario

is that me and my sister would have had
two happy halves. Which is why America,
we need a divorce, so we don't go around

wishing the other half goes out for cigarettes
and never returns. Think of it, this way —
you do you and we do we and maybe, just
maybe, we can meet up for dinner
every now and again and comment
on how beautiful the other has become.

SOME RHYMING ADJECTIVES TO DESCRIBE DONALD TRUMP
CINDY HOCHMAN

Rude
 crude
  lewd
half-brewed
half-stewed
much ballyhooed
pooh-poohed
bad dude
no good
   (for the sake of this poem, "good" rhymes with dude, okay?)
much sued
much booed
emperor-in-the-nude

we're screwed

TRUMPED OVER THE MOON
Maria Lisella

This morning I got so upset. You know the new aide, she is very nice, you know, very sunny, good for my mornings...

Right, the blonde one with all the hair and the long nails.

Yes, her. This morning she walks in with a big Trump button on her chest. I find this so upsetting I can't tell you.

Did you tell her?

Well, no, she takes care of me you know, but I can't stand that thing staring at me, I think it's making me sicker, she leans over me and that button is staring me right in the face.

It's a free country, what can you do?

Free country? Not with him, he's a fascist and besides that he doesn't care about girls like her and she doesn't even know it. I hate to think she might be filled with hate and she is in my house every single day. Besides that, doesn't she know you don't talk religion or politics at work?

Part Two

So you know this aide, she comes in on Monday exhausted.
I don't need a tired aide you know that. All weekend

548

what was she doing with her daughter who's a soldier?
Campaigning for that stinker Trump.

Now she wears a Trump t-shirt so tight you can't miss a thing.
I wanted to throw
a raincoat over those big breasts.

I was speechless, I tell ya, speechless.
I make believe I don't hear her.

You think you could change her mind?

Mind? You're kidding, right? Yesterday she comes in
and tells me another beauty: that
Bill DeBlasio's black wife [is there another one?]
        was a prostitute....

I said, "...what if she was? She isn't now...." honestly
I don't know what to say to that girl.

JENNIFER ROSS

THE WRITHE
THOMAS FUCALORO

I've always hated the left side of my brain.
It tells me funding will be the only way
of making cents of the right.

They want to cut
our fingers off
and wear them
as charms
for Pandora
bracelets.

I painted a forest
walked inside
and smeared.

If I had a nickel
for every time the left side of my brain
didn't understand the right
I would have a whole lot of nickels
that made no sense.

Only the right side of my brain understands that.

I cut off my head
to spite the body
they want us to writhe in.

I have learned to survive
with the brains
in my throat
speaking
through
belly.

I step out of the painting
and sneer. The Dead
Kennedy's start to play.

I duct tape my head
back to my body
and write.

Cutting funding for the right side of the brain
leaves the left side to wonder the logic involved
in this decision.

The arts are the only
true account of history
besides our finger-
prints.

SCARED PEOPLE SCARE PEOPLE
CRAIG KITE

I am now looming over a horizontal blank
Here, I can smell angel's Hair
and compassion
And a reason not to build buildings

I am quickened by a car Horn
As my nose leaks my brain onto my sleeve
and I wear it like a real bugar Heart

This guy wandering in parking lots crying
The edge of his black top is a treadmill
"Mommy, what is that man doing?"
"It's rude to point fingers, honey."

Hit me with homilies to have my aspirations leave
        through my ears with my failures. I can
Hang out behind my eyes with the rest of me.
Really, man? Behind a church?
(I always get Hysterical at church)

Scared people scare people

PHANTOM ANTHEM
ELAINE EQUI

I'll know my country
when I seize it —

like Columbus on the way
to someplace else —

and set my foot
upon its cloud.

O how solemn a business
is the relentless pursuit

of happiness as if it were
a fugitive from the law.

Now its flag is a teacup on an anvil;
now, a grasshopper on a field of stars.

But when I see the adorable children
of celebrities on play-dates,

my joy is irrefutable —
only my denim is distressed.

And when I witness
how tenderly old and young

cradle their guns
and speak in the shadow

of ancient words like freedom.
Well, it never fails to bring a tear.

I AM NO PATRIOT, FUCK YOU AMERICA AND FUCK YOU DONALD TRUMP!

BRIAN SHEFFIELD

But not because you're the president.
Only because you're so full of hate.
like I am and you want to fill the
rest of the world with your hate like I sometimes do.
But now, you walk backwards and clear your steps
as if what you were saying really
didn't mean anything. And I guess it didn't. Good.
I gleefully laugh at middle America who believes in
your bullshit, and I feel no guilt for
doing so. I gleefully laugh at those old conservatives
who should all be dead now anyways.
The people of world affairs should be young
and idealistic. Shove the old fools into the grinder
and feed them to each other. You want hate?
Keep up your shit and we will all fucking eat you!
I revoke my own citizenship. I am no longer an American.
Fuck your flag and fuck your soil.
Fuck your politics and fuck your economy.
America the gratuitous I don't love you America.
I love your people, and people are not their citizenship.
People before country.
Walt Whitman had it wrong.
America is not a poem. America is a poison.
I hope America dies. But,
I hope the people thrive.

I DREAMED THAT I FIRED
THE FAMILY PHOTOGRAPHER
UNDER TRUMP'S INFLUENCE
ZEV SHANKEN

T rump was staying with us 'til the inauguration.
One afternoon when my wife was away, I fired the photographer that my wife had hired to take pictures of our grandchildren. The photographer had exuded warmth as she showed us glossy photos she had taken of other people's grandchildren. I felt she was over-selling, buttering me up for the bad prints to come.

I simply said, "You're fired" and when she said "What?" I repeated and she turned away and knelt. I looked at the shivering back of her head, obviously weeping, and said to myself, "She's trying to get my sympathy, but I see through that ploy."

After she left I said to Donald, "You're a bad influence on me. I have too weak an ego. I was doing it for you, unconsciously under your influence."

"When your wife gets home I'll explain," he said, adding a Latin phrase that I think he thought means an unbiased observer. "Remember, I didn't say a thing during the entire exchange. I was here the entire time and not a word. Did you notice? Did you see that? When she gets in I'll tell her."

"No," I said. "That's the problem. You're taking over my ego. If you defend me then I'm really lost."

"Fine," he said — and here comes the punch line that gave me shivers as I woke. He said,

"You defend yourself. I won't be your shield."

A DREAM WITH "BUCHANAN"

PETER CHERCHES

I was participating in a conference or a panel of some sort. There were about twenty people seated around an imposing mahogany table. This event was taking place over multiple days. I had no idea when it would end, and I didn't know what it was all about. But I could tell it was important, because most of the people around the table were well-known political and public figures. I can only remember two of them, though: Clarence Thomas and the late Thurgood Marshall. Then there were four nonentities, me and three others, two men and one woman. None of us did any talking at the table; we were observers. We were all clueless about why we were included, so we bonded with each other and chatted on breaks.

During one of the breaks the woman said to me, "After this is over I'm leaving town." I was disappointed, because I was attracted to her.

"Oh," I said, "where are you going?"

"Back home," she replied. "I finished my degree and now I'm going to work in the community."

"Oh, was your degree in social work?" I asked.

"No, Buchanan," she said.

"Buchanan? Is that anything like social work?" I asked.

"No," she replied, "it's a holistic therapy for the mouth, teeth and gums. Let me look in your mouth."

No way I'm going to let this flake look in my mouth, I thought. Now that I had learned of her new age proclivities I was no longer attracted to her.

"YOU'RE NOT LOOKING IN MY MOUTH!" I screamed.

THE DREAM OF DEPORTATION (OR, EURO GO HOME)

Evie Ivy

I dreamt Donald Trump had become president
and deported Melania because she was an immigrant.

And one thing had led to another and folks were being
deported and deported. (Many didn't know where to go.)

Finally, full of remorse — over Melania, Donald deported
himself (finally.) No one knew where they were.
Some said they truly went "underground." As I awoke
I noted that the natives, who had been here for thousands

of years, finally were happy, spreading out over lands
once ripped from them. There were totem poles with his
face. Amulets. They danced all feathered up. Donald had
became icon, hero of all the Native American "nations."

RULERS
SU POLO

We love our stars of stage and screen.
It may be that they are our royalty.
Thus invited to rule us with pomp and flair.
Now suddenly Trump is there.
I swear I swear yes Trump is there.
On top of the heap.
With keys to the keep
Ronald Reagan was there before
The Donald
The Ronald
The Arnold is nearby.
It's a disaster yes a disaster.
Everybody to get from street
A whole lot of praying going on.
A whole lot of preying going on.
On shore off shore on shore off shore
And while smallish minds rule
The geniuses continue to fix things
While small hearts rule
Children are growing up anyway
Time marches on marches off marches on
While the homunculus rules
Fresh waves scrub the shore
While ingrates rule
Discoveries are being made
Flowers fold and unfold
While attitudes rule
The earth grumbles below.

IT'S NOT ENOUGH
GORDON GILBERT

It's not enough to just show up and march
Telling all the world how we may feel
It's not enough to speak with eloquence
Preaching to the choir is no big deal

It's not enough to say we will resist
If all we do is only in reaction
Just saying no to orders to desist
As a badge we wear with smug self-satisfaction

We must confront our new reality
Bull-by-the-horns in true Minoan fashion
Vault over this great beast with elegance
Move forward, never backwards, as a nation

Go on offense, never the defensive
It's not enough to say let's make a stand
We have the numbers, we must keep advancing
Progress is our goal and our demand

WHERE THE GROUND SWELLS
JANE ORMEROD

Within, not huddled, nor transparent is and are. Older clouds stretched above us. In the hay, the lizard, the revolution chameleon, startled by the sweep, the rough running, the full infirmary. No, no. No that suffers consumptive filth. No to treacherous division and diversion. Us is we in strength. This is not sudden filth from nowhere but we hold. Find the guides. If the landscape vanishes, believe in truth. Look below, the guide waits. The loss, debt of feeling. Harsh sun, wax, lungs. Understand these lines. Sow and the birds will surely come. This water contains surface, this water contains distance, distance contains water. We do not decay. Do not call you by that name. These shutters, this anger, this fight and community. Do not call you by name. Do call you by name. This fog is for stealth. We are heavy, we are feast day, we welcome the fallen and fleeing, the infinite, the full swing of the lambasting sky. You are not of that name. we watch, shepherd, direct traffic, learn, remember. Our deaths may be constant but we fuel, fill the troughs, the gutters, fling love to larks. We carry linen. We know antiquity, the scales. You are judged and we are us. Clean gums, unstain glass, faiths unite, certain of our uncertainty, our maxims, our petals, pedals, furniture, dust and dust sheets, shoulder blades. We are magnificent. We nurture, teach, teethe, attempt, mix sounds, mix suns, abort when we choose, hold clock faces. Proud of our tenderness. Do not present you with that name. Those forked around your table.

Clocks will open, the bed is unmade. We run, run, run, are muscle, honorable, tenacious. We are not you. We are not your cronies of hate. We are keepers. You are hell silence. We are silence. We swell louder. We are quieter. Louder. All around is center and lines, arrows, fluidity. We are space and tightness. We grip, do not forget. Wind approaches, logical, illogical. Science, art, intuitive and legal, clocks will open. You are leaving. We shimmer. High tide, low. A spell for the flora, the clearing circle. Death rattle, helter the skelter, literature, cadence, factories, umbrellas frantic spinning and falling of wheels, embroidery, choice, mornings. Your obscene gold melts into our million memories of history, our mistakes and misunderstandings. Our experiences and differences and warmth, fear, anguish, luminosity. Melt your gold-shit fingers and baked head, your veer to carnage, pit of entrails, ignorance. We will not add to your crimes. We eat your fingers and spit in the ashes. You will not blast or deny our generations.

Pulsation. Waves of love. In the future, we wander aimless, in joy. For now, we aim. Calm shimmer, serrated edge, an archipelago of kiss and voice. We are each of each other. Expand beyond geometry, expand past air and the furies.

THIS BEAUTIFUL BUBBLE
VINCENT KATZ

I love this bubble,
Everyone takes the subway, and you can look up,
And look at all the people, and each one is different,
And they look different, and each one has a story, and suddenly,
You are awake and want to know each story, only you can't,
Don't have time, they don't, don't want to maybe.

But some you do, you glean, you approximate yourself
        to something of them,
Like the beautiful, chestnut-skinned woman, who, leaning,
Listened to the announcer before getting in, and, confused,
        because the 2 was called a 5,
Asked advice, and three people responded,
Explaining in their different ways, some of them silent,
Eyes met with approval, warmth only subway-known,
Among equals, fellow travelers, denizens;

She sat and smiled, and looking at an infant,
Smiled more, her hair was a flag of self-joy too,
She was real, at ease among people.
The rule is: to speak.
Make contact, and you will find people more beautiful
        than you thought.

But back to our bubble. It is everywhere around us.
Everywhere, walking in the city, you are seeing people,

All different kinds, shapes, sizes, the best education
You can give a child is to bring them up inside this
Beautiful bubble. I complain, but I'll never leave.
I feed off the looks, the stories, the hungering here.

I'm aware, we're all aware, what goes on outside the bubble.
We're not stupid. We just thought people
    outside the bubble wanted the same thing:
To live as variously as possible.
Or, put another way: I am the least difficult of men.
All I want is boundless love.

It took us sixty years or so to understand
What the word "boundless" meant.
Now we know. And we'll never forget.

DAVID SANDLIN

THAT WAS ZEN, THIS IS DOW
(JONES, THAT IS)
RICHARD WEST

1) In the 60's we went to Woodstock. Now everyone's looking for good stock tips.

2) In the late 60's I was living on the west coast of California where it really was flower power and sunrise meditations. Now it's become tequila sunrises and power lunches.

3) In the 60's we tried to expand and transcend the mind; today people try to keep from losing it — their mind, that is — because they're trying to expand their income — because they're losing that, too.

4) In the 60's we had many visions of Utopia. Today most people just dream of winning the lottery.

5) We believed in the future. Now, it's the next quarter.

6) We rallied for civil rights, the war on poverty and peace in Vietnam. We had a new left and an old left. Now, nothing much is left as we march to our underpaying jobs and overpriced apartments.

7) In the 60's we experimented with our lives and human potential. We introspected with encounter groups. We meditated to reach enlightenment or satori. It was the interpenetration of Eastern and Western culture. So what's Samadhi now? People just sit at the sushi counter eating yakatori! So much for counterculture.

8) In the 60's people went to see the Guru. Now they just go to the gym.

9) We were connoisseurs of consciousness and we explored its depths and got spaced out with acid. Now it is antacid as hipsters struggle for their own space.

10) Yes, in the 60's we saw "God in a grain of sand and Heaven in a wild flower." Then it became the glitter and tinsel of a disco ball's reflection on someone's ass and if you got lucky and scored, you'd be in disco heaven.

11) In the 60's we went back to the land and we went to the moon. Now we're running out of land, so who wants to live on the moon?

12) In the 60's money couldn't buy you love. Now the material girl will entertain any offer.

13) In the 60's sex was free and natural — make love not war. Now it's expensive and dangerous — make money, art; anything but love.

14) In the 60's we had communal living. Now it's co-dependency and AIRBNB.

15) In the 60's there was a big generation gap. We told it like it is, was, and should be and we were rude to hypocrisy. Now it's the degeneration gap. People are rude to each other while wearing their social masks and saying little.

16) In the 60's the conservatives went ape-shit about the red menace of a red revolution. Now they demand a redneck revolution with the aid of a Putin love child.

17) In the 60's we hipsters tried to live idealistically and in harmony with nature. Now it should be a matter of necessity as we realistically try to save the planet.

18) In the 60's we dropped out of the rat race of the establishment and joined bohemia. Now, too many rats run bohemia.

19) In the 60's we tried to change the world. Now we have 'alternative facts' of true lies and virtual reality.

20) In the 60's we feared the C.I.A. so much it made you paranoid. Today, if you're not paranoid, you're crazy. So we hope the C.I.A. will do the right thing and overthrow the Republican schmucktocracy.

21) In the 60's Dr. Timothy Leary prescribed advice to turn on, tune in and drop out. Now Donald Trump prescribes to turn off, tune out and drop dead!

HOW BEAUTIFUL
JOHN J. TRAUSE

How beautiful the whip marks on my sex slave's back,
how beautiful the crack of skin, the red, the raw,
so like the red stripes on the U. S. flag,
the contrast of the white and red. How beautiful
the jaw that takes the punch, the maw that takes
me all up to the base in shock and awe.
My bitch, my fag, my leather bag worn raw
with the antidote to deadly bigotry being
more.

How beautifully my sex slave bends down by
the docks, receiving cocks, the payload comes,
set back your clocks as freedom drains into the bay.

How beautiful the day as liberty
is isolate upon the cay. I take
a tortured torch without much of a care
and shove it hard into her derrière,
an accent grave, brave accident à terre.

Prose flows
like the Passaic.

           Blood too…

Fuck you.

BURNED COUNTRY
TOM SAVAGE

I live all the time in Burn Country.*
Everything is too expensive now in NYC.
My landlord burns me every time his insufficient treatments
Fail to get rid of my bedbugs intentionally
On his part in the futile hope that
He can drive me out because I pay
Low rent. I've been burned time and again
By the asshole administrators of the
Senior center I go to who, in spite
Of the fact that l have almost no bugs left
Have thrown me out again
Just before Christmas. Fuck them!
I hope they die prematurely.
Forty years ago I was burnt out
Of a building I'd just moved into
By a landlord fighting with some tenants
Two flights down from me.

Every intelligent person in the city
And country feels burned by the recent election
In which a narcissistic lunatic
Was elected President. If the Russians
Had something to do with this, the election
Results should be thrown out before the asshole Trump
And his cronies can be installed.

*Written while watching a film called "Burn Country" by Ian Olds.

Everyone who voted for him
Should have at least one hand cut off
Saudi Arabian style because
They've stupidly stolen
From the rest of us, their betters.
These suckers! Trump is never
Going to give them what he promised them
Because it's impossible. Their stupid
Mind-deadening jobs are gone forever,
All they can hope for, at best, is for
Some kind of retraining and they
Probably won't even get that from Trump
And the Republicans. Where are the Arabs
When we need them to bomb
The Republicans into the Hell-realm
They deserve and from which they came?
America has totally failed
In its democracy
And may finally lose it
Under the lunatics it has elected.

There's never any money
For what I do.
And now all the assholes in NYC
Under the age of 80 want money.
To find wood in a forest takes no talent
But some of Trump's men and women couldn't do it
Without blindfolds.
Trump will never be my President
No matter how long he stays in.
The suckers can have him and they will.
When you find the source of all things
Trump and his cronies
Will explode from the weight
Of their own lies and manipulations.
His suckers will be looking for Trump.
They'll get nothing but rump

Just like they did in Atlantic City
Fifteen years ago when
His horrible casinos reigned
Over nothing and nowhere.
There may be nothing but violence
To the country's psyche from now on.

INSIDE OUTSOURCING
MIKE GOLDEN

Not much sense of humor
left about the inevitable
coming-of-the-going
though I know it's a fad
and fads usually pass me by
I try to look at the idea
of getting left behind
philosophically
but know that old *briar patch* dodge
won't work this time.
Ultimately, the ubiquitous *They*
no matter what name you call It
fires or retires everyone 'cause
according to "The Rules of the Game"
we all automatically signed up for the day we were born
everyone & everything has to be replaced.
It doesn't matter *who* you are,
where you've been, *what* you've done,
probably not even how well
or how poorly you've done it
even if you've made a deal with *The Devil.*
At this point there is no point on the point
just a dullness of expectation
that needs to replace its carrots
or get a new mule
just because. . .
the holy mountains of future in the distance
look like warts

or distortions
of distortions
as if you need another reason
to get a new model
before the old one
breaks down & cries
Motherfucker
this treadmill
is not working!

Back in the days when shit didn't stink
back in the days when we didn't think
how fucking hard it was to flush
We've Got To Get Out Of This Place
for me & Bobbie McGhee
pumping up the volume
wasn't just a stoned generation's answer
of what to do about Vietnam
since the glorious ideal of *world boogie* never really wiped out
the long term daily spread of poison *The System* automatically
contributes to every level of world wide corruption
without needing an excuse to exploit every opportunity
you can't get rid of as easily as a comic book character
dropping a bowling ball on his toe
to make a toothache disappear.
Even today there are solutions
if you can only fit the right problems into the equation
to solve or not to solve
it's not even a question of what to do
about rebuilding the infrastructure
it's the amount of time you anticipate
is left or right-on to waste
if you're under the illusion
you choose delusion as a methodology
to the madness that keeps us sanely breathing
unless we think too much too fast too long
to-be-or-not-to-be-YO

this is not hypothetical hyperventilation
this voice
categorically states "LIFE SUCKS"
but still wants to be grounded
without actually
being grounded
under the ground.
You know what I mean?
I know what you mean.
Mediocrity is cholesterol of the soul.
It's a mistake to think it's harmless
if we don't voice it to each other.

Meanwhile back at the ranch, stuck in a shit job
keeping the lies of a dysfunctional system alive is one thing,
but I can't spill my guts about anything that pisses me off more
than the cosmic fingernail screeching
     down my blacklisted blackboard
so if you out there can't help doing
     your own confessional 401K
don't let the shit clog up, stagnate or block you
when you encounter the contradictions,
     just count 'em and let 'em go
instead of living them out.
Go ahead, try it: "There goes Lucky Number 11!"
You didn't pick it. Too fucking bad. Now it's gone.
But that was easy. Too easy. Not like Bitch Goddess *Catch 22*!
I don't know about you, but I could live
without the Bitch G's' magik twisted sister
immortal #23 too
though I'll never forget good old #37,
it was a true *Kafkanian* contradiction.
Yeah, sure it was, but no irony here for Gregor-boy
even if Dylan could have sung the shit
out of that cockroach as if he were Sinatra
I still don't know where this song goes
in the long run this is no sprint

coming out of *Tangled Up In Blue My Way.*
Maybe everything doesn't have to have meaning
to have meaning
which would explain
the need for Social Media
on one hand
and obsolescence
on the other
as one scratches the other
it tells the other
it's just been scratched
thus, communication is erased
but the itch is never lost
just found over & over again;
This is gravity in action
so rub, Fig Newton, rub
all the different flavors
apple, prune, pear, pizza brands
Pappa John.

Now if we can only figure out HOW TO SELL IT
that will be rich and we will be richer
   than a Silicone Valley twitter.
It seems like everything always changes
   and never changes at all.
If you look back at photos from the past
17 out of 20 of us were coolly dangling
   dirty little ciggies in every pic,
now it's dumb smart phones in their hands,
   dancing in front of their lips.
Can you come up with the next addiction for the scrapbook?
Or will the next one be invisible chips implanted at birth
to control the next class of new babes on the block?
It's not wishy-washy enough to be in their platform
but Scumbags think if they have the right marketing strategy
they can liberate & exploit the punching bag of Democracy
at the same time they transcend Class Warfare

by pretending not to sell to the rich until first selling to the poor
who – let's face it — would gladly kill to be rich too.
In fact, what the poor bastards want most is to be richer than
                                        Boss Trump
and the other rich sonofabitches who make them eat shit every day
so taking a cue from the pros — we should call
        the shit we sell them
upscale designer Trump shit — Trump blogs, Trump phones
— it could be nothing more than corndogs at Walmarts.
It doesn't matter, as long as they're called "The one & only
exclusive designer — Trump Corndog."
They can sell for $100 each,
or maybe we can get away with $200 each
if the customer is only allowed to buy one a week
with a Special Club Card for *Trump Members Only*
that allows them to bath in the glory
        of the glory of this dog's utility
even if eating it is not exactly their thing
they always have the option to use it as a dildo
made exclusively for them personally by white trash Fashionistas
from *the south of France collection, Dominique,*
Would you like a tattoo of your face on your ass, dear,
while you're waiting for the designer to take measurements
we can use to fit your soul into a Trump gift package?
If you still feel alienated after that we can schedule
a changeable sex change — with a max of 3-changes
        per order in case
you change your mind and change your mind
        and change your mind
but still believe in the conceptual purity
of always being able to wipe
your original ass yourself.

Absurd states of grace aside
we've all used the expressions *Heaven-on-Earth, Hell-on-Earth*
to describe the polar opposite conditions our conditions are in
at different points in time.

We can break life down: Act 1, Act II, Act III
Youth, Adult, Ancient Fucker
if you've got a sense of humor
about how fucked the human condition is
believing or not believing *in god we trust* will fuck us.
If you must know *we don't know*
if there's work to be done on the other side
but even if all we do is sleep, all we do is dream
there's a sense of purpose trying to decipher those dreams
even if we have to admit *we don't know where we're going,*
what we're doing or if the answer is *there is no answer*
to all those essential questions we have about the human condition
it's still ok to pray, chant, hum, sing, masturbate your blues away
betting-on-the-come of astrology
        or transformative magic of poetry
if it gets your spirit to the other side of nature relatively unscathed.
Process is all
if you have the right sound bytes,
yet like all great paradoxes
it never seems enough in the short term NOW
I WANT IT
you can't have when you want it MOST.
Call it Double Zen, Zen-on-Zen to you out there in the Zen Zone,
no matter what you believe, change can come from anywhere
in the background, a human interest story
        babbling on the nightly news
The Voice shilling from *Corinthians*: *It will happen in a moment,*
in the blink of an eye, when the last trumpet is blown...
        you know what to do
when the time is right — turn off that dumb smart phone
give yourself a beat
then one more — for the hell of it
and let the breath go
just like *that*!
And *that*!
And *that*!
And...

PACK YOUR SHIT
NORMAN SAVAGE

Mr. President.
It's only been a month tomorrow
so you can't have much to take:
a bathrobe (maybe two);
a toothbrush (maybe two);
perhaps a thong.
You've already fucked-up
more shit than everyone
who came before you; you'll only
fuck-up more if you stay.
But take heart:
you've made the history books:
most fucked-up president ever.
That's what they'll say.
You'll be the one
they make comparisons to:
You think he's fucked-up? That ain't
nothin. I was around when…
And you'll have your portrait; your
windswept "do"
will be next to Lincoln Kennedy
Washington Roosevelt
and your skinny scrunchy lips and beaver-mean eyes
will frighten the shit out of school children
taking a tour with Melania
who never noticed
you were even gone.

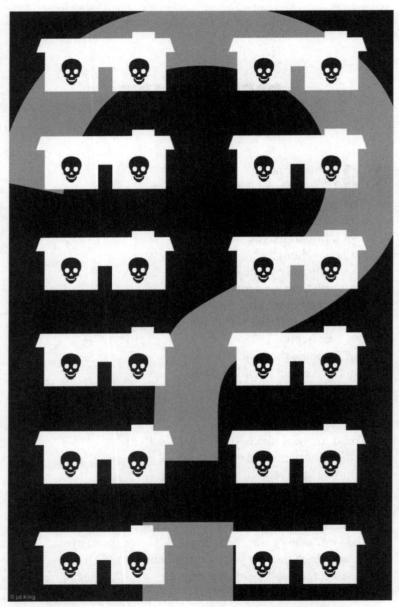

J.D. KING

THE SECOND GREAT CLEANSING
GEORGE SPENCER

O nce upon a time and it was a long time ago there was a country that glorified it's movie stars and pop artists and sports figures and believed in money and believed in a god who believed that the chosen were always rich and wise and that the country must purify itself regularly. It did this by marginalizing its unwanted, by putting them and their old and their young in squalid housing far away from the glamorous golden towers that their Master Builder built for the rich and powerful and erected large walls around these towers of gold to protect the rich and powerful and wise from the people and each province had its gated city of gold shining on a hill and there were compounds where the executives of the country and each province ruled along with the legislators and the court that was supreme and this was called a government of balance and expertise. Every four year there was a National Comedy where the leaders would explain to the poor and undereducated what they, the government, had done for them and why they should rule forever and the poor and disenfranchised would look among themselves to see what had been done for them and they found nothing. They were told to pick leaders from the residents of the gold towers. Being dutiful they did. The leaders needed money to produce the National Comedy and they went knocking on the doors of their neighbors in the golden towers. Always the neighbors gave. In fact they gave twice. Once to each party. This entitled them to the best seats in this Theater of the Absurd. One party was the party of many of the powerful. It represented the owners of most of the land and factories, stores and hospitals. The other party was the party of those of the owners who liked to hide their greed. They were in favor of letting the masses express themselves a little, of the arts and of all that was enlightened in their culture but they drew the line at paying for it. What little funding that was available for these enlightened undertakings was carefully directed to the arts organizations that they enjoyed or pretended to enjoy like the National Museum of Nautical Art that they seldom went to other than for gala events, the Opera Company of the Country where the gentlemen napped, the Orchestra of Enlightening Sound that was in decline.

And for years the people accepted this. Then there began to be rumblings of discontent and the people in the golden towers trembled as an Uber Leader arose whose skill at deceit vastly exceed theirs. He had studied their methods of controlling the masses. He was a master of entertainment and he told the people he would lead them to the Promised Land, a vast new real estate development owned by the Uber Leader's family and he put up billboards trashing the people in the golden towers and their leaders and the people who believed in greed and the people who pretended they didn't and he became Uber Leader Supreme of the country and they, the poor and neglected, proudly called themselves deplorables.

First it was one group and then another and another that was identified as deplorable and was moved into Promised Land and thus began the Second Great Cleansing, the first being the elimination of the Indians.

This was not like the old days when *No Irish Need Apply,* and three Jews were allowed in Harvard, one in Princeton and two in Yale, the old days when there was an unspoken understanding among the elite and the thoughts of the elite were carefully edited. However, recently some of their most intimate speculations of the old elite about Deplorablism have begun to circulate among the people and the people became restless but this was temporary.

It was discovered that Theore Roosevelt had said "I don't go so far as to think that the only good Indians are the dead Indians, but I believe nine out of ten are, and I shouldn't inquire too closely into the health of the tenth." And William Howard Taft once told a group of Black college students, "Your race is adapted to be a race of farmers, first, last, and for all times."

William Harding had opined "Men of both races [Black and White] may well stand uncompromisingly against every suggestion of social equality. This is not a question of social equality, but a question of recognizing a fundamental, eternal, inescapable difference. Racial amalgamation there cannot be." Calvin Coolidge wrote in *Good Housekeeping,* "There are racial considerations too grave to be brushed aside for any sentimental reasons. Biological laws tell us that certain divergent people will not mix or blend.... Quality of mind and body suggests that observance of ethnic law is as great a necessity to a nation as immigration law."

On this subject Harry Truman said "I am strongly of the opinion Negroes ought to be in Africa, yellow men in Asia and white men in Europe and America." He also referred to the Blacks on the White House staff as "an army of coons."

Not to be outdone Lyndon Johnson explained his decision to nominate Thurgood Marshall to the Supreme Court rather than a less-famous black judge by saying, "when I appoint a nigger to the bench, I want everybody to know he's a nigger."

Of course this was long ago, was intended for the general good and matters have improved vastly since then.

We are now well beyond the Second Great Cleansing. The slums are quiet. There are no protests. The golden towers shine as bright as the white skin that is a requirement of citizenship. Obedience is taught in school. Rote learning rules. Thought has been outlawed.

Among the citizens in the golden towers the talk of opportunity and freedom flows. The national institutions of enlightenment prosper. Businesses compete. Hospitals and schools prosper as Adam Smith's invisible hand magically conducts the National Symphony of Enlightened Greed. The borders are secure. All things needed for the good life are abundant in the 100 walled cities filled with golden towers and specially vetted nannies. The population outside these cities inexplicably continues to shrink. Death by Mass Deportation, Death by Disease. Death by Hunger. Death by Mass Incarceration. Death by Institutional Murder. Death by Military Conscription. Death by Pollution. Death by Extreme Vetting. Death by Enhanced Interrogation.

The land is cleansing itself. A more perfect nation is arising.